James is a lawyer, inventor, musician and lifelong student of the martial arts.

He and his family travel extensively and share a love for all things ancient.

This second book in the *Loura Lure* fantasy series presents a forgotten time and people whose only evidence of existence now resides in the stone monuments left behind across Western Europe, the U.K., and Ireland.

Walk amidst the dolmens and stone circles of old and hear the whispers of those who lived there. Magic was everywhere!

To my wonderful wife, Lisa, and my incredible children, Meaghan, Connor, Tara Maeve, and Callum; you have supported me every step of the way in this long journey, standing always at the ready to pop a champagne cork at exactly the right moments. I could not have achieved this and so many other things without your trust and belief in me. Thank you to my parents, Joan and Rae, for the gift of a great education. To my best friends, Stuart and Rob, you never once doubted that I would do something when I told you that I had set out on one of my creative paths. To my mentors, and to my departed brother, Joe, we will see each other again. To my grampa (Silver) who passed the art of storytelling on to my dad. To the people of Ireland and the U.K. who have seen fit to protect ancient sites so that we may all be inspired to ponder the civilization that once was and wonder at its elusiveness.

To you all, I am deeply grateful!

James McMahon

THE LOURA LURE
BOOK 2

The Awakening

AUSTIN MACAULEY PUBLISHERS®

LONDON * CAMBRIDGE * NEW YORK * SHARJAH

Ordering Information
Quantity sales: Special discounts are available on quantity purchases by corporations, associations, and others. For details, contact the publisher at the address below.

Publisher's Cataloging-in-Publication data
McMahon, James
The Loura Lure—Book 2

ISBN 9798895430286 (Paperback)
ISBN 9798895430293 (Hardback)
ISBN 9798895430316 (ePub e-book)
ISBN 9798895430309 (Audiobook)

Library of Congress Control Number: 2025901214

www.austinmacauley.com/us

First Published 2025
Austin Macauley Publishers LLC
40 Wall Street, 33rd Floor, Suite 3302
New York, NY 10005
USA

mail-usa@austinmacauley.com
+1 (646) 5125767

Thank you to the people at Austin Macauley Publishers who have once again worked with me in bringing this second book in the Loura Lure trilogy to fruition. I am amazed at just how many different contributors are required to take an author's work and shape it into a piece of artful literature, which must then be packaged, presented and marketed in such a way that readers might be inspired to proclaim, "I'd like to read that". Many thanks!

Chapter 1

There was a period of darkness, a type of jet-black that occurred only in the most airtight, windowless chambers. Shamus couldn't see his hands or hear any sound of any kind. There was a cruelty to this kind of sensory deprivation that incited an escalating panic within him. Had he not felt the churning of his organs, he might have had to accept that he was already dead.

Erladoch might easily have been two inches from him, or, as Shamus seriously considered, he might have gone altogether somewhere else. It occurred to him at once that such a porthole may lead to many different timelines, and that he could end up somewhere other than Erladoch's Age of Loura! He had no clear idea how far back in time he was actually going!

What if I exit ten years before I should? Or a hundred years too late? His mind was wrapped with anxiety. Never before this moment had he even considered the prospect of spending an eternity totally alone. The sudden sense of defenselessness caused by his own ignorance was crippling. He pondered whether he would remain trapped in this cauldron of silence, deprived of all external sensation, indefinitely. Leaving this void was suddenly the only thing of importance to him.

A spasm of pain suddenly erupted across Shamus's diaphragm. Its thrust pushed unbelievably high into his stomach, forcing out an explosive, breathless shriek. Yin was giving way to Yang in the most violent fashion imaginable as his internal organs heaved downwards. All at once, there was too much sensation, and he felt himself propelled upward. If this reflected the birthing process, he wished to have no further part of it!

Without warning, his embryonic posture gave way to a flailing of arms and legs. He now felt the weight of the ancient broadsword on his right flank, along with his other equipment, drawing him down.

In the middle of his terror, Shamus's mind began to come back online. His arms and legs instinctively began working together, pulling through a medium that was becoming more and more familiar until his brain issued an abrupt warning—*water!* Every synapse in his brain instructed him to swim *up! up! up!* as his mouth closed protectively to avoid swallowing the sudden pressure of liquid.

The air-like substance that he'd not even realized he'd been breathing was gone. With the little oxygen left in his lungs, Shamus registered that he had no idea how far down he was submerged from the surface of this body of water. He recognized that only one of his arms moved freely. His leg kicks took on a desperate purpose as the drag of his soaked clothes and overstuffed backpack seemed to be fighting his every effort to reach what he hoped would be the surface.

There was no light above or below him. He was beginning to lose the struggle for life. The air he had gulped in before forcing his mouth closed was nearly spent. Shamus knew he would soon have to open his mouth to draw air that simply was no longer there. He anticipated that in moments he would experience the rush of gallons of water pouring into his mouth and nostrils until his eardrums exploded in one last awful, numbing moment of pain. He hoped to see some small glimmer of light above, which might permit him to command his mouth to remain shut just a moment longer, but there was none. The pounding in his ears was as crushing as the sense of his collapsing chest muscles. The silent scream of a man about to be drowned began to make his lips quiver.

At the exact moment the water prepared to ram past his teeth, Shamus felt the presence of a hand touching the side of his cheek. It was warm, loving even. It felt like a woman's hand, stroking softly against his skin. There was intention in the touch, and it drew him upward. The terror of his impending death was suddenly overwritten by a soft whisper. The voice asked him to kick his legs one last time. He couldn't see 'her', but somehow, he felt the familiarity of the presence inviting him to live. Just as his mouth accepted the reflexive muscle pull of his opening jaw, he broke the surface of the water. The presence that had encouraged him to act was gone. In its place was the tumult of Shamus's regurgitation as his body worked to expel the volume of water he had inhaled just before he was finally surrounded by breathable air.

Somewhere close to his side came the sounds of sputtering. Erladoch was but a few feet away.

'*Air*'! he told himself.

He'd made it! They'd made it! He choked and retched while greedily inhaling the freshness of unpolluted air. The light had been absent as a guide to the surface because it was the dead of night. Shamus spat up the last mouthful of water that he'd swallowed while his arms and legs began to work again to keep him afloat. He dog-paddled toward an as yet invisible shoreline.

There were neither stars nor any other light to help him distinguish shapes in the blackness. He felt Erladoch come alongside of him. They latched on to each other and kicked their legs in a coordinated effort to make it to solid ground.

"Keep going", Erladoch ordered. "We're nearly there".

While still not visible, the shore was only a few feet away. The closer he got to safety, the heavier Shamus' swords and other gear became. With relief, he felt his left hand grab the top of the shoreline. With his right hand, he struggled to place the broadsword onto land so that he could then plop onto the dirt like a seal and wiggle the rest of the way onto flat ground.

Erladoch applied an effortful tug to Shamus' backpack to help him complete the steep climb out of the deep pool. Shamus extended his arms too late to stop his mouth from firmly kissing the dirt.

Knowing the danger they had encountered on leaving his timeline, Shamus worried that there might be a similar reception awaiting them on this 'other side'. With all good intentions, he attempted to reach for his sword, but he couldn't even elevate his arms an inch from where they lay still, splayed against the earth. He listened for any movement not associated with the two of them. Nothing stirred. With no further thought to their risk, he felt his eyes close into an exhausted sleep.

***

Chapter 2

Shamus awakened under a beautiful starry sky. Whatever cloud cover had previously obscured this spectacle of visible universe above him had moved on.

A small but soothingly warm fire glistened a few feet from his face. Erladoch had already set up camp. There was a crisp chill to the night air, but it was not the harsh winter conditions they had left behind. The chill was more that of a dessert terrain that simply had no ability to hold the heat of the day. Shamus peeled off his soaked clothing and moved closer to the fire. After wringing out as much water from his clothes as he could manage, he propped them up on sticks as close to the heat as he could get them without burning them.

Shamus was still weary, but strength was returning to his limbs. He sat back down and faced Erladoch. The two men looked at each other for what felt like a matter of minutes, silently congratulating each other on the success of their journey.

Shamus propped his head back to take in the stars now that the thick cloud cover had passed over them. With no light pollution to obscure the million pinpricks of light above, he laughed aloud. The utter magnificence of this dazzling, milky sheet overhead was confirmation enough that he had truly traveled back in time.

Erladoch's emotions appeared muted, almost disinterested. Shamus found this perplexing. He'd wagered that his friend's level of elation would have been unrivaled in this moment. *Erladoch has made it home. Christ, he should be exuberant!* Shamus told himself. A moment of worry crept over him. He scanned the shadows of a great cliff at his back which looked down over the large pool he had recently crawled out of. This seemed like the place Erladoch had described but—*but what?*

"Is this not the place from which you originally left Erladoch?" Shamus asked apprehensively.

Erladoch recognized the tone. "Fear not, friend. This is the place. It's just that…I died here, Shamus," Erladoch offered quietly.

Shamus's stomach gurgled its own surprised response before Erladoch completed his thought.

"Or so my people will have believed. See that ledge so far above us?"

Shamus waited for his eyes to adjust until he could better take in the starlit landscape. He scanned the rise of the rock wall once more until his eyes could identify the clifftop that was at least one hundred feet above their position. He nodded to Erladoch that he could now see it.

"I fell to my death from there four of your years ago after being stabbed by a poisoned dagger wielded by Imrag of Treborg. My band of men and I were on a mission looking for this place of power when we came upon a hundred or more of the Treborgan Scrags while they were out on a border patrol."

Shamus quietly searched for his hand-drawn map that he and Erladoch had meticulously prepared over the period of several nights back at the Browse Cottage. He was relieved to find that it was still dry.

"There were but four of us in my band of Keepers. The closest support for us from any man of the west would have been so many yarricks away. We knew we were on our own and should avoid detection at all costs in such wild lands. We didn't expect to see this large of a contingent of the enemy west of the Elec Mountains, however. We slew many that night, but our mission was not to give battle but rather to find the porthole so that I could jump to your time while the opportunity was still available. Glorf, my captain, gave four long blasts on his horn to make it appear as though he was summoning an army to our side. This was a deception to cause hesitation in the Scrags. He hoped that the Treborgans might flee or at least pause to fortify their position rather than pursue us. Our warning only drew more of Treborg's horde to us. We attempted to scatter in all directions, hoping to lure as many of them away from my intended destination. In a few minutes, the entire countryside was filled with the sound of pounding iron shoes. It felt like thousands of Scrags were actively scouring the area in a part of Loura that they ought not to have been. They somehow had known that we would be there, and they were hungry for the taste of the blood of Dunbar. They hemmed us back together in an ever-closing circle. For a time, I fought back-to-back with Glorf, taking down at least twenty of their warriors before we were forced to the edge of that rock. Imrag of Treborg, a vile servant of the Evil One and an infamous captain because of his giant stature, pierced my side with his dagger. The evil magic of his point coursed through my blood at a fast rate as I felt him twist the ridged blade further into my side. Rather than be able to climb down to the pool where I would wait for the transit, I leaped backward from the cliffs, carrying the Treborgan captain over with me while he dug his blade deeper. Glorf would have seen my fall from the cliff. If by some miracle he had survived and even escaped, he would have not known whether I had made the transit through the porthole or not. He would have only seen my fall. As I tumbled, I heard his horn blow before he likely breathed no more. The two sustained blasts from his lips were a signal loud enough to have echoed through the valleys and the flat lands, proclaiming that the situation was dire. Anyone in our Order who might have heard such a call would know that such a horn call was a death proclamation. It would take little work for those who knew of my mission to conclude that I'd perished."

Erladoch seemed to take in the sacrifice of his comrade a moment. "Alas, Glorf, that man had a spine like an ox! He gave battle like a trapped Manticorn! I am sure that he spent his last breaths proclaiming my death to the land rather than fight to preserve himself. After that, I spent weeks in your world fighting against a poison-induced madness from my enemy's blade. It burned through my veins and should've claimed me!" Erladoch's eyes followed the jagged wall of the hill back to the level of the dark pool, and then he ceased his storytelling.

Shamus noted that the tale had been considerably more detailed than he'd ever heard it before. It was as though any secrets withheld by Erladoch back in Shamus's timeline could now more voluntarily be shared, given that there was no way for him to turn back out of fear. While he understood the importance of his friend's omissions, he couldn't help but feel cheated by not having been trusted with all the facts. At best, he had to accept that his friend did not yet trust in his conviction.

Shamus chose to respect his friend's silence by looking down into the belly of the small fire. His contribution to the silence would be interpreted appropriately as a show of empathy for Erladoch's palpable anguish. His friend was a prince of his people, and by all rights, he was believed to have died despite the fate ascribed to his name by a seer at the time of his birth. Shamus measured the impact such news would have had on the man's father. Erladoch VI, still the reigning King of Dunbar, would have aged immeasurably when the relay of horns over vast expanses finally bore home the tidings of his son's fate—the destiny unfulfilled. Too far past his years to yield another heir, the most powerful dynasty in Loura would weaken. He predicted Erladoch's thoughts as both men collectively read the portents contained in the fire. All too soon, the enemy would be upon them, emboldened by this vacuum in leadership.

The once massive pillars of an altar constructed by the Strahanas surrounding the pool beside where they now rested had long been reduced by time and disuse into crumpled boulders themselves overrun with bramble bushes. The place's general state of neglect told Shamus much about the tragedy of this world without further words being spoken.

Erladoch had previously described this place as having been a forested area. Even in the darkness, Shamus could see that much had changed in four years. There was little evidence of a forest in his vicinity. Instead, there was a presence of decay where they sat. Most of the remaining flora seemed to whisper a collective sorrow into his subconscious, as if the land were registering a complaint against the constant crush of thousands of armored feet that now regularly trampled upon it. He felt a great urgency to get Erladoch back to his kingdom and renew the vigor of his people by letting all know that he was, in fact, both alive and had succeeded—at least in part—in his mission. If trouble were to come upon two solitary men, unhorsed in such unforgiving territory, there would be scant little they could do to bring any glad tidings to Dunbar.

The great weight of this realization suddenly fell heavily upon Shamus. He had to be ready to offer a fight that would support Erladoch in a manner befitting the Keeper's former colleagues at arms. He didn't know if he would be ready for the task. He'd never undergone a true challenge by swords. The near-miss encounter with the menacing Treborgan at the Eternal flame had filled him with doubt. As a last gasping flame pulsed into the ether, he told himself that he'd have to find a way to be more than what he was. *I can be more!* He told himself reassuringly.

Even in the presence of his most contrived self-affirmation, a flood of inadequacy overtook his thoughts. Shamus considered the risk of their being detected in enemy territory as if for the first time. He was powerfully inspired to get under way. Without seeking permission, he rubbed out their warming fire with a stick, no longer taking comfort from its warmth. As though fearful even the crickets might hear their presence, Shamus whispered, "Erladoch, we should leave now; there is little time to spare!"

Without so much as a confirming glance, Erladoch packed his gear and joined Shamus in extinguishing the fire, making it appear as though no one had ever been there. He walked over to the edge of the pool with the sword Shamus had bought for him at an Antique dealer's shop in Ottawa. He dipped it into the pool before giving it a vigorous drying shake. With the light of the night sky reflecting off the blade, it seemed beautifully transformed by the christening Erladoch had given it. To be sure, it did not reveal any of the ancient beauty of Shamus's grand-dad's sword; it lacked the artistically etched runes spanning the length of the former's blade. Nonetheless, it was a fine piece of steel workmanship, and Erladoch's ritualistic bathing of the weapon in the waters of his own time seemed to add an air of strength to it. A brief dance of starlight glimmered across the beads of water that ran down its length. Shamus had never noticed anything special before about the blade. Even when he and Erladoch had been training in the snowbound hills of Calabogie, and the blade's edge had so often come dreadfully close to injuring him, it was just a sharp weapon to be respected. Now, with starlight dancing along its edges, it appeared to him as though a magnificent entity imbued with its own magical spirit had come alive. Bathed in the waters at this place of power, it was now fully fit for the man who bore it.

Erladoch's jaw was agape. He was surprised by the sudden gleam of the blade.

Shamus checked his samurai swords and found that they continued to appear as normal as ever. Clearly, they were made with different materials. He unpacked his grand-da's sword for a moment just to afford himself a quick look. He copied the ritual dipping of the blade into the pool. It was as massive and magnificent as it had always been, but now he espied the most subtle aura flowing from it. It seemed a slight thing, and perhaps could have just been a trick of the eye given the interplay of moonlight and stars. The light continued to be there, however, albeit faint. It gave Shamus the same queer feeling that once had drawn him as a child to try and take it out of its scabbard from above the family fireplace so that he could get a closer look at it. This was a personal family treasure. He felt that it had a story all its own. He mused to his friend that these weapons belonged in this place and had awakened to their new surroundings. Erladoch gave him a slow confirming nod. The action of his confirmatory gesture was accompanied with a quiet grunt. To Shamus's mind at least, the utterance seemed contradictory to the gesture. Unsure of the social graces of his Louran friend, he thought no more about it.

Shamus slid his grand-da's sword carefully back into the scabbard and slung it over his back for easy carrying. This was not the time or the place to delay further. They began to move.

Despite his sense of urgency to leave the area, Shamus was surprised that they walked at an almost casual pace. Erladoch was taking great care in his movement, seemingly to limit the amount of noise they might make. He altered the rhythm of their pace frequently, but never once did he increase it to even a light jog. From time to time, he uttered sounds of night travelers—birds, rodents, some familiar, and some that made Shamus smile due to their utter ridiculousness. He wondered what they could possibly represent, as he was not familiar with any animal that might utter such a call. With each utterance, he couldn't help but think to himself whimsically that if he had ever heard Erladoch make such sounds like this while he'd been a resident of the Royal, he would have likely thrown away the key.

***

Shamus concentrated on his limited range of visibility as they ventured more into the cover of slanted trees. A trip, a stumble of any kind, would surely alert any enemy that what moved in the brush was certainly not a wolf or other sure-footed nocturnal creature. An hour, then two, and then three passed by without another sound being made but their own. He began to wonder if he wasn't constructing an uncomfortable paranoid delusion for himself with his expectation of being assailed at any instant. No matter what the circumstances dictated to the 'Doubting Thomas' side of his brain, his reason warned him that there could be consequences if he disobeyed the silence imposed on him by his host.

Careful baby steps were observed anytime they encountered a change in terrain. In the presence of precarious and trippy tree roots, the two men's strides morphed into slow-motion Tai Chi-like steps, with a deliberate effort being made to never place their feet heavily back to the ground.

17

Shamus pondered the unsettling reality that he had no clear idea of where he was, or for that matter, where he was going. He hoped that the map the two of them had drawn on the dining room table at the Browse compound would start to make sense in the light of day—if ever it arrived. Always within reach of Erladoch, Shamus considered the map more fully. He'd done his best to commit as much of it to memory as he could. He knew from what Erladoch had told him that they were somewhere in the northeast of a kingdom known as Anahimara. This was strictly guesswork, however. Even if he had been a more conscientious boy scout in his childhood (a failing he criticized himself for now), he wouldn't have been able to make heads or tails of the star constellations in the heavens above him. They seemed completely different from anything he'd ever seen. *Perhaps star constellations like the Big Dipper, were just not as obvious at this stage of time*, he considered. In reality, the constellations he did know were there to be seen; they were simply obscured within the exponentially larger number of other stars that could be seen in this place, it being completely devoid of light pollution. Still, it was unsettling to not easily spot a single recognizable cluster long enough to place him here in the dark—at least not without risking a noisy trip over an obstacle on the ground which he needed to pay greater attention to.

***

Chapter 3

The fourth hour of slow march was behind them. The accumulation of dew on the ground signaled that daybreak was near. As this realization came to Shamus, Erladoch stopped their journey and began searching for soft ground. He reached for a small collapsible metal camp shovel the two men had purchased at a camping co-op store before embarking on their journey to the cottage. Erladoch had been very impressed by the many types of camp supplies that the store offered. The notion of packaged dehydrated food particularly fascinated him! In the stillness before sunrise, he directed Shamus to start digging.

Shamus had hoped they could have simply sheltered themselves in a makeshift lean-to. After so much walking in the dark, he was far less inclined to frantically dig a hole large enough for the two of them to sit in. Erladoch was insistent, however, that this hole in the ground was a necessity.

The earth gave way easily enough to the diamond-tipped shovel blades, save for the odd rock, which, much to their chagrin, made way too much noise as it clinked against the metal.

Following Erladoch's direction, they quickly laid their packs into the hole after spreading the dug-up soil around over a 30-foot radius. Covering the hole above their heads with a multitude of twigs and small leafy branches over top of their camouflage jackets, the travel companions were once again in almost complete darkness just as the sun rose on the eastern horizon.

Shamus sat with his legs flat and his back reclining against the cool soil wall. The morning air was warm compared to the slight chill they had arrived in. It was far more welcoming than the deep freeze of a Canadian winter night in March. *I'd take this anytime!* he told himself. While their winter jackets had afforded a comforting warmth, Erladoch assured Shamus that they were more useful as an enhancement to their hiding place.

Erladoch closed his eyes like a cat's, leaving just a slit of light to enter, enough to allow for good peripheral vision. At first, Shamus thought he was actually sleeping in that feline state. Cocking his ears, however, he realized Erladoch was engaged in a ritualized chant barely above an audible threshold. He recognized it as one of his self-soothing chants. Erladoch was comforting himself for some reason. The sound of his voice was nearly subliminal in its flow, and Shamus felt his own eyelids grow heavier. He allowed his chin to drop onto his chest and slowly began to nod off. As his mind faded into somnolence, he remarked to himself that his feet were sore.

***

Whether only moments had elapsed, or it was now hours later, Shamus's last conscious thought of having sore feet had generalized into the thought of other people's sore feet—and not just a few, but a sensation shared by so many others. In this dream-state, he felt each synchronized step being taken by a multitude, one footfall replaced by the next, and somehow, a collective signal of pain. For reasons unavailable to him, this shared pain only fed a form of pervasive madness which, ironically, ignited a craving for the excitement of pain. His senses began to shift focus to the cacophonous noise generated by so many feet, the relentless pounding of heel-to-toe concussions against the earth, as the motion changed abruptly into a rumble somewhere in the approaching vicinity. His eyes opened in fear to see Erladoch with a small dagger bouncing across his lap in anticipation. Shamus was no longer dreaming.

A muffled clamor rose slowly to a resounding pounding against the earth. Soon, the entire ground above them echoed with simultaneous explosions of footfalls crashing in unison. The vibration of so many feet was injurious to their eardrums. Emulating Erladoch, Shamus withdrew the 16-inch short katana. There was no need to guess his friend's mind; any noise coming from them down here in their hole was incomprehensible right now.

Sitting with his legs now poised to allow him to pounce from the hole, Shamus hoped to summon the kind of adrenal surge that might allow him to fight like a wild lion if they were discovered. His body was at least 'this ready', he lied to himself. His confidence in his ability to engage in the actions of a warrior seemed too unreal to deal with. He began to pray that they wouldn't be discovered, then questioned if such a prayer would be heard in this time and place, so far from everything he had once known. Following that half-formed doubt, his predicament told him that it no longer mattered what he thought. He simply had to fight. This sense of resignation reassured him in some small way, accompanied by the knowledge that, with his blade at the ready, he was tipping the odds in his own favor, at least for the first encounter.

The ground shook wildly all about them as the clamor of armored shoes went from proximate to directly overhead. Dust swirled through cracks in the camouflage and descended upon them like an impenetrable cloud, separating the sightlines between Erladoch and Shamus, though only inches away lay between them as the Scraggin soldiers ran overhead.

Shamus felt isolated from Erladoch, as though his friend were suddenly miles away. With both sound and light stifled by the tumult above and the air filthy with unbreathable dust, he couldn't discern if his companion was still beside him or had already leaped from their cache with sword and dagger in hand, expecting Shamus to back him.

He reached out very slowly to see if he could feel whether Erladoch's legs were anywhere in the hole. Reassuringly, Erladoch reciprocated with two pats on Shamus's foot to let him know he was still there. The thunder of the soldiers' footfalls did nothing to drown out the guttural jeers of the officers as the horde ran past.

Oh Christ! There must be a thousand of these guys racing by us! he thought anxiously, considering his odds. The raucous footfalls kept thundering past.

With only the warning coming of a sharp "crack!" the roof of their cache split open. One solitary soldier came crashing down toward Shamus's lap, its abdomen unwittingly straddled Shamus's upthrust sword. The 'Scrag' came down hard. Shamus could tell immediately that the name given to these Treborgan soldiers was apt. The man's appearance was as disheveled as it was hideous. The name captured even more. Shamus knew instantly he was looking upon a Neanderthal man. Beneath the deliberately scarred visage, the hallmark sloping forehead and large jaw were frighteningly apparent. Any quality of 'humanity', however, was not present. This early man now formed part of a warrior race, conscripted from childhood into this station of evil and blind madness. The Treborgan army had been built upon these precursors to Homo Sapiens.

The Scrag's body absorbed the blade until its tip forcefully shot through his back. Shamus expected to see the man's face contort in surprise and pain through the momentary clearing of dust inches from his face. Instead, the soldier appeared enraptured by his impending demise. This reaction only increased Shamus's level of terror and revulsion as the Scrag's jaw snapped uselessly inches from his face, in some vain effort to bite him. Eyes locked on him, the Scrag belched blood from its mouth as its midriff came to a firm halt against the hilt of Shamus's katana. The Scrag's body was adorned with crude, ineffectual armor that did nothing to prevent it from being fully skewered.

Once the initial shock of having fallen into the pit seemed to clear from the soldier's face, a new look started to form at the moment of death. It was a nightmarish grin that suggested contentment over having savored its own end.

The Scrag's body stank of exertion! Blood poured over the sword hilt and onto Shamus's still firmly clasped hands. He would have screamed from the abject horror of the moment had it not been for the dust, which had sucked the moisture from the very depths of his own throat, rendering him mute. Not knowing what else to do, he allowed the body draped over him to finish its death shake before attempting to wriggle out from under its weight and free his blade. A terrifying realization overtook him—that others would be leaping into the now partly open ground which had just swallowed up one of their multitude.

Shamus's conscious mind registered a flood of thoughts in an instant: he realized he had just killed, albeit involuntarily. This was replaced by the thought that he had survived this first encounter with the enemy, which immediately yielded to the realization that he needed to free himself from the body slumped over him as he may have only seconds before he would meet this same fate. As he rolled the body over and withdrew his blade, he felt his hands shake as he tried to steady his katana in an upright position once more.

He had no time to consider his conscience or the fact that this image of his kill might stay with him till the day he died. Instead, he tried to refocus on the thunder of feet echoing warnings that at any second, he should expect to block and parry the incoming assault of swords swinging down at his and Erladoch's heads.

Seconds drew into dusty, breath-robbing minutes. He did his utmost to position his legs under his buttocks while gluing his back tightly against the pit wall, as the lactic acid of frozen anticipation permitted. He would need to make the highest leap he could manage with his heavy broadsword still strapped to his back and his short katana once again free in his hands.

The moment never came. The entire incident went unnoticed by anyone, and the war party moved on until the sound of their thumping feet was but an unpleasant echo in Shamus's mind.

*****

After a long silence had replaced the disappearing thunder, Erladoch leaped out of the hole. He reached down and dragged the corpse of the hideous creature away from where Shamus still sat, unmoving. He was in shock, sitting as he'd been—ready to pounce, or so he had told himself. His legs wouldn't move. All he could do was continue to sit. A pool of steaming residue was soaking through his pants. He wanted desperately to rid himself of the horrid stench that he seemed to be bathing in. All he could feel was the immovability of his own legs and the warmth of another's wasted life against his skin. As he attempted to remove the dust from his face, the scent of the Scrag's spent fluids filled his nostrils. Nausea flooded over him in waves.

After he regurgitated mostly dust and bile from his throat, Shamus felt himself carefully hoisted from the hole. By a strange turn of fortune, they were still alive. Although consumed with the momentary sense of elation which came from this as he gazed off into the back of the disappearing dust cloud of the war party, his eyes caught the stare of urgency from Erladoch, who continued to move swiftly in silence as if they might still be heard over the vanishing clamor.

Shamus watched in fascination as Erladoch selected the sturdiest branch that had formed part of their hideaway and began ramming it through the Treborgan Scrag, into the hole made by the katana. He realized they had to make quick work of covering their tracks. His friend's actions were already focused on this effort.

It was clear to Erladoch this momentary oversight of one soldier disappearing from their ranks would at some point attract the notice of an officer. A party would be sent out to find him, and on the assumption that it was a desertion, the miserable soul would be brought back to the fold and flayed alive for all to witness his cruel punishment, before they would then be allowed to feast on their departed comrade's flesh. The body would be found one way or the other. In such lands, all flesh equaled food for Treborgans. For his and Erladoch's sake, Shamus hoped that the Scrag's absence would not be noted for a long time!

It had to appear the Scrag had stumbled and ended its own life by sheer lack of coordination. Shamus had no clear idea how to accomplish such a feat, but as Erladoch was already attending to that task, he set himself to filling in their hole to make it look less like a hideaway and more like a large, naturally formed pothole.

The unpleasant sucking noise of the corpse re-consuming its final entree was too sickening for Shamus to witness as Erladoch carefully worked the branch through him. Shamus squatted like a rabbit and paddled as much soil in behind himself as he could. Erladoch dropped the corpse in a position that made the accidental impalement more believable. Both men carefully stirred the earth on itself to disguise any blood trail inconsistent with such a trip-and-fall scenario. Shamus showed Erladoch his job of rapid hole-filling, much impressed with himself. Erladoch nodded, acknowledging that his friend had clearly accomplished the important task without words.

In a voice as small as a child's, he whispered, "We'll follow their path backward from here for a few yarricks so only a serious search will reveal our presence." His extended index finger indicated they should run backward among the deep tracks lain down from their approach.

Shamus set himself like a football player, preparing to back pedal when Erladoch stopped him. "No Shamus, you must run like a Scrag." Erladoch then set about leaping backward, one long stride after another, matching in reverse what the enemy had done naturally moving forward.

"Once you begin, you must not stop; your feet cannot come together. No Scrag knows the meaning of rest. They are tortured by night and torment themselves by day. They know only pain and hunger for it. They run to feel their hearts pound like crashing stones, with strides long and heavy. You must do as they have, but in reverse. This is how we hide ourselves amidst their tracks."

Erladoch was already hopping blindly backward in what seemed like an impossible task to accomplish without falling. As he was already getting far off, Shamus began to play backward hopscotch, with the full weight of his pack and harnessed swords thudding against his shoulders and back with each landing. The first few steps were shaky and felt ridiculous, but as he gained some pace, he discovered that maintaining his balance depended on springing backward immediately as one foot rolled into the ground. It was exhausting work.

After crossing stride for stride for what Shamus had figured to have been two or so miles, they bounded off on Erladoch's instructions over small shrubs and down a hill. The landing was slightly disorienting and even painful, but the purpose of not making a parting set of tracks from those of the patrol made it a bearable pain.

They caught their breaths for only a few brief moments, when Shamus espied a small pond a few feet from where he lay. He scampered over to the water's edge to clean his face and drink from the small pool. Covered in sweat and dirt, and still beset by the taste of his own vomit, he longed to clean himself and slake his thirst. His hands splashed against the still water, forming a drinking cup with both hands. He opened his mouth wide to take in the largest possible mouthful. As his upper lip prepared to kiss the cool of the water, meant to cleanse the crust of dust caking his lips and nostrils, Erladoch's massive hand grabbed him from behind and forced the fluid from his palms before he could savor it.

Shamus was momentarily angered and startled in equal measure as he sought out Erladoch's eyes for understanding.

"I see no fish swimming in these waters. We should consider that the Scrags may have poisoned it."

Shamus looked quizzically at his friend. "Why would they do that? Surely they need water just like everyone else?" His throat was so dry that his voice sounded more like a croak. The question seemed a fair one.

Erladoch nodded in agreement. "After they have taken refreshment for their own needs, they poison the places where water collects. The only water safe out here is from a spring or running river. The water which gathers in pools like this here under the domain of Treborg can never be considered safe for any creature. Laying waste to the lands is their best defense from intruders. No army that would challenge Treborg can venture far without carrying with them strong holds of water. This forces them to move slowly and only to the extent of their supplies. Their method is better than the construction of any walls since the juice of life delays the approach of any advancing army."

Shamus was skeptical. He couldn't help but measure his thirst against Erladoch's words of caution. *Was this an expression of paranoia? Or was this a statement of fact?*

Erladoch read Shamus as though there were lines of text revealing his thoughts across his forehead. He snatched up a small rodent in his right hand and cast it into the pool, forcing its jaws open to take in water. Within seconds, after he withdrew the small creature, it began to spew blood from its mouth and then writhe like someone electrocuted until Erladoch mercifully twisted its head in an abrupt and merciful manner.

Shamus's unquenchable thirst suddenly vanished. The cruelty of the poor creature's suffering caused him momentarily to hate both himself and Erladoch. His undisciplined childishness had compelled his friend to prove his point. "I'm so sorry Erladoch," he whispered. "I should have trusted you without making you prove it."

To his surprise, tears began to roll from Shamus's eyes. His emotions seemed to catch the better of him. As drops of the salty fluid managed to cascade over his dust-encrusted cheeks and lips, his insight told him that what he was feeling had little to do with the rodent and a whole lot to do with what he had just come away from a few miles down the road.

Erladoch said nothing. He studied Shamus's face as the emotional display played itself out. He neither appeared frustrated nor surprised by the overt reaction of his companion.

"Ahhh." He let out a slow, pained breath of understanding. "I see. T'is about the Scrag. It is still a life that you took, no matter how depraved. I'm sorry to say that there will be others before we're done. Know that I also take no pleasure from this. It is simply what must be done."

The flow of his own tears comforted Shamus. It reminded him that he still possessed a sense of right and wrong, even though the life he had taken earlier in the day was that of an enemy.

Erladoch handed Shamus his water bottle, understanding that a pause for reflection was a righteous thing. After Shamus took a small ration, Erladoch allowed a few drops to fall into his own mouth before replacing the lid and shoving the bottle back into his pack. Silently, he pointed to a distant hill long enough for Shamus to focus on it. The companions had been forced out of their hide-hole and were now traveling by day in mostly open country, possibly the most stupid thing they could do. With the intrusion of the Treborgan Scrag, however, it was now imperative that they put as much space between the patrol and themselves as they could.

***

Chapter 4

It was somewhere around 60 degrees Fahrenheit as the sun rose to the height of noon. In one of their many talks before coming to this place, Shamus had learned that the sun of Loura had two names: *Inyi,* which described the morning sun, and *Naga* for the second half of the day. The sun was considered a trickster of sorts, a living force imbued with two personalities that bestowed on the people of this world different gifts and varying warnings. Many ritual behaviors were tied to either portion of the day. In the presence of Inyi, there was a promise of productivity for the first half of the waking day. So long as clouds did not obscure her warm face, many great things could be accomplished. In contrast, Naga's face was a warning that darkness approached. Unfinished work due to laziness would be punished by the ravages that lurked in the coming darkness. Animals needed to be brought in from pastures, farming and construction activities needed to be wrapped up, and the fruits of the day's labors—like a Louran's home—had to be secured against the threat of predation by wolves, bears, or worse yet, brials! There wasn't a child in Loura who didn't grow up with this knowledge of what the sun's separate faces required of them.

Beneath the camouflage coats they wore with arms out like cloaks, the two men began feeling the intensity of fast rising temperature under so much clothing. It was necessary to at least have the clasp fastened at the neck, as the weapons they bore had all been housed in compartments specially sewn inside the coats' lining.

"Erladoch", Shamus panted as he slackened his jogging pace, "I have to rid myself of this coat, or there will be nothing left of me!"

Erladoch stopped abruptly and offered a twisted smile to his friend. After all the training they had done for this adventure, Shamus half expected to see a grimace of disappointment register on his friend's face. He was taken aback not to be immediately chided for weakness or laziness.

After a series of huffs, Erladoch spoke through a tight smile of gritted teeth. "In spite of all of the magic of your time, your wares are not at all made with the same magic as those of Dunbar!" To Shamus's continued surprise, Erladoch chuckled lightheartedly, apparently comfortable speaking out loud as Shamus had just done.

Almost in a daze from heat exhaustion, Shamus considered that the display of mirth seemed over the top for his companion. Without seeking further permission, he threw off the camouflage coat and sat with legs outstretched on the arid ground, leaning his back against a small boulder. Erladoch, still standing tall over his friend, continued to hold his grimaced smile. He was clearly sweating as much as Shamus, but the sustained smile made it appear that he was far less affected from their long run. Something about the smile simply wasn't right.

Perhaps he's just better able to handle the exertion? Shamus considered momentarily, feeling that he was acting like a wimp. As he was about to chide himself further for not being capable of withstanding the rigors of their sustained exercise after long months of training, he found relief as he watched Erladoch begin to tug off his own coat.

Erladoch wavered for a moment. With no warning, he crumpled to the ground before Shamus's eyes. Shamus instinctively pulled back his friend's coat, thinking he had succumbed to the heat and now needed to have his body cooled down. His action revealed a wholly unexpected discovery: Erladoch's side was drenched in blood, near to the area of his four-year-old wound, which had long healed. As he pulled back the coat for a better look, a series of small pulsations of crimson oozed down over a patch of dried sanguineous crust and torn cloth. Unbeknownst to him, Erladoch had quietly applied a swatch of his shirt as a makeshift bandage. It now hung by a few dried threads from the wound, seemingly having recently given way.

"No, no, no, no, no!" Shamus exclaimed as he examined his unconscious friend, seeking out the presence of any other injuries. He guessed that Erladoch had been suffering from this wound for at least a full day, if not more. All this time, and he had not uttered one solitary word of complaint. Instead, he'd driven them onward to a more secure region.

Pressing one hand firmly against the wound, he tried to revive him. The force of compression caused Erladoch to let out a pained groan, but he did not open his eyes beyond a flicker of his lids. Shamus pondered the limits of pain that his friend must have been privately enduring. Removing pressure for a moment to examine what had caused the injury, he could see the different layers of tissue that formed around the small circular gashed area, perhaps the diameter of a dime. The wound could only have been made by a bullet. Erladoch had been shot!

"Shiiiiite!" he allowed the curse to slowly whistle from his lips.

Shamus reached back in his thoughts to the final moments before their leap through the column of light from the Eternal Flame monument. *Jaysus! How could I have not noticed this before?* He summoned his memory now, recalling that after having been pulled to the surface of the pool by Erladoch, he had promptly collapsed in the darkness and had wakened sometime later beside a fire which Erladoch had already built for them. Clearly, he had tended to his wound in this blankness of time after he had collapsed, breathless, on the shore of the pool.

Shamus wondered whether Erladoch had even considered the small hole in his side significant enough to mention after the burning sensation of the initial penetration of the bullet was no longer superheated inside of him.

"Jaysus, Mary and Joseph!" he exclaimed to no one as he felt around for an exit wound and found nothing. "He still has the bullet inside him, and he's already hot with infection!"

Physician or not, he knew that as a first order of business, he had to get the bullet out and find a way to stop the bleeding. He went straight to work, extracting his first aid kit and finding tweezers. Luckily, Shamus was discovering that his sense of squeamishness was not overtaking him. The sight of Erladoch's oozing wound did not incite the wave of nausea he had been overwhelmed by after his encounter with the Treborgan soldier. Instead, he was deeply worried for his friend.

Doing his best to keep pressure around the oozing wound, Shamus dug into the hole with the tweezers until he hit metal stuck in partially clotted-over tissues. He felt around until he felt he had a grip on the object. Erladoch barely stirred. On a count of three, which he silently offered to the wind, Shamus gave a yank with the tweezers. To his great surprise and relief, a flattened piece of metal came out. The slug appeared to be in one solid piece.

"Okay. Okay. Good!" Shamus comforted himself quietly, suddenly concerned that the entire world might hear him. He then pulled out two waterproof stick matches from his backpack and broke off the heads, laying them directly over the oozing hole in Erladoch. The blood now ran more like a small tap as a result of Shamus tearing through it. Grabbing another match, he began scratching the head across the 'never-wet' abrasive surface on the side of the match container until a flame leaped off the edge.

Shamus hesitated a moment as the flame danced inside his shaking hand. "I'm so sorry, man!" he mouthed as he dropped the flame onto Erladoch's wound and watched the embedded match heads light up in one quick, cauterizing flash. Despite the agony he knew this would inflict, Erladoch did not regain consciousness in a screaming fury. His friend's body hardly moved in response to the searing flash of fire, which immediately brought the bleeding to a halt.

Years of unconscious knowledge acquired somewhere from a television screen had jumped to Shamus's quick-acting mind to perform nothing less than battlefield surgery on his friend, and it had worked! The source of the bleeding had been forced by fire to clot over.

Shamus dug out the hooked needle and sterile thread from the first aid kit. The only time he had ever placed something like a needle through another living creature's skin in his entire life was when he was no more than seven, sitting on the end of the dock at his family cottage beside his grand-da and his parents. On that occasion, he had been forced to hold a flopping sunfish that could not have been more than seven inches in length. His grand-da was guiding him to carefully but swiftly withdraw the fishhook from the fish's mouth so that he could free the unfortunate creature and throw him back into the water. As it was very small, it had not been the fish's time to die. Shamus could hear the comfortingly calm voices of his parents and grand-da. They were insistent that Shamus demonstrate great care and respect for God's creature, explaining to him the importance of only killing for a clear purpose, like eating one's catch.

Summoning that memory for support, Shamus carefully passed and then tugged at the needle and thread through the two layers of skin and tissue around Erladoch's wound until he had reasonably closed the skin back together. *Jaysus H Christ!* He hesitated, looking down at his handiwork. *I've no idea if this is even deep enough or if I'm just condemning him to bleed internally.* Perhaps none of these efforts would be of assistance, but as he had no recollection of seeing blood either soaking through the winter coat or dropping onto the earth as they moved, he surmised that Erladoch's loss of consciousness might have been the cause of the reopening of the wound mixed with their exertion under the oppressive heat. He tried to reassure himself once more. *If this isn't an arterial bleed, this will work!*

When Shamus had originally selected the field first aid kit in the camping equipment store, he had no inkling of how or even why the contents might have to be used. Everything inside of him at that moment had compelled him to consider this purchase as a necessary inclusion in his pack, however, and he was extremely glad for his having listened to his inner voice.

He poured some water onto Erladoch's lips, taking care to not pour out too much and make him choke. As he pondered his friend's unconsciousness, a sense of horror fell over him. If Erladoch were to perish, his chances of survival in this strange land were nil! Using the best breathing techniques available to him, he let the panic wash over him a moment longer and then told himself to let the negative thought dissipate.

He knew that they had been traveling in a direction toward a far-off series of hills on the horizon. Erladoch had specifically told him that that was their intended heading. He told himself that he could manage to cross that far-off expanse of plains whether Erladoch was awake or not, even if he had to carry him. Until they reached this destination, he made himself a promise that his worries about his friend's survival could not occupy any place in his mind. By then, he hoped that Erladoch would regain consciousness, and they could get back on track.

"This is not how I was meant to go out!" Shamus proclaimed to himself with resolve, looking down over his tightly cleaned handiwork before casting his gaze in all directions. He wasn't afraid of speaking aloud. There were no signs of life for miles in any direction. He formed an intention that both he and Erladoch would live. It made no sense that fate would have dragged him so far from his life's path only to drop him in a semi-arid plain in a land and time that modern man had all but forgotten.

Knowing that they were not going to be moving anywhere for a while, Shamus gathered brush and built a crude lean-to that would provide them shade and some degree of natural camouflage. Settling himself under the sunscreen, he placed two fingers on Erladoch's neck and felt for a pulse. Noticing both its existence and its reasonable strength gave him renewed hope. Prior to passing out, Erladoch had never outwardly acknowledged his pain. Shamus determined to use this as a rudder for his own perseverance. He lay down next to Erladoch, keeping a close watch on the rising and falling of his friend's chest until his own exhaustion finally found him.

***

Chapter 5

Shamus awoke to something nudging his ribcage. Before he could leap into action, his eyes opened to the image of Erladoch bent toward him, still gently nudging him.

The Louran sun was nearly below the level of the rolling drumlins off in the distance. *Naga is disappearing*, Shamus considered. *It will be nightfall soon.*

Erladoch lay on his uninjured side, his eyes scanning across the northwest. Shamus was relieved to find his friend conscious. In spite of waking to this positive sign, it didn't take him long to notice that his brow was still beaded with sweat.

How could he appear otherwise? Shamus rationalized to himself. *I know how I'd feel after someone ripped a hunk of shrapnel from my body, burned me, then ran a needle though my skin like a Thanksgiving turkey, all without a single drop of anesthetic!* He shuddered at the immensity of such a thing.

"You woke me, didn't you?" Shamus asked, pretty sure of the answer.

Erladoch nodded in the affirmative.

"Why?" Shamus asked, realizing that as nightfall was approaching, they could probably remain there and be far safer under the cover of darkness.

"We must leave here, Shamus, at once!" He croaked out. "They will come soon. The Treborgans have many animals to hunt intruders, both winged birds and wolves. Once they find their dead soldier, they are likely to send search parties out to verify that his death was, in fact, an accident. I have been bleeding since our encounter with him. If even a few drops of my blood leaked onto the ground, the smell of me will be like a map to our position. What their carrion birds cannot see by day, their wolves' eyes and noses drive them forward through the depths of night."

Shamus half expected his companion to next say that he should leave him there to give himself a chance. The pragmatic sense told him, however, that

Erladoch would not say something as daft and dramatic as all this. He alone knew the direction to be followed in their quest. Despite any mapwork they may have done back at Calabogie, it occurred to Shamus that he had no clear picture of why the distant hill indicated hours earlier by Erladoch was, in fact, the direction to go. It was certainly not as though every hill was depicted in their maps.

Thoughts about the mission that had brought them to this place and time were utterly irrelevant right now. Any discussions concerning their one day defeating the evil that was spreading over these lands seemed so far off as to even be out of reach altogether now. The only consideration that Shamus could bring into focus in this moment was to confirm their direction, lest Erladoch lose consciousness again. Grappling with the possibility that a Treborgan war party might very well be closing in on them right now had to be secondary to knowing where the hell he was headed.

"Erladoch, it would be foolish to walk all the way to Dunbar in your state. You're in no condition to make any movement tonight."

"I will have to, Shamus. There is no other way." He tried to roll over and get up. Pushing off his elbows, he began to growl in pain, catching himself before he might cry out in a louder voice.

"Holy shit, Erladoch! You're being stupid! Don't move! You will open your stitches, and then the chances of infection will be even worse." He considered his surroundings. "I have an idea. Lie there a little longer, please!"

"But!" Erladoch protested, "We need to go!"

"I know!" Shamus snapped back at him out of frustration. "I'm working on it. Just give me a moment, okay?"

Erladoch lay back down, trusting in the earnestness of Shamus's advice. In actual fact, Shamus did have an idea. He began assembling an A-frame style of litter that would allow him to bear Erladoch. During the 20 or more minutes in which it took for Shamus to scavenge materials sufficient to bring the litter together, Erladoch made no comment to him. Instead, he watched his friend with pleased fascination.

Every time that Shamus moved more closely to his friend, he could hear Erladoch muttering the song of self-healing. He'd taught this to Shamus over and over again during their training at the Browse Family Cottage. The regularity of the pitch changes and intonations reverberated into Shamus's mind like the subtle waves of a tuning fork on the lower end of the scale.

Listening to his friend sing as he continued to busy himself, he allowed his thoughts to wander in pace with the chant. Suddenly, Shamus's sense of dread became flaccid and empty; the anxiety about his and his companion's circumstances left him. Instead, his mind rode on the waves of Erladoch's serial chant. So long as the humming continued, he did not fear that Erladoch was still grievously at risk of a life-ending infection. He thought nothing of the impending threat that could fall upon them at any time. He was no longer sure whether he was listening to Erladoch's voice or whether the tones in his ears were the product of his own contribution to the chant. His pace at building a suitable litter to carry Erladoch increased to a point where the time taken to twist fabric and branches into a sturdy enough shape seemed like fleeting moments instead of the hour it might actually have taken him.

Even in his diminished state, Erladoch was lifting him along, maintaining Shamus's focus on the single-mindedness of the task.

When he was ready, he carefully arranged his hands underneath Erladoch's shoulder blades and ever so carefully eased him on to the stretcher. The tightly toothed grimace from his friend confirmed that he had not been gentle enough.

***

Chapter 6

The light of day had vanished only to be replaced by a few very bright stars. The brilliant sky of the previous night had been obscured by fast-moving whisps of cloud that made the landscape less visible. As Shamus hooked the arms of the newly made litter inside the straps of his pack, he wondered where he should be headed. *Anywhere but here!* his inner voice directed him.

As he took the first steps to drag his comrade across the plain, the scarring scrape of wood branches across rock and sand invaded the quietude of everything, including Erladoch's self-comforting chant. He would not be able to focus himself again as the rattle and scratch against hard earth made focus-shifting an impossibility for now. Erladoch would thus be left to deal directly with the pain of his torn and re-sewn flesh.

Shamus confirmed the direction of travel before setting off. The course they had been on continued to be their path. They would make for the distant hills. Even in the dark, the unmoving North Star poked out of the cloud cover often enough that Shamus could fix on this as a guidepost. It was the same heading they had begun earlier during the daylight, and Erladoch seemed sufficiently present as to ask for slight course corrections when it appeared that the path might be diverging.

Although the litter was somewhat of an awkward contraption, it was balanced well enough that Shamus found himself relieved to only have to support a fraction of Erladoch's total weight. The mutual desire was to cover ten to fifteen miles in the time before dawn, and Shamus felt that his months of training and his ingenuity in building the litter made anything possible, so long as the litter held up and the terrain cooperated.

Midnight came and went uneventfully. Save for a few minor starts caused by small, curious eyes of thankfully small nocturnal creatures that would mark Shamus's presence, and then dart off out of reach, there were no large predators about. Each time he felt the aching burn of exertion in his back and shoulders,

Shamus would force himself to consider whether he would prefer to be the one with the gunshot wound or the one who was healthy enough to help the guy with the gunshot wound. He recalled the 'zip zip' sound of bullets buzzing past him as he leaped into the porthole and now considered himself to be lucky enough to even be alive.

Somewhere back in his timeline, the media was having a three-ring circus over the corpses of the two men whom police officers had obviously managed to take down, but not before the former had slaughtered several innocents and police. No one could piece together why two darkly clad men had attacked a peaceful demonstration of First Nation Algonquins in the midst of their performing a peaceful ancestral celebration. More importantly, no one had even tried to figure out which officers had managed to end the lives of these horrifying terrorists in such dramatic fashion. This was what they were now being called in the media, despite any clear motive. Armed with swords as their principal weapons, some bright light would likely report that they were members of some Dungeons and Dragons-like cult who had run amok. None of it would ever really make sense, no matter how the story got spun!

The scraping across the hard terrain resounded in both men's ears. Even though it could not be helped, they recognized that any patrol within a mile of them would probably hear them grating across the plain. Erladoch took pains to draw out his short sword and let it rest on the litter beside his uninjured flank so that it was close at hand in the event of a sudden surprise.

Shamus recognized that his friend had taken this precaution without looking back over his shoulder. He wondered how much contribution Erladoch could actually lend to a battle given his injured state, but he knew enough about him now to not count him out. Shamus himself would likely not survive such a swift surprise attack, given the time it would take to get out from under the litter handles he had made for himself. The hope of having enough time to draw his sword out to present a proper defense in such circumstances was, at best, a long shot. With his shoulders already so stressed from the effort of bearing his friend, the thought of lifting or swinging a blade right now was nearly beyond him. He did his best in that moment to disregard the thought of being set upon and continued to focus squarely on moving one foot ahead of the other on his course.

At least an hour had gone by in relative silence. Shamus wondered whether Erladoch was asleep or had passed out. He hoped that any infection Erladoch might have from the wound would not overwhelm his body and leave him alone in a world that he knew nothing about. The anxiety of this pervasive thought was infectious! He had to find a different focus.

Simple adjustments in the positioning of Shamus's arms temporarily allowed him some relief as he felt his larger muscle groups fatiguing to a point of quitting altogether. This body shifting had permitted him to continue. He wondered how many miles he had covered as the dark of night continued to blanket them from anyone's long-range view. The continuous squelch of litter scraping across hard ground was, however, too damned loud for comfort.

Erladoch began to oscillate between feverish sleep and utterances of a multi-toned hymnal. Shamus found himself trying in his usual scientific manner to analyze the fragments of the chant, hoping that his copying of it might assist him as well. At the minimum, it would keep him distracted from his effort.

In his moments of wakefulness, Erladoch recognized and appreciated the intention behind Shamus's efforts to hum in concert with him, even when his friend went completely off on a tangent. It was through his own similar approach at mimicry that he had ultimately come to master the English language. He slowed the chant down so that the language fragments of the old Louran tongue might seem more discernible. While there had been sporadic efforts back in Shamus's time where Erladoch had expended effort at helping his friend speak the 'old tongue', he now worried about what would happen to Shamus if he passed away. Acquiring the common language of the people of Loura would be essential to Shamus's survival, and they had really not spent any effort toward this. Erladoch chided himself for not having considered that he might not be around to act as Shamus's interpreter. His friend from the future was not going to have the luxury of time to communicate his mission to anyone!

Unlike Erladoch's sojourn in the S.T.U., where months of his imitation of sounds could progress to a point of language acquisition, Shamus would likely be slain the moment he began uttering gibberish to anyone. Any member of his Order whom he might come across would absolutely fear that Shamus was a servant of Enilorac who was intent on casting a spell and cut him down before he could complete a sentence.

***

The discomforting strain on Shamus's shoulders began to wear heavily. The pull of the straps he had fashioned around the litter poles now bit angrily into the small fibers around his neck. He half-closed his eyes in answer to the mounting muscle strain, carefully repeating the slow inhalations and exhalations of his own breath, doing his utmost to bring them back in line with what Erladoch had been so invested in hours earlier before succumbing to fevered sleep. It was likely a good thing that his friend slept, but Shamus's sense of loneliness was a launch pad for anxious thoughts and now, more compellingly, the punishing exertion of dragging a man of his own basic weight along with both of their weapons and small provisions.

The rhythm isn't right! he chided himself. *I've got the words down, so it has to be 'how' I'm doing it.* Shamus adjusted the straps for the twentieth time in the last hour. He tried to get himself to take his throat out of the chant altogether, compelling his inhalation to fill his stomach and then his chest fully and completely before allowing his lungs to resume graduated out-breaths. To his great relief, a change began to occur. His breathing slowed as he allowed the sounds of the chant to leave from the pit of his stomach. A warmth flooded across his shoulders where there had only been painful pulsations. Calming reverberations danced over his previously clenched jaws as they echoed out from his eardrums. He quickly began to forget about the pain in his arms and the stretching burn in his neck and traps. *No way!* he assessed the physiological changes which washed over him from the discrete adjustments he had made. *Nailed it!* Shaking his head in utter disbelief, a smile formed on his face for the first time in days.

Erladoch's chant on this night, just like it had been at the Browse Family Compound, was old science. Erladoch the Keeper was imbued with the knowledge of his own 'ancients'. He had been trained his whole life to respect the science of nature. Having maintained his chant over the hours where he had managed periods of wakefulness, he had passively guided Shamus into accessing the healing magic of song. Through repetition and left with no choice but to truly focus down on what Erladoch had demonstrated, Shamus had discovered a piece of his own natural healing magic. Were he able to see himself in a mirror, he was sure that he'd see his own aura reverberating around him.

As he plodded on more comfortably now, Shamus knew that chemicals in his brain were unlocking from within to help with the strain. So much of

Shamus's education had come out of a textbook or the even more immediate results of e-learning. Without realizing it, in his own lifetime, so much of what he knew and believed about his world had been orchestrated by mass media that itself was highly scripted and edited. Trial and error for children of his modern age had come to an abrupt end by the time he could begin to recite the alphabet. Parents of his generation had become so terrified of the 'error' component of their children's learning processes that they had found a way to banish risk without assessing the rewards which the experience of failure often provided. Skinned knees, scrapes and bruises had been replaced far too often with simulations, tech gaming and virtual goggles.

The kind of learning that had been made available to Erladoch was altogether something different; it was by comparison at least, limitless. The latter's entry into Shamus's life had started an unraveling process. So many things connected to Shamus's self-image and the life-path that he thought he had worked out for himself were now completely laid bare. As a student of psychology, he had often read of ancient cultures that accessed methods of generating high levels of endorphins under physically difficult conditions. Buddhist monks and Aboriginal cultures alike on every continent all seemed to possess this knowledge, but western men who could not reproduce the same results in the sterile surroundings of a laboratory all too often gave up. Because of this failure of science to identify the 'how's' and 'why's' behind this healing phenomenon, investigation often ended in the modern world. It had really only been in the past 80 years that more open-minded members working in the fields of psychology or medicine began to reconsider the power of hypnosis. Its ability to replace the need for anesthesia in some instances began to reopen doors of learning that had been closed for generations. The reality continued nonetheless to be that hypnotherapists who achieved such practices were small in number, themselves considered outliers in science. Whatever they were doing to achieve true altered consciousness in others still looked more like magic than science. *And that,* Shamus reasoned as his musical breath flowed out of his lungs filling him with renewed vigor, *was the true reason why modern society continued to fail. The people of my timeline have all but eviscerated faith in their quest for empiricism.* He measured the disconnect between the two worlds with each lofty stride. *If you can't weave your understanding of something inside the very narrow confines of science, then it was nothing short of being 'magic'. Expressed another way,* Shamus postulated to himself as though he were practicing a presentation to a bunch of students, *magic, like faith, are really two words to describe the same phenomenon.* "Man! Science can really suck!" he said aloud, causing Erladoch to stir a little. *Erladoch has shown me how to tap into a power I didn't know was even within me,* he considered as he marched along. *I will have to let him know how he has helped me, assuming that he regains consciousness again. He will regain consciousness!* he assured himself. "Steady on, Shamus. Steady on."

***

The effort of dragging his friend was no longer a growing burden. It was simply a thing that he had to do.

Shamus was renewed. He smiled in the knowledge that he was on a path of 'becoming', and that for the first time in a long time he wasn't calculating the world on book knowledge. Instead, he was scanning his feelings, and in doing so, was finding wisdom. Whether he had known it or not before, Erladoch had been giving him back the power to think for himself—an autonomy that he had long before unknowingly surrendered. As dust kicked up into his nostrils from the quickening of his footfalls, he felt unspeakably enriched at that moment. Even if he were to die in this desolation, he would do so with the knowledge that he was suddenly a free man. He wanted to yell into the empty darkness of the nightscape that he was 'there', truly present in the universe. The sense of personal power overtook all sense of dread that he had born in his stomach. It was replaced with a longing to discover what else lay within him. He smiled as the chant rolled up from the depths of his innards, and his pace quickened further still.

***

Chapter 7

Morning was somewhere near. Shamus could smell the approaching daybreak as the flowers in the field he had entered began to open in anticipation of being bathed in dancing fingers of sunlight. All through the night's long journey, he was brought back to his situation's reality with the faint sounds of what could have been distant drums, but it may have simply been the sound of blood pounding in his ears from sustained exertion.

He felt the softness of short grasses beneath his feet now, replacing the hard clay he had been traversing for what had felt like an eternity. Sliding out from under his shoulder straps, he gingerly laid the litter down. Erladoch had been beyond consciousness for some time now. His breathing continued to be steady, however, and he did not seem to be laboring through a fever at the moment. Shamus did his best to preserve whatever rest his friend could attain by moving carefully. Without permitting himself the luxury of sitting down, he stretched his core in every direction before using the emerging light to locate and start gathering branches and shrubs for camouflage. As he stretched forward to retrieve a long and already broken branch of a flowering shrub, he felt the utter emptiness of his stomach. It became a pressing and important thought that he should sit down and eat to renew his strength. He rummaged through his pack and came up with some dried meat and fruit, doing his best to open the vacuum seal on the bags as quietly as possible. The oddity of the sound was all it took for Erladoch's eyes to open hastily, not knowing the origin of the quiet 'woosh' made by the opening of the second package. Before he had hammered two bites of dried jerk chicken into his mouth, Erladoch was looking at him with a clear intent to attempt something more solid than the water refreshment Shamus had been giving him at regular intervals during the night. While he had drifted into sleep for the last part of their trek, his mouth now flew open wide like a baby bird's when the smell of food crossed under his nostrils.

Shamus had not dug a hole within which to hide. There was enough ground cover around now that he felt assured a lean-to made with local flora would afford them the camouflage they needed without the effort of having to dig like a gopher. He pulled the final branch over their packs and their bodies, the packs being used as the outer walls of their shelter. He then joined Erladoch in the very pleasant act of eating. A handful of food for each of them was all that could be spared until fresh game could be caught.

"You seem to be on the right course, Shamus, we covered much ground overnight!"

This was the first thing he had heard Erladoch say in many hours. The sound of his voice gave him a small start after their having both been under an imposed silence for so many hours.

Erladoch was obviously in a weakened condition, but the returning color to his face was a far sight better than it had been the day before. At first, nothing was spoken of concerning his wound. Only when Erladoch had drawn back his dried blood-stained shirt to inspect the curious patchwork of stitches under his ribcage did he finally make mention of his injury. "Our return to Loura through the hole did not go as well as I had hoped. The hole made in me by that bullet did not feel the same as the filthy Treborgan dagger that had pierced me on my way out of here, but it still burned something terrible!"

Shamus recognized that in Erladoch's pain and fleeting consciousness, he did not have a grasp of the fact that Shamus had set a small cauterizing fire in his friend's wound. Shamus chose to say nothing to correct this understanding. He was just happy to have conversation again.

"In my dreams, it was as though I had never left here. It felt that I had only just fallen into the pool from the far cliff moments before, instead of four years having passed from my life and my mission having failed."

This was the first time that Erladoch had even approached discussing any part of the beginning of his voyage. Shamus did his best to listen. He was truly interested in knowing more about how his friend had been the one tasked to make the time jump to the future. Try as he did, he could not hold his eyelids open much longer. He felt guilty that Erladoch now wished to chat, but he couldn't seem to help himself. The need for sleep had crept up and taken him by storm. His eyes complied with the weight of his fatigue effortlessly, even as Erladoch appeared prepared to unburden himself by trying to share his tale.

Chapter 8

Shamus awoke feeling refreshed after what had felt like a long sleep. The scent of the juniper-like shrubs over him made his first moments of awakening pleasant. His eyes searched slowly through the cracks of the bushes to find their focus. The terrain was certainly more pleasant than that of the day before. What vegetation there was consisted of prickly but not unpleasant green shrubberies and stunted trees like the ones he had used for cover. Many of them held small blossoming flowers in random clusters about the branches.

He began stretching his limbs and realized that he could fully reach sideways. This gave him a start, as Erladoch was not beside him on the ground. He pushed his head up and out of the cover a little to scan the immediate area. Erladoch was nowhere to be seen. Shamus's heart gave several worried skips as he took in the implications of his friend's absence. He sat up more fully, noticing with rising trepidation that Erladoch's sword was also missing. There were no signs of struggle or foul play on the ground around him, and he realized that his hiding place was still intact.

As it was near sunset, he hoped that whatever Erladoch was up to, he would find his way back to him soon. Shamus was somewhat annoyed by his friend having wondered off so. With the wound he had sustained, Erladoch was at risk of having it reopen and possibly render him unable to return from wherever he now was. The plane he found himself on as Naga was approaching its descent stretched only a few thousand yards, but obviously, there had to have been drop-offs somewhere not far off. Wherever Erladoch had wandered off to, Shamus was apprehensive that the exertion of walking any such distance so soon after having been operated on would weaken his friend. He chose to sit and wait, trusting that there was some actual purpose to why Erladoch would risk this action. It wouldn't have been for the purpose of relieving himself; they were long past any sense of embarrassment over attending to bodily functions.

As he pondered his companion's thought process, Shamus caught sight of a fair-sized bird settling to earth by a clump of flowers about twenty feet away from where he was sitting. It was sufficiently out of reach that he accepted that he would not be able to catch it. It squawked menacingly for a moment, noticing Shamus's presence for the first time under the bushes. Defiantly, it shook a wing at him as if to say, "Nice try, but I could see you from a mile off!" which, from the sky, it probably could have, given that Shamus had clearly disturbed the cache in his initial frantic search of the landscape for Erladoch.

Without giving him any more obvious consideration, the bird with its extensive red plumage quivering from the slight breeze, waddled over to the flowers perched at the top of a small shrub. It plucked up the insides of the flower in its jagged beak, swallowed, and then went for another one. It never reached the flower. From between the legs of the bird, a sharp knife fired out of the sand from a point directly beneath it, the tip of the blade piercing its throat at the same time as a second hand took firm hold of the doomed creature's legs. Shamus could have laughed out loud at the obnoxious creature's fate had he not himself been so surprised by the rapidity of the attack of the well-concealed hunter.

Shamus didn't have time to consider whether this hunter posed danger to him, as the figure emerging from the sandy cache was clearly Erladoch. As Erladoch rose to his knees out of the dirt and began to half-crawl toward him, one hand still wound around the fowl's now limp legs, Erladoch blew the sand off his face with a strong upward puff.

Shamus was in awe. He had no idea that his friend had remained so close to him. '*Quite a rugged practice for the Prince of Dunbar,*' he mused to himself only. He sniggered aloud this time to display his amusement at his friend's appearance. "You certainly never showed me that hunting technique back in Calabogie! What d'ya call that? The invisible sand monster?"

Shamus wondered possibly too late that he might have just insulted Erladoch with his last comment, but the appearance of his friend emerging like a Mudman of New Guinea was all too humorous for him to conceal, and he started to laugh in spite of himself.

After a moment's measure of Shamus, and the initially dazed look on his friend's face as sand fell away from his body, Erladoch began to laugh as well, knowing that he must have looked ridiculous with twigs and dirt sticking out of his hair. He gave his head a shake to free himself of most of the mess and crawled closer to Shamus, clearly still too injured for much sudden or sustained movement.

"I suppose that is as good a name as any," he remarked, still smiling at his success. "You'd never catch a rabbit by lying under the snow. Besides, snow is way colder than sand."

Shamus knew that Erladoch was doing his best to be practical with his reply. Regardless of the intention, Erladoch found it amusing how surprised his friend was by his camouflaged appearance.

"Guess you've used this hunting technique more than once, then?" Shamus queried.

Gauging that Shamus was still utterly tickled by the experience, Erladoch screwed up his face with feigned seriousness, then uttered his best Jarhead answer: "Booyah!" He spouted out, inviting both men to share a further chuckle.

Before their next march, they would at least have a nice meal to reward themselves with instead of having to access one of their freeze-dried meal packages that clearly neither was loving. Shamus assembled twigs as Erladoch immediately set himself to the task of plucking feathers from what would shortly become their dinner. As soon as nightfall overtook the light, Shamus struck a match to the dry wood pile.

***

Chapter 9

It was nearly the midpoint of their night voyage. Shamus's mind was blank, the delight of still feeling a good dinner in his stomach dominating his untroubled mind. He was pulling Erladoch once more, and at a reasonably solid clip, thanks both to his rest and the restorative meal.

Erladoch had initially attempted walking, expressing that he felt like useless baggage. It was no mean feat for Shamus to convince him to stay off of his legs at least another day or two to allow for greater mending. Given that Erladoch ultimately complied was confirmation enough that his friend was not yet capable of such travel. Regardless of his earlier display of hunting prowess, Erladoch had rolled himself to the soft earth where he had constructed his hunting cache. The infection, which was still vying for control over him, was made worse by any effort at real exertion, and he possessed the common sense to not push it.

As Shamus pulled and dragged the litter over softer earth, Erladoch recounted tales of his people to help them both pass the time more comfortably. Shamus soaked up the information greedily, and the distraction offered by it. The night was breezy and pleasantly cool, like a late spring morning might have been at home, rather than the still potentially punishing cold that more often hung around Ottawa in early March. If not for the warmth caused by his exertion, Shamus might otherwise have needed to put his jacket back on. Still, he assessed that the climate of this place was at least a month ahead of what he was used to for the time of year back home.

All night long, he could tell he was progressing through a ravine of sorts. Soon, he felt the beginnings of a slope underfoot, pressing back to meet the effort of his legs. Shorter, more wide-legged strides became necessary as the additional effort required to move forward announced to him that the terrain he was coming into was a form of rolling foothill. With the darkness looming from one side somewhere just up ahead, Shamus wondered whether he was skirting along the edges of a tall forest. Whenever possible, he did his best to stay on flat ground unless Erladoch suggested a course change. Shamus wanted as best as possible to afford himself the longest view possible despite the surrounding cloak of darkness. The more opportunity to espy shapes approaching them, the better. With stars entirely obscured by clouds overhead, such a long view was impossible.

With trees on one side of him, Shamus constantly misperceived the subtle movement of tree limbs to be bodies coming at him through the darkness, ready to end his life. His sense of apprehension and vigilance grew ever higher. He took comfort, however, that with the dawn, he would at least be able to take cover under the treetops when it was time for rest.

***

After having traversed at least 3 more miles with the forest still on their left, Erladoch bade Shamus to stop and find him a sturdy and leafy branch. He cautioned him to avoid cutting one from a tree as this would be noticeable to anyone tracking them. Shamus would have to gather it from the forest floor. The intent was to begin stirring up the dirt behind them once into the forest proper to make the tracks left behind from the litter less obvious.

"We are fully in the midst of the kingdom of Anahimara now. A land comprising some of the most ferocious and noble warriors among our Keeper brethren. Those Anahimarans among my Order meticulously watch the borderlands between themselves and Treborg. They, more than the rest of us, have ensured that nothing comes over the Elec Mountain range without their notice. Alas," Erladoch sighed reflectively. "I thought that by now we would have made contact with scouts from my Order, Shamus, and that you could have been relieved of the burden of having to bear me along. I wonder about the fate of the Anahimaran people given your dark dreams. Unless what you witnessed was a vision of the future, they may have already been vanquished. I have read the signs over the past yarricks and found the presence of iron shoe prints made by Scraggin soldiers. There are no imprints of the mighty Anahimarans interspersed with those of the Treborgans. This would have at least fired a hope in my belly that Treborg has received some measure of challenge over these lands. I am very troubled indeed!"

Shamus pondered the news. "*I'm sorry, Erladoch. I don't have any way of knowing what I saw in my visions. I don't recall ever having visions of the future before, so I just can't say.*"

Erladoch sighed. "The Anahimarans told the fable that the bravest of their warriors walked deepest into the soil, nearly growing roots like the trees of the Dead Forest from the weight of their own valor." He chuckled bitterly at the tale. "Twas nothing but a boast, of course, but there is no sign of anything other than the presence of the enemy here."

Shamus looked around in vain for the evidence of what Erladoch had been describing, but it was too dark. As they walked along, he felt what could only be described as mini potholes from time to time—not deep enough to trip him up, but uneven spaces that could easily have been created by heavier feet than his own in a soft soil. He surmised that there were, in fact, impressions in the ground all around them. "Erladoch, I can actually feel what you are talking about; the ground around us does seem to have deep foot prints. So, the fable of which you speak is kind of real, is it not?"

"Sadly, no, Shamus. What you are feeling beneath you is the impressions of metal shoes that mimic and disgrace that valor. These are made entirely by Treborgans." At that, Erladoch spat into the earth where one of the more obvious shoe prints must have lain, given the punishing bump that the jarring of his litter had just delivered to him. "The cities you described to me in your nightmare encounters with the Evil One closely resemble the Kingdom of the Anahimarans, and I fear, some of the other cities of Loura. When I came to rescue you in the dreamscape, I did not have the clear sightedness of your surroundings. I had only sought your essence out." Erladoch paused as though tallying the distance they had traveled. "It should not have taken us this long to reach the shrub lands and finally the fruit groves of Anahimara in our journey, even with me not able to be afoot. The waste of Treborgan invasion has not only begun; it has spread far in my absence." Erladoch spoke in more dulcet tones now, clearly saddened by what he was discovering as Shamus trudged on.

"I have fond memories of these lands from when I was a child. I came here often enough to know the lands well. I had my first instruction in the use of the Scabber here. The Anahimarans were the true masters of this weapon."

Shamus recalled Erladoch's description of the Scabber from one of the nights back in his home at 21 The Driveway. He had meticulously described it while they had enjoyed a plate of meats and cheeses accompanied by a hangover's volume of Irish Whiskey. His mouth watered at the thought. The Scabber looked like a wooden staff that could be used as such in combat. It also housed a long blade two feet in length, when opened up like a jackknife. Out of this staff, the blade could be set straight out at the top like a lengthened spear or locked in perpendicularly to resemble a scythe for cutting ripened wheat. This multi-use weapon extended the reach of the Anahimaran warrior to nearly twice the length of any broadsword Shamus had ever seen. In his own mind's eye, he conceptualized the Anahimarans as an army of grim reapers, cleaving their way through their enemies like a farmer cutting through a field of hay. He wasn't surprised to learn from Erladoch that the weapon was indeed developed from such a grain-farming practice. It explained the presence of such soft and clearly arable soil beneath his feet for so many hours now.

"We must be near to the brother cities of Taroc and Ataroc. Every sign I have detected over the ground suggests that these once-great cities have now fallen. We will have to exercise great care when we cross the plain between them. Ach! I pray that the pain of the Anahimarans and their proud King Séoin O'Mara passed quickly, and that none lived to be taken prisoner."

"Although I am reluctant to ask, Erladoch, why would you wish death upon someone so readily?" Shamus interrupted.

"If any were to survive, Shamus, particularly children, they are made into but a few things: food for the killing, or slaves. Some would beg for life only to be driven mad with torture until they themselves would be no different than Scrags. While not born as such, and certainly not having been bred over generations into these filthy, twisted creatures, the evil of the unmade Treborgan king from the Pit is said to be so horrible. The torture inflicted on the bodies of those captured is so unspeakable that the madness of accepting fidelity to the Demon Lord and joining the ranks of his armies would be the only relief from suffering.

"At least, this is what my fellow Keepers recounted about what had been observed of those humans who once composed the House of Treborg when the great Evil was confirmed to have returned to Loura. Prisoners are tormented by burns and must run across white-hot coals to reach water to extinguish their suffering. Once the nerves in their feet and most of their bodies is burned away over time, their minds are twisted with the horror of it. They are shod like horses with iron sandals that make the tracks you see around you, just like the old wild people who became the first Scrags. Whether a Treborgan Scrag or simply made into a Scrag through torture, the enemy's captains whip and flail the bodies of their ranks to toughen the skin of their soldiers by overlapping the scars until their soldiers feel nothing but the lust to kill. By speaking the name of the Evil One and allowing him to claim you is the only relief to a human prisoner."

Listening to this repetition of what had previously been a much more abbreviated story when he once sat in the comfort of his modern home, Shamus felt his now long-consumed meal twist uncomfortably in his lower guts. He now understood his friend's prayer for the swiftness of death to have fallen over the Anahimaran people when they met their Armageddon head-on. Shamus regretted having asked for clarification. He resolved that rather than allow himself to be captured, he would have to seriously find the courage within himself to fall on his own sword rather than be taken.

After a time, Erladoch redirected their course into the cover of the forest. After an hour of skirting the inner edge of tree cover, he directed Shamus to stop as they were getting close to the City of Taroc. From a seated position, Erladoch helped Shamus fashion a hiding place for the day. They climbed inside a lean-to wedged between three closely wound trees just as Inyi made her first appearance on the horizon. The companions hoped to achieve sufficient rest for the next trek, which would take them directly between the twin cities at dusk. While Shamus harbored doubts about Erladoch's ability to walk very far at all, let alone with any degree of pace, he understood that somehow this would have to happen when they awakened. If they were to have any chance of crossing this perilous plane alive, he could no longer be dragged.

***

Chapter 10
The Fields of Ataroc

Shamus was surprised to have slept through the balance of the day, given his feelings of mounting dread. The wear on his body from having borne his companion over countless miles on little food rations over the past several days was enough to permit, if not command, rest from himself.

As his eyes opened to embrace the fading light of Naga, he found Erladoch already preparing for their journey. At first, Shamus went about almost mindlessly attending to his own routine. It was only when he realized that the litter upon which he had dragged Erladoch was now disassembled that his attention turned squarely on his friend.

"What the hell are you doing? The litter was working perfectly well, Erladoch!" Consternation hung in his voice.

Erladoch looked up from his labor. He paid no heed to Shamus's scolding. "Agreed, but neither you nor I can afford such slow travel tonight. I'm making something else that will help me travel without yer having to break your back. I'm growing stronger now." His head went back to the task of twisting the torn-off sleeves onto the tops of the two longest beams of the now broken litter. He methodically twisted vines from the tree floor around this until he was satisfied with the tautness of his fasteners.

"I'm glad to hear this. In fact, you have no idea how pleased I am to hear this, Erladoch! Still, I can't imagine anyone making such a quick recovery. I had to dig deeply through skin and muscles to get the bullet out of you and repair the tearing that it caused. I don't know how well a job I really did, as I'm not a medical doctor. I may have injured you more. At best, the stitches that I put into you probably only stopped your body from bleeding on the outside. I have literally no idea what might be happening on the inside of you, infection being but one of the worst possibilities!"

Erladoch didn't look up. Instead, he continued to wrap the jacket sleeves tightly. He proceeded to fasten the scabbards still containing his swords across the top third of the poles which Shamus had previously used as the main frame of the litter. It was apparent that he intended on making himself crutches. Arranged so, the handle of each sword would be readily accessible in the event of a skirmish while lending solidity to the crutch.

Shamus stared in fascination at the industriousness of the design. Even so, he was both annoyed and more than a little worried about his friend's unilateral decision to unmake the litter when he believed that Erladoch was too unwell for extended walking.

"I have less fever, Shamus. I hurt less than I did yesterday, and we have no choice but to move over this ground as swiftly and quietly as possible. I saw these when I was first in hospital after coming to your timeline. It helped me to move around when I was allowed out of bed. Tonight, I shall walk. When I struggle, these will keep me upright."

Shamus examined Erladoch's weave work. He was good at it! He smiled at the crutch-swords, recognizing that there would be no room for further argument. He checked the hand-drawn map and tried to guess the distance and terrain that the night's trek would present them with. Based on where they had come from so far, and the advice of their having to traverse the entire plane between the cities before another rest would be possible, he estimated. "How far do you think we have to go, twenty miles maybe?" he wondered aloud.

Without consulting the map, Erladoch surveyed his surroundings before the light disappeared entirely. "Thirty yarricks," Erladoch offered back. "Possibly a bit more."

When they had first attempted to compose the map that they had drawn in Calabogie, Shamus had learned from Erladoch that a yarrick was a unit of distance that roughly fell midway between a kilometer and a mile in length. His best guess from running 'yarricks' with his companion while they were training for this journey was that a yarrick was effectively 1,400 meters.

"Right. That's what I meant." Shamus's mind was a flurry with the math as he tried to calculate what that entailed for the two men. Traveling thirty or more yarricks signified that they would be walking close to a marathon distance, and in Erladoch's best case, he would be hobbling. "Thirty yarricks? Erladoch, we'll never make that in one night! That's, that means, we're going to have to cover at least one yarrick every 15 minutes at a minimum to accomplish this walk in total darkness. Even if we get close to covering so much terrain, I see nothing on our map that would provide us a place to hide when the sun rises tomorrow!"

Erladoch looked straight into Shamus's eyes as he used the top of one of the crutches to prop himself to his feet. The action looked effortful. The pressure he was imposing on his ripped-up and re-sewn flank muscles made him grimace in spite of his stoicism. The area of Erladoch's flank that had been damaged was not available to support his torso without inflicting suffering. As he leveled himself onto the second crutch, he winced with the effort but made no verbalization of pain.

"I know, Shamus," he replied in a smooth, matter-of-fact tone, steadying himself until he was fully upright. "If I'm right about who now occupies this land, then we will not be able to stop for the next three days if we are to find safety."

If Shamus had heard such an utterance three or four months ago, he would have laughed out loud at the preposterous nature of such a suggestion. However, having spent as much time in close contact with Erladoch since then, he realized that the training the two men had done together was truly about to be tested. Shamus had found untapped strengths within himself while cyclically inflicting deprivations of food and sleep at the Browse compound. He measured the seriousness of his companion's assertion and accepted there was no other choice. Back at the cottage, he also knew that he had a refrigerator full of provisions if the going got too tough. All they had to rely upon now were a few airtight bags of dried camping dinners to last them for whatever duration still lay ahead. The added complication of Erladoch's current condition made the prospect of continuous travel for three days all the more gloomy.

With less than a half an hour of daylight left, they started on their journey, staying within the northern edge of the forest canopy. The pace was slow for the first mile or so as Erladoch tested his strength and the degree of support he could rely upon from his homemade crutches. He worked himself into a rolling pace, never fully putting his weight down on the crutch on his injured side. With some deliberation motivated by pain avoidance, he found he could slide off the crutches as his feet touched ground, propping himself up again before his torso stretched to a fully upright posture. When they came across uneven ground, lingering on the top of the crutch was necessary for balance. Without even looking at his friend in such moments, he knew that the extra time taken to prevent a fall equated to a stabbing reminder to Erladoch that stitches still pulled against flesh.

By starting out while there was still some light left in the sky, Erladoch was able to carefully plot their path, taking them as straight down the middle of the gap lands between the twin cities as possible, keeping no less than eight yarricks between them and either city's earthen walls.

✝✝✝

Hours passed in silence. When Erladoch surmised they were at the epicenter of the gap between Taroc and Ataroc, he did his best to break into a clop-hop-clop pace. While it appeared both awkward and painful as hell, it permitted him to move considerably faster than before. Shamus was surprised that he was struggling to decide whether to fast-walk beside his companion or slow jog.

Looking left and right, both men could see long lines of fires burning from high above the walls of the now-occupied cities. There were also notable encampment fires somewhere out in the wilds between their position and the more obvious blazes of the cities.

Had the Treborgans managed to figure out the reflecting-fire and mirror technology used by the Anahimarans, they would have reflected significant light across the plain between the cities from the crude arrays positioned on the outer walls. The close horizon would have been emblazoned into a near daylight setting anywhere the light would be pointed.

Thankfully, the brutish nature of the creatures that had overrun the kingdom of Anahimara was entirely a function of overwhelming numbers rather than stealth or advanced strategic thinking. After sacking the principal cities of this kingdom, the Scraggin hordes of Treborg were too busy defiling people and property to devote time to figuring out the purpose or application of the light reflection devices which the Anahimaran's had invented. This inability—or lack of interest—in deploying the lighthouses of Anahimara was a calculation Erladoch had hoped for. It afforded him and Shamus the cover of darkness they needed. They just had to make sure they did nothing to attract the attention of a night patrol.

Even though the companions had traversed the midpoint of the gap land, Shamus felt his anxiety building. Every noise outside of the rise and fall of their own feet gave him tremendous starts. But there was something else setting him off. He could not place the source of this other anxiety-provoking cue, yet it began to hang on him like a weight.

Erladoch sensed it as well but maintained the silence. Other than blowing more forcefully through his mouth and nostrils, he hobbled along without a word, doing his best to put as much distance between himself and the cities as he could muster.

For most of their trek through the gap, Shamus had jogged alongside Erladoch, keeping pace with his friend's labored hop, clop, hop. Without knowing why, he quickened his pace. As he felt his breath labor, he realized he had broken into a run and was now somewhere ahead of his companion. He didn't want to lose Erladoch behind in the darkness, but a voice in his head implored him to speed up even more.

Just as Shamus recognized he needed to stay with his friend's slower pace, he found himself without footing. For a terrifying moment, he was no longer on solid ground. He was falling. Thankfully, this sensation of dropping over a sudden change in terrain proved not to be a cliff but rather a shallow ditch that was invisible under the night sky. His chest and arms thudded against the soft earth without pain as the ground came up fast on him. His gear thudded on his back but, thankfully, caused him no harm. Relieved by the forgiveness of the terrain, Shamus identified the thought which had danced at the edge of his sensation which had been vexing him. It was the smell of sweat. So subtle had been the sensation that, until he was being launched closer to the ground, he simply could not have put his finger on it.

Fortunately, Erladoch had not met with the same fall on the uneven ground yet. Such a tumble could prove punishing to his less-than-perfect stitches! Surmising that Erladoch would be approaching his rear in seconds, Shamus sprung to his feet and made for the edge of the ditch, determined to warn him of the fall hazard. With nothing more hurt than his pride, he surveyed the darkness. He didn't wish to raise his voice but had to prevent Erladoch from falling. Just then, he saw the brightness of wide-open eyes closing in on him. He expected Erladoch would give him the glare of a smile to signify that but for the imposed silence, he would be laughing at Shamus's clumsiness. However, the approaching eyes were not friendly. Nothing about their intention was pleasant, in fact, they were utterly fierce. This was not his friend! Erladoch was nowhere to be seen.

Shamus instinctively shifted his weight with a quick dodge to his right. The wind next to him whistled in the darkness, followed by the clanking of steel striking ground near where his feet had just been standing. The blow would have been fatal.

Shamus hefted his grand-da's mighty sword from its long scabbard in an instant, stabbing and searching the air from where he last heard the grunt of disappointment from his attacker. He then began a tirade of controlled figure-eight swings and turn-overs of his blade through the air. Another 'shhhhsh' flew past his neck and left ear, still not finding purchase in Shamus's skin.

The faster he swung his grand-da's blade through the night air, the more a purply-blue light formed around it, lighting up the air within a foot or so around the sword as it moved, proclaiming itself to the night sky. A second of hesitation elapsed as Shamus's opponent became puzzled by this sudden appearance of light in the otherwise oppressive darkness. The aura surrounding the blade was momentarily mesmerizing to the still unseen enemy. Shamus capitalized on this, and as much as in guesswork as in knowledge, he plunged his sword forward, driving it into solid flesh. As the Scrag's mouth opened briefly to belch out a song of pain choked by blood overflowing high up in its throat, Shamus heard what sounded like two other voices shrieking in pain in rapid succession only a few yards away from him. The impacts followed by death gurgles so close by in the darkness sent a shiver of adrenaline up one side of him and down the other. He leaped out of the ditch, feeling his body kick into full gear as he steadfastly moved to come to his partner's aid. The hues of color surrounding his sword showed him the way to Erladoch, who was battling what looked to be as many as ten Scrags.

Erladoch spun with the precision of a dancer, swinging his one crutch with unsheathed blade at neck level across the field of battle. Several sallow heads were already dislodged from their hideous frames, thudding to the ground in cascades of blood across the terrain. Without wasting any time, Shamus swung ferociously, not even considering his own sense of panic at the grim scene. The figure-eight rolls of his wrist kept coming down on his enemies with surprise and lethal accuracy, cleaving body parts from torsos with razor sharpness. The

Scrags seemed frozen in time as they dumbly found themselves staring into the dance of the light rather than understanding the light was announcing their deaths. Over and above the changing nature of the sword's light came a hum, which was like a voice shooting from the blade's tip. It wasn't musical exactly, but it was not a singular tone of steel whirring and whomping through the air either. It flowed in time with the alterations of color, emitting tones which matched the pulsations of light surrounding the blade. Grand-da's sword was expressing itself. It was wholly the reason why Shamus and Erladoch, who continued to cleave at anyone stupid enough to come within his reach, were winning the field.

The more swiftly Shamus swung, the more brilliant it became, as though a spirit all its own was taking control of the sword. Shamus marveled how his body seemed to be moving in harmony with the wishes of a force now compelling his clutching hands and body to follow its lead. Part of him felt he was in control of his actions, but his pragmatic mind told him he was bearing witness to a feat of mortal combat waged by something beyond himself. The glow generated by the complex physical movements so dazzled the Scraggin soldiers that their dumbstruck reactions afforded Erladoch the opportunity to play lawn trimmer with his 'sword-crutch' almost unchallenged.

The more he dodged, danced and swung, the more Shamus's mind informed him that he was not a willing actor so much as a 'participant' in the ferocity his body was displaying. There was a level of detachment from everything taking place, and he recognized the erection of a dissociative wall within himself—one he realized might have appeared before in his life. On one side of the wall was Shamus Bergin, Doctor of Psychology; on the other side, a warrior entity danced effortlessly. It cleaved through enemies in the dark as naturally as breathing. Without warning, he felt himself race forward toward his next opponent, who was leveling his sword at Erladoch's back. Like a possessed animal, Shamus set upon the Scrag, utterly unconcerned for his own mortality. As he dispatched the man with a single angled cut, he sensed the culmination of the training as a young martial arts student, recently honed by Erladoch. And yet, there was so much more happening in each instant that belonged to neither set of learnings. An archaic warrior in Shamus's past was running the show now, and he gave himself willingly to the task of slaughtering the evil surrounding himself and his friend.

As Shamus hewed the final Scraggin soldier across the belly and raised his blade for a final chopping blow, he caught sight of Erladoch watching him in disbelief. As the blade fell, parting shoulder from chest like scissors through thin paper, the blade came to rest.

Shamus was covered in sweat and blood spatter. He could taste the acrid saltiness of his enemies from the arterial spray still running down his face. Despite the darkness that enrobed both men, Shamus knew that his clothes were bathed in the results of his life-and-death struggle. As his breathing began to slow, he felt he was still not fully himself; there was still a sense of indifference inside him over the sudden, violent display he had just managed. The only thing that felt like his persona was the sensation of his knees buckling involuntarily under the weight of his grand-da's sword. He sat himself down on the earth, utterly spent.

"Er...ladoch," he managed through still-huffed breath. "I smelled them as they approached. At first, it was not smell, but like a memory of a smell. Were they tracking us, or was this just bad luck from our having come across them?"

Erladoch balanced himself over the crutch-sword a moment. He looked over the killing ground around his feet, where he had stood moments before, spinning his makeshift weapon, each contact with his foe tearing a bit harder at the stitches in his side. "No, they are armored too heavily for trackers. We are near a camp or a patrol that guards the cities perhaps. If but one had escaped or sounded the alarm, we would most certainly be dead, as more would have arrived by now."

Shamus wiped at the moisture covering his face. He hoped what ran down his cheeks was more composed of his sweat than anything else. His breath had returned to a quiet state.

"The hill I fell off was very abrupt; there was no warning in this darkness."

Erladoch walked to the edge of the sudden drop in the plain where his friend had fallen, ruminating over the irony that it had likely saved Shamus's life. He looked across it and then up and down, doing his best to pierce the darkness with the acuity of a nocturnal animal. He looked across the gap to a place parallel to the trench. His eyes sharpened, and his face became grim.

"Shamus, this is a track left by the wheels of a great moving platform. I look out and can just make out another trench like this over there." Erladoch's right hand pointed and tracked left to right in parallel to the ditch beside them. "This is some kind of giant wagon, perhaps even a machine of war, certainly not one that has ever been seen in this world! Much has changed since I left!" He grunted. "I'm not sure that you smelled the advance of the scout party at all. It would take many men or beasts to move this object. I think that what you smelled is the sweat of the multitude it must have taken to move whatever this is. The air is filled with the stench of their efforts, and the ground is coated with the sweat of spent efforts."

Shamus could not duplicate the long-range view Erladoch seemed capable of, but he could faintly make out the trench opposite from the one he had tumbled into. As he tried to register what he had been told, a bundle of questions began to bubble up. "But what is it? Why here? How long ago do you think this happened?"

Erladoch rested his hand on Shamus, steadying himself. "Though the scent was weak until we came near to the edge, it tells me that this thing came through here within the last few days. I fear the armies protecting it are nearby still." With definite urgency in his voice, Erladoch, still balancing one shoulder on his sword-crutch, reached over and tapped Shamus's left shoulder as if to wake him and compel him back to action. "We must leave the bodies where they lie. There is no time to conceal this meeting, and they will be missed soon enough anyways. Onward, Shamus! Our presence is no longer a secret in Loura. We must travel in haste, or tonight we shall surely perish!"

Before Erladoch's hand left Shamus's shoulder, Shamus felt fully himself again. He sensed the return of his fear as he measured the pure horror of the battle he had waged almost blindly. Despite the darkness of the overcast night, his vision was brightening. With its improvement came the lifting of a veil that had obscured the utter gore strewn around him, mostly caused by him. Erladoch was already moving again, albeit at the slow, hobble step of an injured warrior.

Feeling the weight of his grand-da's sword, Shamus sheathed it in his scabbard and rolled it back onto the top of his pack to make it easier to carry. As Erladoch limped almost out of sight, Shamus attempted to shake off the sight around him. *I did this?* he questioned, still not sure how to reconcile what had happened. He scuffed his feet back and forth against the soft earth, confirming he was present. As he did so, he heard Erladoch say in an almost vanishing whisper, "Move, man!"

He strode away without looking back.

Chapter 11

Within a few hours, the companions found themselves wading across what appeared to be a vast riverbed with definable banks. Climbing down the soft bank a distance, they finally stepped into water that barely came up to their knees. Erladoch's only words to Shamus in nearly four hours of slow, labored march were to comment that the water level should have been high enough to stack many men on each other without reaching the top of the waterline.

The Boldar River stretched in a nearly straight line northward to the sea from below Ataroc. Only four years previous to this night, it had been a mighty river with only a few crossing points that allowed a barge to ferry across safely. Its once fast-flowing current made the construction of bridges across it an impossibility. The depleted state of the river did not bode well in his mind.

During the rest of the time they had been walking, Erladoch was entirely occupied by his thoughts. Shamus wondered when his friend might comment on his performance in their battle. While he'd been surprised at the extent of his newly acquired deftness in combat after only a few months of training alongside Erladoch before departing on this journey, he at least expected some congratulatory words from his mentor. Nothing was offered. Instead, Erladoch seemed singly devoted to not feeling the gnawing pain in his side that had partially reopened from their skirmish. Other than the odd grunt that left Erladoch's lips involuntarily when there was a sudden misstep over uneven ground in the continuing nightscape, he didn't make a sound.

Words of congratulatory praise were not forming in Erladoch's mind as he marched, hobbled, crutched and marched again. Rather, he was replaying the battle scene in his mind, over and over. Each time he did so, he tried to understand how Shamus had been able to dodge various blows leveled at him by the band of Scrags that had come upon them. There was a level of agility and skill in the feat that bore no resemblance to the man he had been training with for several months. Luck could not explain the prowess demonstrated by his friend, whom he could barely see in action through the oppressive darkness of the field. Each time Shamus's glowing blade swung in his direction, it momentarily revealed the panoply of rapid actions Shamus engaged in. Erladoch now worked to process those snapshots of the struggle into a workable explanation for how his friend had avoided sustaining any obvious injury to himself. Try as he might, Shamus's ability to dispatch so many enemies in such a short time was nearly impossible to assimilate.

Another misstep, and Erladoch's attention was once again on finding ways to compartmentalize his suffering and pack it away. Only the grimace lines flexing on his forehead and jaw gave away that he was in pain at all, obscured by the poor visibility.

As minutes rolled into hours, Shamus continued to expect bloodshot and maddened eyes lunging at him through the dark. Had he not reacted so fast, he knew his life would already be over, his disemboweled remains lying in the dirt somewhere. Even worse, if Erladoch's tales were accurate, his monstrously disfigured Neanderthal enemies would have been feasting on his remains somewhere back there. The silence of these many hours of contemplative marching allowed his sense of confusion over how he had managed to overcome such an onslaught to be pieced together. Avoiding the first blade thrust coming madly at him in the darkness he could attribute to luck. *Yah, for sure, I could've dodged such a half-assed attack*, he told himself. But as his brain regained its clarity, Shamus struggled to come to terms with the warrior archetype that had so menacingly surfaced within him. The latent personality which had emerged had somehow managed to shut off all sense of fear within him. It had even compelled him to think that it would be a good idea to perform leaps and a running front flip over a surging group of Scrags, only to land behind them and cleave away their heads as his body rotated above and past them. More correctly, Shamus realized, there'd been very little thought involved—just a whole lot of action.

The last time Shamus had ever performed a running front flip, he was 18 years of age and training in his dojo. On that occasion, fully twelve years distant from this moment, he definitely wasn't carrying a sword in his hands at the time! He certainly had not been weighed down by a backpack loaded with other weaponry and provisions that collectively weighed more than 30 pounds. He recalled that when he had previously performed such an action, his landing on the mats had been anything but pretty. He was now 30 years old. Even with his past few months of hard training, the prospect of what he had pulled off seemed out of reach from his rational psychologist's mind.

Trying to find a way to let the scenes of battle leave him, Shamus allowed his thoughts to drift away from the physical movements that he couldn't begin to reconcile for love nor money. Instead, he replayed the mesmerizing sensory display of sound and light that had emanated from his sword. It had provided an ever-increasing display of intensity as he cleaved his way through the enemy. The faster he had turned the longsword through the air toward his enemies, the more they seemed to have been standing still as he moved through them, their eyes and minds locked. Looking at the battle scene from this angle, Shamus realized that for a time during the struggle where he most felt like he was outside of himself, one after the other of his enemies had frozen in action. While he was propelling weapon and body at hard-to-reconcile speeds, they had slowed. The Scrags had been robbed of thought and action just before they were ready to deliver their own death blows to him. None of this made sense!

Shamus tilted the right side of his backpack for a moment to draw his grand-da's sword out a little from its scabbard to see what might happen. Nothing, no glow and no sound. He let it slide back fully into its housing and straightened the pack. As he marched a few steps behind Erladoch in the closing hours of night, he found himself completely without explanation.

***

Chapter 12

The stealth of their passage across the top of the pass between the twin cities of Taroc and Ataroc had been followed by their forging across the nearly drained Boldar River. The river basin was mostly now a dried-up gulley with water pooled only along its center line.

At Erladoch's bidding, they had done their best to cleanse themselves and their clothing by submersing whenever possible in the remaining shallow waters. The stench of battle was nonetheless ground into their garments. All they could hope to accomplish by soaking themselves at each opportunity was to make it more difficult to be tracked by all manner of foul beast that would be engaged soon enough in their pursuit.

As the fifth hour of the post-battle hush was rolling into a sixth hour of quick marching, the faint wail of a horn sounded. This was followed by puffs of fire and smoke fanned into the night sky. The flashes of fire huffed high into the air somewhere behind them. Shamus's mouth was agape. Despite the fire's obvious distance, the horn call was sickeningly discordant to his ears as it resonated over the plain. He was certain that the horn blasts were only a few hundred feet away, but Erladoch counseled that the horn calls and fireballs were many yarricks off, likely coming from the location of their nocturnal battle. "The Evil One's servants are giving an alert that there are intruders in their midst. Unlike your world, which is filled with so many competing noises, horn calls carry for many yarricks unimpeded by competing sounds. The evidence of our skirmish is revealed, and the trail of our footprints fleeing from the scene will be found. All Scrags within earshot on the plain are being ordered to start looking for us."

As the buzz of the blasting horn cleared, the vanishing nightscape seemed to be occupied by an oppressive and eerie silence. Erladoch pivoted on his crutch and took hold of Shamus's shirt sleeve. In as hushed a tone as he could mutter, he looked into his friend's eyes and said, "Run, Shamus!"

They had not taken 40 strides when, from far less of a distance, came the nauseating and discordant call of a different Treborgan battle horn beginning to sound across the fields. It took Shamus a few moments to discern what this next screech was, but Erladoch recognized it all too well. The call to give chase was coming from behind them, meaning their footprints had been found even in the profundity of the night scape.

Moments later, another screechy wail emanated from a different direction. *Was this one to our left?* Shamus considered, *or possibly to the right?* He couldn't be sure. The reverberating echo of the calls seemed to come from everywhere as they bounced across large rock erratics strewn across the fields. Shamus felt his legs tightening from the build-up of lactic acid. It occurred to him that his pace could not be kept up indefinitely. He looked over his right shoulder and confirmed that despite his speedy gait, Erladoch was hobbling and shoving off his crutches like a man possessed. Other horns began to call out to one another. Fainter than the horns themselves at first, Shamus began to hear the *thud-thud-thudding* of drums. Alarms were going out from one Scrag encampment to another all over the Central and Westerlands of Anahimara. Each one of them announced that intruders were in their midst.

Erladoch understood the beating messages to mean that the Master wanted these men found at all costs. He had listened to these drums so many times in his secret journeys across the wastes of the Treborgan frontier that he also knew that the call-and-reply beatings echoing across the plains was a very effective messaging system, going from group to group to guide each war party toward the other; the noose was tightening.

The pace of their march quickened into a sprint, with Erladoch's crutches nearly cracking at the impact he was making to propel himself faster along the broken ground. With no time to cover their tracks, they were leaving a roadmap for any night-seer now moving about the land at the Evil One's command. Worse still, daylight was coming in less than an hour. The companions were running in open country and would soon be visible to every malevolent creature within miles.

***

Chapter 13

The morning glimmer of Inyi was upon the companions. It enrobed them in such a fashion as to make them stick out on the land for any living creature watching from east to west. Unbelievably, adrenaline continued to compel their exhausted legs forward. The motivation to press on was quite literally behind them. Given that they were still among the living, Shamus surmised that their perseverance through the night and their many dips in the diminished river had caused confusion, maybe even enabled them to slip through the closing net.

The horns and drums were not ceasing, but for now, they didn't sound much closer than they had a few hours ago. If he had had enough breath in his chest to describe his emotions, he would have told Erladoch that he felt like 'the fox' in a traditional English hunt. That would have taken too much effort to explain, however, and he had none to spare. The only solace available to either man now was the height of the long grasses they were wading through. It seemed to be the only cover from anyone pursuing them on the ground. In places, the blades of grass were as thick as reeds in a marsh and nearly as tall as the men themselves. More than once they lost their footing while they swished through thicker portions, but at least the landings were mostly soft ones. Before midday, Shamus felt the ground beneath his feet angling slowly upward into hill country. The camouflage afforded to them from the vegetation began to open up ahead. In the distance, Shamus caught sight of what appeared to be a mountain range. The slopes still many miles off were thickly colored by what appeared to be a dense forest. It was still so far off that one color blurred into the other into a monochromatic blob of green.

"Bodeland," Erladoch offered through the huffing breath of a man who was nearly fully spent.

Shamus considered the advice. *I thought that I had memorized everything on the map that Erladoch and I created back at the Browse compound? Why don't I recognize this place name?* Shamus tried to access his thoughts about the word Erladoch had used to describe the mountain range ahead. *Bodeland.* It wasn't clicking with him at all. He wondered whether he hadn't listened carefully enough to his friend's educational sessions back in Ottawa about the map's environs. The place they were speeding to has a 'name'. He felt a surge of anxiety not being able to recall whether this was a 'good place' or a 'bad place' they were effectively being funneled toward. '*Maybe my mind is shutting down?*' he considered. Shamus hadn't eaten in at least fourteen hours. The exertion of his body had burned most of his blood sugar up, leaving nothing for his brain to use for clarity of thought. Whatever the reason, Shamus could not recall anything about this place they were closing on with every footfall. The fact that they were running toward it was unsettling, but Erladoch at least appeared to be encouraged by the sight of the looming horizon ahead.

***

As the land progressively steepened and their pace slowed to a near delirious walk, the first trees, which Shamus had initially processed as a green blob were dotting the landscape. Erladoch warded off his pain with an incantation that closely mimicked the emptiness of a Buddhist "ohm" for its sustained droning. Shamus understood this signified that his friend's resilience was running thin. Erladoch was no longer able to shoulder the burden of his pain in silence, even if it meant detection from the pursuing Scrags.

Shamus worried for his friend's ability to go on. He worried even more for his own expectation of detection as a result of the chant, until he realized that Erladoch only breathed the sound through his mouth whenever the Scraggin hordes pursuing them blew their horns —unfortunately with increasing regularity. If he survived this flight from capture, Shamus knew he would never be able to purge the scar of those horns from his auditory memory. What compounded their impact on him went back to his evening of nightmares several months before, when he first looked briefly into the face of the Evil One. The horns, the thunder of clomping metal-shoed feet crushing the soil were now a part of his reality. Even if he had the ability to stop long enough to put food in his gut and renew his spent energy, he would not be able to keep it down.

***

From time to time, Shamus would slacken his pace to circle behind Erladoch just to see whether the patch of blood from his partly reopened wound had spread any further. He was pleased to see that it had not worsened, and there did not appear to be fresh blood dropping behind Erladoch as he plodded on. By his best guess, what had, at one point, been a pace of about eleven-minute miles, Shamus reckoned that the companions were now only managing fifteen-minute miles. *Not good! Not good at all!* he proclaimed to himself, estimating that if their pursuers still had their trail, they were covering the same distance in nearly half the time. *They are going to overtake us at some point soon*, he realized. Shamus's heart slumped. His will to keep going suddenly began to falter. He considered the questions as to where and when they would be overtaken, and what his death would be like.

Shamus's labored footsteps seemed now to be matched stride for stride by Erladoch's. His mind became cluttered by doubt. One glance over at his friend told him that the same overwhelming emotion of hopelessness had entered him too. They were not going to be able to keep going. Escape was not possible after all. Only 'death'. A horrible death was the only thought occupying both men's minds.

Shamus looked at Erladoch and noticed that both he and his friend had ceased moving altogether. Both sets of feet were locked into place. After countless hours of running, hobbling and climbing, they had ground to a halt. The only prevalent thought was that they should just *sit*, *rest* and *wait* for their pursuers to find them. For the flicker of a lost moment, he wondered why he was not considering suicide as an alternative to his plight of being captured. Surely this would be more merciful than being torn end to end and tortured by Treborgan soldiers in the service of the great Evil from the Pit? A deeply buried thought warned that these were not his thoughts. He couldn't sustain this warning, as much as he hoped to. He wanted to think and act with hope, but a voice was wrapping itself increasingly more powerfully around his will. It told him that he dearly wanted to pull his sword from its scabbard right this moment and position the hilt and handle on the ground so that the upward-pointing blade would just slide through him as he fell upon it. Each time he considered this scenario, it seemed to be wiped from his mind and replaced with an echoing voice that commanded him to *STOP LISTENING AND RUN!* This was a completely different thought, which had the feel of yet another distinct voice within him.

He struggled to make sense of the voices offering different thoughts. *Shite! I've bonked!* he thought. *This is the kind of mental silliness marathon runners experience when they hit the wall. That's all this is! I'm just confused from dehydration and fatigue.* The repetitive thoughts of *rest*, *sit*, and *wait* that had managed to make his legs stop moving even as the separate voice in his head was growing ever louder for him to *KEEP RUNNING!* continued to chime on. Although he wanted to tell himself he was experiencing the distance runners' 'wall', his mind was warning him that he needed to regain control over both his body and his thoughts.

The competing voice inside his head, which had him locked in place was becoming more insistent now: *Rest! Sit! Wait!* Then it dawned on him: "Hypnosis! Someone or something is trying to hypnotize me! Jaysus, Mary Mother!" he exclaimed aloud.

"En-chant-ment!" Erladoch gasped from his spent lips in reply, his eyes staring at the ground.

They were being hypnotized by a powerful magic that was reaching into their minds in a focused effort to slow them down. For the longest time, he hadn't realized that this growing voice was not his own. Its alienness revealed itself for brief glimmers when he tried to have a thought of his own which involved his personal survival. It made no sense to him to stop fleeing when his every motivation for several days had been focused on escape.

Shamus wanted to 'live'; in fact, he hoped for a long life. Sitting and waiting for his doom suddenly made no sense. In that moment, as he finally grasped the nonsensical nature of the repetitive command to stay put, the voice became altogether foreign and invasive. Shamus slapped himself across his face as forcefully as he could manage.

"Son of a! That hurt!" he spoke aloud once more. "Pain! I felt that!" he said in further confirmation. "That's real enough! The only thing that probably is!" He looked over at Erladoch, who was still staring blindly at his feet, lost in a trance. Without another moment squandered, Shamus wound up and whacked Erladoch across his left cheek. The crack of open hand against skin left a red stain on the Dunbar Prince's face. His eyes barely lifted. Shamus hauled off and let another whistler cross his friend's other cheek. This time, color and recognition returned to Erladoch's eyes. Shamus whispered, fearful that the sound of his own voice would reveal him, not knowing who might now be that much closer to them. "Don't listen to it! It's not your voice, Erladoch! We need to go!"

"The Evil One's magic," Erladoch replied in understanding as he rubbed the sting of the second blow off his cheek. "How long have we been standing here?"

"Uh, I don't know, but we have to keep going!"

Hoisting his right shoulder onto what was left of one of his makeshift crutches, Erladoch scanned the horizon of approaching forest a moment, then said, "This way."

***

Chapter 14

The companions' ascent of the foothills had taken them to nearly 800 feet above the level of the plains. They stopped momentarily by a stream and refilled their canteens, pausing to take long drafts of the icy-cold water. It was like drinking fire through papier-mâché as the liquid eroded the dust and dryness of their aching throats. The chill of the spring numbed their bodies to a point where the throbbing of over-taxed muscles began to subside. But the break was short-lived.

Shamus looked down at the low ground from where they had started their climb. He could now see the hunting party pursuing them. This meant they too could be seen, and the howl of Treborgan horns confirmed this almost as soon as the thought crossed his mind. They were a few yarricks away at best, and covering ground at a frightening pace. The breadth of their image as it unfolded across the plain told both men that there was easily a hundred Scrags pursuing them, gaining every minute.

The failing light of Naga receded painfully slowly toward the horizon. One last sip from the stream, and Erladoch and Shamus were moving again, allowing the cooling waters to act like ice packs on their swollen, aching feet as they went. Almost no feeling in his lower extremities was absolute joy after so many days of too much sensation.

They had not marched two more yarricks when the tumultuous screeches of the Scraggin horns began to fill the air. They were furious now, almost like their squelches were insulting the very slopes of the majestic mountain that Erladoch and Shamus were doing their utmost to ascend. The beauty of the place was in such contrast to the filth of the approaching rabble, whose very feet seemed to scar the mountain.

Trees were now all around them, and the soft, pine-needled floor was a comfort to aching feet. However, the forest cover through which they sped left a clear, easily identifiable trail from their footfalls upon the pristine surface, leaving the companions nowhere to hide. Their pace had become snail-like, with Erladoch faltering continuously. Shamus surmised that they would be overtaken soon, despite their best efforts.

Erladoch was visibly weary; his pace had slackened over the last hour to a few hundred feet every ten minutes instead of a yarrick or more every fifteen. The steepness of the terrain and the sliding back with each footfall made it impossible to climb faster. The only comfort either man had was the knowledge that their Treborgan pursuers would have even more trouble negotiating such steep, pine-needle-covered terrain with their traction-less iron shoes.

Considering that he had been shot only a few days before and had been fighting infection, Shamus drew strength from his friend's unrelenting effort to move on. Over the last twenty yarricks, Erladoch had relied on his two makeshift crutch-swords to propel him along. Now that they were doing their best to crest the first peak, he had taken one of the crutches apart, reslinging one of the swords back over his shoulder. As helpful as it had been to propel himself along with two aids, using the crutch on his injured side had caused his wound to reopen with the stretches required for the climb.

Erladoch continued to dig into the earth above himself with the second crutch. It was an agonizing process, using his core strength fully on one side to pull himself up. Each time that Shamus offered him assistance, he gritted his teeth and snarled for him to conserve himself. Intuitively, Erladoch recognized that Shamus would have to be their defender once overtaken. He struggled to not be overwhelmed by mounting fever almost as much as he did to avoid the Scrags closing in on them.

After a few more minutes of climbing, the companions had crested the first peak. Erladoch staggered onto the flat surface of the hilltop, searching for his footing. "Shamus," he called out through ragged breath. "I cannot go on, though I face my end." He crumpled onto a rock that sat beside the edge of a stream, which twisted and climbed in front of them. He laid himself down, completely spent.

Knowing that it would be pointless to insist on continuing, Shamus sat down on the bank of the stream beside him. He looked around, considering their limited options.

For an excruciatingly long moment, as the cool night air filled and emptied his lungs, helping his heartbeat to settle, Shamus's mind was swarming with

73

cowardly thoughts. The compunction to run like hell and leave Erladoch behind could barely be banished from his racing thoughts. Even though he knew that it meant guaranteed death for his friend, it could present a chance that he might still get away. *But to where?* he weighed. *And for how long?* Doubt and fear spread through his veins like a poison.

Even though he had no idea why they were heading over these massive hills toward what looked like an expanse of even higher mountains somewhere behind, it was completely unclear to him. The belief was that friends lay somewhere along that course. A voice like an echo in his ear was imploring him to go, almost at the same presumed pace of iron-clad feet pounding up the hillside from the valley below. He no longer imagined their clamorous sound against the earth. He heard them plain as day.

"We have to hide ourselves!" he said pleadingly. "I'm 30 years old, Erladoch; I'm not ready to die, and neither should you be!"

Not yet lifting his head from the soft earth, Erladoch breathed the first truly defeatist words Shamus had ever heard him utter: "No, t'would be to no purpose," he rasped. "These Scrags are trackers—the best the Evil One has. Their reward for finding intruders is that they get to eat who they capture. They will not stop looking until they feast on our flesh."

Shamus's belly turned over at the thought of this, knowing that time was running short, even as the cover of Naga was nearly upon them. No matter how exhausted Shamus felt in that moment, he was not prepared to quit, and he would be damned if he would let such horrifyingly evil creatures make a meal of him.

Shamus looked at the small pool of blood once again staining Erladoch's clothing. Just as he suspected, Erladoch was not only spiritually weakened, but he was losing blood again. Erladoch seemed to be mumbling deliriously to himself. While Shamus's ability to understand the common Louran tongue was anything but polished yet, he recognized the repetition was trance-like and all negative. Immediately, he realized that in this weakened state, the magic of the Evil One was reaching across the winds and beckoning Erladoch in his weakened condition to quit on himself once again. Suddenly, he knew what to do. In the most commanding voice that he could muster without yelling, he grabbed Erladoch under the armpits and began to raise his friend's full weight upright. When he was eye to eye with the Dunbar Prince, he locked gazes with his friend's clouded vision. Without any warning, he let go with one hand long enough to slap Erladoch across the cheek and then replace it back under his armpit before he could fall over. Unlike the last time, the slap had little effect to rouse his friend's attention. In a fit of desperation, Shamus drove his fingers into Erladoch's oozing wound. Erladoch let out an angered wail of pain. His face suddenly reddened with murderous intent. The cloud in his vision seemed to give way, the unrelenting chant of doubt seemingly broken. It had been replaced with a fixed gaze that was less than friendly. "You bastard! Why—"

Shamus seized his moment to make his appeal before Erladoch's anger might change to punitive action for the harm done to him. "Rise, Erladoch the Brave of Fior Hill! You are the Prince of Dunbar and Son of Kings!" He wrapped his right leg around the back of Erladoch's left leg, forcing it to straighten and prevent him from crumpling back to the ground. "Your duty to your people has not been discharged yet! Your fate is at Fior Hill, wherever in God's name that is. You cannot die this night!" The lost stare in his pupils began to clear, replaced by a small fire. Erladoch was coming back. The charms of the Evil One's whispers were losing their hold. His right leg straightened on its own, now supporting his weight without the assistance of Shamus's leg lock.

The sound of a sucking in of breath broke the stillness of the air, followed by soft and swift-moving footfalls. Shamus whirled around in all directions to locate the source of the noise without success, his heart racing wildly again. Nothing could be seen in the darkness of the forest. He screwed up his ears as tightly as possible and would have sworn that he could hear the rush of light feet moving around their position. In his wearied state, it took a few moments for him to realize that he had still not even drawn his swords for protection, still trying to get a handle on where the sounds were coming from.

Clearly whatever it was—likely an animal—which he had startled with the raising of his voice, it was now getting as far away from the humans as it could. *Or*, he assessed, *it senses the menace that is scaling the mountain toward us and is getting as far from here as it can.* Either way, as nothing had come crashing through the bushes toward them in that moment, there was still time to get moving.

Erladoch pointed to the crutch-sword on the ground, indicating his need for Shamus to place it in his hands. Shamus obliged and placed the crutch carefully under his companion's arm to support his weight away from the bleeding wound. He slowly pulled his hands away from Erladoch's torso, confirming that his friend's massive frame wouldn't topple over as he did so.

"I'm good," Erladoch huffed. "Now…let's get the hell out of here!"

***

Chapter 15

Whether it had been only minutes since they had set out again in their effort to crest the first rise of the foothills to reach the mountainous forest that lay beyond, or whether actual hours had passed, Shamus would never be able to recollect later. All he knew was that the effort had been more excruciating and exhausting than any other he could ever recall in his life.

Step by agonizing step, he half carried his own spent limbs up the next series of undulating hills while doing his best to half support—half drag Erladoch at the same time. The crashing of bushes and rumbling of feet was now heard as a truly sonorous beat across the night air. Maybe because the droplets of blood that had been spattering from Erladoch's wound onto the earth below were leaving an easily discernible trail for their pursuers, or more likely the fact they were no longer zigging or zagging in an effort to cause confusion, the rumble grew ever louder. Even though they were going as fast and straight as they could manage, the echo of many iron-shod feet assaulting the forest floor resounded just like they had done in Shamus's night of horrors so many months ago. There was no rousing speech that Shamus could offer himself to keep going; he too was now 'done'. Erladoch had become a dead weight that he just couldn't shoulder any longer. Even in the darkness, he could feel the heat of Erladoch's fever against his skin. Shamus's muscles burned from exertion, and his stomach twisted from hunger. His feet were so swollen he could barely stand.

Even without the influence of Enilorac's magic, Erladoch was a shell of a man, half-dead from blood loss and exhaustion. More than once over the past day, Shamus had distracted himself from his own suffering and exertion by attempting to calculate how many liters of blood had dribbled out of his friend's partly reopened wound. *Has he lost as much as three liters by now?* he considered. He couldn't lose much more without succumbing to the blood loss, no matter how tough a warrior he was.

Erladoch leaned against a tree and said nothing. Shamus could see a look of utter regret in his friend's eyes; he could no longer conceal his sense of disappointment in his inability to carry on as the powerful warrior and leader he knew himself to be. It was truly amazing to him that something as small as the size of a bullet could have caused so much damage to him, and yet here he was, at the brink of his personal abyss. In a gesture of friendship and understanding, he reached over and swiped the stream of tears forming on Shamus's cheeks.

Until that moment, Shamus had not even realized he was crying. He felt ashamed and embarrassed that he could not control his emotions.

"I have had a hard but good life, Shamus. I know that I will be rewarded in the next life for how I've lived and what I've tried to do."

Shamus considered these words of resignation and faith, himself now resting the back of his legs on a pile of rocks. As he eased the pack off himself to the mossy grasses under his feet, he mused that ironically, he did not know if he even truly had faith in an afterlife. Certainly, there had been times after his parents had died—'*disappeared*', he reminded himself—that he had tried to come to grips with the notion of an afterlife, but in spite of his strong belief in good and evil, he just didn't know 'where' or 'how' all of that fit into his scientific worldview. Despite all the truths that he had uncovered about the true face of evil and its real presence in the universe, the fact that he managed to jump through a porthole and had traveled to another time and place, none of this made any sense right now in the context of him dying. Standing in the thicket of trees on what had to be the crest of another peak, all he could think of was the grunts and snarls of angry voices that approached from somewhere beneath them in the blackness of night. All he could say about this moment was, "It's not fair!" He lifted his face to his friend and spoke more resolutely. "Erladoch, I refuse to die this way. I…"

Erladoch lifted his left hand, signaling for him to stop.

"Ach, Shamus, accept your death. If you do not, your soul will be a negative shadow filled with anger, doomed to wander in the space where the Evil One draws its own power from. It feeds on the self-doubt of others. A Keeper goes into battle believing he no longer has a life to win or lose so that he cannot fear death. This allows him to react to the harmony of nature and place his body in the rhythm of all great warriors whose songs of triumph fill the winds, if but he can give himself to it. Nothing can now be wasted on regret.

You are a Keeper, Shamus. Find purpose with your last breaths by fighting with every remaining swing and thrust of your sword. The moment is nigh, my friend, prepare yourself to seek the light."

Lifted into action by his own advice, Erladoch struggled with his remaining strength to draw his sword from his pack. He chose the smallest of the collection he had brought with him back to Loura, a single-edged katana which Shamus had purchased for him. It was the lightest of the blades in the collection, and it occurred to Shamus that as the fighting amidst the thickening forest all around them would not be conducive to swinging a long blade effectively, he followed suit.

No longer using his crutch for balance, Erladoch propped his back against the tree for stability. He let the short sword slide along the stressed vines which had held his long sword to the tree branch he had been using as his crutch. They crackled and split effortlessly from the slightest kiss of the blade. When they had been training in Calabogie, he had ground the edge of the blade down to a razor sharpness. He pulled the scabbard off the long sword and motioned for Shamus to help him place the tip of the heavy blade into the dirt where it could be picked up, if need be, at the same time as motioning Shamus to follow suit.

Erladoch's sword was not glittering as it had when he had retrieved it from the waters of the pool they had entered from the porthole. There were no stars and no moon to cast light upon beneath the thick canopy above.

Shamus glanced at his own blade and saw only the darkness of cold metal. Perhaps the light he had believed he'd seen had been a trick of the starlight after all. No light was aiding their vision under this canopy. It was pitch black as both branches and twigs started snapping, and whatever living fauna lurked in nocturnal shadows fled madly out of the way of the approaching thunder of one hundred metal-shod feet.

"To die well in the cause of the light. We will meet again in the land of eternal heroes," Erladoch whispered to Shamus, his teeth clenched from raging infection and fiery pain wrenching in his wounded side.

Shamus could barely hear his friend's salute. His eyes fixed squarely on the movement of the bramble bush only feet away from him. In a nanosecond, the first Scrag crashed through the trees, waving a crescent-shaped weapon ideally suited for hacking at a human neck. Time suddenly began to slow for Shamus. Whether there was just enough light to see it, or the angry intent of the wielder's swing created a perceptible trajectory, Shamus recognized that his neck was the intended target of the weapon. Out of sheer revulsion from the smell of the arcing blade closing on him, he dodged left and ducked, feeling the air above his hair giving way as he uttered a wail of defiance from some place deep within himself. His own ears seemed to prick up in surprise at the raising pitch of this foreign voice of defiance, growing ever louder as if it could rumble the earth beneath him.

As the first Scrag kept moving forward, his cleaver-like sickle having missed its mark, he found himself impaled onto Erladoch's sword before he stumbled onto the dark terrain only a few feet behind Shamus.

The second Scrag closed right in behind from the dense thicket, followed by a third and a fourth, all inches behind one another. This was to Shamus's advantage, as his sword was now entirely up and ready. He squared his feet beneath himself and swung with the intent and uncoiling poise of a professional golfer as one head after another left the bodies of the trio that had come through the small clearing. Had they possessed any discipline at all in close-contact warfare, they would have circled the two men and closed on them from multiple locations, making it impossible for Shamus and Erladoch to cover every angle. However, these were not disciplined men of the west, they were half-starved dogs, each more frenzied in their singular and uncoordinated efforts to draw blood.

With trees at their backs and darkness concealing their position until seconds before the bulwark of the Scraggin hunting party could truly locate them, the companions had at least the advantage of surprise. Before Shamus could recover from his powerful beheading swing, another blade crashed against his, rattling the sinews and bones in his hands. He nearly dropped the short sword from the shock of the vibration as sparks flew up from the grinding edge of the Scrag sword, leaving the tip of his own. The face of this attacker was more determined: disciplined. He recovered immediately from his first strike and brought his blade down again from a height above Shamus's head somewhere out of sight in the darkness.

A voice told him to "step right!" even though it neither belonged to himself nor Erladoch. The voice had come from within, and he obeyed it unquestioningly, too startled by its stern pronouncement. The Scrag captain was immense and incredibly agile. The blade he wielded was not unlike Shamus's in that it was designed for close combat in tight spaces. Worse still, the attacker was literally bounding from place to place as though he had a trampoline beneath his feet. Shamus's sinuses were overwhelmed with the stench of the Scraggin soldier as his body closed on him. With each successive downswing of his gnarly-edged blade, the Scrag hammered against an exhausted defensive posture, which Shamus could no longer sustain. The cycle of up-and-down blows against Shamus' weakening parries and counterstrikes grew closer to achieving the purpose of cleaving Shamus from head to groin.

The blur of the blade's motion was nearly invisible in the dark forest, but the sound of it whooshing within centimeters from vital 'kill zones' on Shamus's body gave it a type of shape and form. A burning buzz feeling sent a surprisingly searing pain as the blade edge zipped past his right ear and nicked the back edge of his neck. He had sustained more than a minor cut. There was poison in the blade, and it burned! The shock of this venomous assault to his bloodstream caused Shamus to falter as he tried to find flat footing beneath himself in the darkness. He drew his blade to a 45-degree angle above his head, knowing his sudden misstep had now placed him right under the enemy's downward arc once again. The blade crashed so hard against Shamus's blade as it ground past him that he was now sure that every bone in his right arm might be fractured under the weight of his stronger opponent's violence.

His katana fell involuntarily out of his still vibrating hands and clunked somewhere beneath his feet. The Scrag paused menacingly. It knew that it was about to win this most coveted trophy. Hoping to reclaim the dropped sword before all was lost, Shamus reached backward, attempting to recover it from the soft ground. As he did so, he felt the contact of the Scraggin captain's iron shoe kicking his abdomen, sending him backward to the ground, all air rushing out of him from the force of the impact.

It'll be over in a second, Shamus's conscious mind surrendered to the inevitability of the moment. He turned away to avoid seeing the approach of the blade that was surely closing in on him. As he rolled on the uneven ground, pressing his left hand to force himself back to his feet, he felt the whiz of something rapidly flying past him. It sailed past him harmlessly until there was an audible 'crack' of metal crashing through bone. He waited for the sensation of his neck being severed to catch up with the sound, but instead, he felt only the flat side of the Scraggin soldier's blade bluntly broadside him a millisecond later. It smacked flat across his cheek with enough force to ring his bell but not to cut him. Shamus's vision swirled with stars from the impact, and his knees buckled. Part of him registered that there was no further blade strike forthcoming in the darkness, but time was losing its context, and his mind was shuttering into unconsciousness from the concussive blow. He could feel the sudden thud of his face contacting the ground.

Before his eyes closed, he saw the dead face of the Scrag captain fall almost directly opposite him, a dart lodged deep into his skull between his eyes. His mind registered that at least this enemy was not going to be the one to dine on his flesh tonight. Suddenly, a cacophony of loud bird chatter filled his ears like trumpets. *How strange*, Shamus's final thoughts closed on him like a doorway to emptiness. All about him came the echo of blades clashing with other blades, and the unfamiliar birdsong swirled through the trees like approaching trumpets just as a veil eclipsed his senses.

***

Chapter 16
The Bodeland Foresters

Shamus's eyelids slowly began to flutter, irritated by sunlight. The pain that had occupied his mind when his eyes had gone dark was now gone, and he sensed a presence of benevolence around him. His lids slowly opened onto a room that was at first obscured by the intensity of illumination.

He could see that he was no longer wearing his grimy, blood-soaked travel clothes. Instead, he had been washed and changed into a white cloth outfit made of the softest fabric he had ever worn. The bed he lay on was filled with down and adorned with swirls of ornately carved wood. There was no feeling or emotion inside of him.

"So, this is death?" he puzzled aloud.

"Nonsense!" came a foreign reply from somewhere behind him. The abruptness of the response frightened his muscles into action, and he found himself bounding out of the bed in one go. As he settled onto his feet on the cool earthen floor, his eyes scanned the room for the soft female voice that alerted him to the fact that he was not alone in the room. He tracked across what appeared to be solid stone, non-descript walls, although he couldn't yet distinguish either seams or brickwork. There was a simple table to his left that held his weapons and gear, but no sign of his tattered clothes. He kept taking in his surroundings in the seconds it took to seek out the voice until finally, Shamus's eyes came to rest on the origin of the voice. *Beautiful!* was the first thought that entered his mind as he gazed upon her. However, the docile lilt of her voice contrasted with what he was absorbing into his view. She was easily as tall as he was, muscled, and dressed in what could only be described as 'battle gear'. Leather and light chain mail covered the more vulnerable portions of her body. This was not some maiden come to tend to him. Likely, whomever had tended to that kindness had long departed the room.

"Uh, where am I?" He started with the most obvious question that came to him. "More importantly, HOW am I alive?" Shamus asked, a little embarrassed by the uncontrolled squeak of vocal cords that had not been used for some time.

"All in good time, stranger," she replied, again with the deceptively soft voice. "You're safe."

Shamus sighed with immense relief. He looked straight at his host, taking in the depth of the steel-blue color of her eyes, relieved to no longer be looking into red blood hot eyes of a Scrag bent on cleaving his head from his shoulders. He could see in one glance that her gaze was inquisitive and ready to unleash at least fifty questions of her own.

"Where is Er…?" he stopped himself from asking. Despite what felt like a place of refuge, it suddenly occurred to him that he might be a prisoner being set up for interrogation. Just because the only Scrags he had encountered thus far were deformed and disfigured in appearance, this did not necessarily mean that the Evil One had not co-opted people of other kingdoms to his service. Especially given that his last thoughts before losing consciousness were of his impending death, however long ago that was, he thought it best to not volunteer any information until he was sure of himself and the intentions of his hosts.

The abruptness of Shamus's silence made the young woman in front of him smile. She was perhaps only a few years younger than himself, he considered, but apparently reading his sudden reticence with a professional eye. She spoke even more softly than before as she approached him, placing her hands on his shoulders, bidding him to sit back down on the bed.

"Many cycles of Inyi and Naga have gone by since the Prince was said to have been slain at the hands of the House of Treborg. We know not whether we are now visited with a ghost or a man posing as the great hope of our times in this moment of our most desperate need."

So Erladoch survived as well? Shamus considered with even greater relief. *They obviously know who he is. So why separate us?* He cautioned himself.

She pulled out a stool from beneath the table where Shamus's weapons sat, his means of protecting himself lay out of reach, her elbow propping just beside the hilt of his long sword, somewhat deliberately. She continued in her rehearsed calm. "Stranger still, we find ourselves having come upon this man resembling the great Prince of Dunbar, nearly mortally wounded, but being defended by his ever more odd-looking companion who bears so little resemblance to the men of this world."

Shamus didn't know how to take what sounded like an insult to his appearance by this woman of similar age, who was now quite obviously beginning her 'Q and A' of him. Rather than dwell on her comment about his appearance, it hit him all at once that everything they had recently exchanged with one another was fully comprehensible. Erladoch had gone to some lengths over the months preceding their departure to explain both language and lore to Shamus in hopes of making him ready to survive with or without him in Loura. However, this was not like that.

"What is your name?" Shamus forced himself to say out loud. *Yes!* he immediately realized it. *I am speaking the common tongue of Loura!* He was now completely confused and impressed with himself, not knowing how this skill for the language had come to him when before he had found himself struggling with even the simplest of pronunciations. How such an implausible event had transpired was completely beyond his comprehension! A flood of thoughts entered his mind as he waited for the woman's answer. Before this moment, he had only spoken in English with Erladoch, other than during his lessons. *Right?* he asked himself. *Had he began speaking the tongue the moment he arrived through the porthole, and because he had only had exchanges with Erladoch, he had simply not registered this? Was it possible to have acquired this beautiful language through osmosis? No way! That's nonsense!*

Another even more outlandish thought occurred to him. Perhaps the reason that he and Erladoch connected so seamlessly in the hospital on their very first meeting when almost no one else could was that some part of him knew the common tongue, and this was, in fact, what he had spoken to Erladoch from the very first meeting. However, if that were true, he truly was insane and was suffering from multiple personality disorder as he had no recollection of this other voice, let alone its language skills. The seconds it had taken between the utterance of his question and the receipt of her answer had left him entirely befuddled.

"My name is Nica," she replied pleasantly enough, apparently not noticing the tumult of Shamus's self-dialogue as he lay back down on the bed. He was still feeling a little queasy, but resolved to maintain his gaze over the torso of the warrior woman who might very well dispatch him at any second with his own sword, although everything pointed to her being a friend. Her chestnut brown hair was carefully collected into spiraling braids, but not so much for beauty, he wondered, but perhaps to fit under a helmet more easily, or perhaps to not get in her eyes.

"I am ward to the Foresters of Bodeland. You are in Castra, stranger, the capital of our homeland. Do you not recall any portion of your journey here?"

Shamus shook his head, signifying 'No', and then wondered to himself whether that gesture would be interpreted as a response in this timeline. To be sure, he replied verbally.

"That woulda' been for the best," she responded. "Your voyage would have otherwise been unpleasant to endure given your state."

Shamus continued to gaze with curiosity over the intricate braiding of her hair. It occurred to him that until he had cut his friend's long mane to disguise him in their grand escape from 'the Royal', he too had worn his hair in meticulous braids. He mused that the braids might signify nothing more than an issue of fashion, but it seemed apparent that it might also define a warrior class. Given her elbow so tightly poised beside his long sword, he thought of a roundabout way of determining whether this woman was a threat to him.

"Your hair. Why do you wear it this way? Does it signify something?"

Once again, his question was met with a smile. "You're a curious one," she studied him back. "Y'er not familiar with Bodeland then, are ye?" She responded with lightning recognition of what he had just revealed about himself. "Do you come from someplace south of the Badlands? Or do you hail from someplace to the east?"

The tonal change in her voice when she said the word 'East' betrayed something. *Careful, Shamus!* he warned himself. *East implies that she thinks I might be from Treborg. Oh shite!* Shamus now recoiled mentally, recognizing that any skills he had once cleverly employed to ask probing questions of patients previously as a psychologist were now being turned on him by an equally adept interrogator. The difference, however, in her style over his was that she was quite direct in her approach. He adjusted strategy, seemingly attempting to answer her question with another question about her hair. It was as much to say: *you first.*

Nica Bodelander smiled again, a truly radiant smile that glistened throughout her entire face, save for her eyes. They were totally unchanging despite the surrounding artifice; a steel blue that was all at once beautiful, and moreover, cool and intense. Was she about to unleash holy hell on him? She had that manner about her, which he had so often seen in Erladoch when he first came across him. In a word, she like him, was 'ready'.

"You are a careful man. Your words are spoken with thoughts for your safety." Nica rose from the table, leaving the weapons behind her without another thought. Even this was deliberate, however, to Shamus's mind. She was clearly trying to ramp down the intensity of the circular conversation. She strode to the opposite end of the bed and sat down, still looking at him. "My people are your friends if you are also besieged by the Evil One. Trust me, good traveler, many of our warriors were lost so that you and the prince could be saved."

For the first time, Nica's eyes turned away from Shamus's as though to mask a great burden: the pain of loss.

"Ah. I see." He ramped down the gamesmanship. "So, there was a battle back in the mountains, then?" he offered, understanding somehow that there had been a loss—possibly of someone close to her. "It was you who came to our rescue, Miss Nica?"

"Yes. There were two of our border parties, each comprising twenty Bodelanders who ultimately faced off against nearly a hundred of the House of Treborg's hunters. It was clear they were tracking you without any concern that they had crossed into our lands. They were very motivated to acquire you. Our warriors were coming from two different areas on our frontier, but each of our groups could see that the Scrags were giving you chase. We converged on them just as you made your stand against them. Frod," she hesitated again. "My brother divided our warrior's ranks; one to bear you and your companion, and the other to engage and lead away the Scrag hunters."

For some reason, Shamus half expected her to say "you and your master", but the more she spoke, the more he realized that she was careful not to offend him. *Perhaps*, he was beginning to realize, *she might even be afraid of me, and hence her cautious manner.* This seemed to make no sense at all.

Nica went on with her recounting. "We had not borne you more than four yarricks when my brother's horn echoed defiantly over the mountains. He was summoning all the Scraggin hunt party onto himself. As he employed his Keeper's horn rather than our fluted whistle, it also meant that he was bidding us farewell." Her head dropped in silent mourning at that. She looked at the floor as though to escape the pain that came with saying the words aloud.

Shamus experienced a surge of guilt as he measured the sacrifice that had been made for him to now find himself lying in the safety of this bed. He and Erladoch had been responsible for the death of this young woman's brother and probably other men and women who had come to their aid. He was without words and felt it imprudent to be the first one to next speak; this was his only way of conveying his appreciation for the sacrifice.

At that moment, the door to the chamber slowly opened, and Erladoch walked over to where Nica was sitting. When she saw him, she made a motion as if to kneel before him, but he caught her and held her up. "You must never kneel before me, brave flower. Your family has given up much for the continuation of my line. You are now second in line to a great and noble house. We stand together, always," he added, with what sounded to Shamus like more than an overture of friendship.

The tracks of tears were now plain to see when Nica raised her eyes to meet Erladoch's. She was overcome with grief, and Shamus realized, joyous relief.

"Erladoch The Brave of Fior Hill, I am pleased to see you once again, and to know that you still walk in Loura. The cost of your return has been so great that I cannot but feel confusion in my heart on seeing you once more. Much has come to pass since we last met." Erladoch bade her to sit on the bed at Shamus's side.

"Scrags from Treborg itself ravage our small villages just inside our frontier, and Anahimara is gone. Saban fell in hours as a horde never seen before in all these modern ages swept over their lands in minutes. Almost no one survived, and it is said that the risen king of Treborg himself lead the onslaught." Nica wiped her face clear, and her voice, although urgent in its intent, also became more focused, as a soldier in the field might report to a commanding officer in a strategy briefing.

Shamus's ears pricked up even more intently at this retelling, recognizing that in some way his night of nightmares, which followed after having uttered the Evil One's name in some manner, had made him a witness to the devastation of Anahimara, and possibly also the place she had referred to as 'Saban'.

"Taroc and Ataroc fell in days, and they have employed an evil magic that has all but drained the once mighty Boldar River on its path to the sea. When the muddy bottom dries out, I expect their full army may soon cross westward at will. King Seoin O'Mara was slain," she said in a low voice.

"It has been said that the Evil One himself hoisted him out of the Boldar River as he attempted to flee like a coward. It is said that he and the rest of his family perished quickly. It would have been worse, of course, had he been taken a prisoner. It would be an unspeakable horror for him and his daughters to have been kept alive, as I am certain they would have suffered unbearable torments! Better this way, for sure." She assured herself.

"What of Prince O'Mara Boldar, Nica?" Erladoch questioned. "Did he fall as well?"

"No," she replied. "Prince O'Mara escaped to us along with nearly 4,000 remaining soldiers and horse only because they were not there to initially engage the invasion. They had been called under ancient contract by the kingdom of Nidar for aid. So much as there was of an Anahimaran army left Ataroc to fulfill this service, they were in the southern lands of Anahimara near to the border of Nidar on the day when the twin cities fell. But Nidar's call to arms was but a diversion, Lord Dunbar. When they arrived in Nidar, they found only death and destruction there. Kos had already been laid waste, and no survivors could be found. They immediately sensed the strategy that had been played on them and turned for home. O'Mara reported that the size of the Treborgan army they came upon was so endless in its number on their northern flank that they were forced to flee until they made their way to us seeking refuge. It would've meant certain death to engage them in such relatively small numbers. He said it was as though every foul and terrifying creature that one could imagine composed the ranks of an army that had already raised Taroc and Ataroc to the ground. Wolves and brials act at their beck and call. Large birds of prey seem to work in concert to attack from the sky and peck mercilessly at any living thing they come upon as though controlled by 'his' very will! The size of the army that had poured out of Greno and over the Elec Mountains could be smelled on the winds for an hour before they even saw them!"

"My friend here foretold of this," Erladoch offered in response to this devastating news as he motioned toward Shamus. "We came past the twin cities on our way here, Nica. The once rich croplands and farms are now dustbowls of ravaged and stamped-out earth."

Everyone paused to consider the magnitude of this information. Shamus passively listened to Nica's continuing reports.

"You say that only 4,000 made their way here under Prince O'Mara?"

"Aye, my lord. The prince of Anahimara is still not himself after many moons have passed. As it stands, Treborg regularly sends war parties into different edges of our kingdom to test our strength, and we know that even though we have repelled them, they are simply playing a game with us to reveal our weakest point. Last week, they pursued you and your strange friend into the first heights of the Castra mountains, well beyond any previous incursion, without any fear of repulsion. They grow ever more daring in their incursions inside the borders of our kingdom. They only throw small numbers at us as though poking us with a stick, testing our resolve. Their numbers are nothing like the massive invasionary forces described by O'Mara. They are small and fast-moving war parties that must know that if we come upon them, they will be overwhelmed, and yet it seems they pop up in multiple places at every corner of Bodeland."

Erladoch took her information in, listening carefully to her every word. To Shamus, it was apparent there was much more than a colleague reporting to another about the news of the day here. Nica and Erladoch clearly shared a long-standing bond.

"What of your people, Nica? Why have you not traveled beyond your borders to repel the dark forces?"

"My Lord Prince," she had taken his comment as a reproach and was now inclined to educate him. "When it was said that you had perished so long ago, a great balance was overturned. The Evil One with no name grew in power. His magic allowed him to make the Scrags multiply their ranks faster than verminous rats. Where he began drawing these new soldiers from, no one knows. In all the ages after the Treborgan king's fall, little was heard of the disorganized Scrags who lived beyond their mountain range. This you know all too well. Since his return, he has found a way to call these backward souls to his service and multiply his fighting force. He directs them with a single mind. If the tales which have made their way to us about Anahimara are accurate, as we believe them to be, soon there will be a force so large as to cover every blade of grass for as many miles as creatures of flight can see from above. We regularly meet his war parties at our borders to show our defiance, but old alliances have failed from hesitation after so many generations of peace. After the call from Nidar for Anahimara's aid revealed a most devious strategy to divide Anahimara's forces, none but the Keepers are prepared to continue to honor the old ways."

Shamus was surprised by Nica's ease in speaking of the Keepers. She clearly formed part of this Order. *Perhaps this is why she so readily speaks to Erladoch about all of this?* he wondered. *No, there's more to their connection than that!* he realized as he watched her mindlessly stroke Erladoch's hand, never taking her eyes from his.

We are powerless to repel the Evil One on our own, and the politicians are much angered by the recent revelation that the Sacred Order of Keepers even exists. They act as though they have been betrayed! It is all too much for some to accept this knowledge that certain members of the high kingdoms of the west have secretly operated such an Order of warriors under their noses rather than focus on the danger which forms to their east. Even now that it appears that the Dead King of Treborg has somehow returned to begin anew his mission to destroy all that is good, they waffle over whether to form armies to meet him. They have made themselves into cowards after so many ages of peace and tranquility, and the Keepers pay for their hesitation with our blood!

Erladoch grew agitated by the display of defeatism shown by Nica. "Speak not of such things, Nica Bodelander, as though you have already become the vanquished! That the armies of Treborg have not yet loosed their full might in an invasion upon your lands tells me that the Evil One is, as you have identified, testing its strengths. There must, however, be more to it than this. He is waiting for something else to happen before doing so. This suggests that there continues to be some measure of uncertainty on his end. While it was clear that Anahimara had fallen to me when Shamus and I traversed it, there had not been a sea of Scraggin armies of Treborg camped across the plains of Anahimara. There were instead war parties that patrolled the lands south of the Treborgan Mountain Range. To be sure, the cities of Taroc and Ataroc were occupied and busying themselves with construction of massive platforms. To my mind at least, this tells me that they are still preparing and making sure they are fully ready for what is to come. You must take heart that there is still time."

"But time for what, Lord Erladoch? My joy in seeing you return to me is boundless, but your return and the arrival of this stranger do nothing to rival the menace which forms outside our borders. One thing that is certain, great Lord of Dunbar," Nica's voice now sounded nearly sarcastic in spite of her tone of deference, "the darkness comes not solely in the form of great numbers of warriors such as the Treborgans of old, but also of foul and horrifying magic which he wields. He has claimed dominion over the minds of many even from far away as his mountain keep in far-off Greno. Your talk of immense war machines only troubles me more greatly. To what use will such things serve him? I know not. But the fact that they are being made tells me they are to bring about the end of all that we cherish, and soon."

Nica stopped speaking as a young man of slight and sinewy stature entered the room. His golden hair was caught by glints of sunlight. Erladoch strode to meet him.

"So it's true," the new arrival spoke in a monotone voice which neither displayed joy nor sorrow.

"O'Mara Boldar, you have ripened into a full man in my long absence!" Erladoch said in a happy booming voice. He locked arms with the young man who appeared to be barely nineteen, although his grim countenance made him appear older. "Your silent entrance into the chamber still confounds the wariness of my ears as you did as a young boy." Erladoch smiled. O'Mara smiled back; a relieved smile that was filled with confirmation that the story of the Prince of Dunbar's return was more than just a rumor.

Other than the one stool in the solid-walled room and the ornately carved bed, there was nowhere else to sit, leaving the two Princes and the Princess Ward of Bodeland to stand over Shamus's bed. Not knowing what else to do, Shamus continued to sit in the bed and simply witness the exchange. A concussion headache was forming around the edges of his thoughts, and his jaw was still sore from where he had been struck. He was accordingly happy to be the one with a soft seat under him. He considered that it would be great to find a mirror to examine his injuries more closely at some point.

After conveying both his pleasure to see the young Anahimaran alive and relaying his regrets for the horrible losses sustained by this man of both family and kingdom, Erladoch continued with the discussion, seeking as much intelligence about the status of his world that could be shared with him.

"I have seen the pathways cut into the ground by these machines which you speak of, Lord Boldar, though I saw nothing of what made such tracks in the earth. I know that no matter how great the bravery of the Anahimarans, the people were unprepared for this great massacre by the Scraggin hordes. I made the decision to break off our attack and flee as I could see that the twin cities had already clearly fallen. I'm ashamed that I ran."

"Your engagement of their army after the twin cities had already fallen would have been nothing short of futile, young prince. It would have only resulted in your death and the end of the Anahimaran royal bloodline."

O'Mara's face revealed his appreciation for Erladoch's words of consolation, but he was so clearly damaged from the engagement that, even as Erladoch went on, the look of a deeply troubled soul persisted.

"I was in a far-off place in my travels when this happened and could only see the devastation in the dreamscape. I tried to locate someone in my thoughts to give warning of my visions of what was about to befall you all, but my focus was not strong enough to reach so far. I was only searching the dreamscape in the first place to help another from being consumed directly by the Evil One at the time."

Shamus noted that Erladoch did not implicate him.

"I doubt that I could have accomplished a meaningful communication from so far away."

"Well, we knew where to find you and your companion, Lord Dunbar," Nica interjected, hoping to shift the discussion. "You came thundering into my and my brother's thoughts a dozen times before we finally sent out border patrols to seek you out last week. You practically lead us right to you on the mountain side."

Last week! Shamus registered. She had made a similar reference previously, but for reasons he had not yet grasped, it was only hitting home with him now. *I've been here for a week?* This didn't seem right to him. Shamus heard all of this with immense interest. He immediately recalled the various moments in time where, despite the immense pain experienced by Erladoch as they trudged along in the wilderness, he serially repeated various tones in a semi-trance-like state. *Had Erladoch been calling to them for assistance in his mind? Could they actually 'hear' his thoughts beckoning their help.*

His mind drew back to the night in Ottawa where he was nearly consumed by the malice of the Evil One as its clawed hand began ripping into his chest. He remembered both the voice coming from inside of him, and the voices which seemed to come from everywhere outside of him that ultimately rescued him from this terrifying fate. The Yang and Yin of it; the male voice and the female voice which had come together and filled the ether to protect him. *Was Nica Bodelander the female who came to my rescue at that moment?* He doubted this as she appeared to be hearing these grim tidings for the first time. *There was a woman there!* He confirmed to himself. *Achingly familiar, like the voice of pure love.*

Erladoch had spoken to him of the continuation of the bloodlines of the Angealkind, which had to have been flowing even for him to have borne the physical marking that he did. *My ears*, he reminded himself. *My goofy semi-pointed ears.* That is what seemingly started everything which had led to this point. Erladoch had opened himself to him in the S.T.U. because of what he had believed must flow within him and which still flowed in some people descended from the Strahanas, the Angelic colony that had lived among men for probably thousands of years before this timeline. Erladoch was a 'Keeper'. This he knew. But a keeper of certain traditions, even a keeper of the basic truths about this heritage and the real story relating back to the stones of power. *But,* he now wondered, *do all Keepers possess some aspect of the magical powers of these earlier Angelic people? Telepathic abilities even?* Apparently, Erladoch possessed this power, and he was freely sharing this among those assembled in the chamber that had grown more cramped in the presence of this young Anahimaran prince.

Shamus continued to do his best to assimilate what he was hearing so far. Nica spoke openly to Erladoch about her bitterness toward the 'politicians' of the various kingdoms, whom she described as having been collectively angered and improperly distracted by the discovery that this secret society existed. They were bothered that their power structure had, in fact, been somewhat of a farce and this secret warrior society had operated under their very noses for generations. It did not seem to matter to them that their cause had been one of affording protection for everything that all people of the west had come to cherish.

Erladoch had just shared the narrative of his telepathic event, where he had come to Shamus's rescue in his near life-ending encounter with Enilorac, without hesitation. To speak so openly of these facts and of the mystical abilities which Erladoch shared even in the presence of the Anahimaran prince confirmed to him that these individuals all belonged to this Sacred Order.

Shamus examined both Nica and O'Mara with renewed curiosity. Neither of their ears were visible to his sight, given the placement of each person's hair. *Do they bare that apparent feature which Erladoch had seen in me?* he wondered. He hoped that this Angelic 'tell' would reveal itself as it had when he had cut Erladoch's hair. For now, he was altogether troubled at the freedom by which Erladoch was sharing their story, his story! *This is being too openly shared!* It unsettled him, but that was not what was putting him off. Even though he couldn't put a finger on the 'why' of it, he didn't know these Keepers. While he had accepted Erladoch's advice to him that he had traveled through a 'mindscape' or 'dreamscape' to protect him, he had nonetheless never fully processed the magnitude of the clear disclosure he had been given. His focus had been so myopically directed toward his own personal struggles that it never fully sank in that this man who was then an inmate of a mental institution, was telling him considerably more.

He listened to the unfolding discourse, trying to find out why it bothered him that these other individuals assembled around him were being told of this encounter that had been so personal to him.

"You're right," Erladoch replied to Nica. "I was doing my best to summon you, but my wound was making it difficult to concentrate. I'm very glad that you heard me!"

Once again, there was a subtle exchange of hand touching between Erladoch and Nica as Erladoch shifted back into his storytelling.

"I've been trapped in a fortress of sorts for most of the past four cycles. I only escaped because of the bravery of my companion. He risked everything for me, trusting when I gave him almost no reason at all to do so. So, while he sits there looking at us with slack jaw, with a most alarming countenance, I assure you that he is a friend to all free people of Loura." Erladoch threw a wry smile behind his comment. It was only then that Shamus realized that he was being spoken of.

Shamus struggled to return Erladoch's robust smile with one of his own, embarrassed that his silence till now had made him feel like a non-entity in the room. While eager to join the conversation, he had nothing to contribute. He resolved to simply nod respectfully at everyone, hoping to passively indicate his familiarity with recent Louran history. Months before, Erladoch had provided him with a painstaking overview of the Ages of Louran history. Except for more recent events that were being discussed now, he felt up to speed. He already comprehended that in this most recent age of history, Lourans had had no use for armies. Because of this, the ancient houses had found themselves compelled over time to share important decisions with non-royals. It was not all bad, but maintaining the cause of the light could not remain in the open without the risk of interference. The 'politicians' as Nica referred to them with an edge of disdain, tended to get in the way of even subtle efforts directed at maintaining even a small standing army to protect the kingdoms of the west, particularly when there was no apparent foe. She didn't hate these people. They had performed important functions which, in many ways, had enhanced the prosperity of the ruling houses. Rather, she was bothered by the reaction that the Keepers had encountered from them when circumstances finally required that the Sacred Order reveal themselves to these 'assistant decision-makers.' Given the divine purpose that their Order was committed to, it came as no small disappointment that Keepers were perceived with mistrust rather than embraced in this moment of confusion and need.

With no warning of a change in the conversation's direction, Shamus was taken aback when the young Anahimaran prince interrupted Erladoch. "Eh, by what name does your strange friend go by?" O'Mara Boldar interrupted the exchange on recent events.

The fact that O'Mara had directed his question to Erladoch and not Shamus directly seemed odd. Due to the formal way the query had been posed; Shamus decided to take no insult from it. He sensed that a degree of caution was being exercised toward him, not unlike Nica Bodelander's initial approach to him. It was clear that everyone in the room, including Erladoch, had treated him with some level of 'care' since he had returned to the land of the conscious. As the light in the room had shifted over the past hour, the window had become more of a reflective piece than before.

Shamus pressed himself more upright in the bed with the intention of getting to his feet for a second time that day. As a result of O'Mara's comment, he surmised that this was as good a time as any to add his own interruption to the conversation. He resolved that he should more formally introduce himself to his hosts. As his naked feet made contact with the cool floor, he caught his reflection for the first time in the glass. His legs went weak from under him. Had the bed he had just exited from not been located right behind him, he would have fallen hard backward. Midway down, he steadied on the bedside, pushed himself back to his full height, and looked again into the figure looking back at him in the glass. His previously black hair had turned completely white! Not silvery white or a version of 'salt and pepper', but true snow-colored 'white'! His skin looked different as well; neither younger nor older necessarily, but no longer flawed. There was an air of timelessness to his transfigured appearance. His teenaged acne scars were gone. He had expected to see a massive bruise across his face and black eyes from having been whacked by the flat side of the Scraggin soldier's sword across his cheek, but that too was not present. His eyes were now a flame of intense green, more blazoned than the brightest of emeralds. He couldn't comprehend this transformation. Even the top of his earlobes had managed to sharpen somewhat. The man looking back at him in the reflection was completely alien! Shamus gasped loud enough to halt all conversation buzzing around him in the room.

What the hell? He was both frightened and confused. "How?" he sputtered and hesitated. *Have they done this to me?* he questioned with shock. He didn't know whether to be enraged or terrified, perhaps both, at the same time.

Erladoch realized that Shamus had just now seen his reflection. He stepped over to him with the intent of calming his friend, who was now brimming past the edge of freaking out.

"My friends, I should have done this earlier. This is Shamus. He is a true friend of Erladoch the Brave of Fior Hill. His destiny is tied to me, and I believe, as I stand here now seeing him transformed as he now is, that I was right in my conviction that he accompany me home. There is little doubt that he is going to play a role in our quest for the Great Stone."

"What the hell are you saying?" Shamus spat out reflexively.

Before he could be allowed to show more of his trepidation, Erladoch placed a calming hand on him, holding him fast to the bed but also imploring him with his gesture to allow him to keep the proverbial floor.

It was clear to Nica that Erladoch was now speaking over Shamus to deliberately lay down a construction of his status. She had been fascinated, if not also intimidated, by his bizarre appearance from the moment she had first laid eyes on him.

"Shamus is, at the very least, a riddle master. In my many dreams while in captivity, I have seen a great man of shocking and awesome powers. Through great portents, this man has come to me to tell me that he will play a role in our darkest times to destroy the great evil that has yet to fully realize its own powers. The Wigget whom I saw had this same white hair, the color of mountain snow. When this man in my dreams came to my aid, his demeanor had not been revealed until sometime later, but he bore a mark of the ancients that was unmistakable. It was in that way that I would recognize him and know to place all my trust and the fate of Loura solely into his hands. He reveals himself before 'us' now on this bed. Friends, this is a great moment of revelation!" Erladoch was jubilant. "This enchanted soul will take a special role in the shaping of the future ages of all people of Loura. While I knew him by a different name when I was to first encounter him, his veil has now lifted and revealed the magical being from my dreams."

Shamus did everything in his power to not laugh out loud, entirely amused by his friend's introduction. *What a ridiculous introduction to give me! What the hell is he trying to do?* He had caught the fact that this was Erladoch's way of saying to him between the lines that he too was shocked by his altered appearance almost as much as he was. Almost. *But then again,* Shamus considered his freakishly altered appearance, *I have been transformed somehow. Maybe he does have an inkling of what this all means.*

Erladoch appeared to be satisfied with whatever internal dialogue he had been having with himself as he spoke of Shamus's 'new look'. The sudden alteration of appearance was, in a real way, an apparent resolution of doubts which Erladoch had harbored regarding the shared sense of connection between them. Studying his friend's face, he could see that a piece of a greater puzzle had just come into focus for Erladoch. Some manner of confirmation. Shamus could see this plainly.

He didn't know what to say. He attempted to replay the last few moments in hopes of gaining clarity. He noted that Erladoch had left out the time travel porthole from his discussion. He'd further omitted the time and place where he had disappeared to. *Surely these Keepers knew that we had traveled? Or,* he assessed, *perhaps only some of them get to know certain levels of detail? Best to keep my mouth shut,* he resolved.

He now recollected that his family name had been omitted from this introduction; and, in its place was this new 'title' which Erladoch had bestowed upon him. *This is some kind of a joke! Right?* Shamus desperately wanted to reject what had been said of him. There was a gaze from Erladoch, however, that his more rational and unpanicked mind also caught sight of. The stern but subtle head turn to the left spoke volumes to Shamus. The solitary glance intended just for him seemed to warn. 'What I'm saying is, in fact, true. The 'how', the 'why', and the rest of what they don't yet understand, we will work out in time just the two of us; so, remain quiet!'

Shamus was not content with this. He was the one who looked completely freaky! Why couldn't he be introduced by his full name? Perhaps someone knew of his parents and might even be able to share something about their fates if only they knew his last name?

Erladoch has reasons to avoid connecting more dots for these people right now? I just have to trust his judgment.

He caught another glimpse of himself in the window glass. *Jaysus! There must be another reason for why I look this way!* He needed to fashion a different explanation for himself as to what had happened. It occurred to Shamus that when he was struck by the Scrag's scimitar, he felt a sense of poison entering his bloodstream before the light of his consciousness went out. Likely, the changes were a result of his immune system having gone wild to combat it, resulting in his altered appearance. *Maybe this will be a fleeting look?* he considered with hope.

What was certain was that Erladoch himself was truly surprised by Shamus's altered appearance. As for the rest of the people in this room, this is how he would have first appeared to them. Now was not the time to challenge what his friend was telling them about him. This 'mask' that he now seemed to be wearing, and the further fact that he apparently now possessed the language skills of the Louran people were sufficiently vexing to him on their own. He would have to wait to be alone with Erladoch before he would be able to sort out the truths from the fictional introduction which had been made for him.

Erladoch seemed to be in tune with the mental turmoil that Shamus now found himself working through. That would have to be enough for now.

"Friends, this is the first time that Shamus has awakened after days of tormenting dreams inspired by the poison which ought to have claimed his life. Except for the power that he harbors within him, he should already be dead. It will take time for the effects of that evil to drain from him. My own healers and nursemaids kept me apprised of Shamus's progress when I was still too weak to leave my own bed."

Nica and O'Mara were equally dumbstruck by the revelation that they were in the presence of a person possessing magical powers, powers which Erladoch hinted might exceed their own special skills. Where would such a person have come from if not from within the ranks of their Sacred Order? How was it possible that they did not know him? If he was also the progeny of the Angel-Human mix, they would have come across him within the ranks of the Keepers. From when and where did this Shamus individual come to be with Erladoch?

Shamus was acutely aware of the fact that Erladoch had made some notable omissions from his tale. He surmised the abridged tale being shared with these esteemed leaders was deliberate. Was it possible that they were not as versed in the complete history of Loura as Erladoch? Clearly, he was not telling them everything, at least not yet. *Did they not know of the council of Wiggets, or the mission held firmly by their own Order to find this Anthrac Aran person? How compartmentalized are the missions of the Keepers?* he wondered. He would have to be given answers soon. The lack of clarity was unsettling to him. Shamus's confusion was beginning to fuel an overdrive of self-protective paranoia. *Oh my God!* A rush of realization flooded in. *Do these people think that I'm an envoy from the Evil One? No,* he deliberated, *that's not it. I'd be dead already. They're tiptoeing around me, though. That much seems clear. And Erladoch is holding information back. But why? Does Erladoch think that I'm somehow an important descendant of the Angealkind even though he claims to have failed in his mission? Am I something more akin to these Keeper folks than I know?*

As his mind was heading for its own logical tailspin, Erladoch interrupted.

"Friends, this has been an exacting journey for us. The labors of our having have come so far makes the further telling of our tale too much to endure right now. We should take our discussions elsewhere and leave Shamus to rest."

Shamus could tell that Erladoch was attempting to usher everyone from the room. *Why does he want to leave me alone? What 'tell' am I giving off that he is trying to conceal? I don't like this at all!* Shamus needed to process the madness and disarray of his thoughts. He could feel a heat rising in his skin as the discordant thoughts increased. He must have been giving off a vibe that Erladoch preferred for the others not to see.

Why Erladoch had chosen to splice out certain facts of their collective tale about things like portholes and the future timeline from which they had come made little sense to him. Shamus had been led to believe that the Keepers all shared in such missions. Was he blocking them from learning the whole story, or was he protecting them from gaining too much information? Whatever the reason, he was pleased to see those assembled in his chamber politely nodding their foreheads and beginning to make their exit as he suddenly felt overwhelmed by fatigue within himself.

"Wait!" A voice from somewhere inside the chamber began to speak.

"Majestic Lords and Lady of Loura," Shamus heard the voice addressing them. It was familiar and entirely foreign all at once. **"Do not depart just yet. The Evil One has hesitated because of my return. Hear me now,"** the voice commanded. **"Time is brief, and you require my counsel."**

Nica turned on her heels first. Her jaw went slack. The others suddenly appeared alarmed.

What Shamus had not yet connected was that the voice in the room was coming from him. It was lower and louder than his own, but clearly, it was flowing up from somewhere within him. He backed himself into the wall just to be sure. The soft thud of spine against hard surface confirmed it. He was the one talking. He wanted to say to the source of the sounds, "Stop this immediately!" It was as though his mind had just fractured into parts. He was sure that he was experiencing the telltale signs of a psychotic break. Another personality within him was suddenly emerging. *Erladoch, please look at me and see the man you have known for many months now!*

Those were the words which Shamus wanted to say, but he was not in control of his own vocal cords. The rush of fatigue that had washed over him had 'split' his mind from his own actions somehow.

O'Mara raised his hands to cover his eyes, and the others followed suit, making Shamus even more confused and alarmed. He could see that the room had become brightly lit, but his conscious brain was playing catch-up with what his body was manifesting. He didn't know that an aura of white light was pulsing from every inch of his body; instead, all he could see was the three of them shielding their eyes, apparently wrapped in awe of him.

Once more, he tried to make his lips move to mouth words of consolation to the three of them, but he had no control over his vocal chords. He was possessed by some form of persona, and it was suddenly awake and insistent on being heard. **"I am part of this man who stands before you. He is my vessel. His family has borne me for thousands of ages and kept me safe. In turn, I have kept my hosts safe in their times of need and imbued them with my power when danger presented itself. In such moments, I have been briefly revealed."**

A burst of insight flowed into Shamus as though a dam of knowledge came flooding forth into the empty places in his mind. His competition as an 18-year-old, where he had blacked out and supposedly nearly killed the opponent who'd actually come to the match not with a plan to win a trophy, but the more sinister intent of killing him in the ring. This presence which he now heard speaking through him—YES! He'd been there before to help him! *My escape from Ottawa at the Eternal Flame where I felt myself hovering safely within a cloak of white light above the flames just before me and Erladoch plummeted through the porthole—he'd done that for me! My superhuman display of ferocity when we encountered the Scraggin soldiers between the twin cities. I didn't slaughter those Scrags! He took me over and moved me like a marionette!* All of these happenings now had a nexus point. Surely there were other moments that had not yet occurred to him as well, but now he knew that he had been truly 'guided'. *Just like he's doing now. But who the hell are you?* Shamus asked the personality.

While the voice continued to speak, Shamus seemed able to register and control his own thoughts. He searched for other seminal moments for which he had never fully been able to reconcile. There had been a first time—only a few weeks following the night he had nearly walked off the dock at his family cottage in the middle of a blistering rainstorm. It was his grand-da who'd coaxed him to turn around, but it had not been Eamon Bergin's voice that had beckoned him to return to safety that night? *Had it?* Shamus wondered. There had been two voices that night, Shamus realized for the first time. One that had been sinister. It had slithered through his sleepwalking mind like a snake sliding over wet grass, compelling him to follow. The other voice was further off; not at all like it was now—it had not been coming from within him, not yet. The enchanting voice which pleaded with him to return to a place of safety only reverberated within his own ears later, maybe a week or so following that night, Shamus now realized. The comforting voice which he now recognized as the one speaking within him had been the same one that told him to awaken moments before his beloved grand-da passed away.

"I am Anthrac Aran, last of my colony on Loura." The light was so bright now that it felt as if the room might explode from the concentration of energy. **"I have returned to Loura to combat the King of the Great Pit, who has corrupted the miracle of our magic. He threatens to eradicate humankind by planning to open the Pit into your timeline. If he succeeds,**

he will erase all that is of this dimension. He has chosen this time when man is not yet advanced enough to protect itself because of the folly of the king of Treborg. The Treborgan opened the time portal, and it is through that link that the Master of the Pit will bring forth his servants to lay waste to man. My self-exile from living form was designed to hide my light away from the corruption that was taking hold of the final living members of the Angealkind. You are all the descendants of the Angel-human merging. I created your Order to protect the Light before merging my essence within the bloodline of this man's ancestors. This man who stands before you is the last of his bloodline. You are the hope of all men and women who would come after you. I am not yet realized in flesh."

Shamus listened to himself articulate every word, totally unaware of what would come next. Nica and Erladoch had already dropped to their knees in deference to the being of light. Immediately behind them, O'Mara followed suit. Whereas Nica and Erladoch were slack-jawed and transfixed before Shamus's frame, O'Mara seemed to be in pain, the level of his apparent deference causing him to shield his eyes entirely and look away. Shamus worried that the intensity of the experience might cause them harm as they all kneeled before him, unmoving, listening to the hollow voice as it emitted its echo through his vocal cords.

"When the last of my brethren fell to the Treborgan king's blade, it was no longer possible for me to dwell as living flesh lest my fragment of the stone be found. Power over all three of the shards would be cataclysmic. Brought together, they would reveal the location of the Great Stone, which was hidden away when the time of the Strahanas began to fade. Made in Heaven, the Great Itavo bestows immense power to them who would wield it, including opening gateways between times and realms. I left Loura in the hands of you, the Keepers, to safeguard my essence and my secret, hoping that by doing so I could prevent the forces of darkness from ever gaining access to the one thing that could enable the Master of the Pit to escape his eternal prison. The one that you call "the Evil One" is an abomination of living flesh. He alone is the tool by which the Itavo can be wielded by Satan. The Master of the Pit may not himself touch this stone of power made with Heaven's light, but his servant can, and he has returned to your timeline. Anyone who can wield the power of the Great Itavo can control all dimensions. Fear me not! Fear not this human who I have selected to carry me until the time is right. Inside him, like his ancestors who also bore me, lies a great warrior. He will prove himself worthy when he is called upon to make the ultimate sacrifice. The time of my awakening approaches; you must safeguard him with all that you have, as he is of me as I am of him. He will bear me to my rebirth. Trust in him to reveal all secrets."**

The audible voice ceased speaking from within Shamus. In its stead, pure thoughts resonated out of Shamus, bypassing his conscious mind altogether in a focused and private fashion that he was not being made privy to. It still had the shape and texture of dialogue, but there was no longer sound to the messaging. "**Dunbar**", Anthrac Aran had summoned Erladoch to participate in this private conversation, "**Though you and your colleagues may not know the words that will be spoken, my vessel will. You must heed him when he does. He will guide you to the place of greatest spiritual force in Loura. You have been entrusted under oath to find my carrier at great cost to you, and you have guided us home. Your task, however, is not complete, Keeper. You must help Shamus Bergin find what he needs to fulfill his destiny of bringing me back to my own corporeal existence. I will guide him where and insofar as I may, but I must stay hidden from being perceived by Enilorac within the dreamscape or he will know that I have returned to face him and make all effort to capture and kill me in this latent form. I am ready to return in this hour of desperation, but I need to be born of a woman who still carries the mark of my race inside her blood. She awaits this man alone. I cannot emerge and bring forth the Stone of Power without such a union. There will be times when my Bearer will be uncertain of himself, times even when he may wish to divert course to fulfill personal longings. Time is nearly run out for the presence of Light in this world. You must keep him focused on this singular task."**

Nica was still shielding her eyes as Anthrac spoke directly to Erladoch's mind. O'Mara shifted gaze and looked right into the light pulsing from Shamus with fascination. Shamus's body continued to glow brightly, but he now appeared to be unconscious, suspended from action by the force occupying him. Even as he stood bolt upright, eyes closed, the audible voice resumed for all to hear. "**Dunbar has battle readied my Bearer. I have further opened**

him to the lessons and skills of his forebears. He is solid and made steadfast for the task by this gift, and the magic I have imbued in him to summon the warrior skills of his many ancestors will in turn aid each of you in defending me. My strength now fades. I go back to my chrysalis to prepare. Guard him well; he cannot perish until his destiny has been fulfilled, and each of you must serve him in order to now fulfill the fullness of your oaths as Keepers." The voice was beginning to fade now as the intensity of the light around Shamus dissipated. As it did, Shamus's consciousness returned in time to hear what his vocal cords were still announcing to all assembled. **"Find your guidance in the shrouds of the old library. Shamus will know where it is to be found, and you shall follow him there. Once he has resolved this task, you will then take with you that which is older than the ground you stand upon. The elder king possesses that which holds fast all others. As I recede to sleep, I call on them that know to bring forth my gift to men once bestowed upon them for safe-keeping. Reunion is nigh, even as time is now short; the journey is yours now to take. I am nearly ready to be made flesh once more. Do not delay."**

Shamus awakened to the sensation that he was once more alone with his consciousness. His entire being had been completely drained of energy. Whatever physical reserves he might normally have had to apply to the basic act of living had been diverted to allow the Angel to reveal itself and its intentions to them. All vital sugar in his bloodstream had drained out of him, causing Shamus to rapidly enter a state of hypoglycemic shock. "Need sugar," he managed to mutter before his eyes suddenly clamped shut and he collapsed into a deep, involuntary coma.

***

Chapter 17

When Shamus reawakened in what felt like seconds, the chamber was now packed with people bustling about the room. Many more unfamiliar faces were fussing all around him. One woman was gently rubbing a cloth bathed in a sweet nectar over his mouth in hopes of reviving him. He sputtered at the sickly-sweet taste. Surprisingly, he felt a sense of incredible refreshment, an 'openness'. He also now had so many more answers in his grasp than ever before to the gnawing questions of 'who he was', 'what his family connection was to this place', and 'why he had felt compelled to come here with Erladoch'.

A great weight had lifted from him that day, even though he was mindful of the burden which lay ahead. As his eyes struggled to find their focus on those gathered around him, he considered that many people go through life never being able to comprehend their purpose on Earth. Even at the end, they are often forced to resign themselves to the possibility that their presence in the world might very well have been futile.

Shamus was awakening to the fact that he had been injected into the epicenter of what might prove to be humankind's greatest struggle. It was more purpose than he had ever expected and, likely, far more than he would have chosen for himself. He now recalled the faces of the faith leaders who had assembled to meet him in the private dining room of Hy's Restaurant in Ottawa. The memory of their looks of appreciation directed at him came into a level of focus for him even as he was trying to fix his vision on those who were physically in the room with him now. He considered himself to have been an educated but simple man, who had not done anything altogether special in his thirty years of life. The people who had come to see him in that restaurant so many months ago were themselves Keepers, descended from an ancient order that connected back to this timeline. They had possessed a knowledge that had been conveniently obliterated from the records of modern man. The importance of their secret lay with him—'within him,' in fact. He wondered whether his father had ever carried the White Wigget within himself or whether that mantle skipped directly from his beloved grand-da to him. The words he last recalled his grand-da ever saying in his presence moments before he never spoke again resounded now in his ears: "not ready". Shamus had been only eight. Is that when the transference happened? Or had it already happened following his birth? The newly rekindled memory of his family having fled Ireland when he was five suggested it had happened earlier, but his supposedly mentally ill grand-da must have maintained some aspect of the magic and was trying, from earliest of Shamus's days to acquaint him with his role. *Or*, he was connecting the dots for himself, *some faceless enemy had become knowledgeable of my family's secret and were attempting to slay both Grand-da and me to prevent the transfer from ever happening.*

He considered that his parents must have been devastated to have had to leave him when they did, but clearly, they had both accepted their fates and their son's role in the coming days.

There were people busying themselves in every corner of his small chamber, taking little note of him as he lay there. Food was being laid out on the table, which had formerly housed his travel pack and swords. His trusted weapons now lay scrunched up in a corner of the room. *Actually,* he realized for the first time, *there aren't any corners in this room*. His eyes scanned the solid wall, confirming that it was in fact a slowly unfolding elliptical shape with no defined edges. *Curious*, he thought.

Until his feet hit the cool ground, the faces, both familiar and new, took no note of him at all. As his toes sensed the presence of flower petals beneath them, all activity ceased. Erladoch walked over to Shamus, addressing him as he would have normally done so on any regular day.

"It is so good to see you up and well!" Erladoch embraced him in the way which Shamus had seen his friend do with O'Mara and Nica on the previous occasion in this very room. He was a bit taken back by the show of emotion from his friend but very much gratified to be greeted by him, nonetheless. Nica ushered the servants from the room and proceeded to close the door to ensure privacy.

Erladoch spoke in a soft voice. "When I first went through the void to look for Anthrac Aran, I was pursuing an ancient mission based on my sworn duty. I came back here with you, not appreciating that I had, in fact, succeeded. I honestly considered that I had failed, but I took consolation in the belief that your return with me was nonetheless going to be important in some way that might later reveal itself given your, and your family's apparent connection to our timeline. The facts of my mission were known only by few of my brethren given the risks involved with where I had to go to access the porthole. Non-Keepers would never know where their Prince had fallen, only that I had likely perished. What Keepers know they may only reveal among themselves. We have kept your presence hidden as best we could until now. Using your expression, my friend, I guess you blew that secret right out of the water, didn't you?" Erladoch laughed then. It was hearty enough of a laugh but one which Shamus sensed was a bit forced. Erladoch was clearly not happy about his sacred position having been revealed in the presence of any uninitiated folk who might have passed by the chamber as the White Wigget was revealing his presence from within Shamus. The event was so all-consuming that it was all too possible that others passed by and bore witness to the event without having been noticed by Erladoch, Nica or O'Mara. Nonetheless, Erladoch was once again filling the air with his own voice as though to instruct Shamus.

As Shamus's head was now clear, he was fully attuned to the fact that he was indeed being told by his friend to follow the lead he was giving him.

Erladoch looked like the peak of health. Shamus thought back to his last moments of wakefulness before Anthrac had taken control of him. Whenever that moment had been, the memory came to Shamus that Erladoch had previously looked pale, albeit clearly well on a path to recovery.

"So," he answered back, "how long have I been asleep this time?"

Everyone in the room laughed at this question.

"Twelve days," Nica replied from over his right shoulder. "You slept so quietly that we often had to hold a glass to your mouth and nose just to be sure that you still lived. The appearance of the White Wigget exacted a mighty toll on you, Shamus of Fior."

Shamus scratched the top of his head thoughtfully, considering this information. By the degree of activity in his chamber, it was clear that much had been going on during his hibernation-like slumber.

Most of the former occupants of the room were themselves Bodelanders. Shamus quickly surmised that they were a very attractive race of people, but all of them carried that look of ferocity that he had first seen in Nica's gaze, which was slightly unsettling. He wondered whether this was genetic or something that had been developed due to the gravity of the era these people found themselves now living in.

He saw now that each person who had been rummaging around before having been ushered out had been preparing various components of travel gear. Shamus had nothing left of his original travel pack. Next to his samurai swords lay a whole new set of clothing, not unlike the incredibly soft garment he was currently wearing. Not having to put back on his disgustingly soiled garments came as a relief. He didn't think that he would ever be able to get the stench of blood and filth out of them again, and obviously, neither did his hosts.

Shamus lifted one of the over shirts and examined it closely. It was made of a tightly woven material that was heavier than it appeared. He couldn't make out the nature of the fibers, but he mused by the garment's softness, that it was some type of silk. He was about to examine the trousers when he was beckoned to leave the room and follow Nica and Erladoch. A pair of soft leather sandals were waiting for him on the floor. He slipped them under his feet and tied the fasteners around his ankles before hurrying to follow them out. It felt good to be on his feet after having been in bed for so long, but his legs cramped and wobbled in protest at first as a result of weeks of disuse.

From his chamber, Shamus was led down a series of winding passageways until he stepped into a small hall that appeared to be comprised of reinforced earthen walls. He noted that they bore carvings which revealed detailed and refined workmanship. Other walls were entirely made of a polished smooth wood surface that also bore carvings. Figures leaped out of the sculpted and carved surfaces from every corner of the hall, in fact. They clearly told stories, but Shamus had no way of knowing where such stories began or ended. He thought back to his undergraduate studies at Carleton University for a moment. He wished now that he had selected the Ancient Civilizations course in the Anthropology Department as his option instead of choosing French 101. It occurred to him that this might have at least given him access to a way of knowing how to interpret these magnificent stories.

Food was laid out on the table, and it, like the sculptures and the carvings, was prepared with excellence. Shamus noticed, however, that as delicious as the meal presented to him was, there was hardly enough to go around to the people assembled there. He got the sense that the people outside of this hall probably were going with even less than what was placed before them and would have considered what was being spread out before him as a feast. He correctly assumed that someone had been taking care to feed and attend to his bodily functions while he slept for days on end. This was an uneasy, if not embarrassing, thought, and he resolved to thank anyone who attended him hereafter. The fact that his body did not seem to have reduced in muscle tone or apparent weight implied that he had received meticulous care. In deference to his hosts, Shamus fussed over the meal provided to himself and Erladoch and chewed thoughtfully on every bite. This act of appreciation pleased his hosts greatly.

Conversation was minimal while each person assembled shared the molasses-flavored black bread. There were bowls of meats mixed in with what appeared to be some type of gritty but fragrant wild rice. Shamus couldn't help but notice the polite but nervous glances that he kept getting from the men and women who were seated at the long table on either side of him. The servants who came in and out of the hall to serve the meal looked downright nervous when they caught sight of him. *I suppose these folks aren't used to strangers*, he thought to himself, momentarily forgetful of his alarming countenance.

When Erladoch spoke first to those assembled, the topic focused entirely on their departure. This seemed to be of great interest to all, but it was of special interest to Shamus. In his mind, he had just arrived in this safe haven after having endured nothing but peril since arriving in Loura.

He kept his mouth busy with the food laid out before him. Based upon where the participants were in this conversation, it was entirely clear to Shamus that his extended slumber had excluded him from a multitude of previous conversations on the same topic. Once Erladoch had started, everyone else assembled began wading in.

After having been out in the wilds and narrowly surviving to arrive in this place, Shamus expected that if they now had to leave, they would be doing so in the company of a large and heavily armed fighting force for the journey to whatever their next destination was to be. As conversation went around the hall, however, it was clear that this was anything but a settled issue. The majority, however, was leaning toward a more covert group that might go less noticed in the wilderness. What was incredibly plain to Shamus was that everyone believed that the once-safe road systems spanning the western kingdoms were now all at risk. Whatever had come to pass in Erladoch's four-year absence clearly represented a dramatic shift in the fortunes of Loura.

O'Mara Boldar rose to say his piece. "My friends, I was given a vision in my dreams last night. I saw that the Bodelands would soon fall to the House of Treborg in as swift and horrific a manner as did my own countrymen " The room grew silent in reflection of this tragic turn of events. "My vision also revealed, however, that the people of the Great Forest could yet survive this devastation by fleeing their homeland and spreading themselves among the refuges of the various houses which still stand in Loura."

A great tumult erupted in the room as clearly the Bodeland Foresters assembled in the Hall considered this an unacceptable notion.

"Aye! I understand that your ancestral homeland will be laid to waste," he said while gesturing with his hands in a conciliatory fashion, hoping to regain the floor.

"You would have us run away from the land that is part of the Forester's very soul out of fear and spread ourselves thin? This makes no sense!" Nica pounded a fist into the table, already infuriated by the suggestion. She was mad that he had not come to her to discuss such a portentous dream in private.

"But you would live, wouldn't ya?" O'Mara offered replied respectfully.

"Only to fight on foreign lands for another kingdom's ancestral home? That leaves our people divided and weak. O'Mara, this is precisely how your lands fell!" This latter comment stung as harshly as a blade in O'Mara's heart. As soon as she said it, she knew that her friend would be overcome by his own guilt and regret.

O'Mara steadied himself, then sat down, realizing that he was a guest in this Hall, and his surviving soldiers and countrymen who had made it to Bodeland were, each of them, refugees. The argument fizzled out of him. Those assembled didn't have to be reminded that O'Mara Boldar's decision to ride to the aid of a neighbor had already presented itself as an example of why not to spread one's forces out too thinly. The people assembled at this grand table all evidently were 'persons in the know'.

***

Since the time of the White Wigget's departure from Loura, the leadership of the Louran kingdoms had maintained a hidden presence of Keepers among their ranks. By this stage of Louran history, however, not all members of the Royal Courts belonged to this clandestine organization. In fact, many didn't.

Even inside royal families, only some members would be chosen while others were entirely kept in the dark, having been viewed by the Keepers as 'not suitable'.

With the passage of time, the Keepers' active efforts to conceal themselves afforded increasingly greater numbers outside the royal houses to begin to occupy important roles inside their courts. These civilians did not know of the threat that loomed beyond their borders. They would have been astonished to learn that people who lived and worked right alongside of them maintained this membership and that for every generation since the all-but-forgotten time of this now mythical Angelic being known as 'Anthrac Aran', they had continued to devote themselves to protecting the safety of their lands.

The civilians certainly had no idea of the portholes once used regularly by the Strahanas or the uses put to them now by the Keepers. The travels and trials endured by the Keepers to maintain a balance in all the world throughout time would never be shared, even though disclosures were being made over the past four years of the Order's existence to those in power who needed to know, given the belief that the Evil One had returned.

Those who didn't need to know had no appetite whatsoever for maintaining a state of battle readiness. To them the apparent scourge of Treborg had seemingly been erased from the map so many generations before their births that the notion of maintaining a warrior class seemed counterintuitive.

Following Erladoch's believed demise, those who had heeded the advice to start building armies had barely begun the undertaking, and only grudgingly so. Before this time, and for nigh on a thousand years, the only obvious presence of a military at all revolved around ceremonial guards for the Royal houses, together with small police forces designed to maintain the peace among neighbors. Outside of the royal families themselves, these had been the additional places where the Keepers had primarily inserted themselves. On their own, their ranks would never be enough to repel what had already begun to overwhelm their unprepared world. The revelation that the long-defunct Kingdom of Treborg had both been reinvigorated and further had been secretly organizing armies was difficult to absorb. The disclosure that the Dead King had risen to oversee all of this was so preposterous a notion as to be unbelievable, fearmongering even! More than a few had accused the Sacred Order of having engaged in an ill-conceived power play designed to wrest authority away from the governing minds of the western kingdoms by raising alarm over something that could not possibly have been a real threat.

It was accordingly not surprising that the armies which had been recently formed, like that of the Anahimaran cavalry, were undertrained and certainly not ready for the ferocity or scope of the invasionary force that had overwhelmed this eastern kingdom only months ago. When the much smaller Kingdom of Saban had fallen to invasion, farmers were conscripted into a makeshift army that never really had a chance. The Evil One's distraction of sending a relatively small force of Scrags to Nidar had been a test designed to assess the battle readiness of its neighbor immediately adjacent to the Elec Mountains. If Anahimara could respond to Nidar's call for aid and still marshal an army to stave off invasion of Anahimara proper, other venues of assault would have been merited. Instead, the undefended Anahimaran kingdom fell with ease. This was no longer a matter for speculation. It was a time for action.

***

Shamus was enough of a student of history that he had already concluded that the kingdoms of Loura, represented by the various emissaries assembled here, had to come together and fight as one. In theory, this made sense, but much was being thrown onto the table in this meeting of elders. It was becoming clear that no one would want to yield their lands without a fight exactly where they lived. He thoughtfully patted himself on his left breast for a moment. His mind went back to that awful night of torment when he had found himself trapped in the dreamscape. He had been forced to witness, with the force of his own senses, the horror that had come to the Anahimaran people, one community at a time. He had seen, heard and felt every moment of the devastation and had been helpless to free himself from the dream until voices had reached out to him from afar, just in time to rescue him and bring him back to the conscious world. The scars around his chest were more than ample reminder. He wondered how many of the Bodelanders who had tended to his care had seen the clawed scars surrounding his heart while he lay unconscious. By now, many people had to have been whispering among themselves about the mark apparently left on him by the Evil One. He postulated that they likely wondered collectively how he had been involved in all of the recent goings on.

Shamus looked around at all the eyes of those seated, only to notice that they all looked away from the Anahimaran prince who now sat quietly, having nothing more to say. It was not as though they thought him to be a coward or were ashamed of their brother; rather, they all knew that the very discussion they were debating would result in a solution that would come all too late for him and his people.

Nica started in again. "The soul of the Bodeland Foresters resides here!" Her index finger swept the hall to define her territory. "We should fight where we stand strongest—in the great trees of old. Our people's stand should be here so that when the killing is done, there will be a home to return to. The Treborgans have not been able to gain ground here. Obviously, they fear encountering us where they cannot move so swiftly."

A tumult erupted in the room once more. Over the din, a small-framed woman with prominent green eyes interrupted. "Yer foolin' yourself, Nica! They are toying with Bodeland. They're assessing where you are weak; you must know this? You have heard what the Brave of Fior Hill has shared about Anahimara, have you not? Ach! O'Mara is livin' proof of this mischief!"

Erladoch pushed back from the table. The scrape of his chair legs forcefully screeched across the hard floor, signaling that he intended to quell discussion. "Much has been shared over these past days. We continue to come back to the hardest of decisions because it is what is right, what is necessary for all."

Many heads were quietly nodding now. "Your homes, like those of Anahimara, will be laid waste whether you wish it or not. The force that comes is of pure evil, and its ranks are soon to be limitless unless we can fulfill our mission. It is the people who must survive to retell the tales of our forebears. Do not spend your blood on preserving the structures and the halls. This is an hour that will re-shape our entire world. The Evil One is but the emissary of the Master of the Great Pit. His Master seeks to pour out its endless legions from the Pit itself into our realm! Make no mistake, my brother and sisters; that is what will come to pass." His statement rumbled through the room. It would have drawn utter laughter and ridicule from any other audience that didn't hold their shared membership. Nonetheless, this statement was almost unfathomable to those assembled, and Nica could not help but interrupt.

"What yer saying to us should be impossible, Lord Dunbar! We acknowledge as brethren that the Pit is a place where the malevolent find themselves traveling to after one has died. Our mission to preserve the light has kept us focused on suspicious activity, and we all see plainly with our own regretful eyes the horrifying strength that has flowed out of Treborg. But to suggest that the Evil One himself is not only back but actually making a way for the Master of the Pit to bring out his multitudes to devastate all will be considered by anyone outside of our ranks as, well, utter madness! They won't believe it. Aw! I barely believe it, and my very oath requires me to know what you say is truth." She hesitated to find the right words. "With respect, Lord Dunbar, how do you expect the people of Loura to believe a word we say when those in leadership, not part of our ranks, are still grappling with the revelation of our existence? To ask them to bide your words when you yerself are now just back from the apparent dead—ach! I know not what to say! For so many, the very notion of the Great Pit is considered a faith statement almost the way that the stories about Mountain Scrags had been thought of until so few recent years, nary a generation even—more of a tale used to keep errant children from straying too far from home after dark. It's too much all at once to think that the people of every kingdom will suddenly listen to our society's proclamation that the end of times is coming and that the only way to combat it is to leave our homes behind and unite on some field of, of what? Glorious, unprotected slaughter?"

"Nica, I know that they won't immediately comprehend this, as there is much in the way of secret knowledge that has been kept from the people of Loura. It is our duty to not just heed the portents, given the direness of this hour, but to act as a clarion call to action. Though we risk revealing so much so fast, it must be done, and a plan must be launched into action!"

Nica absorbed Erladoch's words. In a practiced calm, she addressed him once more. "The revelation to the people of the west that our forgotten mythical Society of Keepers and our sworn mission is real—that be one thing, aye, but the rest? Make yerselves ready for a war to end all wars or be swept away by the minions of hell? That's another matter altogether, isn't it?" Her voice was steely now as Erladoch was preparing to interrupt. "I heard what the White Wigget said through Shamus's lips." She tried to maintain the floor. Again, the volume of grumbling and murmurs threatened to end all sensible discussion, but Princess Nica pressed on.

"Before today, I would scarcely have believed that such a creature as the fabled Anthrac Aran was even real, and I am sworn to his cause. So, I am persuaded, at least, that there is another layer of discussion for our consideration. I remind you, however, that you are in my house as a guest. I consider it of great puzzlement that our society had pursued this perilous mission without any whiff of it ever being shared with me." She looked directly at Erladoch now and did all that she could to control a rattle of emotion, which was threatening to overwhelm her voice. "I'd have hoped for more from you, knowing that you were undertaking this task. I mourned yer death like no other," her voice trailed away at that moment. Nica could not go on. Everyone in the room seemed to understand the force of the comment; the relationship which had pre-existed between the two of them perhaps being the one secret which no one in the Keepers had ever tried to keep.

Erladoch shot her a stare of regret and sorrow meant entirely for her. The room grew respectfully silent.

"Erladoch the Brave of Fior Hill," Nica gathered herself. "The existence of our secret society is revealed to the world, that much we can abide. I just don't know how we move forward. Beyond the strength of all bonds of fealty and of openness, I believe the kingdoms will all agree that we have shared. I canna' see everyone getting behind this plan, though. The politicians whom we readily allowed to run aspects of day-to-day decisions in every House across Loura—they are mad as hell that we kept all this from them. I learn of yer mission myself only now. Even as I look upon Anthrac's Bearer with my own eyes, I barely believe it!"

Nica was nothing short of bitter as she began to pace about, trying her best to contain a mixture of anger and disappointment in Erladoch.

Shamus felt her emotions as though he was being prodded with a stick. He knew that what she was saying represented a debate within her. She wanted to trust Erladoch. In fact, she did trust him implicitly, and yet he had let her down by not sharing what he had had to do before going off and doing it. It was an intimate struggle for her, and she was doing her best to set aside her sense of having been slighted so that she could get on with the business she was there to confront.

Erladoch did nothing while she placed her thoughts into the air for all to hear. He knew that he had let her down by not sharing his mission with her in advance, but it had been his mission nonetheless, and he knew that in time she would have to forgive him for not at least saying goodbye to her.

"Ya ask me in this Hall to take a leap of faith that would have my people abandon an ancestral home that has been lived in for almost as long as the

Great Forest itself has stood. And do what? So that we can make a stand together elsewhere far from our homes on the strength of stories? Quite honestly, for those who would have any memory of the stories at all outside of our brethren, I think most would consider what we're now asking of them to be too incredible."

The speech which Erladoch had embarked upon carried so much information into the light that the Hall's occupants were clearly rattled. It brought a heavy and seething buzz over the room, which fed off Nica's own dismay.

Shamus and Erladoch exchanged glances, both registering that emotions were brimming, and voices were raising. Amid the tumult, O'Mara Boldar had remained silent, looking into the bottom of a drained wooden cup. He had received Erladoch's news differently. There was no comfort of ale left to occupy him as he brooded over Nica's verbal lashings. His lands and most of his kingdom were already forfeited. He had already been shot down by the outspoken princess warrior of the Bodelanders, but as the debate began to rage on, he struggled for a way to re-enter the conversation while Erladoch was dropping another stipend that would be difficult for her to process.

"Say what you will of how the Keepers' legacy will be received by the masses, Nica. Say even that for some folk, the tale of the predicted magnitude of the coming war will be too much to absorb as to be believed. Your people will abide you, Princess, no matter what. They needn't search for long-forgotten memories. Bodeland lost its cherished Prince but weeks ago in this struggle. Yer own Da was forfeit to the Evil One. That which is left of Anahimara sits at this table and is billeted amidst the homes of your folk. This is the easiest of places for the plan to commence from. They will not worry themselves about the importance of our society or its message of woe. They know what lurks just beyond their borders as they have living proof before them. They will listen to their princess."

Nica took to her chair once more. Erladoch's wisdom and calm words were having their impact.

"I ask you only to take hold of your own thoughts now. You and your dear brother would disappear on long journeys throughout your youth. When ya both returned from these journeys with strange trinkets to give to your kin, did the people not question whether such tales were complete? Did they not remark the bumps and bruises you had sustained from your many months of training

117

or from the skirmishes with Scrags that you'd overcome? People know of Scrags that lived in small mountain caves away from our modern communities. Enough people have seen them with their own eyes to accept that these old marauders live in hiding from us. Would it then be so hard for them to accept that they have been organized into the Treborgan army which now rises against us? Your own parents, when they still lived—the people questioned why the work of their beloved monarchs would require them to be away from them for such long periods of time. Your association with the Order will be believed because it will all make sense to them. The fact that you began initiating groups of Bodelanders into small bands of fighting units these past four years. Certainly, to the warriors whom you and your brother personally have already trained, Princess, it will all be more meaningful to them now. Your own brother was among my squad when I went to find the porthole. He bore us to the frontier of Treborg itself before heading home. He kept this from you in the same way that I was required to do. Despite the secrets, you knew that he had seen me go, didn't ya? You trusted him. Your people trust you, and they will follow your guidance, Nica. They will understand that you have been preparing them for this moment."

Nica knew immediately that Erladoch was speaking truthfully. It made her hesitate, and her desire to fire back a retort was bridled a moment.

Erladoch drew in a deep breath. "My friends, I have come back to you to tell you that what you have devoted your lives to preparing for is upon you. The Pit is a real place!" He slammed his hand into the thickest part of the grand table. "As real as this table." The impact of his hammering slap reverberated like a tuning fork in the room. "The Master of the Pit and the Evil One, that accursed and nearly forgotten king of Treborg, are joined through a most evil of pairings with the Master's Serpent Prince. We all have been taught to accept that the Pit is not just a concept and the beast's minions as real. He is looking for a way to enter the world, and he plans to do it here in this time. The inner council acted on the advice of one of our brethren who had traveled far to warn us that he believed the time was almost at hand. Yes, this was kept from some of you. I went under great secrecy to verify this information at the loss of four years of my own life. Four years that I will never get back!" Erladoch paused long enough on this comment to let the Princess of Bodeland know that 'this' was his apology.

"The pride and interests of your own kingdoms aside, I return to you, as it is now clear to me that the fabric of time will be peeled back to permit beasts most foul to fall upon our world—and soon. The Master is bringing forth an army from that eternal hole and seeking to make Loura into a place as foul and loathsome as that which he is trying to crawl out of. He had located, in the human timeline from which I have just returned, the great power which would make manifest his plans. He had nearly killed the Wigget Seed more than once in that time and all but located the final stone that would help him to open his pathway. I believed that I had failed to find the White Wigget's Bearer and instead was permitted my escape by future members of our order and this man, my friend, Shamus of Fior. I did not yet know that I had actually succeeded where I thought that I had failed, but he now sits among you, the Bearer of the White Wigget. It has been our task, as Keepers, to keep the devil from uncovering our secrets and keeping safe the last living Angel until his strength is once again whole. We have dedicated ourselves to this sacred task, as have our brethren for thousands of years after us. I return to tell you that our line has remained unbroken. Our sacred cause has continued where societies and civilizations have long since failed and been covered over by the sands of time. It is only because the Keepers continue to exist in Shamus's time that we are now given warning that 'this' will be the time and the place where the Master will come to extinguish the light from the universe."

The room was now overflowing with unease.

"There is no time for me to school you in all that is necessary, but I ask you, nonetheless, to heed what the White Wigget has already revealed and mark this tiding as the path which must be followed if our world is to hold off the darkness. It is our duty to make all kingdoms understand their peril and then make them ready to meet it."

After a long silence, Nica, now more reserved in her demeanor, asked, "What then do you ask of us?"

"Yer all my kinsmen." Erladoch was now addressing everyone assembled there, even though only a few had waded into the dialogue thus far. "If not by actual family blood, by the blood of the Strahanas that we continue to carry within us. We are made kinsmen by blood spilled on fields of battle that people of our world have never witnessed, over timelines that none could but imagine as real. As Keepers, it is not about the Dunbar taking up swords alongside another kingdom. We are a family unto ourselves. We must now get each of

119

our own countrymen to join with our Order in repelling the darkness. We must do this in unity, lest we all become consumed by it. On the passing of but a limited number of new moons, I fear the Dead King will stop testing us and proceed to unleash the menace we all fear. We have little time to prepare. Beyond what Lord Boldar has suggested, all our neighbors must be brought under one banner. Every fortnight we waste in argument and uncertainty is spent by the Evil One and the Master of the Pit creating new armies through the magic they wield with their portions of the Itavo Stones. Satan's mind courses through time looking for the place where the third fragment of the one Great Stone lies. He knows that if the White Wigget has returned to this timeline, then the stone be not far from his grasp. That is the key to unlocking his prison realm. He will come, and he will unleash all of hell before him to once and for all free himself from his eternal banishment."

"Say that we agree, Lord Dunbar. What exactly do you propose we do?" A voice from the slight and petite woman seated at the far end of the table broke the silence.

Erladoch smiled a grateful smile. His friend from Galagan had spoken to attract oxygen to his cause.

"We will need time to complete our task. You will have to buy us that time by slowing the onslaught of the Treborgan forces. Our strength should be focused in the most distant reach of Loura so that the Evil One will be forced to take time in his strategy rather than pick each kingdom off one after the other, only to replenish and re-engage. Make him stretch his resources. The people of all kingdoms must move to Loura's most extreme westerly refuge in High Dunbar. Shelter in Dunbar's high mountain capital. Baldréimire awaits."

"So, let them sack our lands and destroy our homes while ensuring that the greatness of Dunbar is safeguarded then?" Nica offered in what sounded like a sarcastic and aggressively paranoid tone.

"Ach! I know that this is hard to hear, Nica, and that your faith in me is rattled, but you must find the wisdom in this plan. I ask even more of you and will similarly ask each Lord of the High kingdoms of Loura soon enough as we set out on our travels. I not only wish for you to leave your homes; that will be the simpler task. To slow the onslaught of the coming evil, you must take every item of foodstuff and provision that can be carried, leaving nothing of your remaining crops. In fact, ya should leave nothing that Treborg may use to resupply themselves with on their ultimate campaign to vanquish us all."

Tears of frustration were now glistening down the cheeks of the noble warrior princess.

"But what you ask, Erladoch—is it not helping the Evil One to accomplish at least part of his task by doing this? Lay waste to all that is great and good? What shall we have to come back to if we succeed? Will Dunbar nay be accused of creating a play to break old ties and dominate the lower kingdoms in much the same way that the House of Treborg once attempted and now seeks to do again?"

Something about Nica's demeanor had gone awry. Her sadness had somehow converted itself into a new vessel, one filling with a level of anger that made no sense for the person that she apparently was. Whatever force it was that lay behind the behavioral shift, it was gaining momentum for reasons that Shamus could not comprehend. The air in the room was suddenly heavy with a general presence of ill will. He had been sitting as a passive observer all this time, doing his best to content himself with the food that he felt he might not see again for a long time. He smelled the venom surfacing in the room, however. The presence of an evil entity was palpable to him, and he sensed from Erladoch's reaction that none of this behavior was normal for Nica or the Keepers assembled there. Whatever it was that was moving her to suddenly speak in this manner was entirely foreign.

"Why would anyone believe in the words of a prince believed to be dead nigh on four complete passings of the yearly cycles? And himself now returned in the company of a supposedly pure-blooded descendant of the Strahanas to declare that the Dead King returns from the Pit? Or is this all just evil magic?"

She growled now as if ready to leap at Erladoch, even though no part of that made any sense. It was as if the dark force that had entered the room was trying to win over not just her thoughts but to escalate everyone assembled there into frenzied violence. Other people were stirring angrily. He felt as though another wrong word from anyone might collapse the decorum of the room to an all-out drawing of arms. Even when there had been passive expressions of doubt moments before, this had not troubled him. It was the sudden surge in the emotional temperature of the room which finally made him feel compelled to do what he had so often done in first meetings with violent psychotic patients under his care: pacify and deflect.

"My Lords and Ladies!" he croaked in an initially dry and squeaky voice that slowly rose above the others as he cleared it. He remained seated, keeping his hands deliberately rested on top of the table. He'd already taken note that others' hands had disappeared below the table, possibly even thumbing at sword hilts now as he attempted to distract them from what had merged with their thoughts.

"Uhm, look. I'm not a person of your station. At best, the decisions that I have ever been asked to make in my calling as a healer was for the benefit of but a few people. The words that you say out of fear is a pestilence that attracts the attention of the Evil One this very night. I do not believe these words spoken in anger to be your words! Heed my caution, please! These words of doubt and mistrust are the enchantment of the King of the Pit weaving its way into your waking thoughts. I have felt this darkness myself previously, and I know the breadth of the Evil One's reach. You must not let doubt cloud your judgment. This man"—he extended his right index finger toward Erladoch in the most benign fashion that he could muster—"you've known him your entire lives. He clearly is not dead. He, however, risked death many times to leave his home to fulfill a noble and most sacred responsibility that he alone was charged to fulfill for all your benefit. Even though the tidings he brings with him are hard to hear, I sense that you are all trained to receive difficult news."

The room was now his. The more compelling he chose to become, the less there was a looming threat hanging over everyone. He felt the pestilent haze dissipate like air rushing out of a balloon. "Truth is often hard to hear because it requires so much of us when it is revealed. I had no idea that my destiny would call on me to place my faith and my very life into this stranger's hands but trust him I have. And when that trust was given, other Keepers revealed themselves to me to let me know that, as difficult as the sacrifice I was being asked to make was, and for a purpose that extended so far beyond my greatest imaginings, it was still the only path that I, as a man of the light, could follow. It is only now that my full part in your world's story is becoming clear to me, even though parts continue to reveal themselves. The doubts that stir in your bellies are the work of the Evil One. I do not believe that these doubts come from you. I have faith in Erladoch the Brave of Fior Hill." Shamus reached over and placed his left hand on Erladoch's shoulder.

"He has asked me to trust in you as people to do the work of the light. I therefore trust you." Shamus let the silence hang as he took the measure of every man and woman at the table. "The White Wigget is real, and everything that he has revealed to me, with Erladoch's help, is done at great risk. We have but one chance to get this right. You belong to the cause of the Light; you must vanquish dark thoughts from your minds by reminding yourselves of your life's missions."

O'Mara Boldar looked squarely at Shamus, assessing the measure of him.

"Did ya know that once the House of Treborg was a noble house of men not all that different than any of the kingdoms west of the Elec Mountains?"

Shamus sourced the stories shared with him by Erladoch. He nodded affirmatively.

"Who's to say that they can't yet be reasoned with? Even when they could no longer be trusted and were chased back over their mountains, they left us alone for these many ages. Perhaps there is yet someone among them with whom a truce can be crafted?"

"Young Prince," Shamus countered. "I hardly know you yet, but I would ask you to look upon your neighbors who sit quietly in this hall for your answer. I know you despair, and that your loss is immeasurable, and you would have your neighbors avoid such a horrible fate. But, with respect sir, your mind is not yet clear of whatever madness sought to fill this chamber. If I have learned anything from Erladoch at all, it is that the Treborgans have not carried inside of them the blood or reason of men for many ages now. They carry only the torment of madness and service to the greatest of all evils found in all worlds. There will be no mercy shown. It is not the way of evil to become less so."

O'Mara knew his words to be true. He had slain enough Scrags in his young life already. He'd seen first-hand the madness raging in the eyes of his enemies. Despite being younger than Shamus, he'd engaged in enough warfare to fill many lifetimes. He was simply grasping, perhaps still impacted by the pestilent charms that had finally been vanquished from the room by Shamus's calming but direct tone. The room was no longer animated. The shadow that had been present in the room was gone. Shamus knew that his words may have done some good, but they were likely much reinforced by his startling appearance.

"Nica," Erladoch's voice was lowered to a whisper, as he did not want to invite back in whatever specter had filled her thoughts previously. He wanted, however, to ensure that if anything of what she had said had come from her, rather than from the malevolent influence that had inspired her, it now be fairly addressed. "If we succeed at all, the world we know will nevermore be like it was, but we will be alive and able to build anew. That is the only solace I may offer you."

"What else is going to happen, Lord Dunbar?" O'Mara finally found his opportunity to rejoin the dialogue.

"Shamus and I have a different path to follow. Two of us traveling alone for now makes little sense, as we are clearly too close to the danger that will be assembling on your borders already. We will need a sufficient fighting force to at least manage Treborgan patrols. But we must all make preparations, and without further delays. Also, we should create units of volunteers to form lightning attack forces who will also be used to slow the campaign of the Treborgan army as well as provide reconnaissance for the other kingdoms. In this way, whatever paths are taken toward the refuge of Dunbar, they will not be intercepted by the enemy so easily."

"By 'volunteer', I assume that yer suggesting that we accept that those who form such units should expect to not someday return to their kinsmen, do you not?"

"Aye, t'is what will be requested of them, O'Mara." Erladoch confirmed.

Nica was now seated again. The fight drained out of her. She wasn't angry at him at all. She had been sad for herself and now ruminated on how easily her emotions had been co-opted by something from outside of her. The longer she sat in quiet reflection, the more she came to accept that Shamus was right. Something ill had wound its way through her thoughts and had made her react beyond her normal character. She considered her recently deceased brother, Frod, himself a Keeper same as herself. He had kept the secret of his involvement with Erladoch's departure from Loura from her. She had trusted him unquestioningly. She knew Erladoch as well as any man—better even. But he'd been gone, dead for all anyone had known. Now here he was, changed but still the same man she had loved, in the company of this striking individual. Shamus's apparent story was itself so compelling that, if taken on its face, it involved the fulfillment of her most sacred commitment. She had borne witness to the transfiguration of Shamus with her own eyes. She now reasoned that if the mission of the Light was to have any chance of success at all, other tasks and duties now lay uniquely with her to ensure that the news of his special status be safeguarded before anyone set one foot outside of her capital.

There had been but a few of her trusted lieutenants assembled in this hall in the presence of O'Mara Boldar, Erladoch, Shamus and her other very well-known guests. In typical fashion, these other guests had sat relatively silent off at the end of the long table, offering nothing; just listening to the exchanges. There had also been servers who had entered and left the Hall, but they were all trustworthy Bodelanders themselves. Nica considered for the first time that the magnitude of this grim conversation would require her to seek their oath of silence as to the tidings that had been revealed here this night. Her mind conjured the vast mountain walls of Dunbar for a moment. They were admittedly impressive, ascending outcroppings of natural and human-enhanced stonework that meandered upwards across a many-terraced mountainside. The terraces had been constructed by nature, but they had been skillfully enhanced over several ages of men for the primary purpose of stepped agriculture. The retaining walls at each height would be their best fortification against invasion.

She considered further that to take her kinsmen out of the Great Forest didn't simply entail leaving their lands to the invaders. It meant laying waste to their homes in and around the forest, maybe even burning them down. These trees had been shepherded by her people in a shared symbiotic relationship with nature for more ages than could almost be recalled. *Burn it all down, and retreat to a haven that will put our backs to the sea?*

Even after hearing the calming words offered by Shamus, she spat on the floor, the taste of her choices so foul they had soured in her mouth. They would leave the forest kingdom to the invader, she told herself, but she would be damned if they would burn it down!

"Erladoch," Nica lifted her head to meet his eyes. "I have your counsel on this, but my people will need to hear my decision directly from me. While I doubt not that the walls of Dunbar are truly the greatest in all of Loura to withstand a sustained siege, I do not choose lightly for my end, or the end of times for my people, to come in a foreign land, despite our great and long-standing union. Whether I take this to the people on the morrow as an order or whether I provide each with their own choice as to where they wish to meet such an end, I know that this means that word will find its way to our enemy of such a massive plan. I will give you my choice on how I shall choose to manage this as soon as I can."

Erladoch chimed in, recognizing that Nica was still wrestling with this decision. "You are right to consider this a grave request, Nica Bodelander. But you are also right to recognize that once all have been told outside of this Hall, there will be no hiding your exodus if that is indeed what you choose. The choice must be made swiftly. We may all fall to the axe and twisted Scimitars of Scrags at the end, but let us stand as brothers and sisters when that end comes—not divided and alone in our homes. To Dunbar you should hasten."

"There are others who should thus be called upon to wade into this conversation even though it is not their way." She gestured toward the hulking creature, inviting him to finally participate.

The squeal of wood scratching the floor was commanding on its own as the fullness of his weight rose from his chair. He glanced over respectfully at Shamus and then Nica, but it was most apparent that his eyes sought out Erladoch, requesting his permission to gain the floor for the first time with much formality. Erladoch nodded in approval, imploring the as yet unfamiliar individual to Shamus to speak. Shamus absorbed the colossal image of him into his visual field as the latter stretched up to his full height. The man's eyes were chestnut brown. The gleam inside of his gaze was darker and more sullen than a wild tiger's right before a kill, and yet there appeared to be a softness behind them. His hair was braid-knotted into great curls and locks of brown hair that draped onto his massive shoulders. When he finally spoke, it sounded as though his words echoed on the inside of Shamus's own lungs.

Erladoch offered a half smile. "Finally! The Sethian traveler wishes to speak. I welcome you, Andor. As I have said my mind, I leave it to you to answer my challenge."

The large man scanned the room before addressing his comrades. "Ye-all know me well enough," he began slowly. Even his quiet and reserved voice was booming in nature. "I have passed over many yarricks to find counsel. My princess sends me with tidings of danger. I'm her word and her captain. There is activity on our north-eastern border from the foulest inhabitants of this world. I will send word to my people this night saying that the Dead King has indeed returned, as has been rumored. My runner will inform the princess and her brother, the Prince, that the mind-dancers did not err and that Dunbar calls Seth to bring all citizens to its capital, as was done in the youth of the first Erladoch of Dunbar in times near forgotten. Seth will come to you, my lord, as it did to your distantly eldered forefather."

Erladoch bowed his head in gracious and silent respect for the giant figure. Nica had now regained her composure at the end of the table opposite Erladoch and Shamus. She questioned the Sethian. "Andor, my friend, why do you not carry the news yourself?"

"My Lady Nica, I am not required to lead my people from Seth to the rich lands of Dunbar when my Princess Aloine will wholeheartedly support the missive of an elder Keeper such as yerself. Her brother Abin, as you know, is not among our Order, as he is soft and was born without an ábaltacht. Even if she is away and answering the affairs of our Order in our sanctuary, Abin will at the very least heed the missive of our Order out of respect for his fallen father. He knows that I have come here to seek counsel on his sister's bidding. I will send such counsel homeward. My duty fulfilled, I'm free to let my allegiance go where it will." Andor paused to look upon the faces of those assembled once more. "I thus answer to the needs of the ascending King of Dunbar, a duty for which I answer willingly. All Sethians remember the 71st age of men before the time of insignificance. We would not exist without the sacrifices made by the people of Dunbar."

"I thank you, my old friend. I admit you to my aid and service," Erladoch responded appreciatively. He was humbled and grateful for Andor's gesture of unquestioning support. "My Lords and Ladies, we must now draw our daggers and cast them as a pledge for our course of action. May the good spirits of the forest permit a harmonious choice."

Erladoch and Nica drew their daggers out as a sign that it was time to cast their votes. Erladoch drove his blade solidly into his end of the table. Each guest, in turn, cast their daggers. They all went to Erladoch. Looking at her colleagues, Lady Nica effortlessly spun her dagger in the air until it came to rest beside those of the others.

"Forgive me my doubts, Lord; my sadness in recent days has clouded my mind. The weight of leadership has fallen heavily upon me. Your return to us is entirely a welcome event. Accept me as your servant."

Erladoch rose slowly, a blank look in his eyes as he gazed across the table.

"My friends, Lady Nica, the Foresters have suffered a great loss with the death of your brother. He was my friend also. I feel the pain of that unquenched sorrow and the abiding hatred that burns for the enemy. I know you to be as prudent a warrior as he was." Raising his voice to the room as though to remove all doubt, Erladoch trumpeted. "I call you to my service, Nica Bodelander, to stand at my side without reservation."

Matching the rising of cheers from each of the assembled, her eyes nodded in gratitude for the swiftly given forgiveness, and she, too, rose to adjourn, just as Erladoch's voice raised above the din to make a parting statement.

"The morning takes from here a small band with a weighty mission. One that will be fraught with perils well beyond what any of us have likely ever faced, as I expect that we will be hunted from the outset by the enemy. I cannot request that any follow me on this journey despite daggers that have been committed. Instead, I expect the dreams of this night will inform each of you as to whether you join our company or return to your home kingdoms to give guidance to those who may still need convincing of our decision. Determine best how to organize your countrymen for the hard task that the free kingdoms of this world now face. To those of you that pursue the latter duty, I bid good fortune, speedy travel, and also," Erladoch's voice lowered in a moment of somber reflection, "and also, quite likely, goodbye. I dare say that in this moment of parting, most of us will not survive to come together again in the final conflict. To those who shall find the revelation, meet here on the morrow, ready to depart at the sixth position of Inyi."

Chapter 18

Hours had passed by with Erladoch and Shamus arranging, packing, then repacking their new gear and clothing. A fire roared and snapped in the metal-bowl hearth, cutting through the biting, damp chill of Shamus's room.

"Erladoch." Shamus shattered the peaceful silence in an uncharacteristically loud voice. He could not wait any longer to sate his curiosity. "Why haven't you told people my family name when you have spoken of me?"

The Prince of Dunbar looked at his friend squarely. By the rapidity of his answer, Shamus wondered whether Erladoch had prepared himself for the question in advance. "Because no one other than those to whom you have already revealed yourself must know your full identity. Nor, I dare say, should they know your importance to this mission until we are safely away. You have burdened enough people with the weight of this revelation already through no fault of your own." He gestured toward the transformed hair and strange color that Shamus's eyes had taken on. "I fear that spies are lurking about. Best it would be that no others share in this knowledge and risk hastening the Evil One's plans even more."

Shamus was sufficiently satisfied with the response, but as they were alone, he decided to press for more information. "What happened in the 71st age of men that made the big one, the Sethian traveler as you referred to him, speak so highly of your ancestors? Was it something your father did or maybe your grandfather?"

Erladoch chuckled and turned to face Shamus head-on. He was obviously amused.

"You will have to forgive me, Shamus. I sometimes forget that you are a stranger to this world and its conflicts. You see, history is a large part of the life of all Lourans, and to members of our Order, well, it informs everything that we do. When I recount a story to you, it is painfully detailed, is it not?"

This time Shamus laughed; the opportunity for sarcasm was too available to be missed.

"Exhaustingly so!" he rejoined with his own smile.

"Recall that we do not keep history with written words like the people of your time. Accuracy is accordingly essential." Erladoch chided his friend in a playful enough voice to let him know that he accepted his point.

"We have both witnessed and measured the time of men and other creatures through a direct line of tales told of kings, queens, their people and the struggles they have engaged in as our way of marking time. While that line leads to me and those who bore my name before me, what Andor of Seth spoke of flows so far back that it is easier to measure time through the ages of a royal house rather than try to number seasons and moon cycles. His answering the call based on Dunbar's service to his people is a duty that has been passed from one life to many kings who came after. The tales that still get told endure because of debts yet to be repaid. Such is the honor of the high kingdoms. Till my line vanishes from Loura, songs will be sung of my ancestor's deeds and the Sethian's fealty will endure."

Erladoch took a seat at the foot of Shamus's bed. Respectfully, Shamus stopped tying down the edges of his pack and waited. *I asked for this!* he reminded himself sarcastically.

"That you speak of the Sethian's pledge is coincidental. He reminded me of a tale of the struggle in the 71st age which I had not heard since I was but a small child. Because of their honor pledge, all Sethians of high birth would know the song in the same way as your people would have written it down in your books as though the happening had just come to pass. Those were sad times, and thus a melancholy tune carries the story. As I am not responsible to maintain the songs, I remember but parts of it, and I doubt not that my version is weaker than the way that a Sethian might tell it. The historic facts remain firm with me, however, even though twenty ages of my ancestors have come and gone."

Shamus nodded as much to say, "Go ahead. I'm listening."

Both men sat down by the small hearth. Erladoch unstoppered a flask of liquid, which proved itself to be a nice fruity wine that refreshed Shamus almost just from smelling it.

Erladoch looked into the fire and slowly eased his way into a song, summoning its words from the edges of memory. It started very softly, and the clarity of Erladoch's voice made Shamus feel momentarily happy.

Ne'er was land so green,
The world so serene,
When walked the Sethians and Samarans.
Children of a brethren race,
The women all so fair of face.
In starlight they danced with grace.
The men of Seth and Samara were brothers all,
A young race of men, welcome in either's Hall,
A bond of blood that each would defend,
and they would dwell as brothers till the very end.

Erladoch hesitated, doing his best to recall both the melody and the tale. The fire in the hearth rose up in response to Shamus's pokes from a long stick. He stirred the embers until the fire licked freshly placed branches and formed a refreshed, high flame. Sparks sputtered and vanished inside a venting hole of a clay pipe which loomed directly above. The rising of the flames seemed to restore recollection to Erladoch as he resumed.

"Those days were swept and trampled asunder
When evil from Nor' East came to them down yonder.
House Treborg offered a plentiful dower
If Seth would but conquer its brother
It would be paid with handsome plunder.
But Seth and Samara were brothers
Of a young race of men.
No promise of spoils could cleave them,
Or break the bond of kin.
And they would dwell as brothers,
Until their very end."

The kindred in strong defiance
Marched on Treborg in great alliance.

131

To Treborg's gate of ancient Fedoor.
It opened out upon them.
And T'is said that none among 'em
Expected what would lay behind.
A host of Treborgans came
To cleave Samara and Seth like grain,
Laying the brothers on the soil.
The blood of fifty-thousand drained,
Their lives spent on the Treborgan planes,
Too late, too proud to see their foil.

For The men of Seth and Samara were brothers
Of a kindred race of men.
No wedge would be driven among them;
Against Treborg's evil they'd defend,
For these men all were brothers
And would stay so until the very end.
Samara's rank fell first to the greedy King,
And only crows would be heard to sing
In a battle that raged for five days long.
The brothers refused to yield,
And with crushed helm and shield,
Stood knowing their death would not be long."

Erladoch paused for a long draft of his wine, and then plunged back into the tale—his eyes still fixed inside the fire, which licked above the top of the bowl. He described the battle in this tale to its unhappiest detail, naming the titles of each of the memorable captains who gave up their lives in defense of their homelands, even as he kept his rhyme in as tight a pace as he could recall it. Shamus could feel the sickening sense of an unrelenting massacre having taken place, even though it had been wrapped in song. Of lesser men Erladoch also sang, for it was told that many performed equally brave deeds. As well, he sang of the twelve messengers, some who went on foot on the very first day of the battle and others on horse, in great haste, to all the nearby capitals of the world to plead for their assistance. None would come, assuming this to be a simple border war, not yet realizing that the king of Treborg had a more expansive agenda. Erladoch's song described how the battle raged into Samara to the southeast of Seth as the enemy drove westward. The killing went on for days till all the people of Samara and many of the kingdom of Seth were cut down where they made their stands. They were tilled into the earth like so much chaff; the very lifeblood of its youth poured upon the fields to water a most foul harvest. As the closing days raged back and forth in salvo upon salvo of brigades going out to meet each other across numerous yarricks, all hope for victory was replaced with a struggle for survival. Shamus could tell from the lengthy lament that the light was going out on the Kingdoms of Samara and Seth.

Erladoch's voice became more consistent in tune as his recall of the words flowed more readily from the remote corners of memory.

"Funeral fires whirled, as the enemy
Continued to set upon them,
Spilling over Samara and Seth with unrelenting fervor,
Driven back to fair Traffin.
So little left to save of Samara.
'Twould be there that the brethren were
To make hopeless stand upon desperate stand
Before the Treborgan horror.
But Seth and Samara were brothers,
A kindred race of men;
No enemy could win o'er them
As brothers they pledged to stand
And fight till the very end.
Treborgs' army was made of lowly men,
Consumed with the foul yearnings of a maddened King.
They were happy to pay the blood price,
On promises of becoming lords o'er everything.
Their lust for murder became so consuming
That even the rats would er'more call them 'Scrags'.
Nary could quench such lust,
For blood lust is for the dregs.
But Seth and Samara were brothers,
A nobler kind of men

Who were made of something better,
A bond far more than friend.
And no foul pact for riches
Or Treborgan's empty promise could bend,
For they would stand as brothers,
Until the very end.

War o'er field and meadow
Passed into the dawning of the eighty-fourth day,
Whence came the final siege of King Traffin.
Their last stand to come at Blé.
In crept rising Inyi
To reveal a Treborgan horde.
The good people of Seth and Samara
Knew they'd die this day by sword.
But so stood the finest of Seth and Samara;
Even with backs to the wall they wouldn'a bend,
For these men were the greatest of warriors
Who would fight till the very end.
Captains of Greno summoned their soldiers for the final assault.
Mountain Chieftains of Elec all now aligned to Treborg,
Swelled the enemies' ranks with spear and sword.
Scrags one and all, such a miserable horde.
Horns began to echo o'er field and hills at first light,
Filling the dumbstruck ears of Treborgan
and mountain tribesmen alike.
But t'was not the harsh shrill of Scraggin throat horn
That met the day upon the fields,
But music of the approaching trumpets,
Blazing aloud and causing enemies to yield.
Happy tidings caused the foe's blood to chill.
"Dunbar comes!" the weary chanted.
And so it t'was that Dunbar had sent
Its four Princes armed and mounted
To lead an ocean of warriors, clad in Silver on Green.
The knights of Dunbar brought with them battalions;

T'was the greatest army all Loura had e'er seen!
Their ranks swelled with the warriors of Ara,
And fair Sioubaghn marched beside 'em,
All on their way to war
In friendship they now stood beside them,
To silence the Treborgan menace,
To stand as one for evermore.
Take heart, o brothers of Seth and Samara!"

Erladoch's voice now sang so loudly that it echoed through the halls outside the chamber. His left fist rose in the air as if he stood with an army right then and there in those days of hellish warfare, countless generations before his great-grandfather was even born.

Shamus thought to himself, relieved, *Okay, so this is how the lament will end,* as Erladoch continued defiantly.

"Today is not your end;
All Loura comes to Seth and Samara's call,
And here in the land of Seth we shall defend.
We shall stand as your kindred,
And Treborg's reign of terror will end.
Go back with ye o'er mountains of Elec!
Go back to Greno and relent!
For all the kingdoms of Loura
Have answered the call of their friend.
'Tis ye who'll die on these fields, Treborgan,
And your horrid Kingdom will meet its end!"

Erladoch settled now, very pleased that he ultimately had been able to recall this song of woe and triumph after all. His spirits had noticeably picked up by the retelling of this great triumph.

Shamus was surprised at his own reaction to the song. He had particularly liked the part which told of Treborg meeting its end; their campaign of acquisition broken under Dunbar's broadsword. The notion of it gave him hope even as they readied themselves to face the day. It mattered little to him that he knew that the story of that age had not actually ended there. Shamus was already versed in what had come after. From Erladoch's previous telling of the saga, ancient Loura had experienced months of additional battles across many kingdoms. It was only after a solid defeat within the borders of Dunbar itself that the fleeing remnants of the Treborgan armies had been finally dispersed in every direction. To find their way home at all, Enilorac the Treborgan king had continued to battle fiercely in several more skirmishes until he came upon the last of the Wigget counsel, themselves having been exhausted by their own battle for dominance in far-off and forgotten lands. This last part Shamus knew all too well, but he was pleased to learn of the struggle that had come before.

Erladoch now explained that while the Great Lament of Seth and Samara had come to an end on a happy note of victory, it was not nearly the whole telling of the story that had given rise to the sense of debt that the Sethian colossus had spoken of. Andor's ancestors still held the memory of the ancient debt owed to the House of Dunbar, not simply because they summoned all the western kingdoms to answer the call for help before Seth and Samara risked vanishing altogether from Loura. It had been the specific cost paid by the Captains of Dunbar. At the conclusion of that glorious battle against Treborg, there lay three of the four sons of Dunbar's King, taken in battle. The names of these young princes were only remembered now like those of so many others who never got to achieve their full potential and, instead, were no longer even memorable because of how quickly they fell against the Evil King. These young sons, Hølf, Morg and Baldo, would never sire bloodlines of their own as they still were nearly children themselves, only having barely reached a warrior's age in time to go and be sacrificed on foreign lands. Their deaths were not glorious; rather, they were horrible and immeasurably rapid as they spearheaded the charge right into the heart of the Treborgan army. Those brave princes were cut down in seconds after leading their horses directly into the spearmen of the enemy's front lines. They didn't stand a chance, but their collective bravery in the face of the foe was what all agreed had spurned the combined forces of the Louran kingdoms to rally to victory that day.

Erladoch paused for a long draft.

"A further sadness that didn't even find its way into the telling of the Great Lament was the fact that the House of Samara all but disappeared from history. They had been the first to receive the crush of the Treborgan invasion. The few who survived the many days of massacre were subsumed into the kingdom of Seth."

Shamus was amazed by the incredible sadness of this tale. He now understood better why the Sethian traveler felt an enduring obligation to the Dunbars regardless of the passage of time. "Such great sacrifice should never be forgotten," he offered in full answer to Erladoch's long tale before examining the few hot coals remaining in his hearth.

Erladoch offered nothing further about the ancient story to his friend. He had answered Shamus's question as best as he could.

He noticed that Shamus's attention was now fixed on the dance of small flames still active in the fire bowl. Whether this act of quiet reflection was being led by the White Wigget or by Shamus himself, he decided he should allow this act of detachment to continue uninterrupted. Feeling his own sleep-heavy eyes, he rose, placed two sizable logs in to the back of the hearth and quietly said his goodnight.

Shamus seemed to take no note of Erladoch's departure. Instead, he stretched backward across the down-filled mattress while his eyes continued to examine the portents that lay concealed within the spaces between the dances of light and darkness.

***

Chapter 19

Sometime, long after Erladoch's massive back had cleared the doorway and gone out into the darkness of the dimly illuminated passage, it occurred to Shamus that he was still unsure of where they were going next, or even what his friend's plan going forward involved. The fire in his hearth was now just coal. There was nothing more to study there. He decided to catch Erladoch on his way back to his chamber. It had not been long before he realized that he had no idea where Erladoch's chamber even was. He found himself instead wandering aimlessly along narrow halls deeper into the ground until he was back in the hall where he had supped. Now that he was no longer studying the many faces assembled around the table, he turned his attention to the inlaid designs of the walls. He once again noticed the brilliant detail of the carvings and further realized that the wood blended with the cool rock walls in a very erratic manner. In fact, there would be rock or wooden archways randomly looming over areas of the room where it made little sense for them to be. He remembered thinking how curious this all was, but aside from trying to follow the storylines depicted in the carved walls, he continued to move silently through the corridors. The shapes of all the miniatures etched in wood and stone were so exact that the walls became animated with the indecipherable tale of the thousands of people and creatures that seemed to have been frozen in time.

Shamus knew that many important stories were hidden within these designs. He felt deeply troubled to think that he would not be able to get a chance to absorb them all, let alone understand their significance. The intricacy of the wood carvings was spectacular! Somehow, he knew with great certainty that this would all vanish in a matter of a few weeks. He was not certain what type of castle he had found himself in as he had been unconscious when he arrived. It occurred to him for the first time that he had not been outdoors since arriving in the Kingdom of Bodeland.

As his eyes continued to scan the intricate carvings in the walls, he only knew that centuries of artistic labor had gone into the creation of this beautifully unique hall and that soon it would be callously desecrated. As he moved toward the exit, he remarked that his feet had no sense of warmth or coolness. He took one final look to solidify the images of the Great Hall in his mind forever: forgotten pitch battles expanding out from hallways leading into greater spaces to reveal even more epic battle scenes. These seemed to be followed by the ages of prosperity depicted by images of children and farming. At the very edge of the dark, for but a moment, he thought he saw the silhouette of a woman watching him from a distance. Her face was impossible to see so close to the edge of darkness, but she felt familiar to him, and Shamus sensed that she wanted his attention. There was a lightness to the woman even in the vast darkness of the corridor, which no longer contained shape or form.

Come to me.

He wasn't sure in that moment whether he 'heard' her speak or whether she had implanted a thought in his mind. "Uh, hello? Are you speaking to me?" he replied aloud to the distant shape obscured by the darkness of the corridor. As he moved closer toward the silhouette, she receded into the darkness of the corridor, making no sound as she left.

Shamus attempted to follow in the direction where the woman had vanished but found nothing there. The corridor was pitch black. Not a single candle illuminated the path where she had backed into.

"Hey! Wait! I can't see which way you went! Come to you where?" He spoke to the emptiness. He turned into another corridor that also wound back in the direction of his room. This had candles protruding from the walls, but once again, still no sign of the woman. The place was a labyrinth of corridors that opened out onto other passageways of varying heights and widths. There were no straight lines anywhere! It became evident that he was not going to catch up to the woman who had briefly spoken to him, nor, for that matter, find Erladoch's chamber. Before he could become utterly lost in the dimly illuminated maze, he felt a compulsion to return to his own room.

Recognizing the one corridor from which he had come, Shamus strode back in the direction of his bed chamber. Midway back, he passed two guards clad in pants made of soft leather. Their thin woolen tops dyed in brown and green came to just below their hips. A single short sword was lashed to a scabbard secured across their chests.

Shamus remarked that the mix of colors in the warriors' garments made the two men blend into the scenery like any modern camouflage he'd ever seen. As he passed, he considered that he should say 'hello' to them. Their faces were stern, however, and they stood at attention beside one of the few doors that the castle appeared to have, seemingly taking no notice of his presence. He thought better of extending the formality where there appeared to be no intention to reciprocate his pleasantry and elected to continue on his path.

Having passed the men without any acknowledgment however gave Shamus pause. *Surely not everyone knows who I am?* he considered. *I'm too freaky in this altered appearance that there should've been a challenge from them of some kind.* He paused momentarily to look back at the guards. They continued to look down the dark and narrow corridors, entirely disinterested with his presence. "Hmm, weird!" he huffed.

As Shamus proceeded, he considered the strangeness of this lack of interaction. All too recently, he had had foreign sovereigns bowing before his brilliantly flaming, silvery-haired appearance in a state of awed reverence, if not fear. These fellows had given him nothing!

He recognized the frame of his chamber ahead. It was unmistakable, as it bore the antlers of a massive creature over the top of the entry, likely those of an elk. He suddenly remarked that there were guards on each side of the entry, patiently standing in the shadows. Likely, they had been there when he had first left, but as no conversation had been exchanged with them previously either, he was forced to conclude that they were either instructed not to speak to him, or alternatively, simply chose to avoid him for reasons entirely their own. There it was again, however: that same empty stare. Without further delay or necessity to exchange a pleasantry, he walked through the doorway seeking out his bed, frustrated by his failed ability to locate Erladoch, and even more flummoxed by his chance encounter with the woman who had apparently run away from him.

As he approached the bed, he had the sudden feeling that he had entered the wrong room. From the apparent hump, he identified there was someone lying beneath the sheets. He looked around, startled, wondering how it was that he had made this mistake, only to catch sight of a travel pack lying on the floor beside what were absolutely his weapons. Placing his hands on the sheets with the intent of pulling them back enough to reveal the sleeping visitor, he was at once confronted with the realization that his hands failed to grasp the sheets at all, and that the person lying beneath was himself. A momentous burst of confusion and anxiety overtook him. That was his body beneath those sheets!

"What the?" he exclaimed aloud for the first time. He tried in earnest to pull the sheets back again but could not. He had no sensation of touching them, and yet his eyes told him that he was doing that very thing. None of this made any sense to him! Shamus yelled, almost for no other reason than to verify that he could hear himself shout. He could hear it, but was this only 'thought', or an actual vocalization? His rational mind tried to work the problem. *I just think I'm screaming. Otherwise, the guards would have already been inside the chamber to see what the raucous is about. Oh Jaysus! Have I died in my sleep*? he considered. *Am I looking at my own corpse on this bed?* He was completely petrified. None of this made sense.

"Hey!" he yelled again at his unconscious body beneath where he stood. "Wake the hell up!"

He leaped onto the motionless figure reposing on the bed and began shouting over and over again, "Shamus! Shamus! Wake the hell up! What's happening?" Suddenly, he could hear the actual utterance loud and clear. His lungs felt taut as he was nearly out of breath from shouting at himself. In a nanosecond, his door burst open with two frightened guards scanning the borders of his room for intruders, only to catch sight of Shamus now sitting up in the bed, holding onto his face as though he was making sure that it was on right. The bed sheets were still draped over most of his lower body but were clearly twisted from a struggle. He looked at the two very youthful but grim and determined warriors, taking in the fact that their swords were out and ready to deal with trouble.

"Can you see and hear me?" Shamus croaked out through panted breaths.

The guards looked back at him, clearly puzzled by the question. The younger of the two, who might have been as young as 15, said with a sense of realization that he had rushed in on the tail-end of a nightmare, smiled and replaced his sword. "Aye, Lord, that's why we're here. We heard you loud and clear. I thought you were in need of help."

The other warrior simply nodded and was already turning to give Shamus his privacy.

Shamus offered the two guards a thankful glance for their speedy reaction and then said, "It's alright, it was just a nightmare. I'm sorry for having alarmed you."

They bowed their heads and uttered synchronously, "Yes, m'lord," closing the door behind them.

Shamus knew full well that this had not been a nightmare. His nocturnal wanderings had happened. His proof to himself was that he had recognized the faces of his two guards before they had entered the room to look in on his erratic shouts. There was no denying the experience to himself. This had not been one of his sleepwalking episodes either! A splitting of body and mind had happened. He had traveled the castle's corridors in the form of a spirit, and yet now here he sat alive and intact. The splitting seemed to have occurred when he'd risen to catch up with Erladoch. The Wigget within him must have taken over somehow, sending Shamus's body to bed, and allowing his consciousness to travel without restraint or detection. Why had it been so important to enter the Great Hall instead of his own intention of simply catching up with Erladoch? What was behind his going out at all? And who the hell was this elusive woman? Was she part of his dreamscape, or was she flesh and blood like the guards he had passed in the corridors? None of this made sense!

The woman, unlike the guards, felt his presence and communicated with him. *Or had she?* Shamus tried to sort it out. She had been there very much in the same way that he had been in that one corridor. Every other individual he had passed had been plainly oblivious to his presence; but not her. She knew that he was there. She told him to find her. *I wish I could remember the sound of her voice. It seemed so warm and familiar. She definitely called to me!* he considered. *Had she drawn me out of myself, or was that the work of the Angel? What the hell was the point of all this?* His mind didn't know how to process the experience beyond accepting that it had been real. Instead of feeling comfort from this conclusion, Shamus felt troubled. In sheer frustration, he took his head in both hands. "I, don't, understand!" he said to the now-empty room. All that he'd done in his wandering was examine the sculptured wood and tried to commit to memory the sequence of the stories that the woodwork depicted. *Or was I just responding to the woman's call?* He was sure of nothing now. He considered that he'd made no real sense of the carvings other than to record images of farmers, children and war. *No. There was a symbol too.* he realized. *But of what? Had there been angels depicted in some portion of what*

I saw? Were they performing a ritual? Did I see a stone of some kind? What the hell importance could a bloody stone have in all of that?

"Aaach!" Shamus protested, shaking his head for a clarity which refused to come. He was no closer to seeing that image again in his memory than he was to figuring out the point of his nocturnal frolic. At the edges of his thought for one last lingering moment, he thought he could hear his grand-da reciting a poem. Before he could access it, the thought evaporated as quickly as it had come. Even though it had made no sense, sitting in his bed not yet able to regain slumber, he felt that the journey had to have been purposeful. *Perhaps I, no, not me, not Shamus*, he considered, *but the White Wigget, wanted one more look at the magnificence of the walls*? He half chuckled to himself of the strangeness of the event and said to the ceiling, "Sure, whatever, man! Have your way with me."

He reclined on his soft mattress till he felt the soft, down-filled embrace and closed his eyes, hoping to rest. He wasn't taking the event lightly. He just somehow knew that this was not necessarily for his benefit, and that if there was a point to why the Wigget had 'animated' and guided his mind to take this information in, it might someday be revealed to him.

What of the image of the woman beckoning to me, however? He couldn't reconcile this as part of the White Wigget's plan. He felt proprietary about this part of the experience. That had all been his. He knew this somehow. No internal dialogue came to his aid that would confirm his thought, however. The only thought which occupied him was that he should let it go for now, hoping that it might percolate in his unconscious for a while and make more sense after some much-needed sleep.

Had he been thinking with the scientist's brain that had defined his life on the other side of the time portal, perhaps he would have even relegated these thoughts to delusional thinking. Instead, he allowed himself to be blown away by this para-psychological phenomenon. *I legitimately astrally projected!* he confirmed to himself. And, he realized, whatever he might think of the space he occupied, or even the form with which he traversed it, he had briefly encountered another entity who was more than coincidentally doing the same. *Perhaps, she was a ghost?* Shamus wondered. Either way, he was taking this all in. *How cool! How very unscientific of me!* For sure, the Doctor of Psychology whom he had been would have tried hard to place logical explanations around the experience. But Dr. Shamus Bergin was no longer sitting in the comfort of his modern condominium in Ottawa. Shamus of Fior, Bearer of the White Wigget, was in a world entirely unfamiliar, one in which magic was vibrant. He had come too far to turn back.

***

Chapter 20

The warm embrace of Inyi's rays stirred Shamus from sleep, forcing his eyelids to take notice of the subtle intensity of morning activity stirring in the castle. He lay on his mattress for a long time, contemplating the uncertainty of the day. His eyes half open, looking without any intended focus on the solid wooden ceiling. Like the walls, there were no discernible beams overhead to support the ceiling. He surmised that the very smooth surface he gazed up at had been artistically plastered over with some type of mocha-colored mud that hid the seams from view. Unsure as to what his thoughts were telling him about this, or for that matter, why he would even care how the place was constructed, Shamus realized that the force within him was entirely detail oriented. *Maybe the Angel is telling me to be more observant?* he wondered casually. There were so many other considerations, however, that were going to have to be addressed today, that he gave the issue no more thought. Knowing that he couldn't just wait indefinitely for Erladoch to arrive in his chamber, he grudgingly forced himself to pull away from the comfort of where he had been lying and scampered across the cool floor to collect his clothing and other necessaries. A few embers glowed in the bottom of the pot hearth, but they no longer afforded any comfort.

He pulled out a tunic of radiant bone-white color. It felt at the same time to be as soft as silk, yet sturdier than the tightest knit fabric he had ever known. As he pulled the vestment over his shoulders, he felt momentarily 'un-ordinary'. The color of his clothing was hard to make out as he moved about. What seemed like a white sleeve suddenly took on bluish hues, which changed to green as he moved his arms back and forth. "Weird!" Shamus said to the empty room.

He moved to the center of the room to catch a glimpse of himself in his new clothing in the shallow clay basin of water that had been brought in for him while he had slept. He looked at the strangeness of his visage, still startled by the flaming gray-green eyes and raised brilliant whiter-than-white-haired image that stared back at him. "Jaysus!" he muttered aloud. "I'm a lot!"

The door sprang open without a knock, bringing in an unknown figure with a tray of food for his breakfast. He never got a clear look at the servant's face as the latter maintained a respectful downward glance from the moment he entered the room, until he departed seconds after dropping the tray on the small table. As the servant made his exit, Erladoch passed through, shutting the door behind himself. He greeted Shamus with his usual kind smile, walked to the small window and looked his friend over.

"You like your new garments, I hope?"

Shamus nodded his approval.

"Such garments will serve the needs of your body even as the seasons change."

Shamus noticed that Erladoch was similarly attired, his clothes also making subtle color adjustments as he approached.

"Uh, come again?" Shamus questioned.

"Your tunics and other wear are fashioned of olden days when the beauteous Ika sheep roamed these lower mountain lands. They were uniquely wondrous beasts, as rare as any you might encounter. They could be seen in front of you as plain as day, only to vanish the moment they detected a threat. The colors of their wool would appear to change to match their surroundings. Unlike other sheep who could be shorn regularly to produce fabrics, the Ika only ever grew one coat for their entire lifetime. The older they got, the more colors emerged. Simply by moving themselves in variable directions, they could escape a predator's detection as the waves of their multi-colored coats would confuse the onlooker's eyes. To surrender their wool would bring about their deaths; however, as the special properties of their wool only remained if you could take it from them while they still lived. Their sacrifice of life has made for old magic in every fiber. I can tell ya, Shamus, that by the very act of our hosts having bestowed this upon us, we've been afforded one of this kingdom's rarest of treasures."

Erladoch reached deep inside the new cloth pack he had brought into the room with him. Slowly, meticulously, he withdrew a full-length cloak, which he unfurled from its tightly packed state. It contained a large hood that impressed Shamus immediately as being one of the most unusually captivating articles he had ever seen. It was black-green, with an interweave in every thread with what looked like threads of golden silk.

"This, Shamus, is for you alone. You must always be the one and only person to ever wear it. It was made for none other than you. I mean to say, for the Wigget."

Shamus immediately placed his hands on the shoulders of the garment, intent on trying it on when Erladoch stayed his hand.

"Not so quick as all that!" he warned. "It is said that this cloak, after having been gifted to our Order for safe-keeping was stolen many ages ago, only to once again be found in a place of hiding by a Bodelandish shepherd. He claimed to have found it beneath a carefully constructed cache by a stream. Whether this was true or whether the man simply did not wish to admit to himself that one of his ancestors may have been a thief, he came upon it by some measure of chance. Not knowing its former owner, but instead having been captivated by its radiance, he tried to don it. He perished in torment merely by attempting to dress himself with it."

"In his dying words, he is remembered by those who witnessed the happening as saying in a voice that was not his own, *Here exists the cloak of an Elder of the Wigget Council. It was fashioned in the time before men. Take heed. But one living man may wear this garment of the Angealkind. It is for he who can bear the Hope Seed. Any other human who would defile this sacred garment will die an accursed death.*"

Shamus removed his hands from the table where the garment lay as though fearful that his skin would be infected with a lethal toxin. "Shiiiit! I'm not going anywhere near that thing!"

"All these portents the man was said to have proclaimed, even as he shriveled into disfigurement and death, speaking in the ancient tongue of the Strahanas at the same time as being heard by multiples of people of different lands in their own tongues. The Keepers have left this in the custody of the successive Kings of the Bodelanders for generations. They have kept this ancient treasure for you, Wigget Bearer. It is yours alone to wear, like the burden itself that has been bestowed upon you."

"Uh, I don't know, Erladoch, I..." Before Shamus could offer a further word of protest or anxiety over coming into contact with the cloak, Erladoch wrapped his friend in it without warning. Shamus began to shout curses to the air, believing that his friend may have just dealt him a horrible death. Before the third expletive could leave his lips, however, his body felt a quiver of energy overtake him. The quiver was not unpleasant. It made every cell in his body tingle as his anxiety and elation competed with one another for dominance.

Am I about to shrivel up and die like the unfortunate shepherd? He felt himself wondering as his emotions began to settle. *Or is this just another step in my unrevealed journey of self-exploration?* Warmth rushed over him now.

Erladoch watched as the pores of his companion's very skin seemed to emanate a momentary burst of light from beneath the cloak. Shamus suddenly brimmed with a sense of confidence. The garment vibrated with a life all its own, and he experienced the power of it as though a voice was indeed confirming to him that this had been made for his use. The voice pulsed in harmony with the rhythm of Shamus's own energy. While he was certain that the language could not possibly be known to humankind, there was an entirely understandable aspect of it he realized was pure thought. It was at once calming him while assuring him that this garment was 'his' for the taking. Fear was replaced by understanding. He knew that the White Wigget was within him and that he was being endowed with heavenly purpose. The voice dissipated, and the light excreting from his cells faded to his regular human pinkiness.

Shamus sat down on the edge of the bed to take the magnitude of the moment in. He was filled with a sense of destiny. As quickly as the strong emotions had entered his being, they left him, and he found himself simply sitting at the edge of his bed in a cloak, his cloak.

Erladoch's face displayed nothing short of wondrous admiration. He was happy with his hunch having been correct. Shamus, who was only moments ago both horrified and absolutely livid, turned from looking at the floor into Erladoch's eyes. "You couldn't have given me more time to think about this before testing your theory, hunh?" he said in a tone that revealed his annoyance.

"What do they say in your Ottawa world?" Erladoch responded in a resigned voice. "Sometimes you just have to rip off the band aid?"

"Hunh!" Shamus huffed. "Just had to see if it would work, eh?" He was bugged by the cavalier attitude of his friend, despite being impressed by his appropriate use of a modern expression.

Erladoch hesitated. He didn't want Shamus to be angry with him. He served up the best retort he could muster. "Boo-yah!" He let the two syllables out in slow motion.

Shamus erupted into a fit of laughter. As ridiculous as the expression still seemed to them both, it had become theirs. As hoped, the utterance had tickled Shamus's funny bone and eased the tension. "I should'a never taught you that word."

When they had settled down, Erladoch was all the way back to the serious guy that Shamus knew him to be.

"Whatever the past life you had once lived, it is no more, my friend. You, Shamus Bergin, are the hope of this and all future generations of the free creatures of this world. You will be a prime mover in all that shall come to pass. And all will know, without being certain of why they know, that you are the herald of the greatest being that ever walked these lands. I believe that you, and the life moving within you, will equalize the imbalance that the Evil One has created."

"Hell of a pep talk!" Shamus offered, still feeling playful even after Erladoch had gotten back down to business.

***

Shamus actually did feel different after having donned the cloak. It was as though he had come into possession of a level of wisdom that was not all his own. He remarked to himself that it was like a file download that had upgraded his own user experience. He realized that whatever had been unfolding within him, perhaps over the entirety of his life, was now magnified by having been welcomed by the White Wigget's cloak.

"Join me in this meal, Erladoch, would you please?" He wrapped a piece of black bread around some type of deliciously fragrant cheese and popped it into his mouth. Erladoch picked up Shamus's long and short samurai swords, pulled the outer layer at the back of the neck of the cloak open, and quietly slotted them inside along Shamus's back as though there were ready-made slings ready to receive their varying sizes.

"Unfortunately, you will have to eat as we proceed to the ground. It is time to join with our escort."

Shamus stood upright and allowed the entirety of the cloak to unfurl.

Erladoch assessed his friend's appearance. "Your modified appearance and now the wearing of this cloak will take some getting used to. Remember, for most people of my world, the age of the story of the Wiggets is now at the level of near-forgotten mythology. You're about to reveal to the world that this particular myth is real." He picked up Shamus's pack that already bore his grand-da's long sword and carefully harnessed it to the outside of his friend's back. Once on, the long blade would rest in its scabbard without so much as a bounce against Shamus's flank when he walked.

"Come, let us go now to meet them," he said, leading them out of the chamber.

As they entered the dimly lit hallway, Erladoch collected his gear that was resting against the entrance wall and slung it over his left shoulder.

Chapter 21

They followed a winding corridor that became increasingly illuminated by the penetration of natural light from Inyi's face. As they finally saw the outside world, Shamus was taken aback. He had not exited a castle at all! Before him were row upon row of massive trees. Some of them were better than a hundred and fifty feet in diameter. Looking back from the door from which he had just come, his eyes traced a perimeter of bark that suggested this was the largest of them all. He had misinterpreted the interior surfaces for stone, as they had been hewn and rubbed smooth over countless generations. Extending away from where he now stood transfixed by the sheer beauty of these ancient pillars, he surveyed what he now understood acted as the homes for the Bodelanders. Long boulevards of tree homes went off in all directions, with ground level foot paths meandering around their bases. At ground level, no doors were apparent, but well above normal eye level he espied entrance ways and natural bridges of intertwining branches. "Jaysus!" He whispered in complete awe of the natural spectacle. *Of course!* Shamus realized. It all made perfect sense why the "castle" he had spent the past weeks in seemed so unusually built. The entire forest around him was, in fact, the capital city of the Bodeland Foresters. Looking back a further time at the exit he had come out of, Shamus processed that the door was made entirely of living tree root. The Foresters had spent countless ages building their homes within the non-living portions of the outer rings of the trees and the sprawling spaces found under the root systems. Dwellings and walkways protruded amidst interwoven branches of the dizzyingly high monuments to nature. He was awestricken by the sense of natural harmony achieved between humans and flora.

For any of these trees to have grown so thick and long, they would have had to have endured thousands of years unaffected by man, beast or even natural calamity. He felt himself being emotionally overtaken by the wonder of these monuments to time. They rose so high above him, that he had to nearly lie on his back to see straight up to the sunlight.

Erladoch did nothing to interrupt Shamus. He was pleased that his friend felt the profundity of this natural wonder and permitted him a few moments to soak the sight of it all in. After an appropriate pause, he finally spoke. "Beautiful, is it not? This one is the mother," he said, pointing back to their home for the past several weeks. "It is called Firren. From its highest point, there is a look out which allows you to see over the entire forest."

As Shamus's eyes traced the lines of the bark walls back toward the ground, he saw a guard draw back a barrier door still far above him. The woman walked out onto a branch which served as a parapet. She raised a multi-ended horn to her lips. Shamus braced himself for a thundering trumpet blast, but none came. Rather, what sounded like the call of hundreds of chattering birds echoed in the branches, though not a single winged creature was in sight. He recognized the call as the same kind of sonorous announcement which had echoed in the darkness as he and Erladoch prepared to meet their presumed end in combat against the Treborgan hunting party. This was the distinctive horn of the Bodelanders.

In a short time, all the trees were active with invisible doors opening to the outside, allowing virtually thousands of people to file out onto the forest floor. As the people came out, they formed up on what must have been the main 'road' among the stands of trees. This summoning seemed to be a call to every resident of this forest kingdom to present themselves as though to be counted. They naturally formed a line on either side of what they knew as their main thoroughfare around the trees. Shamus remarked that had this assembly of Foresters not been called out into the open, it might actually be impossible for a person unfamiliar with these lands to even know there was a massive community perfectly camouflaged from sight. Even the sentry posts, some of which were at dizzying heights far above, were hewn right into the bows and branches of the network of trees.

A second form of bird call, equally peaceful, rang through the air. It was answered by every Bodelander assembled turning their backs to Shamus and Erladoch. Shamus could no longer see the faces of the people nearest to where he and Erladoch stood. There was no doubt that those who were close by to Firren had seen the cloak of the White Wigget, if they happened to know what its unusual color array signified. Shamus being seen wearing the cloak and standing in the company of the prince who was believed to have been dead but now lived was deliberate. It had been orchestrated by design.

None of this made sense to Shamus. As ranks of Bodelanders were now answering the command to avert their eyes from him, the whole affair seemed contradictory. He surmised that Nica Bodelander had a purpose for all of this; it simply was eluding him in this moment.

Once this action had been carried out, another hidden door in a tree opened upward like a large garage entrance some fifty feet from them. Slowly, a group of people stepped out into the light which filtered in in dapple shade through the great arms of the trees. They would not be seen by the Bodeland Foresters, as the order for all assembled to turn their backs had been an obvious prerequisite before the newcomers were to exit the nearby tree.

Shamus could not identify the party that appeared to be joining with them as they all were adorned in the same natural forest-colored cloaks that were also being worn by Erladoch. Each of the hoods in the travel party was drawn up to make facial recognition very difficult. The order for all Bodelanders to be present and with backs turned was now a bit more understandable from a strategic point of view to Shamus's curious mind.

Only once they had met up and were within feet of Erladoch did Shamus recognize among them the fierce steel-blue-eyed princess of the Foresters, O'Mara Boldar, and Andor Seth. The colossus of a man was hard to hide even under the natural camouflaged color of his cloak. There were two others who mystified Shamus by their very appearances. He was only to learn their names later in the day; however, since at this moment, all members of the travel party were observing a deliberate silence. The unusual two members of the travel party were obviously fraternal wins: the male whose name was 'Nida' having more severe eyebrows than his sister 'Alida'. Apart from this, there was little else that obviously distinguished the two Galagars. As Alida closed in on Shamus, the latter gawked awkwardly at the twins. The strange beauty of both of their faces was startling to look upon at first. There was an absence of a beard from Nida's jawline. Shamus had more than once remarked that nearly all the men he had seen so far in Bodeland were proponents of such manicured facial hair. Both Nida and Alida greeted Shamus soundlessly with their emerald bright falcon-like eyes. The lines of their jaws and cheeks ran into their noses, making their countenances more bird-like than human, even though they clearly were. They were also less tall than the people around them and seemed, even under their cloaks, to have distinctly petite frames.

Erladoch signaled with a smooth roll of his arm that the small group should begin to walk. Shamus did his best to break his child-like stare to avoid being offensive. He came in step with Erladoch. Princess Nica led them away, and the party passed by innumerable backs of Bodelanders of every age. The forest people stood like lifeless manikins amidst a dense carpet of pine needles which lined the forest floor. From time to time, Shamus caught sight of what had to be acorns. Some hung precariously overhead, and other freshly fallen ones lay on the forest floor. Elsewhere, pinecones lay about in neat piles. By comparison to anything he had ever seen before, they were the size of small boulders. Given the skyscraper-like trees all around him, the enhanced magnitude of the cones made sense to him. He recalled the scent of them before his meal in the Great Hall. The Bodelanders used both the acorns and pinecones as fuel for their cooking fires. Nothing of what the Earth yielded was squandered by these people; everything around them was utilized in some purposive way.

As the silent parade wound through the throngs of people, their eyes glued in obedience to the ground, Shamus didn't know what to feel about the bizarre spectacle. Thousands of men, women and children; their eyes guarded from their view. He wanted to see hopeful faces. Because he felt that this ensemble of travelers who had volunteered to go (*God knows where*, he considered), with Erladoch and himself, they must have been an esteemed collection of warriors. One would have thought that this would be a moment of demonstrable hope, even joy. Instead, the entire scene was ostensibly tense.

The Bodelandish people should witness the departure of this party, Shamus considered. As if his thoughts were being read by someone in his group, he suddenly heard the voice of someone in his midst, "**Do not stop to engage or address these people, Shamus of Fior. Walk!**"

He realized that he hadn't heard a voice at all; he had 'felt it' like a wave flowing gently over the sand till it crashed up against rocks. It had clearly addressed him and receded back into whatever consciousness it had belonged to. It was altogether unsettling the way it had intruded and was then gone. Shamus complied by maintaining a steady stride, not knowing why he had just been cautioned in such a fashion.

Every few minutes, as they proceeded farther away from Firren, which had, in fact, been located in what Shamus now confirmed as having been the center of the greatest and tallest of the trees, Shamus's senses seemed to play tricks on him. From behind him, perhaps as much as 30 yards away, he was sure that he had heard a whistling sound followed by a discernible 'thud'. He broke stride momentarily and began to turn to follow the noise to its location when he felt the simultaneous placement of hands from both Erladoch and O'Mara Boldar on either of his shoulders, preventing him from turning to follow the sound. "Just keep going," came a whisper of reassurance. "Eyes forward".

This advice made no sense to him any more than the polite shove forward he had just received from the men in his party. He was sure now that he was detecting movement in the tops of his peripheral vision, somewhere above his direct line of sight. Every effort to focus his gaze forward, with the apparent restriction of not turning his own head or body as they marched along, made it hard to track whatever it was he was sensing as motion above him. His forward gaze landed onto nothing but dense greenery above him. Branches were sometimes swaying above, but with the cool breeze that was winding through the lands, that seemed to be all that was moving through the forest outside of their party.

"Fsssssst!" came another whistling interruption to the imposed silence, this time closer and somewhere just off his left flank. When he heard a further thud, he also heard the reflexive moan of sorrow from someone else coming from the same area. Shamus once again felt the hand of reassurance both gently shoving him forward and compelling his straight-line path with the group. A surge of anxious breaths seemed to ripple across the wall of humanity as they passed the turned backs, and Shamus remarked to himself that one of the small child-like backs on his right, only a few feet ahead, was shaking in actual fear as the sounds of his group's footfalls approached them. Shamus could tell without seeing any facial features that the little boy was clearly terrified! It occurred to him for the first time as he walked along that the whistling sounds were the sounds of death taking flight through the air. There were archers perched everywhere above them! That was the movement he was detecting! The sentries perched high above their position were under clear orders to rove over the masses. Their bows were strung, and their arms drawn back in ready position. Shamus was mortified when he realized that the back-turning exercise came with lethal consequence for whomever defied the order.

Ssssffflt! came the call of another arrow. It sailed somewhere overhead into the neck and out through the throat of a man only a yard ahead of Nida and Alida. This individual had been obvious in his head-turning gesture. His reckless and brazen disobedience of the princess's order to avoid looking upon the company met with immediate death from above. Shamus had to step to his right to avoid stepping onto the man as he crumpled to the ground. The deceased's distinctive clothing suggested that he was likely from somewhere else. As Shamus absorbed the look of surprised horror now glued to the man's death mask, he wondered why this non-Bodelander had been among the ranks of these people.

Perhaps he was a traveling merchant? He posited to himself as a flush of guilt for the man's sudden end washed over him. ***More likely, he was a spy***, a thought landed in his mind. The thought was not emotive, but rather matter-of-fact. Either way, Shamus once more recognized it as not having been his own. ***Jaysus! Get out of my head whoever you are!*** Shamus protested. ***You're going to make me into a paranoid schizophrenic!***

As you wish, came the reply, which fell away like a handful of sand rushing past open fingers. As the presence vanished, Shamus realized that something about the properties of the cloak magnified his connection to the White Wigget. The notion of having a voice in his head, even a compliant one, was unsettling. *Oh man! This is going to take some getting used to.*

***

Nica, and perhaps Erladoch (Shamus still didn't know who was privy to the plan, in fact, but obviously there was a plan nonetheless), had wanted the Foresters to gaze upon Shamus and Erladoch immediately upon their exit from Firren. There had been a buzzing for the entire time they had been there that the Dunbar Prince had returned from the dead in the company of a very odd stranger. Seeing 'them' leave the principal City of Castra was accordingly unavoidable. Under no circumstances, however, could the populous be allowed to hide in their homes and look through their windows to bear witness to either the magnitude of the party leaving Bodeland, or for that matter, be permitted to see who the other members of the group might be.

While the newly formed military formed a large proportion of the people of Bodeland in these dark days, not all among them had taken a warrior's vow.

The people of Bodeland who filled the ranks of the newly invested fighting force had instead been everything from artisans to food provisioners. The artisans were talented at making weapons like the short bow used by the Bodelandish warriors, and the provisioners were the hunters and gatherers who could fell an animal on land or in the air with their skillful archery skills. They were the first conscripts, but they would not be the last to join. In a time soon enough, all free people of Loura would have to harden themselves into the role of a warrior.

As in all large communities, there had always been some measure of travelers whom the Foresters traded with from the outside world. Even though those foreigners who knew the routes into the city comprised but a small group given the natural camouflage of Castra, they could not be trusted with the same degree of certainty as the warriors sworn to defend Bodeland, let alone the compliant citizens of the forest kingdom. As startling as the entire event had been to Shamus, the weighty edict and its assured consequences began to make some sense.

It took princess Nica's full explanation to Shamus later to clear up some of the questions he continued to struggle with over the strategy which had not been shared with him in advance. As he and the others passed by the last grouping of Bodelanders and beyond the invisible borders of Castra, he cringed, dearly hoping not to hear the signature 'ssssfffflt' call of death from the air above him. If there had been others, they were far enough away he didn't hear them. Shamus was glad to have such a face-covering cloak on himself. He would have felt embarrassed in the company of the hardened warriors in his group of travelers were they to have seen the tears which streamed liberally down his face. He consoled himself that anyone stupid enough to defy the princess's order to not look upon the company had to have been one of the Evil One's spies. He worked to a place of acceptance that any such person had accordingly met an appropriate end. No matter what excuses he made for the spectacle to himself, however, he found himself shaken by the terrifyingly decisive manner in which death was meted out as the one and only punishment. *Could any of the victims of this punishment have simply been weak and overcome by curiosity?* he questioned. *Oh God! Is this cold-blooded destruction of human life all my fault?* Shamus wouldn't know how to take the answer to that question. It bore a weight of moral responsibility that he wasn't sure how to handle. If he were to air his sense of revulsion, would others tell him that this was necessary? Some aspect of his presence in this group, however, made that answer a 'yes', and he knew it no matter how badly he hoped to shake it from his mind. All he had to do was summon the image of the small child terrified by his very approach, and he knew he would wear this on his soul. Had he been able to see into the hood of the Bodeland Princess's cloak, the glistening cheeks of his hostess would have revealed her regret for having had to make such a decree in the first place.

***

Nica Bodelander led the six other members of the travel party for several yarricks through the maze of Bodeland. The scene had become tranquil as the party of travelers walked along surrounded now by nothing but the awe-inspiring trees and the animals, which made their homes within them. Shamus was uncertain if they had finally left the City of Castra behind or not, as there were no distinguishable limits. No castle walls marked the perimeter, and no obvious defensive barriers presented themselves; the best defense was the fact that an invader would not know if he was actually in the city or not. A simple strategy to Shamus's mind, but he thought it might have been effective, at least to the non-discerning eye of an invader who had never been there before. *But what of those who had scouted these lands surreptitiously before?* he wondered. Surely, a seasoned Treborgan scout would discover the forest's secret.

The average newcomer would likely never see the Bodeland Forresters in their own domain before it was too late. The clothing of, at least, the newly minted warriors and their tactics made them blend organically with the canopy of the forest. Invaders never stood a chance against this hidden death from above. The only weakness that placed Bodeland at risk at all was one where a conqueror would have no interest in the subjugation of the forest kingdom and its people, only their annihilation. If and when they arrived in force, it would matter little to Enilorac that a few of his conscripts would be sacrificed in order to lock down the Bodelanders' homes.

***

Chapter 22

The woods were eerily silent. Few animals stirred as the seven adopted a course south by southwest. No one had spoken, but they all were aware of the intended direction. Shamus pulled up close to Erladoch and whispered sarcastically, "Since I seem to be the only one who was not privy to the night's dream of revelation, perhaps you could tell me where it is we are headed, my friend?"

Erladoch turned to Shamus slowly, making no effort to confront the sarcasm, "We go to Gol to find transport."

"Oh. Is that all? We're going to Gol then?" Shamus asked, feeling no better informed than he had been moments before.

"Yes", came the matter-of-fact reply. "From there, we will follow your guidance further."

That took Shamus so by surprise that he almost tripped over his own feet. "Uh, Erladoch?" He said louder than he'd intended; his voice filled with surprise and apprehension.

"I don't even know where we are now! This all just looks a lot like a forest to me. How can I direct us? Surely you realize that I don't know where Gol is!"

"Trust the voice beneath your skin, Shamus. The White Wigget is moving you, and we are following. Though you feel lost in strange lands, we all recognize that this is the fastest course to Gol Bodeland. When we left Castra, you took the lead; did you not notice?"

Shamus scoffed at this suggestion like it was the most ridiculous assertion that anyone had ever made. *You want me to trust in the voice that I told to shut up and leave me alone a few hours ago? Yikes!* He shook his head in disbelief. He traced his thoughts back over the past few hours. It was undeniable that he had, in fact, been out front of the group for a good part of the time, but he had thought that the Travelers had been walking astride of him. *Hunh!* he thought to himself. "Most unsettling!" he couldn't help but speak the words aloud. "Do I have any control over my own body?" he asked the air, and possibly whatever 'thing' was somehow magically paired to him.

"Why are you so troubled, Shamus?" Princess Nica asked as she caught up to the conversation.

"Er, I don't even know how to express it," he stated in response as he considered the irony of his current circumstances. "Maybe one of you would be cool with having some Angelic being hiding out in your DNA, but I haven't quite gotten there yet. Since I arrived in Loura, I don't know from one minute to the next whether 'I' say or do something, it is actually me, or this 'other guy' who is driving the bus."

Nica said nothing in response, mainly because she lacked comprehension of some of the time-bound references which Shamus had just employed. She made a mental note to ask Erladoch later about "being cool", "DNA" and "driving the bus." Erladoch had been in Shamus's timeline; he would know what these references meant. For now, she just sighed in such a way as to politely acknowledge Shamus.

Erladoch continued to stride purposefully beside his friend down the gradual slope of the hill as the clearing they had just entered had already begun to close back into a tighter pattern of trees. The warmth of the sun overhead was as fleeting as the opening in the woods had been. He looked quizzically at Shamus. "I understand 'cool' as I saw people say this on your television. I have no idea what this 'DNA' means. Explain, please."

Nica was pleased to see that she would get a faster answer than she had expected. She decided to continue to stay astride of the odd-looking Wigget Bearer a little longer even though she still felt uneasy around him.

Shamus recognized that this was one of the first times in a long time that his friend was once again the pupil and himself the teacher. Rather than slough it off and just say something placating like 'it's your body', he decided to take the time to give Erladoch a real explanation of the term, knowing that his friend was both incredibly intelligent and would also not take kindly to being offered a child's simplification. As he had nothing else to do but walk anyways, he found being a scientist again comforting, and it helped him to pass the time. The others in the group paid no obvious attention to the conversation, with possibly the exception of Alida, who listened without contribution. The minds of the others were entirely occupied with maintaining vigilance and their own private thoughts. At what seemed regular intervals, two members of their party would split off and disappear into the trees in opposing directions for upwards of twenty or more minutes at a time, only to reappear ahead of them and then take position at the back of their small platoon. Shamus understood without having to ask that they were scouting the area for spies, or worse.

There were no sounds other than the occasional crush of twigs beneath the group's marching feet. Shamus felt a need to engage the Bodelandish princess. "Nica Bodelander, I'm fairly certain I know the answer at least in part already, but can you explain to me why it was that your people had to turn away from us as we left your capital?"

She looked at Shamus, assessing him for a moment, and then lowered her head before offering a soft reply. "My lord, t'is actually a custom of our people to turn away one's eyes and their minds from departing groups, although not in such large numbers and certainly not on pain of death."

Shamus sighed. He now had confirmation that he was at least partly responsible for the death sentences carried out earlier in the day.

"While this day has witnessed the leaving of some of the most significant leaders of our time, only the trees which have no mouths will have seen who these persons are, and where they were headed. T'was a necessary measure of security today and not simply a show of respect." In recognition of Shamus's obvious emotional head-hanging gesture, she added: "It's not yer fault, Wigget Bearer. It is mine and mine alone. All they had to do was obey the damned order!" Her voice faltered. She drew a heart-heavy breath. "Before today, this had always been a symbolic gesture of respect for anyone who would depart. The whole city was ordered out to bid us farewell as we now need to be sure who might be against us."

Shamus slowed his pace slightly and looked directly into her deep-set, steel-blue eyes.

"But is there so little trust in your world that this was the only way to handle it?" Still stung by his own guilt, he recognized that his judgment of her was overly unfair. "Forgive me. It's not fair for me to judge."

"Thank you," she replied with compassion. "Do not think us cold, my lord. We're in fact a very happy people that devote our lives to the tending of nature's great garden. Warfare is a tragedy of our world that is based on the evils of men and other beasts to possess what is beyond their means. As a Keeper, I've been hardened to the life of a warrior. My people have been protected by my Order's hidden sacrifices and have been left to live their lives without such worries till recent times. Only a few years ago, we'd put our youngest and strongest to the task of hewing homes out of the inner workings of our great trees. Each such man and woman were both artist and constructor. We now send our best out to patrol our lands to protect ourselves from the roving hordes of Scrags who would foul the beauty of our forest. They take from the world indiscriminately, and now roam in multitudes just beyond our bloody gates!" She spat on the ground to emphasize her hatred for these aggressors. "When we turn our backs now on departing Bodelanders, there is a level of sadness that was not there before. Our traditional sign of respect is now also an acknowledgment to all that our warriors may never come back. Our warriors understand that they should not look upon the sorrow of their family and friends as they leave, and those who remain behind should not be allowed to see the route by which they go."

Nica stepped closer to Shamus to speak in greater confidence; not because of the members of her group, but rather because it was as though she feared by saying such negative words aloud, she risked inviting whatever malevolence they had recently experienced toward herself. Her superstition was palpable and entirely reasonable.

"There are some among us who have been corrupted by the Evil One's influence and disobey the old ways that have protected our lands for as long as there has been a Bodeland. Our warriors had no choice but to enforce my orders without hesitation, lest the number of our party and our intended destination be guessed and communicated by foul means."

All the talk by Nica with her air of sad resignation to the harshness of current events could not erase from Shamus's thoughts that arrows flew in some numbers today. He could tell, however, that she had been troubled deeply by the loss of life. Her knowledge that it was getting harder to keep the venomous enchantments of Enilorac from finding purchase in the few addled minds of her own people was troubling. He accepted that Nica was completely sincere in her advice to him that the Bodeland Forresters were happiest being stewards of the Great Forest lands, and any other role occupied by them was discordant from their core values. There was so much obvious harmony between man and trees in Castra that he accepted that the newly formed warrior class was borne entirely out of a need for self-preservation. Harkening back to this thought, Shamus shifted his focus to the magnificence of the treed capital in hopes of not dwelling on the scene of his morning. Even with context now firmly encasing the experience, it had been a painful truth that he no longer wished to think about. He directed himself to consider that the largest and most magnificent of the great Sequoias of his own time paled in their size to the tree he had spent several weeks living inside of.

"Yours were the first people to walk in this forest world, were you not?" Shamus questioned Nica, hoping she would welcome his changing of the subject.

"Aye, m'lord." Nica replied, pleased with his insight. "T'is always been our home. We didna' have to fight to claim it, if that's what ya mean. The Scrags are an older people still, though. I canna' say how long they've walked in this world, but all agree they were here before us. To almost the last of them, they've never wanted to take part in the communities of Loura, even as we flourished, became more organized, and began to develop communities which blossomed into kingdoms; they kept to themselves. But I should tell you that there'd been a kind of peace between us in the early ages of our past memory. That is, till the Evil One began collecting them."

"By 'collecting', do you mean 'influencing', Lady Nica?" As she had continued to address him formally, Shamus decided that he needed to afford her the respect of her own proper title if she was ever going to accept him.

"Aye. The Scrags are, well, less advanced than the other people of the west. They already loathed our kind and elected to shy away from our developing towns and cities. When the Dead King returned to Loura, these scattered and disorganized cave-dwellers were easy to enchant and be turned to his purposes. That is not to say that Lourans are immune from his influence; you've seen with yer own eyes that he has found ways to make his malevolence dance into our minds in moments of weakness."

Shamus nodded in acceptance, hoping that she would not take the conversation back to recent examples. He decided to change the subject once again in hopes of avoiding further discussions of unpleasantness. "Uh, Lady Nica. This may seem an odd question, but I mean it with great respect. Your eyes. They're not like any I have ever seen before."

Nica looked at him with puzzlement.

"They're blue," she replied matter-of-factly, not understanding his point. "Surely there's lots of Keepers with blue eyes from where you have come from? I might even say it's you who have the odd ones in fact, wouldn't you?" She smiled.

Shamus laughed awkwardly, realizing that her observation wasn't wrong. "Yer right, of course. I'm still trying to reconcile my new look actually. I'm still a bit freaked out by it!"

"Freaked out?" Nica queried.

"Yah. Sorry. Freaked out means surprised to a point of being frightened by something."

"Fair enough," she offered.

"But my lady, your eyes are more than just blue, they are unlike any color of blue I have ever seen, and I couldn't help but notice that many of your people whom I have seen up close have a similar steel blue. It's beautiful, of course," he stammered embarrassedly as she continued to look placidly at him.

A thought occurred to her now. "Ah yes. Now I know what ya mean. We retain a special gift of our early ancestors that makes our eyes not unlike those of night dwellers. You know, like brials for instance. Our people have always lived beneath the forest canopy, Lord Shamus. Seldom did we witness the light of Inyi and Naga in the same way that other kingdoms have. We love this land, and the forest is our home, but to be sure, our eyesight is better suited to darkness than people from the other Houses of Loura."

The explanation made total sense to Shamus. The pigmentation had an adaptive function based on her environment.

"You know, Shamus, I'm greatly sorrowed to leave Castra as will all of my people be soon enough when my lieutenants shall deliver my edict to bid all of Bodeland farewell. There is small doubt that the Evil One who sits re-made in the House of Treborg will destroy our great forests with his horrible black arts. When the Scraggin armies cross the Boldar River in force, I've little hope that that they will leave the east part of the world's oldest forest unblemished. That is but a child's fantasy. If they do what I expect, I wonder what my children's children's eyes will look like then." Nica's voice faltered. The verbalization of such an admission caused tears to stain her cheeks.

Shamus felt terribly awkward, not knowing what to say next. He could give her no comfort. Before he was forced to come up with something that might offer consolation, she took leave of him, politely bowing her head and slowing her pace to create space between him and the rest of the group trailing behind. Despite his sense of guilt for having exposed this raw nerve, he knew that

Princess Nica would not be angry with him. It was clear that he was not from their time, and he was simply struggling to learn all that he could. The young warrior princess's face may have become wet from grief, but the fire burning in her heart that would soon solidify her resolve was burning ever more passionately. The ache of knowing she likely had seen her home for the last time inspired a fierceness within her that would later give way to the courage that she would need to survive when all else would seem to go against her.

Shamus warned himself that his probing questions of the members of his group would likely alienate him somewhat. For reasons that he was not processing, however, he felt a compulsion to keep singling out each member of the group to learn their personal stories as best he could, doing his best to not become offensive. Even if they collectively perceived him as ignorant of their ways, or worse still, alarmingly uninformed of their personal dramas and how they had impacted the land of Loura's unfolding tale, the voice inside of his mind gave him no choice but to press on with his interviews. As the Travelers came closer together from time to time in tighter clusters of forest, Shamus went from person to person in his band and proceeded to ask lists of questions that seemed to form spontaneously the minute he came into close contact with the next of these new companions. He knew damned well that the White Wigget was running 'the show' on so many levels right now. Having nothing else to do and no reason to doubt that he was being directed to conduct such interrogatories, he gave into the whispering thoughts that bubbled up into his consciousness as if texts were forming on a PDA behind his eyes.

***

Shamus began to speak more openly, unworried of who heard him. His conversational partners, however, chose to maintain stifled voices. After hours of slow marching through the trees, he realized that he had never once not been in the lead; his feet making sure footfalls as though they were guided by a compass. If he had indeed maintained the lead position as now seemed apparent to him all this time, then his sense that 'he' was singling out members of the party was not altogether reality. It was more likely that each member responded to a summonsing of sorts to take their position alongside him. All who were being called upon seemed to be prepared to share the knowledge that his inner mind was directing him to uncover.

The Travelers were not perceiving the flawed, and entirely mortal man known as 'Dr. Shamus Bergin' when called upon to converse. As a highly educated and modern man, Shamus ought to have connected these dots entirely on his own. In reality, however, so much about what had happened to him recently was, at some level, still being processed by him. It took time for him to assimilate that the members of this group shared the understanding that Anthrac Aran was no longer an individual confined to their myths. Rather, his essence was animating and informing the actions of the man who was walking among them. It was even more foreign to Shamus that he was one and the same with this mythical figure! Even though he should have been able to accept it, given what he had already experienced since arriving in Loura, the notion of carrying another soul within himself was disarming. The professional psychologist that he believed himself to still be on some level was at odds with the concept of himself housing more than one personality. He'd seen how others had mistreated the mentally ill. Even members of his own profession maintained unconscious biases that often interfered with their insight as to how to help patients in their care.

Despite his own best efforts to embrace his new reality, a part of Shamus continued to attempt to maintain dominance over the emerging personality within him. Even his very scant recollections of his grand-da revealed a man fraught with a battle for sanity. From the first moment it was revealed to him that he was bearing the White Wigget, he had been constructing walls around what he now sensed was the Angel's personality to preserve his sense of self. As he listened to himself ask questions of each of the Travelers, he sent a warning to the entity within, *I'll let you share space with me, Anthrac Aran, but you're a guest in my house, don't forget that.* He cautioned.

Those who had joined this esteemed party cared nothing about a man named Dr. Shamus Bergin. They were in the presence of someone else whose life and mission they had sworn their service to at their coming of age. It was entirely the Angel that they were delivering themselves up to. The 'White Wigget' had been absent for so many Ages of Loura and was now calling upon each of the Travelers to summarize the great history that had unfolded over his long absence. Because of his self-imposed exile, Anthrac had only witnessed flashes of this place and its deleted history through very rare and incredibly taxing conjured visions. Such efforts had drained him so greatly, or more correctly, drained his human hosts so greatly. His reawakened mind could not possibly assimilate a clear picture without gaps being filled back in by the members of his Sacred Order, and each of the Travelers was anxious to interact with him.

With the limitations presented by the brains of the hybrid hosts that he had hidden within for tens of thousands of years, Anthrac was now organizing the linear progression. He had roused himself to a heightened level of awareness in this host named Shamus Bergin in a fashion in which he had seldom ventured to do. He had only briefly permitted himself to exert control over his hosts when there had been imminent physical peril to their mortal bodies. He did not automatically know that Shamus was the last viable host of the Angealkind after so many millennia. Like any fetus that had almost come to term, he simply perceived a pressure that informed him his return was imminent. The fact that he found himself nearly all the way back to within only a thousand years after the time when he had first gone into his self-imposed exile had involved decisions made by the members of the Order he had founded. There had to be a reason for everything, and his disciples could provide at least some clues to sate his curiosity. The further revelation that the Master of the Great Pit had not yet found a way to enter the world of humans but had chosen to reinsert the Treborgan king into this moment in time told him so very much. There had to have been discoveries made by Satan's disciples regarding the True Knowledge. A congruence of that enemy's emerging knowledge around time portholes and the Itavo Stone clearly related to this moment in history. It would all come together eventually for Anthrac, but only if Shamus got out of the way long enough to allow the Angealkind to assimilate the knowledge being offered to him. The timeline all the way to the 2000s of the Christian Era had been maintained without a breach of realms by Satan; and yet, every instinct informed the White Wigget that were he not to have returned here, to the forgotten time of Loura, something cataclysmic would soon occur!

His efforts to bring clarity to the experiences of his hosts down through the ages had diminished them all so much that they often lost their sanity. The ritual of transference sometimes had to be brought on years before planned with some of Anthrac's previous bearers. This current host was a different sort altogether. He 'recognized' the presence of Anthrac's personality and was managing to share it better than almost any host he had experienced by attempting to lay down ground rules for when and under what circumstances he would permit his persona to be secondary. The blood which coursed through this Shamus Bergin was surprisingly pure despite the linear timeline—purer somehow even than the man's grandfather. *He must have been refreshed along the way*, Anthrac calculated. *This is good! It will afford him a better chance than most.*

***

Rather than protest further, Shamus once again decided to listen to the distinct voice echoing in his own ears while Anthrac spoke through him to the members of the group. Hours passed as they traversed descending valleys which spilled into new rises of heavily tree-covered terrain. Perhaps because of the absolute stillness involved with the empty activity of walking for hours on end, Shamus decided that becoming a passive listener to the Q&A which the White Wigget had imposed could afford him some insights. He grudgingly accepted that had he not permitted the White Wigget to move through him, he would likely be dead already in this very strange land. *Maybe if I give way a little, it might provide me a sense of intimacy or at least a better understanding of the thoughts and intentions of this Anthrac person,* he finally reasoned.

As he considered this sharing of understanding with his 'guest', the image of his grand-da kept returning to him. *Grand-da Eamon had volunteered for this role. I wonder how long he had borne the Angel's essence; how long before he began to lose himself?* he wondered. He knew so little. In fact, he realized he knew absolutely nothing! *Did Grand-da struggle the whole time as a Bearer of Anthrac, or was there a triggering moment? Going through his life hiding this incredible secret might have always been a struggle. Or maybe the Wigget was less noisy a lot of the time inside Eamon's head than he is currently in mine.* As his ears absorbed the soft crumple of pine needles beneath his steadily moving feet, Shamus realized that he had seen first-hand those moments where his grand-da's own self had become so diminished that it appeared to any reasonable observer that the essence of him had been lost. In those times where the White Wigget must have been focusing his power, everyone around Eamon Bergin couldn't help but treat him like the Village Fool.

Shamus's mind floated back to his childhood as the light of Naga was beginning to disappear from the trees overhead. His grand-da's efforts at preventing him from being enchanted to walk to his death into black waters as a child now became clear to him; it had been as though Anthrac was choosing this moment to allow Shamus to explore his own personal childhood story with greater clarity. His mind went straight to the moment of his grand-da's intervention. Utterances of completely incomprehensible chants and words of incantation flowed into Shamus's child-like ears, calling him back from an enchanted somnolence. The power of the words alone embraced his mind and compelling his body to stop moving toward the dark water! All of this was there in his thoughts now like text on a display for Shamus to consider, followed by the last words Shamus would ever remember hearing his grand-da say, "not ready". The malevolent force which had compelled him to the water's edge had burst like sparks from a dying ember in a bonfire, and then they were gone. Shamus's grand-da's life force was fully spent not long after, the apparent victim of a human's effort to call upon and channel the White Wigget's power. A collaborative effort to intercede in the attack against him as a child had become necessary, and it had worked. *But*, Shamus now saw, *the cost of an old host like my grand-da forcibly awakening the Angel within to intercede on my behalf cost him his life as it had taken all of his remaining personal power to do so on my behalf.*

Tears began to well up in his eyes as Shamus now recalled his unexplained 'flu', which had kept him in bed for weeks following the near-drowning incident. He had remained in a state of feverish delirium. There had been an exchange that was years too early in the making between himself and his grand-da. The exchange of the White Wigget into his body through a blood transfusion, which swapped blood for blood, must not have been safe or anticipated for a child so young. The sudden discovery of the Bergin legacy by forces of darkness; the attack which led to the rush to escalate the timetable for the rite of transference—all this made waiting for Shamus to achieve a stage of proper maturity for the exchange to have taken place voluntarily an impossibility in the blink of an eye. So much was beginning to make sense to him now. Since the arrival of Erladoch in his life, there had been a slow evolution of learning that was coming to him from elsewhere; first in half-captured memories, then in whispers, and now almost in direct dialogue with this entity's conscious thoughts. It shook Shamus to the core knowing how hard paranoid schizophrenics struggled with sorting out the voices inside their heads.

Shamus walked among his fellow Travelers now, connecting with the need to comprehend each of the life stories of the respective people in his group and those of their important ancestors, all the while feeling the full weight of the responsibility which had been bequeathed to him. He reached out his arms as wide as they would extend, brushing the soft green needles of Spruce and Pine which reached out to each other on either side of him. He felt as one with the air as he inhaled the fragrance released from the idlest contact of the bristles against his fingers. Flecks of light dappled through the trees to the ground beneath his feet in a way he had never before noticed. To those who walked directly behind him, his gesture of extended arms looked like no more than a stretching action, a physical shift designed to take the load of his pack and his weighty swords momentarily off from where they rested against his back. For Shamus, however, this was a moment of awakening.

Erladoch and Nica had just fallen back into the group after having each performed their own circular scouting missions. As they approached the rear of the group simultaneously, both found themselves having to adjust their eyes to the spectacle that was passively playing out ahead. At the moment of full 'stretch' where Shamus's hands made contact with the trees on either side of him, both of them saw a charge of colored electricity surge from his fingertips. It spread through the boughs of the trees, producing shoots of fresh growth of needle and cone alike on each of the trees contacted.

The Travelers looked from one to the other before boiling over with gleeful responses to Shamus's unexpected action. This momentary display of the old magic from the stranger within their midst had just rewarded their enduring faith and belief in their oaths. Anthrac Aran, last of the Angelic earthly colony known as the Strahanas had returned to them in Loura's time of need. Shamus Bergin would not have to do another thing to convince any one of them what his importance to their group was. They would each of them surrender their very souls to ensure that he would be kept safe to fulfill his part of the mission.

Chapter 23

Shamus listened to each of the Travelers' tales. There was unanimity that Anthrac had made the right decision to flee by hiding himself within the bloodline of a Human-Strahana host. For him to have remained in corporeal form in Loura would have surely risked allowing the Treborgan king to find the third Itavo fragment within a very short time. That would have spelled the end of days then and there.

By Enilorac of Treborg having blindly experimented with the two stones he had plucked from the hands of the murdered Wigget council members, he could go nowhere other than the place where a person consumed by malice and greed could go: the Great Pit. He arrived in the demon realm alive and, ironically, won the gift of immortality from the Master, a power he could not possibly have foreseen. The torment that he would have to endure for this, however, meant that he would cede control of both his soul and body. He was combined with that of the Serpent demon most loyal to the Master.

These stories Shamus knew well enough by now, but by hearing his travel companions speak of this tale along with their own unique storylines telling how they themselves were born to the cause of the Keepers allowed him to understand both the linear connection back to the Strahanas themselves and the meticulous nature by which each Louran House worked at maintaining purity in their bloodlines.

From the very moment that Anthrac had constituted the Sacred Order, which would rely on these Human-Strahana hybrids to defend the cause of the light, there was an understanding that there would have to be a continuity of bloodlines traceable back to the Angealkind for there to be any chance that Anthrac could remain in hiding, even if this meant bearing such a responsibility for millennia. He would stay hidden until the moment where Satan was most likely to find his exit from the demon realm. No human without this mix in their blood could survive having the White Wigget within themselves; nor, as it turned out, could the White Wigget continue to thrive unless his host carried some measure of connection to the Angelic bloodline.

The math involved with being able to sustain such a pristine continuity for as much as twenty millennia was mind-boggling to Shamus! No matter how he tried to calculate the number of generations it would take before all presence of Angelic blood would vanish versus his understanding of the Mendelian combinations of gene pairs necessary for it not to do so, he simply could not see how it had been feasible for the Keepers to have kept sufficient purity in their lines to arrive at his birth in the twenty-first century of the Christian Era.

The missing fact that he was going to have to come to terms with, however, was that Anthrac had also gifted the Keepers with the 'True Knowledge'. This understanding of the time portholes was carefully guarded by the Keepers and used as sparingly as possible was, as he would come to realize, integral to the Keepers' success in re-perpetuating their own lines across time.

But what of the third Itavo fragment? Shamus wondered. *When Anthrac went into hiding, what happened to this? Surely this stone left Loura at the same time as the Angel; otherwise*, he reasoned, *it would have been there to be found by Enilorac, and the Great Stone which the Strahanas had gone to such trouble to hide away from humans would have been located long ago.*

The rupture of space and time would have already come to pass had this stone been found by those committed to the cause of darkness. *So where the hell is it?* Shamus wondered.

As far as he could tell, this stone would have to have been hidden somewhere else in history so that it could not be found by the Evil One. There was scant little said to Shamus about this third fragment, however, and yet, the Keepers in his midst had every confidence that this heavenly artifact, in a manner similar to the return of the White Wigget himself, was going to make its way back to them in this timeline. *But for what purpose?* he asked each of them without receiving a clear answer. *Who was responsible for this additional piece of the puzzle, and when and by what means would they return to join their cause?* Again, no one could offer anything to these questions. With the Keepers being masters at compartmentalizing information, Shamus had to accept that all would be revealed by someone else, hopefully at the appropriate moment.

When the Strahanas were still a robust and thriving presence in the world of ancient Loura, their explorations across the dimensions of time and space had always been used for the sole purpose of briefly inserting themselves into future earthly timelines to foster a continued desire for people of goodwill to work in the cause of the Light; 'a sort of auto-correct', Shamus considered. He conjured what he knew of ancient history around the world. He noted that there had indeed been times in recorded history where God-Like creatures had appeared to mortals. On notable occasions, the myths of every race contained tales of such deities dwelling for a time among them, even fathering the odd child with them; the 'demi-gods' as they all too often became known by the ancients. Accepting that the Strahanas had indeed revealed themselves to other civilizations beyond the Age of Loura, Shamus then also had to confront the truth that demons had also found their way into the fabric of recorded time. Grotesque, terrifying creatures which drove fear into the hearts of mortals had been along for the temporal ride too. His own timeline knew of multi-limbed, sometimes half-human, half-monster entities that had dominated entire cultures, forcing the civilizations of the day to receive them as gods. This thought unsettled Shamus immensely. Even if Satan had not yet breached the barrier which contained him, he'd found a way to send emissaries. Somehow and somewhere in Earth's timeline, those connected to the Great Pit had acquired some aspect of the 'True Knowledge'. It was undeniable that demons had acquired an ability to travel to the earthly realm using portholes of their own, even though there had never been any evidence of Satan himself having stepped foot out of his eternal banishment. This was a truly vexing puzzle for Shamus! It had to lead back to the Itavo Stone. That had to be the one thing which held the Master of the Pit in captivity.

Everything that the Travelers shared with him confirmed that, at least until the present moment in Loura, with the very notable exception of the return of Enilorac, no one had ever encountered a demon in this stage of the human timeline.

As a pure race descended from the Light, the Strahanas were entirely formed of goodwill. They used their individual pieces of the Itavo to travel to prepare each culture they encountered to repel darkness from their lives, never knowing when or how it might appear. With the stones hidden away from man, the Keepers imbued with the 'True Knowledge' erected monuments over the places of power where the light of the Strahanas had been seen to come and go. *Perhaps those were all the breadcrumbs that those invested in the cause of Evil had needed?* Shamus considered. The Keepers founded a science based entirely on predicting how, even without the Stones' power to direct their own will to travel, they might still transport as the Strahanas once did. This had been integral to their mission as Keepers. They knew that there would be future times when men of ill intention might be in such numbers as to overwhelm those of goodwill. Beyond protecting the White Wigget and his stone, the mission of the Keepers included their being able to insert themselves like the Strahanas themselves had once done to defend the Light until the final battle for the earthly realm would come, and the White Wigget would have to return.

In every sense of the word, the Sacred Order of Keepers represented a complete paradox: the members were selected and schooled from an early age because they demonstrated the highest examples of kindness and devotion to missions of goodwill, and yet, they were carefully molded into the fiercest of warriors, ever preparing to protect Loura from an evil they believed would inevitably return.

The Keepers were considerably more than just warriors of the Light, however. As proponents of peace, they resolved to make themselves the greatest scholars of their times. Each member had to choose whether, in addition to their learnings in war craft, they would bear the verbal record of the people's laws and traditions, the arts, the lore of healing, or the sciences of earth and sky. They called this individualized lifelong devotion to their studies the 'ábaltacht' or special skill. While some ábaltachts' were obvious soon after their toddling years, others only revealed themselves later. Either way, no Keeper living didn't possess such specialized gifts passed down from the Angealkind.

As the Travelers continued their journey, Shamus listened in fascination to each of his companions. He was committed to learning their personal tales and, by so doing, he also came to understand how each of them came to acquire their additional obligations in their lifelong secret education as Keepers. Each of them in turn discussed the nature of their own ábaltachts so that the Wigget Bearer could gain an understanding of how they might uniquely be able to support him in his part of the mission.

For O'Mara Boldar, it was agriculture. The young prince could grow anything edible and assess the right type of soil to derive the maximum benefit for each of the Louran houses' diverse terrains. Nica Bodelander had been schooled in the laws and traditions of Loura from its earliest days. She maintained the verbal record of all laws of property and civil order, such as they were.

Andor Seth's ábaltacht involved Metallurgy, but he did not hesitate to add that he also dabbled in making various alcoholic beverages. Not only did he take great pains to construct the most lethal of weapons; he had a great love for making jewelry. The very first piece that he ever made was a necklace of interwoven gold ropes which held an embedded emerald drop when he was only sixteen. His beloved friend Alida never took it off.

Nida of Galagan was a master healer who knew every property relating to Herbology. There wasn't a poultice that he couldn't combine from things other persons would walk over without taking any notice of thousands of times. His twin, Alida, small though she was, possessed a level of fighting craft and deftness in the wielding of every conceivable weapon. Without a doubt, pound for pound, she was the most capable warrior among the group.

It did not come as a surprise to Shamus to learn that Erladoch's ábaltacht revolved around mind-dancing. His friend's telepathic skills were both a natural gift from his Strahana ancestors, but also a highly disciplined craft which he had worked carefully on all his life. With the return of the Evil One from the Great Pit, however, wielding such a power had to be used both sparingly and for the briefest of moments wherever possible. Entering the dreamscape meant risking detection by Enilorac himself. Many of the strongest mind-dancers of this age had already become ensnared by the Evil One's dark enchantments simply by having ventured into this ethereal space. Shamus had seen for himself the toll which had been taken on his friend's vitality when he had come to his aid the night that he had nearly succumbed to the black magic of Enilorac.

***

The more the Travelers walked, the more conversations returned to the importance of the Great Itavo Stone and its three fragments. None of the Keepers had ever laid eyes on the stones, and it was abundantly clear that the hiding place of the Great Itavo was outside of their knowledge. This secret was too great to be entrusted to men. The stones which had been combined into the one Great Itavo or Heaven Stone, were hidden here on Earth in an ancient Age of Loura that had been lost to all memory. Only Anthrac himself would know how to find it, as all other members of the Strahanas were now long dead. It was horribly ironic that by the Strahanas having come to Earth from the heavenly realm with their stones, they had placed all realms in the universe at the greatest possible risk of being swallowed up by darkness now that they were no longer present to protect this treasure.

Shamus had arrived in this timeline with an understanding that he would somehow play a role in this struggle. With his recent physical transformation, more had been revealed to him. This march alongside some of Loura's greatest and noble warriors connected further dots for him in a way that he was not yet able to fully process. But there it was. They were racing against a clock to bring the White Wigget back into the world and find a way to harness the power of the Stone against a force of pure evil. That evil was ready to spray over Loura like a pressurized pipe threatening to explode. He was that carrier now, as had been at least one of his immediate ancestors, if not countless of his forbears before him. They would have to learn more about the fate of the Wigget's fragment. Shamus reasoned that it would be needed somehow in assisting their collective efforts.

Returning now to Loura was entirely purposeful. Shamus considered his own personal experiences. There had been both portents, and even Biblical warnings during the ages of 'recorded history' where the Master of Hell was feared to one day find a way into the corporeal world of humanity. Armageddon, at least in Shamus Bergin's timeline, was a known and feared phenomenon shared by many Faiths. His own Catholic upbringing spoke of the end of days in tremendous detail.

"The End of Times", Shamus voiced. "Hell, back where I am from, we even have a Doomsday Clock that measures whenever we edge closer to it." Despite the religious portents, that day had simply not yet arrived. Even though many Hollywood stories had been told of unrelenting efforts by Satan and his legions in utter horrifying technicolor, no one could say when or under what circumstances the Darkness would finally swallow up the Light.

Shamus trudged along. He hadn't noticed that he had pulled ahead of his group or that conversations had ceased. His mind was busy with his own thoughts. His head was beginning to spin with what he was learning for himself and his 'guest'. Even though Erladoch had taken time soon after they had become friends back in Ottawa to reveal his most dire quest, the notion that the Evil One had already found a way to inject even a single of his servants into this world was unsettling. By combining the Snake Lord with Enilorac of Treborg as he had, Satan was already so close to bringing about his plan. No one of Shamus's Modern Age had any knowledge of the people of Loura. Nothing of their civilization had been found, or at the very least, nothing of their age was associated with this age, other than perhaps the few stone relics scattered across fields in places like Ireland, England and parts of the European world. These dolmens and stone circles had been misinterpreted, *or possibly* Shamus thought, *deliberately misrepresented.*

Certainly, these magical places had never been properly associated with anything of merit, not really. The people of the Modern Age who continued to unearth the Dolmens and places of significance like the stone circles seemed to consistently 'get it wrong' on every level. They were wrong on the level of sophistication of the people who had constructed these places, and they certainly had no clue what these places represented. *Or did they?* Shamus calculated again. *Could modern people of my time really have had no idea and no evidence of these people? Or did the Keepers simply conclude that it was just better to let historians spin their wheels?* He mulled these thoughts over for some time. The Travelers left him to work through this as they followed along.

Shamus had only very briefly been exposed to modern-day Keepers. He could not discern from the very brief interaction he had experienced with these people so far what the full extent of their knowledge even was. *Perhaps* he assessed, *they didn't possess all the facts either about the use of such places of importance. Nah! That's crap!* He concluded. *At least some of them possessed the True Knowledge. I wouldn't be here otherwise.* Accepting this basic truth, Shamus was suddenly awestricken by how careful and meticulous the Keepers across the ages must have been to start erasing clues surrounding the Standing Stones in such a fashion as to befuddle the people of his own timeline. His mind went into overdrive. He began to question not only the details around Armageddon as spoken of by St. John and others, but also why such details were even allowed to be shared. Was it accurate at all? Or was it just a reminder for all people to not take the Light for granted?

How could the dice have already been cast? And here? Shamus puzzled. *the final battle for all the souls of man would happen in 'this time'? Not 20,000 years forward in the age of modernity from which I've come from?* Shamus felt his heart begin to race even though his walking pace was beginning to slacken for the first time in many hours. *Was the timeline already fractured in some way? What did the Keepers of my time know? Or Not Know? Or...*He considered further, *Could they not have known what happened here because...because...*he hesitated. The answer was elusive, *because whatever takes place will cancel something or everything from happening.*

Shamus needed to bring order to his thoughts. Conclusions were forming, but his scientific mind doubted whether anything of what he was working through was even reliable.

The Master of the Pit has worked out a way where he might enter Earth in a point in history, a time where man would be least able to resist him. The future timeline was at stake. The Age of Loura would become the entry point for Satan and his legions to overcome the Light. To win, however, he would have to find the last part of the Wigget stones cleaved from the Great Stone under the mountain. *Anthrac's Stone is the key to everything!* he told himself. The devil's human puppet Enilorac has been sent here to prepare the way. He is on a quest to find the stone so that he can free his Master from his eternal prison realm. He is a physical 'toehold' in this moment in time for the Master of the Pit. Until this minion recovers Anthrac's last piece, the Itavo will lay lost and unfindable. Shamus reminded himself that he was bearing the White Wigget within his body, here, in Loura. "Oh! Sweet Jesus!" he exclaimed in a voice loud enough for everyone in his company to hear him. He was ostensibly astonished, confused at his blindness in not fully realizing his full part in this struggle until right now.

"How did I not see this?" His feet suddenly planted firmly in the soft earth, unmoving. The weight of his intellectual effort caused him to stop as though there was a conversation moving too fast in his mind from his guest for him to both control his bodily motion and still work on 'the details' he was now coming to grips with. "I'm no less a puppet than Enilorac himself! Oh, Good God! I'm going to have to face this creature that nearly ended me in my dreams!"

The Travelers had stopped dead, looks of complete horror building in all their faces. Shamus caught sight of their reactions. Too late, he realized that he had called the Evil One by name aloud. He had summoned Enilorac's attention to him. To all of them!

The pain of realization suddenly erupted inside Shamus's head. He instinctively attempted to physically defend himself from the anticipated attack by covering the scars surrounding his heart. They seemed to suddenly burn as though acid had been dripped over their surface. As though a blanket had covered his eyesight, Shamus no longer knew where he was, let alone where he was going. He was no longer in the company of the Travelers. It was as though he had stepped sideways into a different reality.

Shouts, which sounded like whispers from his companions, buzzed all about him. This was the only confirmation that he would get that while he could not see them, they were still with him, albeit detached from his experience. Chanting voices broke out and pinioned themselves like a shield against the approach of shrieking, guttural howls he could hear climbing over hilltops and ripping through tree boughs. Shamus was immediately engaged in a conflict with a force that was invading his mind from the air.

The members of his company were fully attuned to something most foul descending upon them, its intention fully focused on the Wigget Bearer. They did not have to be mind-dancers themselves to know what had befallen their strange colleague.

Shamus started flailing his hands, hoping to fend off the invisible attacker as though wasps were flitting about his head attempting to sting him. By uttering the forbidden name aloud, he had permitted the Evil One a laser-guided focus on himself. As he panicked, Shamus experienced a part of himself chiding his weak-mindedness. He registered that a mortal man was defenseless on his own in blocking the malevolence which was hammering down upon him. *Idiot!* he told himself before his thoughts and senses shifted again.

Shamus's eyes filled with dark clouds. Flames erupted across his field of vision as if he had stepped into the mouth of a volcano. Even though his travel companions did not see this splitting of worlds, they felt the massive approaching dread and struggled not to cower in terror. Shamus was suddenly caught between two planes of existence now, and he saw the middle space in technicolor. He heard it too; as though he was right back in his bedroom at 21 The Driveway in Ottawa, picking up right where he had left off with the thunder of the metal-shod feet of thousands of Scrags parting for the Evil One to make his acquaintance with him all over again. This time, as the clawed hand drove toward his already scarred chest, Shamus could feel the skin giving way to burning talons sliding into him. The pulse of his heart was hammering out of control. He knew that in a matter of moments he would feel the light of his life go out with the further penetration and ripping out action that would claim his heart.

Chants from within him suddenly rose up and washed over the rush of venomous thoughts stinging him all over. The pounding of blood in his ears and behind his eyes was so intense that Shamus didn't know whether he could fend it off further. The enchanting voice of Erladoch, which Shamus had heard in this wavelike form once before, began to bellow through the trees nearby. The latter's tune was flowing through the ether and synchronizing with the song that was trumpeting inside of his own head.

The Travelers were all around the upright body of the Wigget Bearer even though he felt nothing of their efforts to prevent him from being sucked up into the air. Erladoch marveled at Shamus's body lifting off of the ground as though he had been picked up by a giant invisible hand. The Travelers' swords had come out, but this would not accomplish anything as the struggle the White Wigget and his Bearer were engaged in was not being waged on this plane. As no Scrag could be heard approaching on the wind, blades were dropped to the ground so that the Keepers could exert the strongest possible restraint of Shamus's limbs. There was little most of them could do to assist the Wigget Bearer in his struggle but tying him to earth against the unseen pull was at least something palpable.

Erladoch shouted directly into Shamus's right ear to bolster the Wigget's protective incantations bubbling up out of Shamus's diaphragm. He hoped that both his own proximity and vocal volume would serve to outplay the cacophonous caws and clacks of the Evil One's chants, which Erladoch heard as clearly as though he, too, were surrounded by such dark-winged creatures.

In an instant, Shamus no longer saw or heard any of the tumult around him. The only sensation left to him was one of falling into an abyss of blackness. O'Mara Boldar had only been a few paces behind Shamus when the latter had first called out in apparent pain. He could see the physical manifestation of the Evil One's psychic onslaught before anyone else. He had been the first to rush to the Wigget Bearer's aid and the first to wrap his strong, youthful arms around his waist. While he remained in the physical presence of the other Keepers, he experienced the buzzing susurrations attacking Shamus on a deeper level than anyone else. Being first to take physical hold of Shamus, the Evil One had somehow managed to become aware of O'Mara and was tormenting him on a level of consciousness which none of the other Keepers were experiencing.

Erladoch was first to notice that there was something amiss with the Anahimaran prince. He resolved, however, that he needed to maintain focus on his repulsive incantations and that this represented the very best possible outcome for all of them.

Shamus's head began to rattle at a furious rate. As each of the Travelers took hold of a part of the Wigget Bearer to keep him firmly on the ground, an overwhelming sense of dread overtook them. Even though they were not connected to Shamus's experience, they were still set upon by the medium which carried the menace to their location. It was as though patches of hot and sticky molasses were slapping down onto their skin only to tear away as an all-encompassing buzz of invisible insects threatened to sting every inch of their bodies.

As the dark enchantments persisted, the volume of Erladoch's voice rose and fell in the tongue of the Angels. Shamus's eyes were open but entirely vacant. His mouth opened and closed, but he made no utterances which could be heard above the din of the psychic assault gripping the Travelers. Without warning, his feet came back down to rest on the uneven terrain of spongy moss-covered rocks. Shamus buckled at the knees and began to drop. Nida and Alida moved in concert with his fall on either side of O'Mara, just in time for the three of them to soften Shamus's crumple.

As the Travelers released their hold from Shamus, Erladoch drew his sword and yelled to the air, "Seo e Fiorling! Blas a gearradh!" (*This is the sword Fiorling! Taste her cut!*). In one singular arc, he swung Fiorling straight across Shamus's chest, coming as close to his friend's body as possible without so much as trimming a fiber of his friend's cloak. A pulse of light exploded outward from Shamus's chest that was so powerful the entire party was thrown off their feet. All about them went dark as Naga finally dropped beneath the horizon.

***

Chapter 24
Conversations

Shamus was adrift. His mind was combing through Louran history. The stories that had been told to him seemed to pass by his consciousness as though he were flying above the ground, watching movie reels that were set to fast-forward play. He mulled over the several conversations that he had already engaged in with his travel companions earlier in the day. He pondered the existence of Anthrac Aran and the devotion to this near-mythical being that they seemed to revere, even though one insight he was experiencing suggested to him that the Keepers absolutely should have rejected him for his having abandoned the world. With the passage of time, and so many ages having elapsed in relative tranquility, the stories of Anthrac Aran and his people who could fly through the air, disappearing and reappearing at will, had all but faded into obscurity in the minds of Lourans. A thought imposed itself that the Strahanas could have done more for humans in the Age of Loura and instead, they were self-occupied and not worth all the trouble. Shamus found the negative judgments he was making about what he had been told 'curious', but his mind was moving too quickly for him to dive more deeply into the reason for why he was even assessing such ideas.

His mind shifted to the people of Loura. The societies of Loura had enjoyed much progress after the Strahanas had vanished. They made advances in everything from construction to agriculture. Houses weren't simply made of mud and twigs or piled stones anymore. Complex geometry was emerging, and houses were often being made of enduring stone and wood combinations, with tunnels of clay pipe for plumbing running through them. Water from mountain lakes had been redirected through systems of aqueducts to multiple catchments in many of the towns. Even the obscure Bodelandish people of the trees took to making their communities amidst the trees of the Great Forest, finding ways over time to hollow out dwellings and passageways inside the non-living portions of the massive thousands-year-old pillars. Music, the making of fine clothes and even commerce between kingdoms was emerging over the past centuries to a point where the Louran kingdoms were engaging in active systems of barter for materials not readily available in their own kingdoms. Humans had done this! Not the Strahanas! They were useless to the world, each and every one of them!

The telling and retelling of stories of the White Wigget and the Strahanas simply faded from lack of relevance until the notion of an Angelic colony living among humankind was no longer even believable.

No one needed them!

Shamus felt a gesture of punctuation aimed at his thoughts again that didn't feel organic. These double-edged and layered interruptions to the narratives his mind was replaying were becoming pervasive, but he didn't know why they kept coming or whether he could even stop himself from editorializing.

There had been so much woe and suffering in the world of man, and yet the Keepers had hitched their hopes to a forgotten and redundant being who didn't care about the fate of humans one little bit! *He hid like a coward and paid no attention to their suffering! I should be done with this irrelevant leach on my soul!* Shamus heard himself proclaim. *For that matter,* he realized, *who do the Keepers actually serve? No one but themselves. They are a bunch of murderers who should be wiped out of existence for all time!*

None of his thoughts made any sense, but anger was roiling within him in a proportion he had never felt before. The building rage was entirely directed at the Keepers. *The Keepers are deceivers! They are the enemy of all men!*

The active voice in his mind told him that he wanted nothing more than to kill something right now, to strike it down, starting with the Keepers traveling with him.

Hold on! Shamus exerted himself. *Do I though? Why would I want to do such a thing?* He hesitated, trying to sort out his emotions that were feeling completely out of whack.

An answer seemed to flash to him as though he should accept this as his rationale. *Only the Keepers remain to continue the memory of the Strahanas, the Stones and all of the conflicts which once threatened to overwhelm the lands. They are the ones who make all the trouble! With them gone and the stones taken away by someone who would know how to dispose of them, all of this would simply go away. You can do this.* The voice had grown even more emphatic, and probably because of the sudden discordance, a part of Shamus awakened to the fact that he might not be the one thinking the thoughts which kept pushing themselves across all other conscious reasoning. *That felt like someone else telling me what to do rather than me actually making such a conclusion*, the rational voice took momentary hold within him once more. His head was starting to pound as though different parts of his brain were processing stimuli from multiple points that threatened to tear his cortexes apart.

Ah yes, the stones. What of the one remaining Stone, Shamus Bergin? You know where to find it, don't you? came the question in his mind, momentarily interrupting his efforts at assimilating the points of conflict. *Why would I know this?* he protested to himself. *These are not my thoughts! Who the hell is asking?* He asserted himself just as a familiar song was gnawing at the edge of his mind. It was remote, almost inaudible, but it was like the hand of a frozen child rapping on a large wooden door in a violent storm, imploring to be let inside.

As if in answer to his question, Shamus drifted immediately back to his fateful night of black dreams in his condominium in Ottawa. That had been the most terrifying moment of his entire life! As the song increased in volume, he recalled the dream once more. He had come face to face with the Evil One. Suddenly, Shamus was no longer floating freely in his thoughts, and certainly he was not walking now.

Where am I? he asked the distant voice in the darkness as he reflexively clutched protectively at his chest. Immediately, he was afoot in a forest so dark he couldn't see anything but shapes of tree trunks surrounding his field of vision. Shamus now heard a voice which he identified as that of O'Mara Boldar. The Anahimaran prince was not speaking to him. Instead, he was passively narrating the devastation of his kingdom over his own thoughts of horror which flitted away under the pressure of competing voices. The speech was being delivered to someone, *no*, Shamus adjusted his focus, *had been delivered to someone*. O'Mara seemed resigned to the destruction as Shamus heard the tale being told in his ears, *no, not my ears, in my mind*, his own voice interjecting in an effort to sort through the muck. He was not walking with

O'Mara Boldar right now; he didn't know where he was at all. But there it was, the replaying of O'Mara Boldar's discussion continuing undaunted like a broken record. It sounded rehearsed, like a whisper telling him that he had to accept the narrative and comply with everything he was hearing. *Comply? Comply with what?* he flailed momentarily again as if to clear away the claws of an aggressor from his chest, then he was drifting through the narratives again, unconcerned about anything.

By O'Mara's telling, the Anahimarans simply had had no time and no chance to organize a large force to repel Treborg, even though, like all those assembled in this group, Boldar was indeed both a Keeper and a member of the Royal Bloodline of the people of Anahimara. Navigating how to not reveal his position in the Sacred Order and still find a way to convince his kinsmen that a threat was soon to be imminent following the apparent disappearance and believed death of Erladoch Dunbar was almost insurmountable. *And who cares anyway?* came a remote whisper once again. *He can't help you, he can't help anyone; he is but a man!* gurgled the voice, which instantly changed back again into tones of O'Mara simply carrying on with his tale.

"Erladoch the VII of Dunbar, the Brave of Fior Hill, was known to be a well-traveled and outspoken politician, with skills beyond his years, but he is dead," O'Mara's voice answered in the darkness.

No, he's with me. Shamus countered.

Impossible! Shamus heard the voice dominating him reply to the unseen voice of O'Mara. *He was traveling in lands adjacent to the kingdom of Anahimara when news of his death was caught on the winds. The horn calls had proclaimed him as having been lost.*

O'Mara's voice also felt it necessary to correct the understanding of the questioner inside Shamus's head. "The Prince of Dunbar lives, Lord. He comes ready to challenge the darkness which has afflicted these lands, to end this conflict once and for all."

As this conversation echoed through the dark mindscape, Shamus experienced a sudden thrust toward his heart.

Conflict? Conflict, is it? came the bitter cackle of a voice Shamus finally identified as being utterly foreign to himself. *There need not be any conflict, Shamus Bergin!* It was filled with venomous rage now as it came at him again. *Enough games! Submit to me! Place a dagger in Dunbargin's brain and then slit your own throat. You will be free from the White slime within you! Doooo iiiit!*

"I won't! Get out of my head, you evil bastard! I see you now! Be gone!" Shamus's mouth worked for the first time. The proclamation of his will against the darkness invited an immediate response in the form of crushing pain. He felt as though a massive hand had wrapped around his back and was driving him forward into knives that were breaking through the surface of his skin.

Before the expected punch-through of his rib cage could occur, a barrier made entirely of light surrounded his entire being. It was an animated energy source that lunged back against the plunging knives. Something, or someone, was shielding him from harm with a protective spell, which gathered light into a psychic barrier. Upon its assertion, Shamus's mind shifted once more, taking him away from thoughts of his imminent death. He was no longer in a dark forest; he was sitting on his bed in Castra. Nica Bodelander was recounting the story of her having heard the news of Erladoch's death and how it had been received.

Jaysus! Shamus thought to himself. *How did I get here, and why is Nica telling me this right now? Why does the conversation keep coming back to Erladoch?* As he mulled this over, the pain, which had been searing into his chest, eased. He imagined himself as being fully in Castra, a safe place which Erladoch had taken every ounce of his remaining strength to guide Shamus to only a few weeks ago. He was back there now.

Nica's voice was the only sound in the room. The room, which looked every bit the one he had first awakened in at the heart of the Bodelandish capital. Nica was telling him a story. Her story. Shamus saw her sitting on the stool across from him as though they had never left this place of refuge, even though he seemed to comprehend on some level that this was not possible.

"The passing of Erladoch the Brave of Fior Hill, First Son of Dunbar, had sounded from kingdom to kingdom. But, by the time this message arrived here from Anahimara over the winds, the facts explaining his demise were carefully filtered out to not set off a chain reaction that the Keepers were not yet ready to reveal to the masses. While the news needed to be carried forward to far-off Dunbar, it had to be refined. I saw to this endeavor personally the moment the news found its way to me. Even as it crushed my heart to admit the loss of him to myself, I knew that we had to control the messaging before it traveled further westward."

Deceivers! Dirty, dirty liars! A voice interrupted somewhere behind in shadows.

Nica continued to speak over the competing personality, which continued to slither through Shamus's thoughts, trying to re-assert its dominance.

"Telling the general leadership of any of the free kingdoms that Erladoch the Brave of Fior Hill had apparently met his end while on a secret mission to find a porthole to another time in hopes of finding a being that most people didn't even know was real, was simply not a tale that could be shared! The common people did not yet fully understand the threat that was forming. Revealing the secrets of our Order in hopes of justifying the grief of Erladoch's loss at the same time as asking for the indulgence of people who had lived completely unaware for generations of the evil that returned to Greno in far-off Treborg was unfathomable! Asking them to believe our advice that a great danger was coming was not going to be well received." She hesitated a moment. "It wasn't well received." Her voice trailed off a further moment more as though static was interfering with the message. "The politicians who had come to share power with the ancestral royals of our houses were angered even by the much-edited version of what we started to share."

That's because you are all liars! the other voice spat. The image of Nica sitting in front of him faded momentarily, then reconstituted.

"Don't forget that royal birth is not necessarily the basis upon which the members of our Order are chosen. It is a question of bloodlines staying tethered to the Angealkind, plain and simple. That means that even some members of the royal houses themselves were kept in the dark about our existence. They were none too happy to receive our disclosure, and they were angered beyond words that the prince of the largest kingdom in Loura would recklessly venture off and disappear as he did. Ya see, Shamus, the thought of a prince journeying into a land known to be inhabited by crazy Mountain Scrags was, on its own, hard to explain to regular folk. It made no sense at all really! It was an accepted fact that Lourans who were daft enough to challenge the wild Mountain Scrags in their harsh and desolate domain would meet an untimely end. No one ventures upward, let alone over the Elec Mountains! Not for hundreds of years had anyone thought to undertake such an act, or so t'was thought. T'is a place of pestilence, Treborg. The things which had been said about the fallen kingdom after the war were true enough when we let such stories be spread to our people. Only foul deeds could be expected for you if you were fool enough to venture that way."

It's what they deserve for interfering! came the guttural voice that was so discordant from Nica's intonations.

"One would be assumed as foolhardy to do such a thing." Nica's voice resumed control even as it ironically seemed to agree with the competing voice. As Shamus listened to her, a part of him could now see past her body. The wall behind that had been present in the room of his tree castle was not there. He knew that he was simply replaying a sound file from his recent memory. Nica had told him these things much earlier in the day as she had strolled alongside him. This was not a conversation which had happened inside of Firren. "As generations passed following the Treborgan war, Scrags became fewer and fewer in the kingdoms of the west, or so it had been said. Non-Keepers had no idea they had been drawn over the Elec Mountains and were now serving the dark purpose of the Evil One. Breeding an army, they were, as we now know. But, to common folk, the advice of a parents' warning to children was simply designed for them to behave and never stray too far from home, lest they actually encounter a beast that they couldn't best with their farm implements. "Tend to the flock close to home, or you'll attract the crazy mountain marauders!" That was just a thing people said now that Scrags seemed to have died off. So long as people bordering the Elec Mountains didn't climb its slopes, they were unlikely to meet an actual Scrag. If such backward people as they were still walked in Loura at all, they had become shy of us to the point that common folk assumed they had migrated elsewhere. The Keepers kept a watch for them if they happened to come over the passes. We kept our borders safe in secret. That had been enough until the Dead King of Treborg returned. After there had been evidence of greater-sized hunting parties of Scrags pushing into open country in Loura, rumors rose of the forgotten threat to the east. What the good people of Loura had no concept of was just how many Keepers were standing against this emerging threat in the shadows. Full-blown warfare was coming, and we knew it. Erladoch's very mission was designed to seek out our founder and savior while there would still be time. Of course, I didn't know all these facts myself till Erladoch's return. He still has some apologizing to do, that one." She spoke as though no forgiveness was truly required. "When he was believed to have fallen, enough was shared among the ranks of our order that we did begin to organize armies beyond ourselves, though. I think now that it may have been too late, however." Her voice trailed off as the screech of the competing voice overlaid itself on this memory trace.

Of course it's too late! The voice cackled and roiled, utterly amused by all the information it had managed to pull out of Shamus's mind. *You, you impotent fool! I am coming for all of you! You will bow before me and beg me to cut off your heads rather than let my beasties make a meal of you while you still breathe your last agonizing huffs! Now get out of my way and let me finish this dog from the future realm or suffer my retribution!*

Nica's silhouette was gone, as was the vision of the room in Firren. Shamus was back in the wilds and the sting of sharp nails pressed for their advantage against the light barrier protecting his chest once more. Erladoch had to have been the one maintaining this protective spell; that's why he kept coming to Shamus's mind. Shamus could sense that his friend's efforts were weakening. He needed to stop allowing himself to drift away as his means of self-protection. The strategy of self-detachment was an ineffectual one. The Evil One would soon win. He needed to find a way to join Erladoch in repelling the imposing darkness while the latter could continue to remain inside the ever-changing scenes of the mindscape in which Shamus had lost himself. He wanted so desperately to add himself to the struggle, he truly did. Each time he felt the surge of the Evil One's claws against his mortal flesh, however, he chose escapism as his option. He did not want to be where the Evil One was, even if that meant his soul might come away from his living flesh.

***

In the four years between Erladoch's apparent demise, O'Mara Boldar had managed to convince his father and his uncle that more of their strongest folk should be schooled in warfare. The practice of wielding a grain farmer's commonly used tools for the cleaving of grains could easily enough be re-purposed into the 'weapon' it had once been. It had been a thousand years since the Anahimarans had turned their scabber spears and single-hand-wielded collapsible scythes into tools of agriculture. It would not have to take long to change the practice back. Every Anahimaran knew how to swing such implements! The men and women of O'Mara Boldar's land were fully adept at the swaying motions required to cleave grains from the ground on a short-stroke pole and fruit from the trees overhead with a longer one. They simply needed to be instructed on how to do so as they fought alongside their kinsmen on a field of battle so that they could function like an army. Changing farmers into warriors overnight, however, required more than technique. It required a grit that peaceful folk lacked. (*A sour cackle reverberated over the sound file playing in Shamus's head.*) *Like it would matter!* echoed the sarcasm.

Shamus recalled that he had eyed the long pole carried by Boldar that, at first appearance, looked entirely like a six-foot-high walking staff. The leather tie about two feet from the top carefully held the lethal blade in place, which was almost entirely folded into the body of the staff. It fattened at the top end just above the hand grip. It bore a hinge of sorts at the top, which allowed the blade to pivot outwards at either 90 degrees for a scything motion, or, if flicked into a secondary recess that was oblong in the pivot area of the metal, it could recess a few inches into the straight line of the staff and become a spear.

Only in this generation had Treborg and its hordes of Scrags, once spoken of as the wild people of Elec, given rise to the renewed discussion in the kingdoms bordering it to once again begin the process of constructing fortifications and armies. These Neanderthal throwbacks, who had once lurked in shadows and were known only in children's tales of marauding cave-dwellers who attacked farms to steal livestock, were now 'organizing'.

It came as a surprise to certain members of the leadership of these kingdoms that this threat had always been there, simmering. Because the numbers of the Keepers had so greatly diminished over time, and because even the most high-born carried out their missions in secrecy, they had little to no influence in the kingdoms of Loura. Their bonds of secrecy had proven to be the undoing of the first kingdoms to encounter the power of Enilorac as his battalions began to spill over the Elec Mountains.

Oh! came the seething laughter of the other voice. *I have so many plans for you all!* So many of the spent lives of the Keepers who had each in turn kept watch for signs of activity beyond the great mountains were lost to deliberate obscurity. Even their tales of pitched battles against the growing evil simply could not be told, as there were not enough indications of the magnitude of what was happening in this other land to support the risk of revealing the existence of the secret society. *No one cares about them, Shamus! They are vile and sneaky cowards that only get in the way! Join me, let me in! I will free you of these deceivers and the pestilence that has robbed your body! You cannot resist for much longer. Join me or die!*

"Nooooo!" Shamus managed a trailing whimper of defiance. Intrinsically, he knew that these were not his thoughts but rather a cruel distraction designed to silence the internal Wigget's voice that was trying to join with Erladoch somewhere out there under the great trees. He momentarily felt the pain tearing more deeply into his chest. He 'felt' this sensation! He also now felt the warm, sticky ooze of wetness that was beginning to come to the surface. *Blood*, his mind warned him. *He's getting through to my physical body!* Blood was beginning to flow as psychic claws were working past the layers of skin and fascia to drive through his rib cage. *How is this possible?* he protested.

Hiding himself inside the narratives of the Travelers was no longer drowning out his thoughts of his own death. He needed the White Wigget to come to his aid, before he passed out. The pain became so intense in his chest that he was suddenly lost to a wholly different kind of drifting. For the first time, he felt his life slipping away.

***

Chapter 25

Shamus found himself moving toward a being, or at least a consciousness, full of pulsing light. The voices of the Travelers imploring him to fight back seemed to have faded from his ears. So, too, were the interjections of the acrid and snake-like tonalities that had been editorializing over his thoughts. A voice within Shamus told him to take respite beside this figure, as if he were pulling up a stool beside the sheltering warmth of a fire set in a large hearth after being caught out in a lashing storm. He felt calm beside this very old man. He couldn't really see him, but his mind told him that this was what the consciousness was. The voice began completing a very different narrative—one that he realized all at once he had long been waiting to hear. It was the voice of the 'counter-point'—the answer to the malice which was still trying to whisper in the other reaches of his mind.

The figure of light seemed to flicker from time to time, leaving Shamus with the impression that he had met an old Irish traveler out on the road—a figure his grand-da often described as the 'Shanachie'—a wandering storyteller. Part of Shamus knew that his life was hanging in the balance right now, but time was irrelevant in this 'in-between' space, and he felt great comfort being in the presence of the being of light as he began his tale.

He began by telling Shamus that he needed to complete the gaps so that a choice could be made at the end of their meeting. Anthrac Aran had kept as close an eye on the affairs of this world from a very long way off, as he jumped from time to time and, later on, from host to host. He wandered in and out of humankind's struggles, deliberately unengaged from their affairs, to maintain himself hidden away, knowing that even though there had been at times much evil in the world, such events did not constitute 'the time' for his return as 'The Light' was nevertheless finding a way to prevail over such incursions. Anthrac had to allow his corporeal form to diminish to truly hide from detection.

The further away he traveled in linear time from the final Age of the Lourans, the more he had found a way to better hide his essence and yet still maintain an access point, out of which he could one day re-emerge—along with the most powerful of the stones.

Some of his human hosts were so clearly descended from the people of Loura—and more importantly, the Strahanian bloodlines that continued to flow through the descendants of the kingdoms of Ara and elsewhere—that the couplings occurred consensually and without question, given the unbroken line of the Sacred Order of Keepers. Other times, as society's ability to refresh bloodlines waxed and waned, Anthrac's hosts, while still willing believers in the cause of light, were not always able to handle the burden. All Wigget Bearers who had come before had been much older than Shamus when they had accepted Anthrac's essence in; whereas he was fully unwitting, given the extreme youthfulness at which the transfer had had to take place. It had nearly killed his child-like body to accept the transference of the White Wigget from his grand-da in the old man's dying seconds. It was a ritual of blood and light magic that few Keepers would ever see—although all of them knew of its existence and were schooled in the ritual in case they might ever be called upon to join in it.

It was thought best to not initiate Shamus into the Society of Keepers, given the risk of detection. Shamus was thus deprived of some of the talents that his colleagues were schooled in from a young age, with the only exception being that of his martial arts training. This he could do without attracting any attention to himself or his illustrious family, and so, his education began early. The Evil One's plan was escalating, and his presence through human devotees in the modern era had become much too powerful. The existence of Satanic covens was even popularized under the guise of entertainment! This fact alone proved how disturbing and pervasive 'His' influence had become.

Anthrac could no longer truly hide from Satan and simply ride out the timeline. The Master of the Pit's earthly followers had become so powerful with the aid of technology that the Wigget Bearers' detection and destruction was becoming more likely. Shamus's grand-da had had no choice but to come to the boy's rescue when he had, and in turn, Shamus would have to bear the burden of his family's secret in order to protect humanity.

Even before that moment, the Master of the Pit's earthly disciples had reasoned out that Eamon Bergin was the host. All they needed to do was locate the child, and kill both him and the old man before he could grow strong enough for the jump to take place, and Anthrac would be no more.

Enchantments had been placed by the White Wigget around his fragment of the Itavo Stone, disguising it from detection. The continued power of such enchantments, however, was intrinsically tied to the lives of Anthrac's hosts. The only problem with such enchantments was that the Itavo fragment taken from Loura by the White Wigget would briefly reveal itself in tiny echoes that would reverberate into the ether as the lives of the human hosts weakened with advanced age. The Master of the Pit could sense those reverberations, and he would scour the minds of mortal men anywhere that he could when he felt its echoes, calling upon the most fragile mortals close to it through dark enchantments to do his bidding. Children were perfect puppets—easily influenced. The Master of the Pit's human devotees were determined more than ever to bring about the end of times. They had traded away their souls for lives filled with immense wealth. By the twenty-first century, they possessed both the technology and the power to wield that wealth any way they were directed.

Hiding in linear time had proven to work for thousands of years for Anthrac—tens of thousands even! As humankind became increasingly more modernized, so, too, had the risks associated with remaining in such a space in history increased dramatically.

Shamus's grand-da, Eamon Bergin, was born in 1923. In this elder's lifetime, people were still using guns, swords and bayonets on battlefields when he had been directly engaged in such conflicts. This had not been that different from the way wars had been waged for tens of thousands of years. In the century of Eamon's birth, however, war had evolved so quickly that one could now wage it by delivering bombs through the air at supersonic speeds on civilian populations with no regard for whether soldiers were even the casualties. And then, there was "the A-Bomb". Where Eamon had begun WWII by rushing an enemy position with a repeater rifle in house-to-house battles in Holland, by the conclusion of the same war, America had dropped the first nuclear bombs on Hiroshima and Nagasaki. In Eamon's lifetime, the stakes for Anthrac Aran remaining hidden within the modern timeline were growing ever more complicated by the decade. The next host would have to be young and strong enough to make the jump back in time closer to where the conflict had all begun, and strong enough to fight actual aggressors one on one.

The Keepers had resolved that Satan's earthly followers could not be allowed to kill the White Wigget and intercept the last stone of power in a modern timeline. The Master of the Pit would be enabled to rupture the prison wall encasing Hell and enter the world using modern man's technology in nuclear science against them. Mankind would be decimated in seconds, rendered into a heap of smoldering brimstone—a perfect revenge for Satan's eternal damnation.

***

Anthrac injected images into Shamus's mind. These were memories long relegated to a part of childhood that few could retain into adulthood. The Bergin family had been forced to flee their ancestral home outside the little hamlet of Doolin, Ireland. His parents and his grand-da had been forced to use one of the ancient portholes to escape a pursuit that was about to close the noose around them. The Bergins didn't know who those people were, only that they had arrived at the village's one and only church in Lisdoonvarna early one Sunday morning before the beginning of Mass, seeking to find a man named Eamon Bergin. They were men of multiple accents, none of them Irish, all dressed in business suits. They stuck out like cactus plants in a rainforest in this three-pub village.

Poulnabrone! Shamus offered almost simultaneously to the images conjured from Anthrac's internal utterance. *I knew it!* he congratulated himself. He referenced the memory of the ancient dolmen, suddenly recalling his research on the internet, which had displayed an image of the place. It had been one image embedded within so many others when his research kept leading him to places with similar geomagnetic anomalies. This image had been so eerily familiar, however, at the time. When it had popped up on his computer screen in his home, the 'Deja-vu' he had experienced had been palpable. At his tender age, he would have had no memory and even less understanding of the sacrifice that had been made for his well-being on 'that day'. He likely didn't even recall the priest that baptized him and came to visit his family regularly in their home, which looked out onto the Cliffs of Moher.

Monsignor Frank Nolan, the parish priest, had an instinct for men of ill will, himself having fought in the Second World War before coming to the cloth. He had known the Bergin family for years, and he knew that old Eamon was considered nothing more than the town drunk since returning from the war. People liked Eamon fine, but they left him to his ramblings when he was on a tear. Eamon's lapses in sanity were understood for what they were by the monsignor, however. He alone held a different opinion of Eamon, having fought alongside him in that war, and other conflicts most would never learn about.

Many a damp, salty night, locals would puzzle themselves over an all-too-regular scene of the two men quietly enjoying a pint at the back of one or another of the Doolin pubs. In those moments, Eamon Bergin seemed to be on his best behavior; sober-looking even. Just as anyone might consider the old man's behavior to be downright normal and start to muse over what the two men might be talking about, he would fall into expected character and start a rant while the priest simply looked on, his face placid, his hand reflexively reaching forth to the elder Bergin to draw a sign of the cross toward him. That was always enough for the townsfolk to go back to their own business lest they be accused of eavesdropping, which, of course, they were doing to the level of a sport.

Monsignor Frank Nolan still proudly displayed a cherished photo of his comrades-at-arms from his platoon on the mantel of his small hearth in the rectory at the back side of the Church of the Holy Rosary. It was a simple enough church, not even two kilometers outside of Doolin on Route 479, right at the crossroads. Its smooth, white exterior walls gave no signs of the opulence found in some churches, but it was a center for the community all its own, and there was a wealth that came with being the spiritual leader of such a community.

Oftentimes, the old monsignor recognized the irony of so proudly displaying a photo of his warrior side in the heart of such a holy place. Such was the complexity of the oaths he had taken in his life, however, both of which he held in equal reverence as the rudder to his life's work. It never occurred to him that he might ever regret identifying this other part of himself. Many Irishmen had gone to war after all. The men he was most closely bound to in his life served as a constant reminder of his own burden, one that would not be erased with the years.

As he heard the creaking of the door to the Sacristy open an hour before anyone was due to help with preparations for the early morning Mass, he instinctively suspected that trouble had found him. He turned from his vestments closet and caught sight of the group already positioning themselves around him. He could think of but one solitary reason why men dressed in thousand-dollar suits that failed miserably at concealing holstered weapons would come to this tiny spit of a village, steps away from the coast. They were looking for the old drunk, and they were entirely unconcerned about the priestly clothes worn by the old man or the place they were standing inside of. The punches started landing on Monsignor Frank with fast and vicious ferocity.

Shamus realized that he wasn't being told this by the being beside him so much as he was being provided 'images' of these details. The images of this man's sacrifice were so real as if he was being enabled to stand in the room where the monsignor met his violent end. He could see the old priest's hands and legs had been tied to his chair, blood from his puffed-out left eye and both nostrils spotting his white frock. He could feel the man's thought just then, *When they are done with me, they'll search my house. Damn it! I'm so stupid!* Frank Nolan had no thought for his own survival. Even had he been able to sense their approach in time to release the Sig Sauer pistol from beneath his desk, his advanced age would have left him only enough time to maybe fire off one shot before becoming overwhelmed. His secrets were too important to be disclosed.

Had the suited men had time to do so, they would have seen the tattered 'black-and-white' photo of Eamon resting up against a Sherman tank beside 'Frankie' Nolan, each of the men's names scrawled underneath them together with another of their dearest comrades. Beside them in the photo was a civilian and a child. Beneath that, someone had also humorously inscribed in bolded letters, "THE MICS", which had been the title their platoon mates commonly referred to them as. They were flanked by a Canadian guy nicknamed "Browse the Mouse", who was their medic. He was somewhat short, but his nickname was more about his ability to get in and out of tight places quickly. His friends in his unit loved to introduce him as "Browse the Mouse" or "Silas, for short". While their joke didn't make any sense to anyone else, these brothers-in-arms would break up all over the place thinking that they had said the funniest possible thing ever, no matter how many times they said it. The two civilians depicted with the trio of soldiers wore the obvious garb of death camp inmates. Their arms were interwoven with each of the other men's shoulders. Beneath the boy's feet was inscribed 'Yacov'. Under the adult male, who looked like the child, was written the name 'Hyman'. While it certainly appeared that the people depicted had been brought together by complete happenstance, the photo commemorated a lifetime bond that would never be broken. For the three soldiers in the worn-out picture, there was already a bond forged by comrades-at-arms. They were members of a most ancient society, the oldest of such organizations, one in which the rescued man and his nephew had been identified as belonging to and who required rescue. All of them would be joined in a most singular purpose; that of ensuring Eamon Bergin made it through the war, and for that matter, his entire life in one piece. Keepers all.

As it turned out, however, the reason the malevolent figures assembled in the church rectory even knew how to look for anyone named 'Eamon Bergin' at all was because of an intercepted communication between a high-ranking priest in the Vatican and a Rabbi in the Synagogue of Rome, which had named the monsignor as Eamon's protector. 'Protector of what?' These dark figures had no way of knowing for sure, but they came with the full might of a private army intent on finding out and then wiping whomever this protected party was out of existence.

Shamus's mind vacillated from complete fascination to momentary and fleeting physical flashes of chest pain as the old man's final minutes were conveyed to him by his internal narrator. The being of light seemed to glow more brightly whenever those thoughts interrupted his storytelling, as if he was waving a hand to flick off an errant mosquito. The extension of light would then settle as the voice of Anthrac resumed. Shamus settled back into his state of detached fascination. He had not encountered the White Wigget in this way before. At most, Anthrac had been a second level of thought, which he considered to have been part of his own intuition; not a distinct entity. This 'dialogue' was causing him considerable agitation as he struggled to assimilate all the stimuli that was coming forth, while still preserving the calmness that the space created by Anthrac required for the dialogue to unfold. As he felt occasional flashes of pain coursing through him in the greatest of slow motion, he knew that the Wigget needed to close this loop for Shamus for a reason.

Monsignor Nolan's torture was interrupted only by the sheer luck of his having to say Mass at 9:15 a.m. that morning. The townspeople heard their beloved priest's wails of anguish as they approached, mostly on foot, to the Holy Rosary at the appointed hour. While there was a small parking lot adjacent to the church, few needed to drive there. This interruption would not prove to save his life; however, only prolong it momentarily. Only the backs of nondescript dark-suited men could be seen rushing out the side door into waiting Land Rovers that had been left running just down the lane. All thoughts were on the well-being of their priest; no one thought to give chase. Before he passed away, Monsignor Nolan managed to get one of his parishioners to bring him a phone.

The images flashing like a fast-forward video in Shamus's mind switched back and forth between the church rectory and the home where Eamon Bergin now picked up the phone on the other end. The Bergin family farm sat high up on a cliff overlooking the seacoast not three miles from town. The Bergin family had been planning to attend Mass at 11 that day to let little Shamus sleep. When Eamon drew the receiver to his ear, he could immediately hear the labored breaths of a man dying. All he could hear his friend manage to say through his final blood-strangled breaths were two simple words, "Danger close"—an expression that they had learned as soldiers to signify that the enemy was upon them.

Anthrac now addressed Shamus directly for a moment. Pure thought took the form of an active voice, "I know all of this, Shamus, because what Eamon heard, I heard. Like all my hosts, his experiences were my experiences."

"Eamon shouted to William first, and then to your mother. 'Twas the same message that he had just heard. Your parents, like all Keepers, were highly skilled. They quickly gathered only the most important things that would allow them to establish themselves and their credentials as Keepers elsewhere in less than a minute as Eamon collected you from your bed. You were still in your night clothes when we carried you to the family car. There was a hidden goatherd's path lining the high rock-walled property that was just wide enough for their car to navigate out of sight from the road, which the dark vehicles were already speeding upward. They ascended toward the house like a storm cloud, blasting through the iron gate as they came. By the time that they had arrived, however, the entire home was fully ablaze, leaving no trace of their ever having lived there. The smoke of this morning fire would attract immediate attention for miles. They'd activated small explosives for such a moment so that their attackers would have little prospect of following them or getting the message out that there had been an escape. They had even gone to the precaution when they first moved into the home of placing four medical cadavers inside a grave in a locked shed directly adjacent to the house so that, once explosions and fire overwhelmed the premises, anyone investigating would conclude that you all perished from a terrible gas leak."

"Once they got off of the sheep run, they pulled onto side roads that few, but the locals would even know went anywhere but farms. Your Da managed to make the drive to Poulnabrone to access the ancient passage hole in less than twenty minutes. This passage hole was a place of great power that had been used by the Strahanas and, even later, by the Keepers over thousands of years when the celestial forces coincided with the magnetism of the place. The only way. however, that it could have been used on that occasion was because Eamon carried with him my stone that would artificially create an alignment that would let them—and you—jump. So, this was how it was, Shamus. You probably were too young to remember any part of this having been so wee, but your parents, you, Grand-Da, with me along for the ride, all traveled sideways through the porthole: first to a place of power in Arizona, then to Greece, then to Belize, and then finally to Sweden, all through places of power that your moderns still have no concept of their purpose. It happened in an instant each time, but each time the power of the Itavo fragment opened the gateway to other places of ancient power traveled to by my brethren; it was a confirmation to the Master of the Pit and his corporeal servants that the stone was still in existence. Alas, it couldn't be helped. The pace of the jumps made it impossible for the enemy to know where or even to when we had traveled. From that point onward, they never used the fragment again, hiding it away, traveling only in conventional ways until they landed in the port of Halifax by ship, finally making their way to Ottawa, where they knew they would be sheltered with new identities."

Shamus pondered the Angel's advice. He felt as though he did have some memory of this place after all. He specifically remembered looking at the massive rock standing stones from the side of the road with fascination. They couldn't have been more than seven or eight feet high, but to a small boy barely out of his toddling years, they were immense! The even more massive flat stone that lay across the tops of these pillar stones angled like an Irish country hat, tipped just slightly to allow the rain to fall off it. What he now recalled most, however, was that this place was mostly exposed rock. It could have been the face of the moon for all he could recall. Very little vegetation grew there other than small flowers and occasional wisps of heather. He suddenly remembered the surprising unevenness of what, from a distance, looked like flat rock. He cut the bottom of his foot as his Ma dragged him by the hand at one point to keep him from falling flat as they closed on what modernists believed was a 'tomb'. They were not entirely wrong, of course. Poulnabrone most definitely had later been used by those who had not understood the full measure of the place's purpose for burying their dead. Perhaps it was this that had caused Shamus to hesitate and lose his footing. He recalled the anxious moments shared with his family as the ground seemed to tremble, even make a 'yawing' sound as his grand-da began reciting some incantation, which his parents joined in on. The closer they got to it, the more alarming this had seemed to Shamus's child self. He did recall it! He had been terrified! He struggled a moment as he did not want to go further, and he definitely remembered both the yank of his grand-da on his arm at the same moment that his ma whispered to him in the middle of her chant, "Don't trouble yerself, Shamus. We're all going to be fine." Good God! How he had missed that voice!

Shamus could feel a growing tug at his mind from another direction once again. He felt the voice of the being of light beside and within him beginning to trail off. Anthrac was winding up his tale to him. "I have carried on with an eternal oath to safeguard the very existence of humanity long after all of my Angelic brethren have vanished. Where we find ourselves now is my fault, Shamus! I was devoted to the Great Creator and was, in part, one of the reasons why our combined light vanquished darkness in a battle in the heavenly realm long before your planet was born out of nothingness. We banished the fallen into a realm of eternal damnation, and for my reward, and for those who fought alongside of me against the pestilence that had emerged in the heavenly domain, I was permitted to take a colony into the corporeal world. From there, we could travel through time holes to emerging societies in hopes of showing them ways out of darkness. Never was it thought, until it was too late, that the power of the Heaven Stone could one day be manipulated for the wrong and most insidious purpose: the possible escape and destruction of all worlds by the king of the damned. Many people have sacrificed their lives, Shamus Bergin, to preserve my light and prevent the Master of the Pit and his puppets to claim this prize. I have shown you but one such story. You must now choose to succumb to the dark force that is invading you as we speak or join in this fight with all that you have and channel the light that I now give to you.

Shamus! Shamus! Aach! I am not yet manifest. I can't do this alone!" He shouted from within, as though calling for external assistance.

Shamus felt himself falling backward again into darkness. The Shanachie image sitting placidly beside the fire was gone. The anguish of penetration pain was resurging into his chest, and his eyes clamped tightly shut. Despite the return of crippling pain, Shamus was suddenly filled with a sense of incredible pride as he came to realize he was a prime mover in the great history of this world and his own. *I am the Bearer of the greatest Angel that may have ever come to Earth*, he reasoned. *I'm descended of a forgotten heritage of an even more forgotten people sworn to bear and protect this being from a time that our world has somehow been taught to forget.* His left rib above his aorta felt ready to break apart from an external pressure. *I am singly responsible for the safety of Anthrac Aran! There have been so many struggles in my known world that have passed since the Ages of Loura without his interference because this coming war will be the one which could signal the end of times. My timeline will never happen if I don't fight right now to stay alive!* Shamus yelled at himself. As though standing 50 feet away from himself in a mirror, he implored his reflection to wake from the dark melancholia that had overwhelmed his consciousness. There was no longer the strength of joined voices that Erladoch had been inciting to protect Shamus. All of what had felt like hours of floating through levels of consciousness had flitted past in but seconds!

Either the enchantments of the Evil One will prevail over my fragile mind, or I will find my ability to fight this menace! The thought turned to louder sounding verbalizations. *If I die*, Shamus considered, *the force of Light within me will forever exist in a void as an unrealized potential. The responsibility is all mine! I must live at all costs!*

Suddenly, his fifth rib gave way to burning pressure. It made an audible 'crack' as the invisible menace pressed its advantage. Even with his eyes closed firmly shut, Shamus let out an audible wail of pain that echoed through the forest.

For God's sake man! Fight, Shamus! Fight!' He heard himself screaming in earnest as if it were another person's voice trapped in a hole somewhere deep below. It was now imploring an unknown rescuer to throw him down a rope. He could hear his last words in his own ears now over the echoes of others' emerging vocalizations. The poisonous whispers that had first overwhelmed him seemed to break apart, leaving behind an actual stench of sulfuric fumes that made everyone around him cough. A joining had occurred. The volume of Erladoch's voice had increased once more, along with the voice of the Angel within. To his surprise, yet another voice combined with the others against the force of the malice violating his flesh. This one did not emanate from the Travelers. It came from somewhere far off, that sweet voice which hovered at the edges of familiarity, now joined in perfect harmony with the others. With the appearance of the female voice, his own vocal cords began chanting in a language that his conscious mind most certainly had no comprehension of; but there it was.

Suddenly, Shamus felt a gush of warmth shower over him, coupled with the even more sudden appearance of light—bright light—bursting through a measureless darkness that all at once took hold of him and yanked him decisively from his mental prison. His eyes opened upon his travel companions. They were all standing over his motionless body. He felt the sudden struggle for air as though he had nearly drowned in a deep pool even though he was nowhere near water. He gulped it in hungrily a moment before he began to retch out the sulfur that had managed to pool inside of his lungs. He had come too close to being mortally wounded by the hand of dark magic which had found him in the wilderness. Blood was slowly oozing from his chest. He examined the source of his injury. It was plain that his skin had been pierced. Even as his lungs were purged of the foul air, the effort to expel it had brought with it the excruciating realization that at least one of his ribs was indeed broken.

"I accept my duty," he whispered to the Keepers as he worked to regain his composure, his eyelids still fluttering. "I'll go, wherever that may lead me," he said to them all before almost succumbing to the exhaustion of his internal struggle.

To Shamus, it had felt as though he'd been away, wandering in a vast empty space with no boundaries around it. How long that may have taken was unclear. O'Mara and Erladoch helped him to his feet from where he had fallen. Shamus looked around at the faces of concern for him and connected that his journey had happened in a matter of seconds, or at the most, minutes; nothing more than that. His legs were still unsure beneath him, and the pain of his broken rib sent numbing shock waves around his chest to his mid-back. He struggled to breathe and fully open his eyes.

Nida rushed a drink to his lips, which he sputtered and coughed at the taste of. The Galagan then pulled out a handful of herbs and what appeared to be a mushroom and the head of a poppy that had been neatly housed in little pouches dangling from the inside of his cloak. He spat into the herbs and then mixed them in his hands a moment by swiftly rubbing them together in his moistened palms. The mess in the little Galagar's hand appeared to bubble up in reaction to Nida's saliva. He immediately pulled back Shamus's cloak, lifted the torn overshirt, and exposed the wound to better view. Without any warning, he jabbed the blob he had made into the penetration wounds in Shamus's chest. Grabbing him from behind, he ground the concoction forcefully with the blob in his one hand and applied a chiropractic-like counter-pressure maneuver that invited a soft yelp from Shamus's lips. The maneuver was designed to reset the fractured points of his sternum back into alignment. The pain of the continued pressure being applied invited an immediate reaction, which signaled to all that the Wigget Bearer was fully back to the conscious world.

"Eraaaagh! What the hell?!" Shamus shouted at him, not even a bit pleased with the sensation. In a few moments, however, the bleeding was stopping, and the searing pain that had previously been there was gone. By the lessening of pressure in his chest, he felt, but could not verify, that the fractured bone in his chest was mending itself as if Nida had applied a glue to the reset bony structure. *More likely*, he told himself, *he'd just managed to set it back in place. Either way, it doesn't kill me to breath any longer.* Whether it was the content of the drink or the 'extra' ingredient of the poppy, his head was clearing, and his pain was no longer dominating his conscious experience.

"Yer welcome," Nida retorted sarcastically as she walked away from Shamus, muttering words that sounded a whole lot like a bird chirping to other birds. Because of Anthrac's presence within him, Shamus was pretty sure that he was calling him an idle and foolish man in his own language. Even as Nida drew further away, Shamus could hear the annoyed chirpiness of his voice going on. "Idiot! He nearly got us all killed!"

Shamus knew that Nida was right; he had disregarded the rules as though they didn't apply to him and recklessly placed them all at great risk by running off at the mouth. He hoped to make immediate amends. "I'm sorry, Nida!" he called out. "And to all of you! It won't happen again! I'm really trying to learn," he added in his defense, which at this point was starting to get old. He pulled his torn and blood-stained shirt back down and re-fastened the inside of his cloak, waiting for the Travelers to make the next move. Nothing. They stood around him, waiting. *Right!* He remembered now. *They're following the White Wigget.* It was pitch black outside now, and yet, it was clear that there was no intention of resting. The Travelers were already lighting torches to illuminate their path; all Shamus had to do now was walk.

***

Chapter 26

The Travelers had marched for hours in silence when Erladoch signaled for them to rest as they entered a clearing in the trees. The light of the torches revealed to Shamus they were no longer beneath the towering pines. Instead, they were surrounded by a variety of leafy deciduous trees. He remarked that they were still incredibly massive and thus equally as ancient as those they had left behind in Castra. Not having pine needle beds to trod over made the ground feel considerably harder on the feet. Shamus was glad to have all the torches come closer together as the party gathered to sit and share food. There was a nip in the air now, cold enough for him to see his breath in the torchlight even though Inyi had not yet risen in the morning sky.

For the first time since starting out the day before, Shamus saw the provisions that had been packed for them. He was pleasantly surprised to enjoy a meal of dried meat and fresh fruit. He couldn't discern what the meat was, but it tasted a lot like beef jerky. He thought better than to ask what it was in case it was something that might alarm him, like rat. It mattered not. His mouth was salivating like a wild beast's when he took his first few bites. The fact that so much of the food packed was fresh suggested to Shamus that their voyage to Gol would be reasonably short.

All the members of the party sat eating in a reservedly quiet manner. What conversation had been exchanged before their break had been brief, in low voices, and not with him. Shamus took it all in stride. *And what could they have asked me, really?* he considered. *They have no understanding of the world from which I come.* Perhaps the only bothersome thing to him was that Erladoch had said absolutely nothing to him since his regaining consciousness. Likely, he was annoyed with Shamus for having made such an utterly stupid utterance of the Evil One's name. It had been reckless beyond all good sense! This he knew. But it had happened, and he had come out the better for it, had he not? Whatever the reason, Erladoch had devoted his time walking in the darkness separate from the Travelers and most certainly out of Shamus's line of sight the entire time.

Shamus began to feel awkward that no one was engaging him. Everyone else quietly whispered to the person next to them. He elected to sit closest to Andor Seth, who happily munched on an apple, making slow crunching noises that impressed upon Shamus that his mouth was literally pulverizing the fruit before swallowing it, so that he could savor every ounce of liquid in it. Between bites, he would whisper to Alida about how impressed he was by her ability to move from place to place with such speed considering how skinny her legs were. She just answered that not everyone was made to swing a battle-ax. Andor pursued this line of banter and told her that he was at his happiest making such weapons, as it gave him a sense of hope and made him feel like a man.

Alida looked over his hulking shoulders and chest for a moment. She poked his arm with her index finger, whispering loud enough for Shamus to hear, "And what a fine and powerful specimen of a man you are, Sethian." She then looked away and filled her mouth with the last of the meats she had rationed for herself.

If there had been enough light in their camp for Shamus to see Andor's face, he fully expected there would have been a considerable blush emerging under his beard. At the minimum, he could see that she had paid him a sweet compliment that had put a momentary smile on his cheeks.

Since Shamus had no rapport with his new colleagues other than as the White Wigget's Bearer, he wouldn't have known what else to say to them. Now that they had all told him their stories, what was there to talk about? As he sat digesting both his food and his thoughts about what he had learned from the Keepers in his midst, he realized that he did not yet have everyone's stories. The twins had said nothing of who they were really, other than what their roles as Keepers happened to be. Shamus had learned nothing of their homeland or their history, which he found a little odd. Perhaps it was only that there had not yet been time for them to share like the others had, especially given that they had spent more time separated from the pack than any of the other members, scouting the nearby terrain.

Erladoch had been conversing privately with the princess for some time when he stood up and menacingly withdrew his sword. Though very little light shone through the trees as Inyi was just beneath dawn's horizon, the light of the torches that illuminated their clearing displayed a frightening beauty to his sword. 'Fiorling'. Shamus had heard him refer to it more than once now. Erladoch had named it and, by so doing, tied his fate inextricably to it.

As Shamus mulled this thought over a moment, another thought beckoned him to attend to the fact that Fiorling was out!

Nida and Alida bounded like rabbits through the trees and were out of sight before Shamus could blink. He was startled by the suddenness of their movements in response to Erladoch's own withdrawal of his sword from its scabbard. He wondered for a moment whether it had been something that Nica said to him, as though she could have angered him in some way, given that he was standing directly over her with his sword out. That would not be in keeping with his personality. Erladoch was a bastion of calm and, for his time, well-mannered. It only took another second for Shamus to realize that there was no anger in Erladoch's face and that he was looking past Nica into the darkness of the grove behind her. In the passage of maybe three more long seconds, everything was made clear. All the others were on their feet and readying themselves while Shamus rose gingerly, doing his best to protect his rib injury. Though he had been healing with miraculous speed from Nida's concoction, the action of trying to push up and out of a seated position hurt more than he cared to admit.

Seeing the hesitant movement, Andor scooped a faltering Shamus under his arms and rushed with him to the center of the clearing before putting him back down. His incredible strength was not nearly as alarming as the speed by which he acted. Shamus easily weighed 185 pounds, and Andor had lifted him to his feet and carried him like an NFL lineman 15 feet away to the middle of the clearing like he weighed nothing.

The Travelers closed ranks around Shamus, watching all directions even as they extinguished their torches.

Shamus still heard nothing. Not so much as the snap of a twig made its way to his senses. The entire company of Keepers were ready, nonetheless. A gush of anxiety filled him. It felt like a full minute had passed with electric anticipation before he first heard the sound of heavy feet rumbling through the forest. Shamus placed his right hand inside his long-hooded cloak in search of his longsword, still marveling that there was ample room for his grand-da's sword, when the voice of Erladoch hoarsely whispered to him from the darkness. "No, Shamus, only your small katana; no time to explain!" Shamus obeyed immediately and ripped out his short samurai, the blade still being nearly two feet in length. He felt strangely impotent compared to his counterparts, only holding his secondary samurai sword.

They stood in the hollow a few more painstaking instants while Shamus considered incorrectly the cowardliness of the Galagar twins. They had run off at the first hint of trouble. *Some warriors they*…As this thought registered, four Scrags came thrashing through the trees into the open. He remembered the face of his first kill, the miscreant Scraggin soldier who had fallen into their hide-hole and impaled himself on Shamus's blade. The sloping Neanderthal forehead and large jaw opened wide in a mixture of anguish and relief. The scarred face, the breath, the blood! The image was overpowering, and now, once more, he had to face these sub-humans. Even in the pre-dawn light, they were once again so horribly menacing in appearance that it sent a shiver of both fear up his spine and a rollicking quiver of disgust through his stomach. To Shamus's surprise, they had not yet withdrawn their swords as they entered the clearing to find the Keepers. The wind, having been at their backs, they had not yet detected their presence. By the time they were upon the company, it was too late for them. Before Nica could slice the first ones with her sword, the first two Scrags stumbled and fell dead before her feet, the backs of their necks already revealing long and obviously poisonous darts that had stung them from somewhere above.

More Scrags began to flood into the opening, also with their major weapons still sheathed. Shamus's fellow protectors made no noise as the enemy came into the open in increasingly greater numbers. Their covert actions would hopefully prevent any warning coming to the company of Scrags, however many of them there actually were, before immediately coming into the Travelers' path.

In the space of ten seconds or less, fifteen Scrags had rumbled into the clearing to be met from behind with darts shot with deadly accuracy. Nica's greatest prowess, like so many of the Bodeland Forresters, was archery. She had already re-sheathed her sword, moved laterally to the left of the company, and started fitting and releasing arrows, one after the other, parallel to the tree line. She picked off as many of their foe as possible, knowing that the more they could take down without the clanging of metal against metal, the longer they would have the gift of surprise. If a Scrag made it through the trees without having been taken down already by the lethal darts from the Galagars' blowguns aimed from some location they had managed to ascend to in the tree branches, Nica was almost sure to get at least some of them the moment they entered the clearing.

Andor Seth had positioned himself to be the first to encounter those who were making it as far as their small clearing. He met them with drawn sword in his left hand and an immense battle-ax in his right. There was a deftness to his movements, which surprised Shamus as the colossus ran his first enemy through with his sword, only to then relieve the Scrag of his head.

The long-poled Scabber of the Anahimaran was now stabbing like a long spear in repetitive jabs into the necks of two Scrags who were still reaching to draw their jagged swords. That noise and the guttural death squeals from having been disemboweled by the others' swords gave those who were emerging from the trees the warning that all knew they would at some point get. Surprise was now gone, and full battle was being engaged. If it had not been so horrible an experience to behold, one would have to call the complimentary and highly coordinated movements of the Keepers 'artistic'. They were not just individually trained; they were clearly schooled in group fighting tactics, which made their coordinated efforts look more like a well-choreographed dance.

By sheer number of opponents, the defense around Shamus was slowly breaking down. O'Mara Boldar broke away from the protective circle the Travelers had formed, and in three wild motions, the blade that had previously been positioned like a spear became the Scabber sword resembling the one made from Erladoch's crutch many days before. It was manipulated with nimble fingers across smooth circular, and mostly horizontal pathways. O'Mara twirled and leaped until he was to the side of the trees where most of the Scrags were emerging into the clearing from. With frighteningly swift twirls of body and scabber, he sliced at various exposed areas of his approaching opponents' bodies as they appeared—cleaving the first at the neck, only to then drop, spin and take the leg off of the next.

Shamus was moved that the Keepers' first instincts were to protect him, not knowing what ability he may have to join in the fight. As he raised the katana to make ready for the first enemy to get past the Keepers, the burning ache around his chest announced to him that he would be compromised if he extended himself too much. A rush of fear made him cough out the deep, steadying breath he had attempted to take in.

With the gap made by O'Mara, Erladoch suddenly emerged from the darkness and positioned himself beside Shamus at the center of the slowly collapsing circle.

"You're injured, my friend. Let's do this together, with me taking the lead," Erladoch encouraged.

The next two Scrags to reach the midpoint of the clearing seemed to travel in slow motion compared to the speed being wielded by the sword and axe of the Sethian. He reaped through Scrag frames effortlessly, even though Shamus noted that Andor's sword had to be a good fifteen pounds; and the double-headed axe probably heavier still.

O'Mara continued to sway and dance in circular patterns toward and then away from the opening of the trees where the majority of the Scrags continued to approach from. Those Scrags with more warning, however, had begun to spread out, making it harder for the Keepers to control the scene.

While darts continued to whistle out of the darkness from Nida and Alida's hidden perches in rapid succession, Nica Bodelander had shouldered her bow and was deftly twisting her sword not far from where both Shamus and Erladoch were meeting the enemy. It became clear that this party had been dispatched to track and find the Travelers, possibly because of Shamus's encounter in the ether with Enilorac. They had been traveling with such rapidity to find the one in the Wigget Cloak that it would have been difficult for the Bodelander scouting parties to have even known they were crossing through the heart of their kingdom.

All effort by the attacking force now focused upon Shamus. A common thought was guiding them, as though someone had placed a laser pointer on his head for the delivery of a smart bomb. In response, the Keepers regrouped into a phalanx-like wedge. This physical barrier did not fully prevent Scrags from getting through, however, and the members of the company could not help but catch glimpses of Shamus's ability with the sword. Although it was a comfort to know that he possessed his own ability to fight, there was a common understanding, nonetheless, that if the Bearer of the White Wigget were to fall in battle, all would be lost.

For five long minutes, they fought on. Andor leaped from rock to rock outcropping. Nida and Alida had flitted through tree branches bordering the clearing, seeking out better vantage points to shoot their darts from until the moment when the Scrags had fanned out to a point where they nearly had the

Travelers surrounded. They alighted to the ground with swords already drawn and swinging.

Shamus was faced with direct confrontation for the first time by a Scrag who had not already been weakened by the blows of the other Keepers before breaking through to him. The grasp on the handle of his short katana was unfaltering in its figure-eight motion when this first Scrag came directly at him, rapidly closing the distance with a cruelly jagged and double-pronged spear. As the left prong of the spear glanced the edge of Shamus's right hand, he felt his entire world suddenly slow. Even the foul creature's low-pitched rumbling howl became but an echo in his ears. The tips of the spear had been pulled back by the Scrag and were now being extended only a few feet from Shamus's stomach, thrusting upward to claim purchase in the soft aspects of his chest and throat. The Scrag's iron-shod feet pounded ever closer, one after the other, digging harder into the ground to bolster the anticipated contact of his thrusting stab. Every muscle in its body rippled in anticipation of the piercing and ripping action it intended to execute; its face covered with the horrible burned boils which reduced the Scrag's eye sockets to slits. Shamus could smell the yellow foam frothing from the jagged and broken teeth in the creature's reddish-black and blue face. As the final moment of penetration was nearly upon him, Shamus's two-footed pause melted into action. He flipped forward at a 45-degree angle to the left of the spear tips as they thrust harmlessly past him. The short samurai sword parried the spear further while Shamus's body continued its sideward rotation. He landed squarely behind the back of the Scrag. As his feet met the solidity of the ground, Shamus's sword followed its path from the parry of the spear across the Scrag's Adam's apple, introducing it to a horizontal shock of cold steel. Without any ability to stop himself, the momentum of the charging Scrag passed him right through the blade. His foul head flew to the ground, still showing an expression of complete disbelief.

The pain in Shamus's chest, which had been dominating his thoughts only seconds before, faded as adrenaline fed his instinctive need for self-preservation. The archaic warrior who had taken over Shamus's body on the plains of Anahimara was not emerging, however; no one was being channeled right now. The man wielding the short katana was one hundred percent the desperate and terrified Shamus Bergin, who was consciously performing every sword kata that he had ever learned in his dojo just to remain alive. The archaic warrior that had appeared to unconsciously guide his movements on the plains of Anahimara had measured no fear, no consequences, and thought nothing of the body count he was creating as he wielded the large broadsword. That individual was fully at one with the air and the ground beneath him. There was no such dispassionate warrior courage flowing through Shamus at all! His only saving grace was the discipline of his early training, which had been made better by the polish that Erladoch had applied to that base of knowledge. Even though the archaic warrior was not moving through him, he was being guided by a bubbling rage overtaking both his fear and his disgust as he stabbed and hacked at his opponents and dodged just in time to not be stabbed or hacked in turn. Just as he was about to encounter another frontal assault, he felt his legs go out from under him from behind as the dead body of a Scrag cut down by Nica rolled into him. It was entirely serendipitous for Shamus, however. He fell as a second unseen Scrag was already halfway extended toward his right side with an Elec spear as he stumbled backward. The spear pierced the empty air, finding no purchase in human flesh. Instead, the abrupt recoil of the attacker recklessly smacked his Scraggin companion clear across the face as he brought it back. In the anger and the undisciplined lust that so occupied the minds of these two creatures, their collective attention turned momentarily as Shamus performed a back-rolling break fall out of harm's way, long enough to make room for Andor's axe to claim the spear Bearer and Erladoch's Fiorling to drive up and through the back of the other.

Shamus's short katana was nowhere to be seen in the pandemonium. A surge of panic coursed through him in recognition he had seconds before he would be set upon by Scrags intent on doing him in. The adrenaline of mortal fear surged until it suddenly surpassed an invisible threshold within him. With no further thought to his peril, Shamus reached over his right shoulder and drew out his grand-da's long sword. A wave of calm replaced the surge of panic and the overriding instinct to 'live'. With the long handle planted securely in both hands, his only thought now was to put his enemy down.

Shamus charged headlong through the phalanx that had been formed by the Travelers for his protection and leaped into the thick of the Scrags, who were still closing around the group. He met them with a violent fury and a level of enhanced skill that caused all around him, on both sides, to look upon his movements with awe.

The first beams of Inyi suddenly penetrated the clearing. Instantly, every fiber in Shamus's cloak projected a kaleidoscopic aura around him. The hood, which had previously remained tightly over his head, fell back as he jumped from one Scrag to the next, springing, flipping, rolling, all the while cutting a horrible swath through his opponents. As he leaped from his last victim's dying body, his silver hair began to emit flames of white light. The sight of him filled everyone present with wonder. As he thrashed about, licks of flame rained down a molten sweat on his enemies. Stung by this inexplicable weapon, any of the Scrags who attempted to engage Shamus immediately lost hold of their weapons and grabbed at the part of their bodies hit with the spatter.

The remaining Scrags who caught sight of this display froze in incomprehension. They had no idea what this marvel meant, but they watched slack-jawed as Shamus cleaved a path through to them, seemingly locked where they stood. This moment of hesitation gave the Keepers the needed advantage. Not possessing the same fear, but only the unified sense of immense awe at the display and actions exhibited by the White Wigget's Bearer, the Travelers powered on to finish the battle.

Shamus wheeled round and round, his eyes aflame with the archaic warrior's countenance, looking for another enemy to confront, but none remained standing in the open glade. In the early morning light, he was terrifying and beautiful all at once. Nida and Alida were already afoot, pursuing those few, who had attempted to flee blowing darts from their hollow stalks in hopes of ensuring that no one would escape to share the details of the battle.

In a moment, Shamus, like his comrades, wiped the evidence of this macabre encounter clean from both sides of his long sword, and then carefully re-sheathed it behind his back in the cache that had been specially made to house it. He felt his persona re-emerge, the one which experienced emotions of horror, revulsion and even remorse at such a grizzly scene. Unlike the battle that he and Erladoch had waged on the plain between Taroc and Ataroc, he possessed a memory of every move that the warrior who came out of his dark recesses had made. He was much more at one with this individual than he knew was possible, and in the last seconds before his own personality was about to fully re-establish itself, he saw in a flash every Bearer that the White Wigget had ever selected for his own continuation; all prolific warriors. He was sure that in time he might even slow that flash memory down long enough to get a clearer sense of who they were and how they lived, but for now, the images had evaporated as quickly as they had come.

His companions were still processing the sudden display of power they had hoped was within this man. Not knowing what else to say to them, Shamus exhaled and asked, "Is that all of them?"

The reply came with Nida and Alida scampering down the walls of the trees and securing their small bows and blow pipes behind their backs into leathery cases that hung snugly over the backs of their travel cloaks.

Erladoch patted Shamus on the shoulder in a gesture of comfort. He could see the expression of his friend's sense of horror over the carnage appear on his face despite the calmly offered question. "You couldn't help but take out the broadsword, could ya?" Erladoch was smiling as he spoke, but behind that expression, Shamus was fully aware the statement reinforced his preference that resorting to this awesome weapon had not been necessary.

"Er, yah, I know what you said, Erladoch, but I dropped my katana and—"

Erladoch raised his hand to signal a pause. "It's alright, Shamus. I saw what happened. I know that your connection to your grand-da's sword helps you to find a way to channel him. We just need to have some luck now that none of the Scraggin troop made it out of here alive. It is clear to us all that you make the Wigget's light more obvious when you summon the aid of your ancestors."

Erladoch stepped over a Scrag's carcass and retrieved the half-covered katana, wiped it carefully, and handed it to Shamus, shaking his head and seeming almost amused. "I have to say," he spoke more loudly so the entire group could hear him, "you and your ancestors make one terrifying warrior to reckon with!"

He stepped over the bodies that Shamus still stood in the midst of. There had to be as many as 70 Scrags that had attacked them this morning. Twenty-five of them had been laid waste by Shamus in less than a few minutes. The number of appreciative grunts of approval and acknowledgment from the Keepers identified that no one was going to be worried about Shamus holding his own ever again. He may not have been initiated into their Order exactly, but his ancestors clearly had been.

***

Andor was utterly pooped. He slumped down on a rock and laid his battle-ax on the ground beside him; his long broadsword already back in its husky container. First, Nica and then the others looked themselves over in a practiced way to assess the personal damage done to them. There were no significant cuts to any of them. None of the Travelers, however, had managed to avoid collecting at least a handful of emerging bruises from the skirmish. It only made sense that even the greatest warriors could not avoid the odd passing punch or kick to extricate themselves from the more lethal arc of a swinging blade. Erladoch had a minor bleeding laceration at the base of his chin, which suggested a very close call with the end of someone's blade. Nida was already attending to him, even though he was politely trying to shoo the Galagar away.

"I will not relent, Lord Prince. This can get infected," Nida offered matter-of-factly, already spitting into his herbal concoction.

Erladoch knew he was right. He gave in to the wound treatment being applied. "Aaach!" he said with an air of disgust rather than pain, as Nida applied the small mixture. "That smells horrid!" he protested.

Nica Bodelander laughed at the irony of his protest. There was so much carnage all around their feet, and yet, it had been 'this' smelly poultice that drew a protest from him.

Laughter. Shamus thought to himself as he surveyed the waste of Scraggin corpses all around them; there were so many! The warmth of their dark life's blood still vacating the dead bodies of some. The steam caused by this slowing ooze in multiple locations on the ground was unsettling in the chilly morning air. The others looked over at Nida wiping the goob onto Erladoch's small wound and all started to chuckle at the ridiculousness of his appearance matched only by Erladoch's less-than-happy facial expression. He appeared grossed out. Shamus joined in the laughter over the sheer irony of Erladoch's reaction.

Laughter, Shamus considered again. *How peculiar that Nica and the rest of the Keepers can move their thoughts away from the horror that is all around us.* He felt that some of the laughter represented the shared sense of relief they all managed to survive the sudden attack, but nonetheless, he knew that these were the most battle-hardened warriors anyone would ever encounter. It must have taken years of devotion to become so matter-of-fact about the job of killing an enemy so molded by their own malice.

Shamus wondered whether the people who belonged to the Sacred Order of Keepers in his own timeline continued the practices of war over and above the facades they lived behind. He was particularly curious about the holy people of various religions, some of whom he had met in person at Hy's Restaurant with Jacob. *Were they equally as schooled to wage war like this? Had they similarly been selected at a young age to go somewhere and train?* His mind drew a picture of so many kids he had met in his lifetime at his dojo, some of whom he had become friends with for a time. *Had they actually been his friends? Or were they Keepers in training?* He reviewed the faces of the kids he had trained. *When some of these kids went off for the summer, were they attending 'summer camp' or were they initiates into this secret society?*

He thought of his longest-standing friend, John Browse, a moment—a devoted friend whom he first met at the tender age of six. Both boys attended the same private school from the very beginning; they were signed up for Jujutsu training by their parents at around the same time—*no, exactly the same time*, Shamus corrected himself. They even studied psychology from undergrad straight through to their doctorates, although their specialties were entirely different. He realized he was missing his friend the same way he would every summer when John moved up to the cottage compound at Calabogie. *Well, at least he wasn't going to Keeper Summer Camp now, was he?* Shamus flippantly remarked to himself as he recalled the understated opulence of this large structure hidden in the woods. He didn't get to go to John's cottage/mansion at Calabogie very much as a kid, or even as a young man growing up, as there was always some function that his parents or grandparents seemed to be hosting that meant there was no room for Shamus in the multi-room country manse. He did enjoy the place very much when the invitation was extended, however.

Shamus considered the magnificence and privacy of the place, so far removed from the sight of any road, none of the property viewable by neighbors. There were none anyway, as there wasn't a piece of developed land within several miles. The sprawling Browse compound was way down at the end of the road. Everyone else that lived up that way tended to congregate either around the lodge, the golf course or the ski resort. But not the Browses. They enjoyed their privacy. Their ancestral country retreat had been off the beaten path.

He remembered himself and Erladoch training under the privacy of the trees. He also remembered how much he hated dragging toboggans full of supplies over many hundreds of meters in the snow through thick and well-forested property when the two of them left Ottawa to begin making preparation for their ultimate departure. He wondered then whether things between John and Jackie would work out. John had never really stayed with anyone for any length of time, much like himself. When they would be out drinking over the years as young men, consoling each other over the last woman who had left one of them for greener and more committed pastures, they literally manufactured a toast to console one another. It had happened so many times, particularly for Shamus, as he never believed he had yet met 'the right one' for himself. He mulled over the toast they offered each other: *Brothers from another mother. The ladies love us, the ladies hate us, but mostly, they just love to hate us. Bachelors again, brothers always, Slainte!* They would recite this private joke to each other often enough, finishing it with the Irish toast familiar in both of their homes growing up. 'To your health!' Regardless of who had just been broken up with, John would, as a habit, slap Shamus on the back and say, "Wherever we go, I'll have your back right to the end." Shamus felt a deep sense of regret in that moment as he remembered that because he and Erladoch had hidden out at John's family's private compound, it was now a destroyed heap of smoldered memories, flattened by a missile strike launched from a drone. Shamus's friend had truly watched his back after all, right to the end.

***

Nica, bruised but unharmed, downed a long sip of water taken from her travel pack. She had been mulling over Erladoch's soft reproach to Shamus. "If any of these Scraggin dogs managed to escape this skirmish, my people will intercept them before they ever leave the Great Forest, I will assure you of that." Feeling that a message of danger should be shared with her countrymen, she pulled out her multi-ended horn and blew in three separate directions: to the north, to the east and then south. It did not resonate like one would expect. Instead, the sad wail of birds echoed each time for a few moments, as if one were in distress from a predator attacking it. Its tone carried for many yarricks, however. To Shamus's surprise, in less than a minute, a reply passed on the wings of the wind to where they were assembled. It could be heard just at the edges of perception. The call had been acknowledged. A Bodelandish scout had intercepted the princess's warning call, advising that invaders were afoot in their kingdom. The scout would diligently pass the message on, but first, she would send her reply southward to where the first call had originated. The answer received back by Nica from both the north and east was clear: "Once found, the enemy would be slain with prejudice."

"Erladoch," Alida addressed the Prince of Dunbar. "Should we not do something with these bodies? They foul the land and air by their very presence!"

"Aye, t'is true what you say, Alida, but we've not the time ourselves to tend to this," he replied. "The Forresters have been summoned. They will take care of it. It is possible that this is only an advance squad of Scrags. Their lack of serious armaments or provision tells me that they were tasked with quick travel rather than a lengthy mission. I fear that there is already a much larger force pursuing us from behind."

"If this is true, Lord Dunbar," Nica interjected, "then the house of Treborg has become more daring than even I thought. By what they carry with them, I think y'er right. There is a larger force supplying them, probably less than a day's quick march from us. The Evil One's forces are apparently capable of doing more than sneaking their way through Bodeland. It looks like they're already prepared to make war where my people dwell. We must expect that he is already preparing to strike again."

"Hmm, you're right to suspect this," came Andor Seth's booming voice as he rolled over one then another dead Scrag with his soft leather boot. "The tribal markings of these Scrags suggests that they are from a point somewhere far east of the dwelling places of the Elec Mountain Scrags. This is evidence unto itself that an army has been organized and put into the field. We should make haste."

Shamus looked over at the Galagans, who were also examining the bodies of their deceased enemies. They were studying them with great interest. He addressed Alida and questioned how she and her brother were able to react so quickly to Erladoch's sudden defensive move before the first of the Scrags had ever burst through the tree line.

"Our greatest strength is our speed," Alida responded. "Our second greatest strength may be our sense of smell. We were downwind of the Scrags, and we could sense something most foul approaching long before they had arrived, my lord," she said as she took leave of Shamus and went over to where they had all been camping prior to the attack in order to collect her pack. Shamus found it hard not to want to look at the Galagars. As the only two examples of their race he had seen, they were a truly unique and wonderful pair. Clearly, they were as human as any one of them, and yet their distinctive features were like nothing he had ever seen in his timeline. With their sharp noses and equally chiseled chins, their petite body habitus, he imagined they would fit the best description of the fabled Faerie people so long spoke of by the Celts.

Shamus looked about the group of Keepers assembled around him. They were all stretching themselves upright, getting ready to move once more. Even if they were in the heart of Bodeland, it was patent they could not remain here. Clearly, nowhere was safe any longer, but these chosen few took this revelation with resignation rather than alarm. They were bonded in their understanding and in their purpose: brothers and sisters in arms, all from 'another mother'.

***

Chapter 27

Shamus had been relieved, if not happy, to be putting distance between himself and the stomach-turning stench of the Scrag slaughter grounds. To him, at least, it served as a humbling reminder that he could just as easily have been still lying there in the dirt with them; his body mangled, his life spent. It reminded him how much he treasured his own life, and this filled him with an actual sense of hatred for these awful creatures who were clearly bred for the sole purpose of ending lives with great fanfare. Still, as they were quick marching now, hoping to make their destination by or before nightfall, his humanity still filled him with regret, even shame, for his own acts of violence the more he replayed the events of the morning. He was processing how easy it was to kill when left with no choice.

Andor looked quizzically at Shamus, as though in tune with the Wigget Bearer's thoughts. "Lord Fiorian," he started. Shamus caught the label which he had been addressed with by the colossus.

Apparently, this is how some will abbreviate my name after having been told back in Castra that I was Shamus of Fior, he realized. *My fate is seen to be tied entirely to that of the Dunbar Prince.* He turned to Andor in acknowledgment of the address as much as to say, "Yes?"

"There is no pride to be won in the killing, even of these beasts. I hope ya know this. But take heart, there is meaning that you have risked yourself for the continuity of all other free creatures of Loura. Had you not raised your sword, and swung it again and again," Andor's colossal head swayed back and forth as though he were replaying the scene in his mind. Catching himself, he at once realized that perhaps he shouldn't replay quite so accurately the grizzly scene if he didn't want to lose making his point to Shamus. "The indignities that would have been given you by these bringers of death would have been unspeakable! Once, when Treborgans were an early form of men running free over the lands, one could indeed pity them. They're no longer that, however.

221

They do not belong to a noble house serving their King or bringing honor to their kinsmen. They are even less than they once were. They have not been 'right' for many ages. Their lives are a misery, lived entirely in the service of a monster. It is for this reason that we hate the House of Treborg and why we are sworn with every life-breath to vanquish them. While Lourans slept, the Keepers have kept watch over this festering and growing sore in this world. Even when Treborg had been a House populated by humankind, they conscripted these unevolved savages to serve their needs. Now, there are only Scrags beyond the Elec Mountains; made to resemble their disfigured demon master. What has been done to them is unnatural. No part of what they have become involves humankind. If the rumors bear out, then the houses that lie to the east and south of what was once the Treborgan stronghold have similarly long since fallen. This we do not know with certainty, as few have ever ventured across the desert lands beyond. Certainly, none of them ever attempted the return journey. We do not know what comes to Loura, but we know they do not come as brothers or even friends. One need only look at what has so recently befallen the good people of Anahimara (he said in a lowered voice to avoid troubling O'Mara) to know that this is a dire time for all people of goodwill."

Shamus nodded his appreciation for the comfort that Andor was plainly trying to give him for his violent actions. Hearing Andor describe the Scrags thusly, he wondered whether this was an effort to dehumanize an enemy to make their slaughter more palatable. He thought on this a while. No matter how long he mulled it over in his mind, however, he could not but see the 'less evolved' countenance of the Neanderthals which, plainly in his own mind at least, was what the Scrags were. What had been done to them in their service to an Evil Master was, he wanted to believe, beyond their ability to resist. No matter what, this was killing, and he took no pleasure in it. The fiery madness in the eyes of these servants of darkness haunted him like a waking nightmare. Andor was right about this much at least. There was no compassion for him that would ever be given. There was only a lust for murder that motivated this enemy; a compulsion to do the bidding of their dark master without any thought to another thing on the side of the Light. He was going to have to make peace with this, and soon.

***

Erladoch came along side Shamus and Andor as they maintained their quick march. Shamus decided to gain a better understanding of his friend's sudden switch from relaxing over a snack to the hyper-vigilant state he had taken up in the minute before the attack.

"Erladoch, the Galagars told me that their second-best gift is that of smell, and that that is what they were relying on when they reacted to you just before the Scrags came through the trees. I was completely oblivious to any approaching danger. How did you know that we were about to be overrun?"

Erladoch assessed what to tell Shamus. He looked over his shoulder to locate Princess Nica and O'Mara before speaking. She was nowhere to be seen as she and O'Mara were doing advance scouting. "About an hour before Inyi's rise, I felt a heaviness in the air."

"Was it an odor that Nida and Alida spoke of?" Shamus queried.

"Hmm, not for me. Not entirely at least. There was an unnatural odor just before they came upon us, and that was definitely the stench of Scrag sweat that I'm sure we all later sensed. But what I was sensing even before that was a feeling that seemed to hang in the air to the south, where we are now headed. It didn't 'feel' right. It had put me on edge. It still doesn't feel right."

"But Lord Dunbar," Andor interrupted. "The winds which gave us warning of the advancing Scrags was blowing from east to west."

Erladoch nodded in agreement. "Yes, Andor. I know," he paused, trying to explain his pre-science. "But the Ators move in all directions, my friend, even when one is dominant."

Shamus began to understand that Erladoch was not just talking about 'the wind'. He had learned previously from Erladoch that 'the Ators' were, in essence, a type of ethereal wind; like a collective spirit that motivated the wind to move in any specific direction in the first place.

"Ah! Now I understand. You speak of yer mind-dancing ábaltacht, Lord Dunbar. From the time we first met as whelps, your abilities to commune with the unseen has left me feeling like a wandering idiot by comparison." Andor was being humble, but he clearly respected the vestiges of the Strahanas' bloodline which flowed so much more robustly through him. Friends these two men were. They had been so for a lifetime. Andor wasn't much older than Erladoch; maybe 35 at best, but he towered over him the same way he did over everyone else in the party. He was such a colossus of a man, standing at 6 foot 8 and sporting a belly that matched the width of his hulking shoulders.

When Erladoch was first taken into the training of the Order of Keepers as a child, he was skin and bones, entirely uncoordinated, and possessed the strength of a flea by comparison to Andor. The children who were put into training possessed gifts. Andor's physical gifts were obvious. If it was heavy, he would lift it simply because he could. What he needed was to find a way to make his massive frame become agile. As he matured, Andor developed a scientist's mind, and it became clear to his elders that he was a natural metallurgist. Despite his massive hands, he could wind metals into the most delicately beautiful and fine jewelry, or, as he aptly showed, exquisite weapons.

Andor's battle-ax was truly unique for its time. Certainly, he was not the first to make a double-headed axe, but the balance of it made it incredibly lethal, whether wielded in the hand or thrown. The handle and hilt bore woven knots of metal that somehow managed to feel like soft wool in the hand. Both afforded a superior grip to its wielder, each metal knot made exactly to the length of Andor's own digits, and the fingertip impressions were hewn in such a manner as to only allow him the grip which could maximize the weapon's full use.

"You are the biggest man I have ever had the great displeasure to wrestle with, but an oaf you would n'er be my friend!" Erladoch felt it necessary to offer. "You cannot hear the tales of the hidden spaces in the air as your mind is too busy listening to the song that sings to your ears when you hammer metals into perfect creations."

Shamus caught sight of the colossus's pride-reddening cheeks. The big man didn't blush often. The first time such a blossom filled his face he was no more than 14 winters. Alida had watched him throw three grown men to the ground in a hand-to-hand training session in their secret enclave of Lorelai. She was so excited by the display of strength that she clapped her hands and giggled like a thrilled schoolgirl as he tossed his trainers like cordwood. The look of glee for his feat of strength made him redden like a ripe berry. He had always loved impressing her after that.

"The air song from the south has subsided, my friends, which in itself is not promising given that we head toward where I first felt its weightiness come from." Erladoch paused to put the sensation into words. "I now think that I know this weighty feeling, and yet I trust that the 'Ators' have misled me."

Perhaps fifty paces behind the White Wigget, and where Erladoch and Andor walked astride of him, O'Mara had rejoined them from his scouting mission. He quickly came alongside Alida. "I am not possessing of your keen nose, but tell me that there is not something foul coming to us through the air, Galagar," O'Mara said with trepidation as the two of them closed in on the lead pack. Nida was off climbing a tree somewhere, perhaps a half kilometer ahead of the Travelers. "What do you think this smell is that rises from the valley to meet us, Alida?"

"It is still too far off yet to be sure, but if ye must know, it is death and burning that I smell," she answered unhappily. "I wish it were not so."

This was the Anahimaran prince's worst fear being actualized. "I know this smell too well then," he shared in a lowered and barely emotionally restrained tone. "I had hoped to forget it, but it becomes more and more plain as we go forth."

This had been the smell which had hung over his homeland and blew as far as Bodeland before it finally dissipated. It hung in the air for more than a fortnight, even after he and his small army had fled across the Boldar River like beaten-down dogs, only a few passings of the moon ago. It was his greatest humiliation to not give his last breaths fighting for his homeland, but he and his men had been too late. They'd been too far off and too small to do anything but give warning to the outlying villages west of where the invasionary force from Treborg had already put every living man, woman and child to the sword.

Erladoch interjected consolingly, but also in a commanding tone. "O'Mara, you could not have known what fate would befall Anahimara while you went to the distress call of your neighbor. Believe this: your presence would not have altered the turn of events. You too would have been wasted, and the world would have seen the end of all Anahimarans. You saved whom you could, friend. Never forget this!"

"Aye!" supported Andor. "Avenging Anahimara has a chance of expression only because you walk above ground. Your people's torment will only haunt you if you do nothing to stand where they fell, man. Be done with these recriminations; their souls have some hope of release. The Evil One knows not that Anahimara was missing over 4,000 of its kin when he unleashed the darkness on your kingdom. He will gain a grand surprise to see your horsemen add themselves to the other people of Loura when we finally stand against their tide. It will come soon enough, yes?"

"Mine is but a small band of soldiers, my friend. Set against tens of thousands or more Treborgans, I'm not sure what we can really do. They sacked my homeland with lightning speed!" O'Mara spoke as if he was already a defeated man. "The paltry number of what remains of our resistance was so evident when my gracious hostess, Lady Nica, could find easy refuge for us in the homes of her people amid their treed capital. T'was like we were nothing of any consequence at all!" He exclaimed as he spat on the ground.

"A small number perhaps, O'Mara, but your soldiers are of the finest metal and will give support to the withdrawal of the Bodelanders to Dunbar."

A voice came from the right of the assembled troupe. "When we get to Gol, Erladoch…" Nica opened as she emerged from her scouting run from their rear flank, "I'll send horsemen and runners alike over all the lands under my seal to proclaim the decision of our meeting. I expect that the exodus will commence before the descent of the old moon. I pray now that this will be sufficient time for my people's escape to be made good."

As they continued their journey, Shamus remarked that the density of the trees in the deciduous forest was thinning out in number somewhat, even though many of them were once again springing up to the heavens to dizzying heights in a manner similar to the massive pines in Castra.

Alida began to sniff the air deeply. "I know now with certainty that there was more about these woods than the Scraggin band we came upon; we're very close."

Nida was coming from ahead to meet them at a fast pace. Looking upon her brother as he approached, Alida's complexion grew more pale than usual, so much as to have become practically opaque, the veins in her face clearly visible. Seeing the expression that could only mean 'bad news ahead', Lady Nica's eyes began to run involuntarily with cold tears.

Erladoch went to her side as she assumed the lead, her feet picking up the pace toward something just out of view through the morass of massive trees. The rest of the Travelers followed behind for nearly two yarricks, all of them now running the last stretch, trying to keep up with the young princess.

The odor was strong enough now it was unmistakable. Charred flesh stung their nostrils as they came around one of the massive oak trees whose multiple trunks extended in every direction like a protective walled entrance into the small village. Nica and Erladoch had already made it around the turn. They'd already stopped, standing side by side, slack-jawed, as the rest of the Travelers caught up. None of them bothered to draw their weapons as they came forth. Their refined olfactory senses had already told them before their eyes could be cast upon the scene that this was a completed event.

Their heads turned back and forth, slowly assessing the ruination of the small but once beauteous enclave. Amidst the lower tree branches, and scattered in places on the ground, parts of vilely desecrated humanity lay strewn about like the entrails of gutted fish on a cutting room floor in a fish market. The gore of perhaps a hundred or more people was everywhere. They had awakened to sudden and terrifyingly swift attackers who dragged the Bodelanders from their beds into the avenues outside. The scene of massacre and violation unfolded in the largest of the village squares, with only the ancient trees as witness. The Scrags who had come through here had taken their time, taking pleasure in the spectacle of it once they were in control of the whole village. The flesh of so many of their victims around their torsos and thighs had been cut away to be used as meat for later, and the blood which had not sprayed out of their victims in the moment of contact with the enemy had been collected for their drink.

The contents of every house were scattered about the previously swept and meticulously arranged avenues. Many of the bodies had been crucified upside down against the massive trunks of their homes and set aflame—a popular method of torture used by the Scrags. They would start by burning the soles of the feet of their inverted victims so that their hearts would pump faster. This made the collection of blood from shrieking victims spill more liberally from their severed carotid arteries. Dried gobs of blood pooled beneath many of the inverted Bodelanders' carcasses due to the haphazard effort of the Scraggin torturers to collect the spilling life force into their flagons. Scrags considered the hot life's blood of their victims a truly intoxicating beverage.

Those who were not burned after having been nailed upside down against the great trees were filleted in ways that made the collection of life blood impossible. Their suffering would have taken long, agonizing minutes while Scrags danced and slid in the pools which dripped onto the forest floor. These victims weren't used for food; they were abused in this fashion to send a message. Murdered thusly, anyone coming upon such a calamitous scene as the Travelers were now doing would know that these Bodelanders were made to die slowly for the sheer amusement of it.

Nica knew from even a quick survey of the scene that a few of the most unfortunate Bodelanders who had been crucified still had a few heartbeats left in them. Amazingly, their hours of torment had not yet come to an end. Beneath them in the dirt, fragments of their tongues lay like so much refuse. Even inverted and impaled against their beloved trees, they had resisted with twists of their heads and gnashing of their teeth to prevent their tormentors from gaining a solid plucking out of what the Scrags considered a delicacy. These brave souls would not be able to tell Nica anything. A few of those with any level of remaining consciousness saw their princess as she and the Travelers went from person to person looking for a survivor. Were they able to ask for anything at this point from her or her companions, it would have been for them to provide a swift end to their suffering, and no more.

Nica unrooted her feet, which had been previously frozen in place from her despair, and sprang into action. Picking up a large branch that was still smoldering on the ground, she went from one crucifixion site to the next, screeching a wail of sorrow that made the Travelers stand fast and watch in horror as she set to the task of putting her countrymen out of their misery. The volume of her rage-filled sorrow powered her shoulders as she began to swing wildly at the heads of the dying, too overcome with grief to even draw out one of her weapons for the task.

Shamus wanted her to stop! He felt the bilious fluid of his own vomit moving upward in his chest, and he was not alone in this. Nida was standing over the corpse of a child so disfigured he fell to his knees and began to sob openly. Regaining himself a little, Shamus began to move toward Nica in an apparent effort to stay her hand, only to be met by Andor and O'Mara.

"She is doing what she must to aid her people in their final moments, Lord Shamus. Do not interfere with this; the pain will make her stronger."

The other Travelers stood fast, eyes wide to the carnage in order to never forget; it was all that they could do for them. Shamus loosened himself from Andor's grip and sat squat over his feet, his legs feeling unsteady beneath him. He wished to escape the horror plastered over his eyes but could not. Tear after stinging, miserable tear passed over his nose and fell to the dirt between his feet as Nica went on shouting and running back and forth to the few that waited for release, still swinging her partially charred branch. The head of each corpse she struck disintegrated at the place of impact. Small clouds of ash puffed from the branch with each sickening thud. The hopes and dreams of the unsuspecting villagers, and now their suffering, all snuffed out.

Alida slowly approached Nica as the fury began to subside. The rest of the band now took places around the Bodelandish princess who had finally finished with her unsavory task of affording the last dignity of a swift death to her people. Covered in sweat and the blood of the innocents, her legs gave way to weariness. She crumpled to the ground, giving herself to loud and heart-sickened shrieks of mourning. One by one, each of the Travelers arranged themselves around her, kneeled, and took hold of one another and her in a comforting embrace. Shamus was beckoned by Erladoch to join himself to the lady of the forest so that he might partake in this unusual ritual. O'Mara Boldar was the last of the Travelers to join the circle. His eyes continued to scan the devastation around them, assessing a scene he already knew too well.

As Shamus's arms wrapped around Nica's torso, he experienced a surge of pain and anger that felt entirely alien to his body. Though it lasted but a few seconds, it was terribly intense; and then it was no more.

The brief ritual, which each member took part in, was clearly for more than to simply offer consolation to the forest princess. As Shamus raised his gaze to meet her steely blue eyes, he no longer saw sadness within Nica Bodelander—only exhaustion. He rose to his feet and walked to the outside of the village square momentarily to process the transfer of energy which seemed to have passed through him. He didn't notice whether O'Mara followed him in embracing the princess's pain, or whether he had gone to check something near where they had first entered the village. He knew that the re-experiencing of such trauma had to be awful for the young prince of Anahimara.

Shamus stared off into the dapple shade of the furthest away tree limb he could find at the edge of the village square. He began speeding away from the scene of carnage around him. He needed to throw up and wanted whatever privacy he could find for himself to do it.

When he was done retching the small amount of food he had consumed earlier in the day, he slowly walked back to the group. He considered for the first time how each of the Travelers had somehow contributed to channeling away Nica's distress. She had been enabled somehow through this process of sharing to shed the wailing, banshee-like shrieks of raging horror from herself like a tossed-away garment. The rage had literally drained out of her with each shared embrace, until she was no longer making any noise at all beyond a hushed cry as she rocked in Erladoch's consoling arms.

The rage and sorrow had seemingly left them all; even the distraught Galagar had found his sense of calm, following the ritual and was now whispering almost absent-mindedly to his sister.

Despite the scene of devastation all around them, it seemed to Shamus that some of the Travelers were preparing to move out. Shamus knew that the scar of this day had already been embedded within each of the Travelers' minds. The next utterances confirmed his suspicion.

"We should assemble the victims and make a funeral pyre, my friends," Erladoch offered in a low whisper, hoping to give comfort to Lady Nica.

"No, Lord Dunbar." Nica's refrain was decisive. "I appreciate your sentiment. I do. But there's nothing left to do here. We should leave this place." She rose to her feet. Drawing from her inner reserves, she began to lead the group away.

"I disagree!" Erladoch protested. "This is not our way!" He was determined to honor the fallen appropriately.

Nica shook her head severally before replying. Her voice was at the border between calm and constrained rage. "The village of Ardehla is no more," she answered his protest through clamped teeth. "The forest is sick with Scraggin Horders well beyond the numbers we've already encountered today. We canna' waste time offering my people their dignity without signaling to whatever army roams my land that we have come this way. The evidence of our battle is likely already known. We go now!"

With heavy hearts, the Travelers grudgingly turned their backs on the destruction and proceeded back toward the unseen path southward. Once they were beyond the carnage, Shamus found himself leading the companions once again. Even if the entity within did indeed have a hand in steering Shamus, he needed to be out front so that no one else could witness the raging turmoil and horror registered on his face. He had watched countless war movies in his lifetime. Many had been graphic in their depiction of violence. Somewhere along the way in his life, he had sold himself on the notion that he would be someone who could 'take it'; that he could compartmentalize horror. Shamus had come face to face with the Big Lie; that moment of self-revelation that every warrior had to grapple with. If he was going to psychically survive, if he was ever going to be right again after bearing witness to such a deeply traumatizing scene as he was now walking ever more swiftly away from with every footfall, he would have to find an 'off switch' that would allow him the ability to not replay every image he had just taken in for the rest of his days. Tears continued to stream down his cheeks unchecked. The bile from his already overturned stomach made his hyperventilation so out of control that he risked fainting at any moment. *Move your damned feet, Shamus! Just keep walking!*

Chapter 28

The spread of the trees narrowed once again, and the boughs and trunks were no longer as broad. It was plain, even to Shamus, who had never trod in this place that at some point in history, a great fire had long ago destroyed large areas of this part of the Great Forest. New growth of maybe a few hundred years in age was replacing the deciduous monoliths that were many thousands of years old.

Inyi crested the highest point in the sky. The coolness of the air ceded its grasp on the land to a warming wind that whispered that spring had fully arrived in this place. The further he went on through this day, the more the surroundings were seemingly familiar to Shamus. He could not help feeling as though he were walking through landscapes from of an old remembrance. *Perhaps not my memory,* Shamus reflected. *Likely 'his' memory.*

The companions increased their pace to a soft jog, hoping to make back some of the time they had lost in their journey. The echoes of familiarity with the terrain rolled more freely within Shamus's mind. He realized that the great Wigget within was both gazing through his eyes and simultaneously funneling the calming emotion of 'familiarity' to him. It wasn't clear to him exactly why Anthrac was choosing to communicate his recollections to Shamus's consciousness about such trivial things. *Maybe,* he considered, *maybe it was important for him to remember this path?*

So this is what it's like to be possessed, Shamus quipped in amusement; half expecting to hear in the back of his mind a reply to the effect of, *How d'you like it so far?* from Anthrac. *Or more aptly, what schizophrenia must feel like,* he rejigged. Nothing was coming to him. At times, as Shamus stumbled slightly over soft earth, he would experience the imbalance twice in a split second, as if the union of the two minds was short-circuiting with such little surprises. It had the interesting effect of slowing the experience of time down while speeding Shamus's physical reactions to the uneven terrain.

Erladoch and the others moved gracefully through the trees, each one enmeshed in their own worlds of thought. Nica, on the other hand, was studying Shamus intensively, as though she alone were noticing a qualitative change in him. She strode to his right side and broke the quiet.

"Ya have more than the Wigget Seed inside you, friend. I reckon you have the spirit of a great warrior coursing through your blood. I see him inside you; he moves like a great cat, each part of him a muscle readying for an approaching kill. Is this a part of your nature, Lord Shamus, or is this an illusion which emanates from the magic of your cloak?"

Shamus assessed her comment and her question with equal measure of surprise. He struggled to supply her with a meaningful answer. "Uh, well, Princess Nica, I have no answer to give to your question. Who I was when I first came here is a very different man than the person you now look upon. I feel that I am indeed 'different'; that much is true. I can tell you this with confidence. But so many new parts of myself have emerged in Loura that I can no longer say whether who I appear to be is anything of who I feel that I am. I've seen a warrior come out of me in times of need that I can't honestly take much credit for. I further hear the voice of the White Wigget whispering in the recesses of my mind from time to time, and it really unsettles me, if you want to know the truth of it." He sighed before sharing a further lament, "Honestly, I fear I'm losing myself."

Erladoch interrupted. "Ach! Think, fear, think. Ya think too bloody much!" He wore a wry smile, but his interjection was educative. "Yer the same man I first met, Shamus! Do not muddle your thoughts with such melancholy. The doctor that you once were is still among us; only that man is being made better. What you now see is the rest of your true nature emerging. All that you are now was present when I was first introduced to you. Just because you are having to get acquainted with those parts of 'you' that never had a reason for expression doesn't mean that it isn't you. In his brief appearance back inside the boughs of Firren, Anthrac Aran told us all that you are part of an endless line of warriors. This is your heritage, friend. This is where you belong. The voices behind the stars have said so much of this themselves to me when I have gazed out upon them."

A defined path was becoming more obvious now as the trees closed their ranks tightly, leaving only a narrow conduit for which the party could run through. As a result, everyone had tuned into the present conversation, looking for a diversion from the monotonous sound of their footfalls and the oppression of their own dark thoughts.

"What do you mean, Erladoch? You know that that makes no sense. How have the stars told you anything? They don't have mouths ya know," Shamus believed that he had said this jovially enough, but his 'Doubting Thomas' psychologist's voice might have overplayed itself as much to say, "That sounds like bull-crap!" All Shamus had truly meant by the sarcastic retort was that he couldn't believe his friend could be so certain about his persona when he clearly was not.

Before Erladoch could answer, Andor broke in with his own contribution. There was no air of humor in his voice, however. "Wigget Bearer, in asking such a question, it is obvious that you are not acquainted with the ways of our people. It perplexes me greatly how you portray yourself clearly as a visitor in some things, and yet in other things, it is at least apparent to me that you are more like kin who has been long away and maybe even craves to become reacquainted. Your ignorance offends. Are ye not a man of honor? Your words leave me wondering."

Shamus found it odd how quickly Andor had just come to Erladoch's aid. He hadn't considered his comments to have been controversial. Andor's interjection was abrupt, and from what little he knew of the man, out of character. The size of his imposing frame caused Shamus to back up. Addressing Erladoch directly in hopes of calming whatever offense he had just given, he noted that his friend was avoiding eye contact with him. Instead, Erladoch was measuring Andor Seth.

"Uh, I, didn't mean to sound as though I doubted you, Erladoch. I guess I thought you'd laugh."

Erladoch continued to say nothing in return.

"Seriously, man, I'm just trying to understand 'how' you acquire information from star gazing or listening for messages from the wind. I guess I know that you do such things, but not being able to do so myself, please understand that I am mystified."

Erladoch briefly gazed over at Shamus as much to say, "Don't sweat it, Shamus," but Andor continued to measure the Wigget Bearer for his apparent lack of understanding of the hierarchy among the high nobles traveling in this group. His stubborn determination to make a point about how Erladoch should be spoken to was coming through, even as he was seemingly struggling to not lose control of a temperature that was rising inside of him. Andor was going to be heard, and Shamus feared that for reasons outside of his comprehension, the perceived slight was going to land him a beating from the colossus yet.

"Over and above the seed within you, you have shown yourself to belong among us as the man that 'you are': a fierce and able warrior. You walk among the Keepers as one of us and display at least some of the ancient knowledge. That is far more than what can be said of so many of our own people. But if you are to be fully among us, you must come to terms, Lord Fiorian, that in this place, to challenge the Prince of Dunbar's knowledge with such questions is to doubt what 'is', and more importantly, what 'he is' to us." Andor's protective behavior was now coming into focus for Shamus. "You walk among the Keepers and seemingly know our truths. You know the secret of our Sacred Order, even when most Lourans had long forgotten that we walk among them. They can be forgiven their ignorance of our ábaltachts because we've protected them in silence o'er the generations, letting them sleep calmly in their hovels even while we have sacrificed to maintain their illusion of a peaceful world. We needed to preserve our Order's sacred mission in the face of politicians who would no longer suffer the belief that our mission was legitimate and our warriors' ways necessary. They do not know what it is that has lived in shadow till now. The darkness is now upon us all, Fiorian, and our secret can no longer be kept. As more have begun to learn of our role among them, we trust they will follow us unquestioningly. They will have to respect us for the lost arts that the Strahanas passed on to us alone. That will not happen when one who walks among us fails to honor our ways!" Andor poked his index finger into Shamus's chest to emphasize his distaste.

Shamus had never heard Andor say so much to anyone in the entire time that he had traveled with the giant. Possibly because of his immense size, Shamus had mistaken him for a bit of a dim-witted brute. Being dressed down in such a fashion, it was dawning on him in that he had likely underestimated the intelligence of all the Keepers he was traveling with, simply because he was a man of modern times who found himself in the midst of people who predated the most ancient races known to his history; a carefully assembled and redacted history, as it turned out.

Shamus felt ashamed in the presence of what had been, in fact, an eloquent little speech from Andor of Seth. He realized his arrogance all at once. He could see that Andor was more than adamant. While he'd been sufficiently imposing with his lecture, the poke delivered to his right shoulder was something more than that; it felt threatening.

"I meant no offense, Andor." Shamus offered to cool what was clearly more than an impassioned speech.

Erladoch and the rest of the Travelers stood quietly assessing the exchange, working out for themselves what was enveloped inside the level of seething frustration brimming in their lifelong friend from the House of Seth.

This is not right. Something about this is over the top. Shamus's inner voice told him to be on guard. His trained mind told him something more: *Don't back down, Shamus, just de-escalate this any way you can.*

"Ya said it yourself, man of Seth. I'm not from here, or at least, I was not born here, even if my bloodline descends from this place." Shamus felt a need to demonstrate respect for what he understood Andor had been trying to impart, but also realized that the colossus would have to take a huge 'chill pill' if he was to learn all that he could about the full legacy he inherited nearly too late in his own life. "While I do not intend offense or disrespect, I cannot continue to learn without posing such questions. I do not yet know what knowledge you take for granted, having had a lifetime to acquire it. I believe that to accomplish my mission here, you will have to forgive me my ignorance." Shamus was now standing under Andor's barrel chest looking straight up at every imposing inch of him. "And accept that I am not showing disrespect for your captain. I have placed my full faith in him and left a life of much comfort to serve in this great mission alongside all of you because I believe in him. So, when I ask my many questions yet to come, Andor, recognize that you are helping me accomplish my part in this struggle, and don't conclude that I am challenging or disparaging you."

Andor stood silently for what felt like minutes, assessing the man standing fearlessly inches away from the middle of his intricately roped breastplate, despite his previous effort to chastise him for what he had wrongly perceived as a slight. He was also now grappling with why he had felt the need to lecture Shamus at all, or why he had felt so suddenly emotional about the matter. He'd witnessed Shamus's decisive shadow warrior in action but a few hours before. Shamus could handle himself. He knew this plainly. He'd also chosen to close the distance between them rather than back away like most persons Andor had ever imposed upon. He felt the weight of his hefty battle-ax dangling at Shamus's midsection. Some voice within the reach of his mind was grating at him, asking him to consider how exciting it would be at that very moment if he drew it out and cleaved the Wigget Bearer's head from his shoulders. The minute that the thought had become so pronounced as to form an image, he knew it was not his own voice that had placed the sudden need to cause conflict. Something from outside of him was trying to weave its way into his mind, and he now saw it for what it was. His training as a Keeper informed him that the invasive thought that was calling him to do unspeakable things in that moment was not proprietary. He felt his left arm suddenly rising.

"Hahahaha!" Andor suddenly burst into laughter, bringing his hand down in a controlled sway, slapping Shamus on the back in an apparent gesture of friendship. Shamus felt his teeth rattle despite the seemingly benign gesture. The tension within the colossus had dissipated. "Now that I comprehend ya, I measure you well, friend!"

Shamus weighed that the gesture continued to be over the top. At least now it was coming from the opposite side of the spectrum. He'd seen this sort of thing in therapy sessions in the S.T.U., dealing particularly with the paranoid schizophrenics. Back then, he'd always had to be on the lookout for the inexplicable and sudden loss of impulse control by any one of his violent psychotic patients. He knew that those with any residual ability to exert control over the imposing voices screaming in their heads could sometimes pull themselves back from the edge. This felt like that. *So very much like that*, he told himself.

Choosing to make no further utterance that could retrigger the Sethian, he managed a respectful nod acknowledging to Andor that the exchange need not continue.

"It's my turn to take scout," Andor announced. He disappeared into the darkness of the tightly hedged trees, apparently finished with the bizarre exchange. In truth, however, Andor was determined to remove himself from a place where the insidious voice might have further opportunity to spurn him into taking actions that he wished to have no part of.

Shamus breathed an audible sigh of relief. He'd had no clue as to what had truly just occurred, but he knew that something had momentarily gone askew. For his and everyone else's sake, Andor had elected to place as much distance between himself and the company as he could. While Shamus was happy for the outcome, he continued to ruminate over the incident. *This felt so like dealing with my schizophrenic patients*, he concluded. Those voices all too often incited them to carry out egregiously violent acts. This had to have involved interference from Enilorac. *Jaysus! I don't even like thinking of his name! I should bloody well stop invoking it!* He chided himself. *Still, I'm not alone in this. The bastard's reach is like poison in the air! It seems like he can afflict any single one of us if we but allow him to do so.* He made a mental note to be wary of any of the Travelers in the future. If he were to see them begin to act out in any kind of discordant way, he'd have to be ready for this if he wanted to survive.

Erladoch and Nica came alongside Shamus, saying nothing, but having measured the weirdness of the moment. Their pace increased as a silent note to everyone that, for whatever reason, they all needed to move more swiftly through this section of the forest.

Once the pace had become comfortable for talking again, Shamus tapped Nica Bodelander on the arm. "Lady Nica, what did Andor mean by ancient knowledge?"

"Ah, that is what ye meant by not knowing everything which we take for granted from our training then?" The light of recognition was apparent in her. "Well, Shamus, t'is simple really. Each Keeper must remember in their own way those parts of the special knowledge that befits their own aptitudes. A knowledge of things not yet seen, sounds not yet or no longer heard, and sometimes, even thoughts and feelings private to each of us. As part of his ábaltacht, the great Prince of Dunbar is a mind dancer. Surely, ya must already have realized this?"

Shamus nodded in agreement.

"And ya know what that means, yes? His mind does not simply dwell within his head like most people. It dances in the wind and is not bound by hard spaces like walls. You've felt his mind song come to your rescue more than once, have you not?"

Again, he nodded. She seemed to know much about what had transpired between the men, and she wished for him to use some of his own common sense in the discussion. While her voice remained soft and pleasant as she assisted him with the answer, there was an admonishing way about her. She could sense that Shamus still struggled with what he could not measure with his own natural senses. If she could have understood the concept of 'science' in the same way that he did, this might have made it easier for them both. As it was, she wondered why Shamus held himself back from fully accepting the nature of Erladoch's power to see beyond the physical world.

Erladoch smiled as he took in the Bodelander princess's diplomatic manner. In her polite way, she was telling Shamus to open himself to the reality of magic. She knew that he had witnessed Erladoch's special gift, but she could tell a part of him rejected his experiences when they lacked explanation. She wanted Shamus to stop trying to retreat from it, for his own future good. Nica was never dearer to Erladoch than in this moment. He could tell she had grown much as a leader in his absence.

"While most men will look to the night sky and see but thousands of flickering candle lights, a seer like our Lord will reach forth with his mind and find another's thoughts as though they intermingled themselves with the stars. He communes with the unseen and the unheard. I wouldna' doubt he speaks to his long-departed Ma, wherever she may be."

"I've never heard him speak of his mom. Did she die?" Shamus asked with great curiosity. He felt bad he'd never asked Erladoch about his family beyond what Erladoch himself had volunteered—not really, anyway. He realized that his preoccupation with his own journey had made him more selfish than he would have seen himself as.

"Don't know really," Nica replied. "He was 13 winters when Fanoola left. Keeper business, to be sure, but she's not been heard of since. He seldom talks about her, even to me, and I've known him all my life. Everything tells me that she still lives, though. I've ne'er heard him utter a mournful word about her. His ábaltacht as a mind dancer came from her, to be sure. She was considered to have no rival in it. I'm sure, however, that he refrains from applying his craft to reach out to her or anyone else now, for that matter. You've seen how it depletes him of late in the few sparing moments that he's interceded on your behalf. With the Evil One's ability to hunt those of our kind who can enter the dreamscape, he may be one of the few who continue to be strong enough to withstand such invasions of the mind. If the Evil One has his way, not even Erladoch will be able to safely dance in the ether any longer. He's nearly the last of our kind to do so who hasn't succumbed."

Shamus knew that Erladoch seemed to 'anticipate' things better than the average person. With Andor's and now Nica's comments, however, he flashed upon several scenes already unfolded since coming to know the man as he had. Even though, he couldn't possibly have known the floor plan of "the Royal", it had been Erladoch who grabbed Shamus's arm to stop him from moving into the central corridor to get to the elevator. He now recalled his friend telling him they should go another way, as if he must have known that they would encounter resistance by taking the shortest path. Another memory presented itself. It was a vision of the moment that John Browse had telephoned him, imploring them to leave the cottage at Calabogie at once. For the first time, Shamus processed that before the phone had ever rung, Erladoch had begun packing their belongings into their travel packs. Even today! The evidence was all around him! Before anyone else reacted to the approach of the Scrags, Erladoch had perceived their peril! It wasn't just refined senses of hearing or smell at play here. It was something far more intricate than that.

"Jaysus! I'm so limited in my understanding, aren't I?" he asked the Travelers walking alongside of him.

Nica smiled at the moment of Shamus's epiphany. "Ah," she said contentedly. "There ye are."

Shamus knew that the Wigget within him was immensely powerful and was definitely driving him along. More often than not, however, he also felt a 'wedge' or a 'movable wall' between his own experiences and that of Anthrac. Whether he'd placed it there or the White Wigget had done so, it felt as though it was there to help maintain both Shamus's sanity and the integrity of his own experiences. He questioned whether there might someday be a way that he could channel some of the Angel's power to help him gain some part of this gift of foresight. He turned to Erladoch for guidance as a thought formed on his lips. "Beyond my physical appearance, what is it that you saw about me, Erladoch, which first told you that you could trust me?"

"I saw only that which I've already told you, my friend. I knew upon seeing you for the first time that you would free me from your world and you possessed great untapped reserves of strength. The ancestors seemed to dance all about you, telling me that you carried important secrets that even you had no knowledge of."

"Erladoch," O'Mara Boldar piped in out of nowhere. "Can you or the Fiorian tell us whether our mission will be in vain, then? With your great magic, can either of you assess whether we shall have sufficient time to organize against the House of Treborg and the demon realm they hope to unleash?" There was an air of self-defeatism wrapped in a package of hope overlaying O'Mara's interruption.

"No, O'Mara," Erladoch answered him back. "I'm sorry, young prince, but I canna' do that. I dare not look so deeply for the answer to such things not yet done." Before O'Mara could press Shamus for his own answer, Erladoch continued, "Neither should Shamus attempt to access the Wigget's mind for such things. The mindscape cannot provide such a detailed outlook regarding such complicated tales. By our being here at all, the timeline may already have been un-set. They tell only of general things, leaving the most important mysteries of man and creatures undecided. I can seek only the possibilities in my wanderings, and now I fear that even that type of endeavor carries too great a peril to be trusted when such images come to me. The Wigget Bearer is a separate man from the one he carries inside. It is not for him to even try to interpret the sights and sounds he is being given from within. We'll have to wait to see what ábaltacht emerges for Shamus, but it is not mind-dancing in any event."

Shamus slowed nearly to a halt. He was confused by the presence of a veiled message being given to him through Erladoch's words, but something more was now pounding at the back of him that he felt he needed to consider with full concentration. The others slowed around him, waiting for what they expected to be a change in their direction of travel or perhaps some piece of wisdom. In spite of his having been dressed down by Andor only a half hour before for having displayed an annoying lack of respect for his friend's gifts, Shamus felt himself preparing to speak to O'Mara Boldar's question. His inner clinical psychologist wanted to confront the presence of the possible double entendre he felt that he had recognized in the Anahimaran's message. His training told him to read the subconscious 'tells' which popped out in normal speech with patients who were plainly in psychic conflict. The undertone of O'Mara's question was one of a man who had already surrendered to defeat despite the careful way he had worded his inquiry with a pretense of hope.

Boldar pressed on. "Erladoch Dunbar, surely you see more than a void in this time of woe which could give us all comfort? Why not gaze for us, your friends?"

Shamus's professional self was devoted to conducting a full-blown psychoanalysis of O'Mara's sudden need for information. The discordance he felt ringing in his ears between the voice tones he heard coming from O'Mara and the wording of the request had him on guard.

He spoke now directly to O'Mara, but in a voice intended to be heard by all as a gesture of authority. "Another mind is also out there searching the heavens currently, is there not?" The Travelers' ears collectively perked up as Shamus pressed with his interrogatory. "The one whose name cannot be spoken of is that other mind, yes?"

Erladoch silently nodded in agreement while the rest of the Travelers listened.

"Andor Seth spoke that few will inherit your gift. What you have failed to say is why. I'm guessing that it is because those who possess the gift of reading the portents of starlight and wind song have been lost to the Evil One. Nica's pretty much confirmed this. Since the devil's minion has returned to Loura, he casts a net with his enchantments and scours the countryside through the eyes of those he has claimed as his personal trophies. Even though they do not wear the demon's brand, their minds are now forfeit, aren't they?" Why it had become important for Shamus to over speak O'Mara was not fully clear to him, but, his inner voice compelled him to dominate the conversation in this moment as though to give warning.

Once again, Erladoch simply nodded affirmatively to his friend's question.

"Hmm, there then is your answer, O'Mara." Shamus shut the topic down before anything more could be brought up. Recognizing the lesson he himself had learned from Andor about the workings of the Keeper hierarchy, he then delivered an authoritative message. "I'll caution you all to not ask your Lord to place himself in peril by posing further requests for him to enter the mindscape. It is like a magnet which allows the Evil One to track us down."

Shamus's interjection had been forceful, directive and as much in O'Mara's face as had been Andor's admonition to himself earlier—minus the inexplicable and mounting rage that Andor had suddenly felt himself nearly overcome by.

Before O'Mara could respond to Shamus's friendly but firm warning, Andor re-emerged to the back of the group, having run a wide and serpentine scouting mission looking for signs of potential danger. He was sweating profusely even though it was probably all of 55 degrees Fahrenheit outside, revealing he had clearly been running at a significant pace.

Alida, who had said nothing since the Travelers had left the devastation of the morning, immediately came astride of him. "Are ya yourself again?" she inquired, with a smile thoughtfully affixed to her countenance. "Or do I need to worry about you, my big man?"

She spoke so sweetly as to disarm him with her obvious affection for him. No one else seemed to be paying attention to this exchange between Andor and Alida, as Shamus's comments continued to percolate.

Andor had known the Galagar female most of his life. He knew that deception would be impossible. "Forgive me, Alida," he said with a countenance that revealed his clarity of introspection. "I don't know what came over me earlier, but every word that I meant to say was intended in the kindest of ways to the Fiorian, and yet with each word that left my lips, there seemed to come a growing and unspeakable anger within me that was not of my own doing. I had to create distance to sort myself out."

"I hear the whispers of a serpent rustling through the leaves, also, big man." She brushed her hand across his forearm consolingly. "It's not you. Just recognize it, shut it out and find yourself." Alida slapped his face playfully. "By the bye, it was quite the speech you made, for a metal smith." She teased him sweetly before leaving the group for the darkness of the forest.

Andor offered a heartfelt and relieved chuckle to her back; he could not see the silent exchange that transpired between her and her brother, who was waiting in the shadows of a branch not far from where Alida and Andor had just been. The male Galagar, like his sister, was completely invisible to all but the most inquisitive of eyes. Nida had waited for a signal that 'their Andor' was once again 'right in his head'. The slightest of approving glances from her upward into the thick leaves was enough. Nida quietly slid his arrow back into his quiver, executed a flawless backflip from his stealthy perch, and landed softly upon the unusually high arches of both feet before rejoining the company from the foreground. He acted oblivious to the exchanges that had been going on when, in actual fact, he'd been tracking Andor from the moment the latter had broken off his interaction with Shamus. Unlike Andor's large and sweaty frame, Nida looked reposed, showing no sign of exertion. His fragile and slight-looking physique was so light and pliable that his pursuit of Andor's relatively louder stomps through the soft cover of the terrain was at no point even sensed by the Sethian.

None of the Travelers said anything to Andor upon his return beyond the usual tacit acknowledgment of his return to their formation. What Shamus had spoken of concerning the workings of the Evil One sat heavy. It was an unengaged conversation that had been simmering for some time among the Travelers. While it had been O'Mara who had launched the party into this awkward dialogue, others were carrying some manner of burden that had, prior to this moment, gone without canvas. Shamus's interjection had exposed a nerve. His assessment of the danger had been spot-on. His counselor voice informed that while he had foreclosed further conversation about entering the mindscape, he, nonetheless, had to find a way to reinvest himself as a member of the group. There was a potency to his unique station. This much he understood about his new place among the Keepers. He resolved to find a way to settle the lingering doubts.

"My friends, what none of you have yet said, I now understand. Your hearts have been allowed to grow heavy and riddled with doubts while Erladoch has been gone. The Evil One's strength has indeed re-emerged. I see it now. His poison has clearly infected and even taken hostage of some of your Keeper brethren."

The shared look of resignation confirmed his hunch. "Yes. I see. Even though you've said nothing to me of it, I'm right that there are perhaps none among your Order left beyond the Prince of Dunbar who still possesses the mind-dancing gift." Even as he voiced this as a fact, everything inside of him told him that there was another mind dancer out there, waiting.

Nica Bodelander sensed what Shamus was trying to accomplish. "Yer right enough, Wigget Bearer, although as descendants of the Angealkind, we all possess some potential for it. The Evil One has altered some of the best among us and turned them to his malevolent purpose. He manipulates the power of the Itavo Stones that he possesses by proxy through the Evil One. He has bound those who previously wielded the gift of mind-dancing to himself, extending his reach ever greater than he once did. Erladoch cannot risk further forays into the mind space without great peril to himself from this time onward, but you now know this part already."

Shamus nodded without hesitation, feeling all too well the scarring of claw marks around his left pectoral area.

For the first time after a lengthy pause, O'Mara chose to re-engage the discussion, seeing his opening. "Perhaps I've over spoken from before, Lord Erladoch," he offered in a conciliatory and deferential tone of voice. "I meant no offense. I am simply stating the point that you alone among us possess this gift which could help us to avoid future dangers on our journey at the very least. It seems a shame to not…"

"Shite, man!" Nica interjected in a huff of exasperation. "Do na' ask him to soothsay or seek again!" She reprimanded. "Measure yer words, O'Mara. Yer placing our friend and leader at far too great a risk! Lord Erladoch's gift could help each of us in our own ways, but ya know all too well that to do so now comes with too great a cost. You saw what happened with your own damned eyes when he was forced to intercede for Shamus!"

Shamus felt the presence of the proverbial 'elephant in the room' as they continued to march along. Even though he was unhappy with O'Mara's continued effort to entice Erladoch, the Prince of Dunbar deliberately refrained from engaging in the conversation.

Somewhere within, Shamus felt a thought bubble up. It felt like a restless stirring by the White Wigget rather than an experience of intuition. Something about the restlessness was telling him to assert dominance over the discussion. "As I started to say, I see now what continues to go unspoken, friends. There are people close to you who are now captives of this force of darkness. The King of Bodeland, your father, he's not dead, is he?"

Without trying to overtly impose himself between O'Mara and Erladoch, Shamus reached out to lay a consoling hand on the Bodelandish princess's right shoulder. It created the physical space that he felt he was being directed to explore further while signaling to O'Mara that any additional probing of Erladoch would not be tolerated. His touch caused her to search Shamus's quicksilver eyes quizzically. She immediately perceived his action as more than just an expression of support. There was kindness in Shamus's touch, but there was something additional which she couldn't quite access: a compulsion for her to follow his lead and free herself from the discussion. In spite of herself, her eyes welled up with tears. It confirmed to Shamus everything that he felt he needed to know; the Evil One's overwhelming of Keepers who could mind dance was not a statement restricted to an unrelated number of members of their Order. This had hit her right at home!

"Where is he, Nica? What has happened to your Da?" Shamus pressed for confirmation.

Alida's gray-green eyes flashed over Nica for a moment, assessing her companion's now exposed torment. She answered in Nica's place. "The Forrester King 'is' dead, Wigget Bearer." There was no anger or consternation in her melodic voice, only pity for all present. "So too is the elder king of Seth, and our Chairman of Galagan, Guanda, last of his clan. I say this to you with all sincerity: 'yes', they are very much dead to us and to themselves. They were each of them mind-dancers, and they've all fallen prey to the Evil One. If any of them continue to live in body still, which is not likely, they're lost in a place in their minds that is so dark they'll ne'er come back from it."

Nica gathered herself. She decided that she should be the one to complete the sorry tale in hopes that by saying it with her own lips, it might unburden her somehow. "When it began to happen, the inner council decreed that any mind-dancers in our ranks be isolated. Sensing the darkness that was reaching out to them in the dream space, some volunteered to travel as far afield of Treborg as possible in hopes that the physical distance might make their detection less easy. It got so that it mattered little whether our brothers and sisters voluntarily isolated themselves or had to be compelled to do so. A madness began to overtake them all. It compelled them to carry out sudden and horrific acts of violence to anyone near them. One by one, they fell to his sway. Those who could be subdued were gathered up and kept safely restrained for their own good. We had no way of knowing how to heal them."

Even though he hadn't erupted in violence against any of the Travelers, Shamus knew what that darkness felt like. He'd been nearly lost to it on two occasions now. The second time he got caught up in Enilorac's web, it had been so much more difficult to escape the grip of his malevolence. He allowed Nica to continue.

"The greatest healers of our world were sent to them in Dunbar, where we had sent them all in hopes of saving them, but they were beyond saving. Their rantings and screams were so overcome with the Evil One's brand upon them. Anyone who simply heard the sound of their voices risked being driven mad from the sorrow of it. When Bodeland's greatest healer went to my Da, he came out of the cell and embarked on a spree of murder. He killed four of Dunbar's warriors before he had to be put down like a dog. This all occurred within the passage of five moons following the disappearance of Erladoch the Brave of Fior Hill. All those of us Keepers who hold the ancestral blood of the Strahanas are blessed with our unique ábaltachts. This blessing has turned into a gaping and ever-widening wound, however, for any whose ábaltacht is to mind dance. We discovered too late that it could be used as a weapon against us by the Evil One from the moment that he was sent back into Loura by the Master of the Pit to open the way."

The pain of her admission to herself of her father's fate was palpable as Shamus continued to grasp onto her shoulder.

"Ach!" Nica said in a truly exasperated but not yet defeated tone. "Perhaps your absence, Lord Erladoch, is what shielded you from having been similarly overwhelmed. Whatever the reason, we're fortunate that you once again walk among us with the Wigget Bearer in tow. Shamus," she set her entire gaze on him, "it appears that in as much as Erladoch has come to your rescue with his mind dances, there is something strong about your friendship that has equally fortified and sustained you both."

Shamus considered these words of appreciation from Nica Bodelander. He briefly reflected upon his first interaction with Erladoch in The Queen Elizabeth II Mental Hospital. There had been such a powerful draw to him from the moment they first made eye contact with each other. He replayed the moments of their perilous trek through the wilderness in hopes of finding refuge in Bodeland. Erladoch's side had gaped from a gunshot wound. His mind and body so seriously compromised by fever that the Scrags who hunted them were bound to capture and kill them. Even when it would have made sense for Shamus to run and hide before they were overtaken, he couldn't leave his friend any more than Erladoch could abandon him in the dreamscape. They were bound to each other.

"Whether it be a quality ye yerself possess or the Wigget's connection to our Lord through you, something about your bond has kept him shielded from the Evil One's reach. Either way, you can be damned sure that none among us will ask you, Lord, to look into the empty spaces from this point forward!" she said in the most scolding of terms, her eyes firing darts of frustration and disappointment at O'Mara Boldar. She wasn't prepared to accept that his relative youth had made him this naive. Instead, she worried that there was a malevolence in the very air around them which continued to afflict him. "T'was a reckless request that will not be made again! Are we clear?"

O'Mara appeared embarrassed. He wasn't accustomed to being dressed down in such a fashion, and it caused him to hesitate before responding. Seeing this, Shamus interjected in hope of quelling the tension among these lifelong friends. "Thank you so much, Princess Nica, for sharing your heartache with me. I now know all that I must. I suppose you did not kill them out of pity for who they were."

"Sadly, Lord Shamus, you're wrong," Lady Nica answered. "Out of pity, we tried to end their torment with flights of arrows from a distance far enough away that the minds of our warriors could not be invaded by their haunting voices. Even in this we failed," she replied, looking down at her feet momentarily. "Death did not come to them from this effort. Even when they had been drained of blood from having been shot full of arrows, the Evil One breathed life into their vacant corpses. Beneath the deepest caves within the Dunbar capital of Baldréimire, he continued to animate them like nightmarish puppets. Beheading our loved ones was the only way to end their torment." Her voice lowered at the memory of it. Something about this admission was ever more personal, as though she herself might have had to have been the executioner. The confession of it gave her no comfort. "T'was the only way to prevent the Evil One from wielding them against us."

Shamus looked long upon his companions, longest of all at Erladoch.

Erladoch knew from his friend's gaze that he was now being studied very closely by him. Shamus was conducting a risk assessment. Having heard what Nica had shared, Shamus was considering the safety of the other Travelers from the possibility of his becoming overwhelmed by Enilorac the longer he remained in Loura. He felt no anger at Shamus' sudden trepidation, only respect for his concern about the others. He spoke to console his friend. "Fear me not, Shamus, for as you see, my friends bear no such worries."

Shamus considered this a moment. "I know that your ability has now more than once saved me from the Shadow of the Evil One, Erladoch. Like Lady Nica, however, this tale of your brethren's fate troubles me."

"Aye, Shamus, as it should, friend. It could have been at great expense that I had come to your aid. Each time, it has felt like I struggled for an eternity to free myself of His black will once I called him off of you. It was then, however, that I discovered two things: the new presence and strength of the Evil One's Magic in Loura tells me that the entry of his Master into our world nears. It also has shown me that my gift is not exactly the same as that of my brethren. I have not fallen victim as they had when they were confronted by the Evil One. I sense the presence of a greater power than that of men is controlling my fate; perhaps it is the Wigget within you that shields me, or perhaps it is the very purity of my own bloodline's connection to the Strahanas, I canna' say."

Either way, I feel the blessing and the potency of their magic in equal measure, and it has permitted me this strength to block the Evil One's invasion. These tidings of the devastation of our elders troubles me also. We will need to find a way to resist."

"I'm sorry for having expressed doubts today," Shamus confessed. "I now realize that harboring such feelings may have started this day's unpleasant and charged exchanges. My heart, like all of yours," he waved a messianic arm over the Travelers, designed to purify them all, "holds nothing but confidence in our mission. While I've indeed learned much, it is painfully clear that each time we speak of woe or access our feelings of doubt and despair, it is as though we are opening ourselves to a poisoning of our minds. The Evil One's spell hangs heavy in this air."

O'Mara Boldar and Andor Seth both knew that somehow, while Shamus was speaking to all the Travelers, he was doing so with particular focus on them. He waved his arm over the group a second time. Aided by the glint of sun rays filtering through the dapple of tree branches, the sparkle of each thread of the unique fibers in his cloak illuminated momentarily. It brought a hush over the Travelers. "From this point in our journey forward, the very moment that a doubt comes to your minds, I am going to ask you all to try and remember the happiest moment in your lives." This was not the White Wigget speaking through Shamus now, or at least, he felt as though he had ownership of his thoughts as he addressed the Travelers in his psychologist's voice. In his short clinical practice, Shamus had mastered the technique of helping seriously emotionally disturbed schizophrenics to create moments of mindfulness, permitting them to drown out the disturbing voices that so often ranted relentlessly in their own heads. If he could have seen himself in a mirror as he advised the group, he would have had to concede that his sage counsel was being helped. "Find that moment right now," he said with command. "Regardless of our future perils, access this thought that is uniquely yours and think of nothing else. Hear the sounds of laughter, breathe in the smells of flowers, savor your favorite meal, feel the notes of a song of love vibrate in your ears, or, the tingle of warm waters rushing over you—whatever that moment holds for you, go there every time you sense the darkness, and let this become your only focus from now on when ill thoughts start to creep in."

The Seekers were highly skilled warriors, each imbued with special training for their own unique gifts. The strengthening of mind and body working as one was second nature to them all, and yet, Shamus had struck a chord.

Andor most particularly seemed to appreciate the Wigget Bearer's advice. He permitted himself to find that 'happy place' within. His thoughts turned to his ten-year-old self, soon after he had been committed into the Sacred Order of Keepers to begin his training. He remembered being bigger than all the other children in his group, although some of them were several years older. Training in the Keeper's secret enclave many hundreds of yarricks south would soon begin. He and his family were traveling across the Kingdom of Dunbar with many other Keeper families, making the journey to deposit their initiates in Lorelai. At that age, he had been awkward as hell! He was beset with a shyness proportionate to his immense size. The first time he set his eyes on Alida of Galagar, she was hanging like a bat by her bent legs from a tree branch ten feet above the ground. He'd not yet met the Galagar, her brother and parents having just joined their encampment on their way southward. Several of the children from the City of Gwail had come upon her in a glade by a tributary of the River Gliff. Like Andor, they'd also never seen such a small and fragile-looking soul as the young Galagar. Like most children, their fascination was quickly replaced by fear, followed by a need to torment anyone who didn't 'fit'. They had chased her to a tree that hung lazily over the banks of the river, where they were now calling her names, doing their best to infuriate her.

In response to their taunts, Alida laughed with the most rolling and delight-filled laugh that the Sethian child had ever heard. She swung to and fro, leaping from one branch to another with the ease of a monkey, seemingly unaffected by their jeers until one of the less impressed members of the rabble hit her in the back with a rock. It had been thrown with a most deliberate and malicious force. Having initially watched from a distance, Andor could not suffer the injustice. Hearing Alida's melodic laughter replaced by a shriek of surprised pain felt like joy had been ripped out of him. In a blink, he came crashing through the trees with fists clenched and ready to swipe at the other children. The older children who had been stupid enough to oppose were thrashed and tossed away like annoying wasps. They soon fled in terror of this sudden colossus punishing them with relish.

Alida watched him with fascination as he came to her rescue. Her little heart surged at the display of chivalry. When he'd finally come to a halt below her, he reached up with both hands and told her not to be afraid. Alida's tears fell less liberally, her silvery-gray eyes transfixed on Andor's brown pupils. She let herself fall from the branch into his hands with complete confidence that her slight weight would be received. She wasn't even half of his almost six feet in height despite her being older than him by at least a year. Wiping the tears from her face, she kissed Andor's cheek with the most butterfly-like softness. The gesture sent a tremble throughout his entire boy body.

"Are all giants as nice as you?" she said without hesitation, the sobs of pain being replaced with soft voice tones. Andor was speechless; the small Galagar's speaking voice was nearly as lovely as the sound of her laughter.

"No matter," she answered to the empty air. "We're always going to be the best of friends." She said this so matter-of-factly and sweetly that he knew her intention would stick. From that day on, and for every year that these two Keepers gathered with their brethren, they would ever more be inseparable.

Chapter 29

The Wigget had been quiet. Shamus knew that somehow Anthrac was reassured, even restive. The hours passed in relative calm since he banished the malevolent buzz that had been attempting to remain fastened to the Keepers. He knew that it had been his own idiocy in speaking the Evil One's name that brought the dark enchantments forth toward them out of far-off Greno. He was accordingly determined to rid the Travelers, and himself, of the negativity. He knew that compelling everyone to only think positive thoughts might not shed the dark cloud that descended over them, but it was at least a strategy to afford protection to them, and, he reasoned, *it might work*. The thought of doing nothing at all was worse, and for whatever reason, his own sense of malaise had passed.

Shamus considered the immensity of Anthrac's self-imposed exile. The Angel had been gone from Loura for more than a thousand years of their memory, and yet through the eye of the void and the protection of hosts who bore him generation after generation in a distant temporal world, he had watched and waited for twenty times that length, wondering when it might become necessary to once more take corporeal form outside of a host. Anthrac had borne witness to every age of humankind through the eyes of his hosts, passively observing the rises and demises of many kingdoms all the way through to the time of Shamus's own point in the timeline. He had lived in a self-imposed exile—a careful, watchful hiding spanning more than 20,000 years of linear time. *How was such a thing even possible?* he asked himself. In a way, hibernation was akin to a plant bulb that gathers energy beneath a frozen, wintery surface only to then press forth a new flower come the spring. *But wow! Such a very long time!*

The White Wigget had witnessed atrocities and great demonstrations of evil visited on the planet by men and women of ill will. More than once, ancient civilizations had been wholly dominated by creatures from the demon realm, passing themselves off as false gods. These moments in the timeline came with great atrocities that had pained him greatly! Never once, however, was evil the dominant presence upon the lands. There had been many moments in time where goodness could be found, and thus hope continued to prevail. The threat of the Master of the Pit's entry into the earthly realm had strangely not yet come. In a linear understanding of time, Anthrac knew that this made no sense. The madness that so often became the profile of the White Wigget's hosts was fully tied to Anthrac's own efforts to look at time using their human brains. He knew that if Satan were to attempt to escape his eternal prison and cross realms, it would be at a time and place that he selected as being most advantageous to himself. All he had to do was figure out a way. The Itavo Stones were 'that' way—the one and only way.

As Strahanas began to diminish on Earth, a solution to protect the light in the universe had to be worked out. It was determined that an intermingling of Strahanas with some humans could be permitted to preserve their legacy. Some of humanity would thus enjoy a uniquely magical birthright. To further protect the mission of the Angelic colony even as it diminished required that hybrids born of Strahana-human couplings agree to only breed with others who had been so favored. The purer the bloodline, the greater the magic of the Angealkind would endure in select families. Anthrac Aran had instituted specific rules for these chosen people before vanishing from the minds of Lourans. It would constitute his only way to protect humanity from meeting an end at the hands of the Master of the Demon realm.

Erladoch Dunbar the Brave of Fior Hill and his brothers and sisters in the Sacred Order of Keepers were the progeny of the pact made with the last living Angel. His genetic purity as such a hybrid was stronger than many of his fellow Keepers. The endurance of Strahanian magic within him presented both gifts but also a heavy mantel of responsibility to fulfill the Angel's mandate. His station both as a Captain of the Sacred Order of Keepers and his honest nature would ever collide with that mandate. Of all the Travelers, Anthrac was at all times preoccupied with Erladoch and his commitment to the imperatives of the Angealkind. Even in repose, he listened intently through Shamus's ears to any and all advice uttered by the Prince of Dunbar. When Erladoch had revealed his personal power for the first time in the dreamscape to save Shamus from certain death in the hands of Enilorac, he had built a psychic bridge to the man. That bridge would be ever-present to ensure that Erladoch remained focused in his priorities—namely, to protect Shamus against all enemies, including himself.

Since arriving in Loura, the White Wigget had tried to occupy a presence of reposed vigilance. He chose to avoid acting through Shamus whenever possible, and only when he deemed that his Bearer's life was at true risk. The more he expressed himself, the more he would act as an unwilling beacon to the evil king of Treborg. Furthermore, every moment that his human host required him to enhance his presence in the physical domain drained his vitality dearly. The past several days of hard foot travel carried out by his host had been peppered with frequent incursions from both physical onslaughts and magical invasion alike. It had caused him to blaze within Shamus more than he ought to have. If he were to find the energy to ultimately ascend into corporeal form once more, he would need to conserve himself. Recognizing the power shown by his human host and that of Erladoch the Brave of Fior Hill signaled to him that he could recede for a time. The White Wigget now slept as the last hours of the multi-day march wound down. As the Travelers closed in on the city of Gol in the southern limits of the Kingdom of Bodeland, an air of calm finally fell over the group. It had only been a journey of 70 yarricks, but the unevenness of the mountainous and heavily forested terrain often made it impossible to go beyond a jog.

* * *

The light of old Naga was almost completely gone from the few openings in the forest canopy above their heads. The Galagars had traversed these parts of the Bodeland Forest to the south often. They were highly familiar with the city of Gol and its inhabitants. It had long been a central point along their own people's thoroughfares for trade and commerce. Of all the populated areas of the world of Loura, one would be more likely to come upon a person from the Kingdom of Galagan in the city of Gol than pretty much anywhere else. It served as a halfway point between Galagan and the kingdom of Ara. Trade between these two kingdoms had been robust for centuries before the other kingdoms of Loura began to participate.

Exotic Galagan silks had been traded in return for the beautifully handcrafted pottery of Ara for many ages. Aranan pottery was desired for its obvious utility by kingdoms that did not have the abundance of clays available

254

to them. Whether it was jointed clay piping, dishes or large amphoras designed to hold water, wine or even exotic oils, the craftsmanship invested in all such products was of the highest quality. Made from the unique clay found only alongside the banks of Lake Kitar (a landlocked lake fed by an abundant natural spring), Aranan clay had no rival. In more recent generations, the amphoras made in Ara were also shipped to Galagan filled with everything from wine to basic food staples. More than any other kingdom in Loura, Ara served as a main food source for Galagan.

Once it had been said that the trees of Galagan had to have been adorned in sheets of gold and silver. More correctly, however, the fabrics produced by the Galagan people were thought to have held greater value than such precious metals. A sprawling forest domain that nearly rivaled the size and age of the ancient forests of Bodeland, it had been populated with many fruiting trees, and most particularly, Mulberry trees. To have walked in the old Land of Galagan would have involved an experience of pure enchantment! The stretching treed landscape was enrobed in silk threads extruded in such abundance that they hung like Spanish moss from every branch. At Galagan's zenith, most of the kingdom's occupants were in some manner invested in the production of silk fabrics, given their high level of desirability. The industry had become so dominant, and its people so reliant upon it, that over time, the silkworm population was permitted to grow unchecked. Where silkworms had once confined themselves to the mulberry trees, however, soon they began consuming every variety of fruiting tree in the area. To survive as a species, they rapidly shifted eating habits that had once been restricted to leaves and berries to stripping the bark right off the trees upon which they had thrived. The once-immense forest canopy of the Galagar people began disappearing at a rate that could not be stopped. The resourceful Galagars attempted to adapt by expanding their trade with their neighbors for resources they no longer had in abundance. This, however, was not sustainable. Ironically, if not predictably, at the time when their silk became most coveted elsewhere in Loura as a garment of value, the Galagars woke up to the reality of the ecological disaster they had brought upon themselves. Within only a few generations, the trees, which had once been so abundant, were nearly gone. The worms were so highly adaptive that they began consuming entire trees for its food source, taking even the largest and oldest trees right down to the roots. Unbeknownst to anyone, those trees sat atop vast quantities of mineral-rich earth. Once the metal-dense soils feeding the roots were ingested by the worms, an entirely new form of silk thread emerged in Galagan. Light, resilient and pliable, the properties of Galagan silk bore properties more akin to chain mail—a garment which would not be created for many thousands of years later. It was said that an arrow shot at a person wearing a Galagan overshirt would not be able to pierce the firmly woven garment.

Galagars faced a horrible dilemma: If they protected their remaining trees by culling the silkworm population, they could end their reliance on other kingdoms to supply them with basic food staples that were no longer in abundance in their kingdom. The alternative was to plant fast-growing mulberry bushes that would sustain the silkworm population at a distance far enough away from the remaining forest lands where Galagars still made their own homes and continue their practices as manufacturers and traders. To accomplish this without allowing their people to starve, however, they resolved to rely on other kingdoms for food until they might someday reinvigorate their own fruit trees. This would take generations. Not even recognizing that they had cast the die against themselves, the kingdom of Galagar was forced to depopulate to such a point that it would be a kingdom in name only, as the land would not be able to sustain its entire people. Once a robust kingdom with several hundred thousand occupants spread across vast forested lands, the people divided themselves into the few remaining towns that had been preserved, with the rest having long taken to the byways of Loura. On any given day, the full-time occupants of Galagan only numbered in the tens of thousands.

The Galagars bore features that were distinct from the other races of men. Like their Bodelandish neighbors, they had both venerated and thrived in their forest homes. Their distinct diet, comprising mostly flora, had resulted in the Galagars being very slight in stature on average. Many of them had very gaunt and bony countenances which chiseled to finely pointed cheeks, chins and noses. Coupled with nearly opaque white skin, they were a people who were considered all at once to be both beautiful and startling in appearance. Deftness and eye-stunningly fast in their movements, they had once been referred to as the 'phantoms of the forest'. The average full-grown Galagar adult stood no taller than 4.5 feet. They could climb trees so swiftly and blend in with the plant life around them so convincingly that even the most discerning eye would be hard-pressed to catch sight of one as they clung to the bough of their once uniquely adorned forest realm. While their slight frame made it appear as though these soft-hearted people could be pushed over by a strong wind, there was another side to them. One was well advised to not annoy a Galagar, however, or trespass upon their property. The unfortunate soul who acted with recklessness toward their diminishing forest would most assuredly get a taste of their terrifying speed and agility.

As the silkworm populations ate themselves into near extinction, the lands of Galagan were beginning to recover. Trees began to return, and the earth slowly healed. Galagar communities were still spread out across the other kingdoms of Loura in large part, as it would take time for the terrain to be once again able to sustain its occupants in multitudes. Nida and his sister Alida happily traversed Loura, fulfilling their oaths as Keepers. Having said this, they craved contact with their own people whenever such opportunities presented themselves. They accordingly now lead the Travelers toward Gol, firmly convinced that Shamus was guiding them there in any event.

***

Shamus had listened intently to the tales shared by both Nida and Alida in the final hours of the Travelers' journey to Gol. They had a very palpable affinity to this place, which had once posed as the trading crossroad for all of Loura, and, most notably, for their people. It was perhaps one of the remaining places in Loura where tales of their great culture still got told with enough regularity that the Galagars who still traversed the Bodelandish city were not looked upon with fear and suspicion.

In the excited exchanges of conversation now flowing among Nida, Alida and Nica Bodelander, it was apparent that the Galagar siblings had been traveling for a very long time, tending to Keeper business before this journey had begun. They longed to meet up with some of their own kind again. Given that the race and culture of Galagan was so closely interrelated, Nida was concerned that his parents would be much worried about their long absence. He hoped to stumble upon kinsmen who would take messages of greetings home for him and his sister.

Nica assured the Galagars that she would see to it that some of their kind would be found and dispatched to them for that purpose. The twins had been sent by their uncle, the overseer of the Galagan council of elders, on a mission of reconnaissance along the distant northern portions of the Boldar River. Their observations of the massive equipping of Scraggin armies had acted as firm proof that the Great War of Loura was finally coming just days before Shamus turned up with Erladoch in tow.

As the mountains between Castra and the ways to Galagan made for too perilous a journey to proceed straight home, their natural course would have taken them close to Gol before turning northward if they had been disposed to return. With this new mission in hand for the two Galagars, they would remain with their new friends as representatives of their countrymen's place in the unified struggle against the impending evil.

***

Nica drew the small, wood-fluted horn from inside of the hip belt, which Shamus had seen previously. This time, he noticed that it had many small, irregularly shaped holes on the outside. Nica thoughtfully placed her lips over the horn, covering but a small portion of the holes carved into it. She blew lightly several times as she moved the device back and forth like a harmonica. An echoing, bird-like chatter pitched and dropped as she worked the horn-flute. This time, its sound was melodious and pleasant; very different than previous intonations he had already heard. The intent was clear—she was announcing her arrival.

While Gol is a slightly more modern city than Castra, the same form of defense, comprising camouflaged perches high above the ground, was prevalent. One might have thought that cities built entirely in the hearts of the mountainous trees of the Bodeland Forest would be nearly impossible for traders and other welcome travelers to properly find. This thought crossed Shamus's mind as he approached Gol with his companions. The Bodelanders had long addressed this issue of maintaining their privacy while still opening themselves to the other kingdoms of Loura. By placing high-perched sentinels at regular distances around the perimeter of each of their principal cities, they could assess the 'visitor' from high above as they approached. Once deemed friendly, a Bodelander would always manage to emerge, seemingly from some unseen hole in the ground, their entire job being to act as a guide into the city center. It was a time-honored method, and any traveler seeking respite among the Bodeland Foresters obeyed the custom of waiting to be greeted, even after they had traveled the same routes and pathways for years.

In a moment, the Travelers heard a response welcoming the princess. This was followed by much fainter whistles. Nica explained to Andor and Shamus, who were both visiting Gol for their first time, that the other whistles contained a variety of simple instructions. One call signaled to the inner city to prepare a proper feast and accommodation for the visitors. Another call was a message to the various newly formed garrisons to strengthen the guard around the city to reassure that no unwanted parties were following the Travelers. This call to action was, not surprisingly, the most discordant of note combinations that Nica blew on her small flute.

The companions had completed a perilous and disheartening third day's travel as they drew within the natural fortification of the immensely thick cluster of trees of the outer city. Erladoch instructed the party to draw their hoods well over their heads to avoid being easily recognized. In the warmth of the day and the hard travel, they had relaxed their precautions a little, but now, for the sake of the Bodelanders, they walked quickly with heads down and hoods closed around their faces. Even this far south in Gol, spies of the Evil One could be lurking. Recalling the spillage of unnecessary blood when they had departed Castra, Shamus knew that it would be easier on the citizens of this city if they knew nothing about their identity.

Nica alone walked with head held high, her hood draped over her slim, muscled shoulders, so that her people could see that the kingdom was still confidently led by at least one member of its ruling clan. The others stayed covered and avoided eye contact. Thankfully, there was no apparent order for the people to turn their backs to the visitors. This was clearly a tactical decision made by Nica to provide encouragement. As a result, the Travelers were not greeted by anxious faces, only polite nods.

Bit by bit, however, men, women, and their children poured out onto what revealed itself by its width alone to be a principal boulevard to cheer for and greet their princess. Her arrival helped dispel the fear that had recently gripped the kingdom, as increasingly more tales came to the inhabitants of Scrags running unchecked within their borders.

As they walked in file along the open-armed masses of people, Shamus held his eyes on Nica. He would catch glimpses of her face from time to time, noticing the very complicated mix of her emotions. She was highly pleased with the expressions of welcome from her people, but the firm pursing of her lips suggested that she was weighing the tidings she was bringing with her. She knew all too well that the happy faces would rapidly change to grim countenances even on the most jubilant Bodelander gathering around her. Once they knew what would be disclosed to them about Ardehla, as well as what would now be expected of them in but a few days' time, she estimated they might even wish to stone her.

Nica did her utmost to display a commanding look of resolve and confidence to the hundreds who were pouring out from hidden doorways in the massive trees. Shamus found himself continuing to marvel over the trunks of mostly deciduous trees that formed the homes and halls of Gol Bodeland. Trees which had grown for thousands of years, sprung up out of the earth. Unlike the Conifers of Castra, the massive leafy branches of maples, oaks and hemlocks ambled and stretched like blood vessels, all of them winding themselves into their neighbors.

Like Castra, the closer they neared what had to be the city center, the bigger the most ancient of the trees were. Shamus guessed that the circumference of the oldest trees exceeded a hundred and eighty feet at the base. The roots of many stood high above the ground like rock walls before plunging hundreds of feet below the surface, supporting the ancient monoliths as they spread their boughs and branches heavenward. While he did his best to keep his cloak closed around his face, Shamus was awestricken. As the Travelers moved into the city center, he needed to take in the utter magnificence of these structures, knowing that he would never cast his eyes upon something so fantastically ancient and beautifully alive ever again.

Reminding himself to remain unrecognizable, he looked back toward Nica at the very moment that her commanding and practiced facial expression faltered momentarily. Shamus had no difficulty reading and interpreting her very briefly uncontrolled facial grimace. It was as clear to him as the sound of a sports car changing gears is to a race car driver. The clinical psychologist read her 'tell'. He knew it to signify a raging conflict erupting within the otherwise stalwart woman. Her nation was in full-on celebration of her unexpected arrival from the wilds. They had no notion that she was soon to make them into homeless refugees, guests at the whim of another ruler. However benevolent their future host might be, she was there to bring this sad news, and it was becoming all too much for her. Her momentary lapse in composure revealed both her sadness and her feeling of intense shame. Nica was so weary from the travel and the sudden surge of emotions boiling up within her that she faltered.

Andor was close enough to her that his massive hand steadied her before she could stumble to the ground. Despite the subtlety of his effort, the people saw. The crowd's merriment spontaneously hushed. She mustered a smile and said something in her ancient Bodelandish suggestive of her being clumsier than a child wearing two wrong sandals. This quickly attracted nervous laughter from those closest to her in the throngs. The damage was done, however. A realization swept over the multitude that this was not a social visit; their young princess was exhausted from her travel, and this meant that she had been moving with dispatch. Over the past four years, that had always meant 'bad news'.

Until she was fully standing in the largest public square of Gol, where the lantern lights suspended in the branches above cast the greatest amount of illumination about the Travelers, the blood stains of warfare had lain nearly fully concealed in the specially woven cloaks that they wore—till now. Before the murmuring of whispers could turn into a rollicking wave of fearful chatter, a door concealed in the root of the largest maple to O'Mara's right heel swung open, and a contingent of soldiers marched out to welcome the princess. With a gesture of her hand to her companions that was as much to say, "Let's waste no time getting inside!" she strode into the cavern beneath the roots, which revealed its immensity the moment she crested the doorway.

Shamus hurried his pace to walk beside Nica. Erladoch and Andor closed in behind, concerned that she may faint from exertion. Shamus reached out empathetically and clasped her right arm. "You know that what you are here to tell them is the only possible choice, Princess, don't you?"

She looked at him briefly and then turned one last time to face her citizens, waving her hand in thanks like the royal that she clearly was, before disappearing inside the corridor.

"Thank you," she managed politely, not bothering to make eye contact with Shamus before she resumed walking.

With the soft slide of a massive door, the outdoor light was completely gone. Shamus stood still a moment, waiting for his eyes to adjust to the light provided entirely by a multitude of lanterns swaying from the hands of their escort. Turning the first discernible corner, he saw ceramic wall torches adorning the walls up ahead. As Shamus looked forward into the long, arcing corridor, it occurred to him that he would be of immediate interest to anyone who looked upon him in this more illumined place, as the sheer beauty of his cloak in comparison to the others was sparkling from the transient light. Certainly, this would have been enough to signal that there was something special about him—a reveal he would have liked to have avoided, if possible, for everyone's safety. As these thoughts flashed through his mind, he was pleased to find that his cloak had in fact turned to the same basic color as the cloaks worn by his companions. It was as though the magic of spells so brilliantly woven into every thread of the garment provided a connection to the intentions of its wearer. The notion was completely illogical to Shamus! To even imply that something not alive could, in any manner, accomplish discreet perceptions—or, more correctly, mirror the thoughts of its wearer—was ridiculous! The fact of this land, however, was that the impossible had become plausible. Shamus simply had to accept that his Wigget's cloak was, in and of itself, another example of the supernatural power of a race of beings he simply knew so little about. He wondered what other tricks it contained.

As each corridor emptied into the next, Shamus noticed that the passage sloped abruptly. By the number of paces he'd taken since entering, he calculated that he had not only walked a distance beyond his estimation of the outer circumference of the tree, which they had apparently entered, but he was also climbing. The feel of this corridor as he walked along reminded him very much of the multiple walkways, he had traversed inside Firren back in Castra. His mind went back to the chance encounter with the ethereal woman during his out-of-body experience. He hadn't chosen to share this story with anyone, lest people think him nuts, or the fact that he had now felt echoes of this same womanly apparition beckoning him during moments of quiet reflection at least twice since then. She always appeared as no more than a dot on a horizon somewhere far away, but he nonetheless recognized her as this same person. Back in Firren, she had called to him, imploring him to close the distance between them. He was sure that she had spoken aloud when it first happened. Now he was no longer sure. No matter how much he wanted to do so in his thoughts, he couldn't seem to get to where she was. The image of the woman's face remained utterly elusive to him; it had been as though she deliberately obscured her countenance for some reason.

Shamus's hand inadvertently brushed the polished bark wall of the corridor, bringing him back to where he was as they followed the illuminated path. By virtue of the changes in angle to the corridors he had traversed, he also reasoned that somehow the largest of the trees that had been around him in the square outside must come together somewhere and form a ring, likely somewhere quite high above the ground. What was actual tree versus man-made edifice built into the trees somewhere high above the city of Gol's major square was impossible for him to resolve. The natural continuity of the pathway appeared unbroken in its lines. Wherever he now was, it still felt as though he was in one single tree. The possibility that it might be joined together via a patchwork of natural catwalks in the branches was imperceptible. *If I'm truly walking outside or even inside tree branches right now, their size and scope is beyond my comprehension!* he told himself as he worked through his awe. The branches were, in fact, so large in places that one could have driven a 5-horse wagon over them. While Castra was formed of older coniferous trees and bore its people's history in carved monuments adorning the living walls, Gol's city center amidst the skyscraping maples, oaks and hemlocks was stunning on a whole other level. Castra was the historic seat of the Bodelandish nobility; Gol was its political and trading heartland.

When the party had passed through to the end of the welcoming crowds lining the expansive corridors, they found themselves climbing up a further 20 steep steps. This was the first obvious thing any of the Travelers had seen that was definitively man-made. Shamus could feel a momentary breeze. It led him to believe that he was outdoors as he ascended this stairwell into what he correctly guessed was the center of one of the tree castles. As they approached the top of the stairwell, the bark of the tree door swung open, layer upon massive layer. The thickness of this door could easily have been the length of a full-grown man laying horizontally.

Being the only newcomers to Gol, Shamus and Andor exchanged glances, which revealed their mutual sense of wonder and respect for the builders of the city. The very act of having hewn such a door, let alone finding a way to hinge it, must have been an undertaking that occupied craftsmen for years.

A procession of finely adorned soldiers filed out of the entrance way. As they came out, they stepped right and left of the Travelers climbing up to them on the last of the stairs.

Erladoch followed Princess Nica through the opening as the others made their way over the threshold, filing in behind. The room revealed itself to be a massive gathering place. Shamus caught sight of the soldiers now standing guard around the extremes of the door. There were men and women alike, all in fine uniforms of softened and sturdy leather woven into an underlying dark green cloth. The colors of their clothing helped them to blend into the background of their forest habitat. These newly minted Bodelandish warriors were not only expected to blend with their natural environment; they were equipped with weaponry that would facilitate speedy movement. With bows fastened to the side of small quivers on their backs and short but sturdy swords on their hips, these were proud and sure soldiers, new or not. Each one stood perfectly straight. Though all of them had reached adulthood, it was obvious to Shamus that they were, nonetheless, young. The concept of a Bodelandish standing army was a very new one; like the majority of the warriors who were beginning to form its ranks. Shamus noticed that each soldier had a different patch sewn into the left breast of their garments. Some patches depicted trees, while others bore images of flowers. The significance of their distinctive patterns was not entirely clear to him, but he guessed that each distinctive patch was worn by a captain of sorts. He wondered how many people each captain might have had under their respective commands. *Is it a handful? Or do they have command of whole legions?* He had no way of knowing.

The companions entered a large and beautiful chamber. Its size defied Shamus's understanding! Knowing that it was 'indoors' and had to have been constructed 'inside' a living tree, he was unable to reconcile the information. As he had approached the Great Hall in relative darkness, he could not have seen that this space was formed out of the junction point of three distinct trees, which had, over many centuries, twisted into each other's embrace. The hall had been hewn out of the midpoint of where each tree had come together, giving the illusion that the parties were inside of one tree rather than being located within the outer exteriors of all three. Either way, the hall was impressive! A table had been set in anticipation of their arrival. It overflowed with foods of all forms common to Bodeland: partridge, rabbit, mushrooms, potatoes, beets and turnips, to name but a few. The Travelers were invited to take seats at the table by three people who plainly had control over the actions of everyone else entering and leaving the hall. Without fanfare or ceremony, they were introduced by Lady Nica after she greeted each of them with great affection. To Shamus's left was Harn Leafcorn, Commander of the Gol army. Next to him sat Anisha El, the Mayor of Gol. Shamus remarked that the mayor bore a resemblance to the princess. Lastly, Nica presented Elhin Overbranch, Steward and royal family's representative in Gol. These were the people of influence in Gol. While there were internal ministers of trade, construction, city planning and industry, it was in this triumvirate where the power over all decisions regarding the life of the city resided.

As Nica and her friends moved into earshot, they rose and bowed courteously and beckoned servants to relieve the Travelers of their packs. Before anyone removed their cloaks to drape them on the wooden notch-hook at the back of the dinner chairs, Nica ordered all the guards present to watch the entrance closely. She took quiet note of the servants as well, counting their number carefully. When she was satisfied that they were all present, she announced to them that if any one servant remained too long in the room, or if it were discovered that they had repeated any aspect of what they were to overhear during their comings and goings, she would see to it that they would have their tongues taken out. Despite what he had seen during his departure from Castra, the order seemed immensely harsh to Shamus. *Jaysus! Not again!* He swallowed hard.

No one else in the room even batted an eye upon receiving her warning. The need for security was high, and thus Nica's command was deemed reasonable. As a result, the entire evening became a test of how quickly the servants could enter, do their task, and leave the room again.

The first matters of discussion consisted of the tribulations of the princess's three-days-long journey. The hosts were very saddened to hear of the demise of the village to the north and ashamed that such a large party of Scrags could have gone unnoticed and unchallenged in Bodeland. Even if they were free-roaming Scrags and not actual Treborgan soldiers—an issue which invited some measure of debate—it was unheard of that such atrocity could occur so deeply within their forest kingdom.

Nica retold their long and sad last day's journey, remarking that the new Age of Darkness had befallen the entire world and not just the boundaries of Bodeland. News of the Anahimaran slaughter had long since arrived in Gol by this time, and the three heads of the city each took a moment to fill the princess in on their preparations for the coming war. The mayor and steward each surmised that great labors should be brought to bear in further hiding the city's existence from the outside world. Signs had already been removed from tree walls; windows that once opened out from the non-living portions of the great trees were covered over with bark panels fitted tightly, like storm shutters. Typical thoroughfares once commonly used in the outskirts of Gol had been wiped daily to remove the prints made by many feet.

Plantings of small shrubs had been placed sporadically along the way to further hide the natural path systems accessing the city.

Nica complimented them in a polite and respectful manner. Her people were new to a warlike footing. They were doing what they thought was best to manage threats. Their efforts had been reasonably impressive, even though what she would soon speak of would render such efforts of little use. She turned to Harn Leafcorn for a report on the preparations of the military. Leafcorn's eyes slowly rose from his tankard of fine ale, meeting the princess with a hopeful glance. "My lady, forgive me if I have erred by not working in concert with my friends. I have been making ready the Legions of Gol to travel great distances. In your name, I've also called upon all able men and women to the service of Bodeland and have, these past 12 days alone, trained as many of them as best that I could."

"What was your intention commander?" Erladoch asked with apparent curiosity.

"To make ready for an evacuation of Gol on a day's notice. My information from the neighboring kingdoms is not good. The Evil One, whose name is unspeakable, is soon to be on the advance. I fear that his forces are of a magnitude that will overcome our newly assembled army unless we unite with our brethren in Loura on one place of battle. I reckon from what tidings that have made their way here about the demise of Anahimara"—O'Mara winced noticeably, as if even a declaration of a known fact was like the sticking of a blade in his guts—"we're no match to stand alone agin' such darkness."

"This is where we have differed in our opinion on what your orders might be, my lady," Anisha El broke in. "Surely we can conceal ourselves from our enemy and just let this madness pass us by?" She was clearly still at odds with Harn's estimation of what Nica's plan would be. "I have made extensive preparations to erase our man-made appurtenances already, my princess. The enemy might never find us here."

"You speak madness, El! Ye canna' think this will be enough!"

Before Harn Leafcorn finished his interruption, he adjusted his tone. He had felt the heat of Princess Nica's expression of displeasure in him. His disrespectful interjection was not appreciated. He adjusted the volume and tone of his voice before continuing, mindful of the scornful gaze.

"Apologies, M'lady. What I meant to say is that my friend is naïve, I'm afraid. Even if the entire House of Treborg knows not the location of Gol exactly, they still know 'of it'. They will scour the forest till they find us. The madness that spills out from behind the walls of the Elec Mountains will not rest until every tree in Bodeland has been destroyed in such a mission."

His tone was shaky now, as he measured the utter scope of such a notion. He had been mad at his sense of defeatism but had worked hard to become resigned to what he considered to be the likely outcome of an invasion.

"Now, I know that you come to us in haste and secrecy because your message is one of desperate tiding." He reached for his tankard and took a long draft of its contents while those assembled waited. "You have come to tell us that we must evacuate our families under the protection of our newly trained legion to safer lands. I estimate that you will command us to move our armies to a meeting ground of the other kingdoms. Aye? Tis not our battle alone, after all, is it?" Harn glanced at the Travelers assembled at the grand meeting table. "Our princess comes to tell us just these very things, I suspect. If I'm wrong, I request your forgiveness." He settled back in his seat.

Nica's beautiful steely eyes flared, but in admiration of Leafcorn. "Surely, there is no better or wiser a soldier than you, Harn Leafcorn. Anisha, Steward Overbranch—you've all done well to do what you have done to hide the city back into its natural state, for perhaps it will buy us time in making our evacuation complete. It may even leave our homes impossible to find when the darkness comes. Your very clever anticipation is not wasted. Harn, you speak the truth, though I wish t'were not so." An audible gasp filled the air in the room. Nica's confirmation of the general's suppositions was hard news to receive. Everyone assembled stirred in upset with the idea of abandoning Gol, for though most of the Forresters were not natural soldiers, they held the pride and love of their homeland as much as anyone. They would gladly exchange their lives in order to preserve it.

"What I find concerning," Alida spoke for the first time since entering the chamber, "is that no runner has arrived before us to deliver this message in spite of your princess having chosen a few trusted soldiers to bring these very tidings ahead of our arrival. You have clearly arrived at these conclusions without having received tidings from Castra, eh?"

The absent stares of the triumvirate gave her the answer she had expected. Nica glanced over at Erladoch and Alida. Unlike Andor, who was quietly munching on a partridge leg, his hunger making his politeness secondary, the others had been sitting in abject silence. Erladoch met both Alida and Nica's sideward glances long enough to read the mental messages exchanged among them—that the Bodeland Forrest was clearly so unsafe that even a solitary messenger had not evaded Enilorac's ever-tightening noose. The people of Gol were not ready to leave. While Nica and her companions had moved with little rest, it had been nonetheless expected that a trusted messenger could have made the journey in two days' time, if they hadn't stopped. Important time had been lost. Without any sign of alarm being shown on her face, Nica Bodelander resumed.

"How long before there are wagons enough to carry out all the provisions and treasures of Gol?" Nica asked in an open-ended manner, expecting that any of her trusted leaders could offer a reply to her question.

"Thirty days at the very best, mi' lady," replied Elhin Overbranch. "We will need to build many wagons to accomplish such a feat, plus we will need tanners to make halters for beasts of burden to pull them."

Nica considered this assessment. "It must be done sooner if ye can. It is my hope that messengers would have reached all the communities within Bodeland by now to spread my command. Now I fear whether any of the smaller boroughs and villages know what is expected of them. The people of Castra, for sure, will arrive within the next 14 days, so please spread the word this night. Any more time taken than this and you may not have time to clear the Bodeland Forest before the Treborgans strike. They are already afoot in our lands with strength. I do not want what happened in Ardehla to be the fate of all my people. We don't know how long we have. I want the entire city informed immediately so that preparations can begin. Secrecy is no longer possible. The order to maintain silence is canceled."

One of the servants who had just entered the hall breathed an audible sigh of relief. Nica eyed the old man with sympathy before resuming.

"Spread the word throughout Gol and surrounding areas nearby immediately. My colleagues and I will require your finest horses and supplies for five days' travel. We leave on the morrow."

Upon hearing this news, Shamus groaned out loud. The volume of his protest was louder than he had intended, the pulsing of his sore feet craving rest. He tried to cover it up by coughing into his beer as though he had been choking on too big a pull from the contents of his fired clay mug.

Alida smiled in spite of herself. She had no trouble in reading Shamus's cover-up of his outburst, and the honesty of it made her giggle. In truth, all the Travelers were smarting from their journey, but unlike Shamus, they were hardened to the rigors of a warrior's life.

Andor also heard Shamus's protest. He already knew the message that they had come to deliver. The princess's announcement meant only one thing to him: eat and drink more! He plowed into his large cup of beer and stabbed at another piece of meat sitting on the platter in front of him.

Nica paid no attention to any of the reactions around the table. Her own muscles were sufficiently weary and aching from their recent battle and hard travel that she herself did not enjoy having to lay down such an agenda. She craved respite like the rest of them and would soon enough find her bed. Till then, however, she would consult with her kinsmen and ensure that all necessary plans would be in motion the minute she would awaken tomorrow.

"In one cycle of the moon, all of Bodeland is to gather here in Gol to commence an exodus. It must be left barren by the next day. Leave no one behind. If anyone resists, remove them forcibly."

The steward rose from his place of honor. "All yer subjects will follow, m'lady."

Anisha El winced noticeably but said nothing. The notion of an evacuation of her birthplace felt like a dagger in her side. She looked down at her feet as Elhin Overbranch continued to seek the princess's guidance.

"Of the traders within our borders, what shall we do with them?"

Nica considered his point carefully. This request posed a different type of challenge. Sending visitors away could spell certain death for such folk if they were to be set upon by Scraggin war parties. On the other hand, if they were to go out in large enough numbers, there would at least be a chance that they might bring the news to their own kingdoms that she had hoped would have already gone forth.

"Tell them to return to their homelands with all speed, and to spread the word that we shall meet in the lands of Dunbar. There we shall then have chosen where to secure our families, and also where to draw our battle lines.

If they fear a voyage back to their own homelands, invite them to join in our exodus. No one shall be left behind or deliberately thrown to the wolves."

Elhin motioned with his hand to request permission to speak. Nica nodded slightly to demonstrate her approval.

"Given your majesty's plan to depart ahead of us, your mission draws you elsewhere, no doubt?"

Once more, Nica nodded affirmatively.

"As the peril of your voyage must be great, permit me to suggest that you take an escort of a hundred or more riders."

Princess Nica acknowledged his offer with grace and appreciation but replied to him, "My Lord Overbranch, yer a faithful and considerate servant of the throne. I thank you for your concern. I assure you that such a move would only place both of us in more peril: you, because the people of Gol will need as much protection as they can find when they leave the cover of our beautiful forest land, and therefore, ya canna' spare even a single warrior. There are yet so few good soldiers in our service, and you'll need to spend the next several weeks making a real and capable fighting force. As for myself and my companions, I am sure you'd understand that we would only be encumbered by having so large a number to ride with. It is imperative that we move unnoticed and with great speed, lest we too run out of time to complete our tasks."

"Lady Nica," the mayor interrupted. "Why is it that no messenger arrived before you with this news?" There it was—the question which could only raise greater alarm, if not actual panic. Deception, even in the form of a small 'white lie', was neither appropriate for the station of a princess of these people, let alone for a Keeper.

"I suspect they were killed én route, or possibly at the massacre of Ardehla village. It is thus important that you dispatch your fastest riders and runners to all the outer communities lying to the south. I had sent messengers to fan out across Bodeland with my tidings as well as to the borders of Ara, Dunbar and Seth. I expected that for any one, if not all of them, their journeys would be long and perilous, but we must pray that some will avoid the fate of the messengers sent this way and reach their destinations unharmed. We cannot light signal fires nor sound horn calls to warn our neighbors of impending war. The Evil One watches us much more closely than we can estimate. If he receives knowledge that we are preparing for his onslaught, he may unleash his forces earlier than expected. This would be disastrous! The very survival of all Lourans depends on stealth. Therefore, my wise friends, even you must travel in silence, and avoid the open country as much as possible despite your great numbers. Though it will be perilous, you must lead our people west along the edge of the Dead Forest until you come together with the exoduses of the other kingdoms on the plains of Ara. There are many different and dangerous creatures which still walk both the forest lands and plains alike, yet I pray the size and strength of our collective people shall discourage most from interfering with your transit. Lead the people as you have led them thusly— together. But, in event of an attack while on the road to Dunbar, I counsel you all to listen to Commander Leafcorn. Of all your collective ábaltacht, he is the most learned in the ways of large-scale combat over all of ya."

With this said, Nica sunk lower into her chair and drew a great draft of ale from her mug. She sighed and then said, "I fear that I shall never again taste the fine flavor of the Bodelander's mainstay. Let us all raise our glasses and drink to happier days, which shall hopefully return someday."

Erladoch rose and tilted his tankard one more time, saying to all assembled, "Yes indeed! I shall toast to the hope of future ages." Raising his beer high, he cleared his throat before addressing the room. "So that our children will'na know of the pestilence which comes to devour us except in the songs of heroes." He drank a hefty swallow, then sighed. "Tomorrow, we make for the lands of Ara. We ride mostly in open country with little cover. Sleep heartily, friends, for our journey must be swift if we are not to increase the risk of detection by creatures in the service of the Evil One."

"Aye, Lord Dunbar," came the Sethian's reply. "Even fair Ara is likely no longer safe with the fall of Anahimara on their northern border. I doubt not that the Scraggin armies prepare to march forth from Taroc and Ataroc soon. Surely, they've laid sufficient waste to those noble cities that they now hunger to move on with their foul plans."

O'Mara Boldar sat expressionless as he processed Andor's observation. Even without having witnessed it himself first-hand, what the colossus had just spoken of was entirely likely. It could not be avoided in conversation just because O'Mara was in the room. Yet, it still felt like someone was twisting a knife into the Anahimaran prince. Despite the display of outward stillness, on the inside, bubbles of rage coursed through his blood, and his face and neck reddened in spite of himself. Even the triumvirate who sat in their ceremonial chairs meticulously carved out from stumps of mahogany trees across the large table, could feel the bubble of rage which surged within the Anahimaran prince. *Rightly so*, they all considered. *This was still a very fresh humiliation!*

Trying to exert his Keeper-inspired control, and in hopes of being able to prove that he was still an asset to his colleagues as a member of their most Sacred Order, O'Mara offered his own thoughts to the chamber. "Certainly, by now the Evil One is spinning in anger, trying to guess at who could have slain so many Scrags and yet leave no victims of their own to identify the victor that engaged them."

Nida perked up. Till that moment, he had been absorbed with his own private thoughts. "It amuses me so that he will twist on this! Let the loathsome beast writhe and torment his servants for their failure to identify the intruders who bested them! I can't imagine how many he's already twisted out of his rage, but I wager his wrath has been visited on many already!"

Alida was taken aback by her brother's remark. As her twin followed his statement by uttering a harsh giggle that was entirely uncharacteristic of him, she tapped him on the shoulder with an outstretched arm. This was not the happy-go-lucky brother that she knew. His comment was thoughtless and wholly uncharacteristic of his status as a healer.

"What kind of half-witted nonsense is this? What did the Fiorian tell us about inviting negative thoughts into our midst?" She spoke just above a whisper as she kicked her brother's foot under the table as further confirmation of her ire and disappointment. "Have ya forgotten all those souls captured in Anahimara who'll also burn because of the Evil One's venomous anger?"

Interrupted thusly, Nida now seemed surprised by his own utterance. His sister's reprimand confirmed the degree of his impropriety. His opaque skin blanched as though any remaining blood which could have fed his cheeks had run away. The look of utter surprise at what had left his own lips was apparent.

"Idgit!" Alida whispered through a soft exhalation from her tiny chest. It was too late for reprimands. Everyone in the room was already privately musing over the unexpected toxicity of his statement. The room felt instantly colder and dark. A tangible weight of despair caused all assembled to hang their heads a moment. Nida's thoughtless comment evoked not only images of the plight of O'Mara Boldar's people, it further invited a graphic prediction of what would befall all their lands soon enough.

Despair was no longer the emotion coursing through the Anahimaran prince, however. Already struggling for control over himself, the imagery created by Nida's thoughtless comment caused him to lose composure. Even though he now spoke in a low voice, it was clearly not his highly trained Keeper persona that now rattled his vocal cords. The tone was baser than O'Mara's and filled with hate and challenge.

"Are all Galagans so quick with their tongues because they are so exceptionally slow with their thoughts? I would cut that tongue of yours out of ya tree weasel, lest I be forced to hear from you again!"

Nida sprung from his seat at the table. In a moment of blurry speed, he strung and fired an arrow, which whistled into the back of O'Mara's chair. The tail feathers of the missile had come to rest precariously close to the Anahimaran's right cheek. Everyone in the room froze in surprise except O'Mara. He was already on his feet, drawing his short scabber sword out of its leather housing.

"In another place and time, a man would have easily perished for having offended a Galagan so! Yer lucky that you continue to breath, horseman!" Nida spat out as the others watched, half-dazed. The exchange had been lightning-fast.

"You'll not be so lucky, you refugee from a worm's nest!" O'Mara growled as he leaped upon the wide oak table. He began the outward jerk, which caused the blade to fly out and lock into place on his short scabber; his swing arc, aimed at neck level, was already beginning at the exact moment that Nida had fitted a second silk-threaded arrow to the string of his bow, the latter's hand already pulling back. The blur of their lethal actions toward each other was rife with intent as they sped toward each other. The other Keepers, the triumvirate and the guards assembled in the room looked on with horror at the rapidly deteriorating situation.

Before the arrow could fly or the swing arc of a scabber could complete its journey, a loud and piercing screech interrupted the flow of violence. A sudden clash of metal on O'Mara's scabber interrupted his swing at the exact same instant that a hand shot out and took hold of Nida's bowstring. Everything came to a dead stop, as if time itself had slowed to a screeching halt. All eyes turned on Shamus, the Bearer of the White Wigget. As breath and sinew hung locked in time and space, Shamus had leaped in-between the two lifelong friends in what was less than a blink. His short samurai sword had appeared from beneath his brightly sparkling cloak in time to arrest the scabber's further movement. Those furthest from the conflict continued to look on as though they had been witnessing a sped-up movie reel that was coming to a violent stop. The sturdiness of Shamus's preventive barrier sent a shiver of pain down the Anahimaran prince's arms. Nida's arms, which had been drawing in opposite directions, suddenly lost all tensile strength and went limp from the energy resonating from Shamus's grip on the bowstring. Even had O'Mara and Nida not been so taken aback by the sudden alarming actions of the Wigget Bearer, the energy which washed over them in that moment consumed them both, making their knees buckle beneath them.

"Ssstttopp!" Shamus slowly whistled a word of mesmerizing commandment. Like his previously shrill scream moments ago, the way that the word left the Wigget Bearer's lips was disarming. Nida and O'Mara alighted to the ground unquestioningly, their weapons falling bluntly into the mess of overturned platters of food on the table.

"Con-trol-your-sel-ves." He lingered over the syllables with a deliberation which seemed to exert its own influence over the two men.

O'Mara withdrew the arrow from the chair and handed it back to Nida as though he was picking up a coin fallen out of its rightful owner's pocket and deserved to be returned. They didn't even look at each other. Instead, both fixated on the figure of Shamus standing commandingly on the table. He replaced his samurai sword beneath the now dull-colored cloak and hopped down.

In the same level of calm that he would have mustered in a group psychotherapy session that had just gone off the rails, Shamus spoke to the two friends who had moments ago been committed to the murder of each other. "Look at each other now." His voice was placid, emotionless and utterly compelling.

Erladoch studied his friend. Shamus's voice was all his own, professional and practiced.

Nida and O'Mara's respective eyes met. No sign of anger remained. The only obvious emotion which registered at all was a shared countenance of confusion. No one else in the room moved. They were still catching up to the scene which had whirled out of control and then had been brought back to placidity in a matter of seconds. Nothing of what had just happened had made any sense!

"O'Mara, think clearly. Did you truly wish to kill the Galagan?" Shamus queried in a calming and dulcet tone.

O'Mara Boldar looked at Shamus as if he had been asked the most ridiculously absurd question of his life. "No. Er, yes? No!" he whispered in an ashamed voice. "I...I've known Nida so many years that I remember not a time when we were not friends. I don't know why I acted so." His face had reddened in utter embarrassment. He continued to look at Nida as though he were searching for whatever it was that he had felt only moments ago that could have inspired so much rage.

"Nida?" Shamus turned his attention to the Keeper from Galagan. "Would you have wanted your next arrow to kill O'Mara Boldar?"

The Galagar's face was similarly befuddled. Nida replied in an empty and overwhelmed tone. "Lord Shamus, I was going to kill him without so much as a thought. It was as though the face of my friend had vanished only to be replaced by a visage so vile that I could do nothing other than shoot an arrow between his eyes. T'was only as I was firing the shaft that any part of me changed aim to graze him rather than kill him..." He hesitated, searching for his next words. "I hated him! It was as if I'd been separated from my own mind, without reflection of the knowledge that I love this man as I do the closest of my own kinsmen." He turned to the Anahimaran then. "I canna' tell you, O'Mara, how sorry I am for what I said. It wasn't me!" He realized the truth of his own apology as the words left his lips. Nida was himself once more.

The others present in the room were still playing catch-up with what felt like the sway of two separate pendulums now coming back into a synchronized tempo. The momentum of thoughts and actions were once again in line.

"Yes, my friends," Shamus continued to speak in dulcet and relaxed tones, still exerting a sense of calm over the room. "The great menace sits in a tower at this moment in Greno and laughs and spits foully upon us. I feel him also. His gaze actively scours the plains and hills alike, seeking both myself and Lord Erladoch out. He is testing our resolve by looking for our weaknesses."

Everyone in the room listened intently to the Wigget Bearer. Shamus was confirming all that they had suspected for so many months now. With the recent fall of Anahimara still stinging, they had suspected that more was coming.

"He has become aware of our arrival in Loura. His projection of negative thoughts is designed to seek us out and turn all of us against one another."

Shamus bade O'Mara and Nida to come to him. They moved to his side immediately. Taking hold of both men by the arms, he went on. "The Evil One seeks to find a way into our minds to channel his poison in moments of weakness when we are all most vulnerable to his influence. When he catches hold of your negative musings, he is allowed, however, briefly to see through your eyes. His enchantments give him glimpses of where to find us in such moments—this you must remember, at all times, henceforth. Foul thoughts cannot be permitted to reside within you—we have already seen this influence during our travels here. He wants the Keepers out of the way as we are his greatest threat. He knows what you are because you travel with us. The only explanation as to how lifelong friends could suddenly turn on each other in such a way is that he feels your strength above the crowds of all minds in Loura. Where I come from, we say that someone is "hell-bent" on destruction. Now that you have seen this, know it to be a real and ever-present danger. Your pride, your despair, your anger are all tools that allow his dark charms access. Do not let them dwell within you, lest you risk being lost the same way I nearly was."

Erladoch came over to his friends. They were still shaken from their recent outbursts. "Hear the Wigget Bearer and know his words to be true, friends. This was not your deed. Even this far from Greno, the Evil One has been able to reach out and control your behavior. He sees our company, though he knows not where we are, none of us having called him by his foul name. Hopefully, he knows not your actual identities. I have hope that he is still not yet aware of our mission or that the heir of Anahimara still lives and has yet a small army that he can bring into a field of battle when the moment comes. Every miscalculation that he makes can come to our favor in the closing hours, so we must heed Shamus's advice with care."

Nida was first to raise his arm to O'Mara at that moment. "Forgive me, Horse Prince. No part of me would ever have wanted you harmed by my hand."

O'Mara Boldar assessed his fellow Keeper's apology. He knew the words were true. Nonetheless, he hesitated another second before responding. A different process was underway within him; trauma weighed heavily on his soul. So much had been taken from him, so much pain endured. His inner voice compelled him to participate in the moment. "Aach! I know ye' too well to have nothing but faith in your words!" With that, he clasped both of his hands firmly around Nida's skinny little extended arm in sign of abiding friendship. "One way or t'other, I know you'll be there with me at the end."

The tension which had so swiftly enveloped the room had evaporated.

"Everyone, finish eating!" Princess Nica ordered in the most artificially jovial voice that she could muster in that moment. Upon her cue, servants rushed to the upset platters of food and ale and tidied the area with haste. An abundance of boar's meat and roasted game birds landed back on the table, along with large jugs of a lukewarm drink tasting of honey with notes of wildflowers poured out into everyone's mugs.

Mead, Shamus realized as he let the fluid roll around in his mouth before swallowing. It immediately took his mind back to a childhood Christmas Day. His grand-da was still alive, but for the life of him, while he could recall the presence of his parents and the laughter in the room that made him think that he was still young enough to have been in Ireland, the memory flash included the voices and faces of others taking in the celebration. One of those assembled was, without a doubt, the man who would become his family's lawyer in Canada: Jacob Greenway. Another face might have been that of John Browse's father Silas, but he could no longer be sure, having been so young. These were not people that he would have yet come to have known. He reconciled that his memory might simply be filling in blanks to enhance the imagery of the memory. He couldn't be sure. Whomever they were, the older gentleman was sitting commiserating with an old priest of similar age while a fire consisting of peat bricks and wood roared in the large hearth behind them. All he really knew for certain was that this had been the first time his lips had consciously encountered alcohol—mead, in fact. He had grabbed his Ma's glass out of her hand in a child-based act of curiosity, eagerly determined to learn what everyone was sharing to his exclusion, only to first encounter the powerfully sugary and yet sour beverage. The expressions of surprise on his own face must have made quite a sensation in the Christmas gathering, as his mind echoed with the joyful laughter of the adults reacting to Shamus as he sputtered out the powerful beverage. The smell and taste of this drink were so close to that first experience, that the memory was entirely vivid now. As the years went by, mead had become a nearly symbolic way for his family to commemorate the homeland, even years after he had been in Canada. Shamus could even see the label of this traditional drink in his mind's eye: *Bunratty.* A graphic of a castle dominated the label on the bottle. As the happy thought faded away, his memory focused on the last snapshots of the childhood vision, his grand-da's broadsword hanging over a massive window (the same sword which was now hooked on the back of his chair in Gol Bodeland), and a view through the picture window providing him a last-second glimpse of the sea. *Hmmm,* he mused with recognition, *that had to have been my home in Ireland where this party had happened. And yet, my later Ottawa connections were present. They definitely were!* He affirmed his recollection.

Shamus's musings were interrupted abruptly by Erladoch, who had been happily filling his plate with a sample of every food laid in front of him. He was to Shamus's right. He laid his strong and rough left hand on Shamus's right arm. "Eat, Shamus. Are you not starved?"

"Er yah, I am, Erladoch. Indeed I am," he replied hesitantly, grabbing a chicken leg from the platter and taking a hungered bite, still a little lost in his own thoughts of days long past and near forgotten.

"You saved some good people today," Erladoch offered, poking a dagger-like fork into a piece of what looked like blue cheese and slapping it onto his own plate. "Your instincts on what was happening and how you handled the matter was perfect. Was that you or him?" Erladoch asked, pointing at Shamus's chest as though this was the location where the White Wigget resided within him.

"I think that much of it was me, but how can I ever be sure?" Shamus responded tentatively.

Without missing a chew of the gristly boar meat, Erladoch offered his appraisal. "Well, your scream broke a very compelling spell which had befallen our friends. That much is sure." He gnashed away at the thickest portion in his mouth till he could speak clearly again. "Maybe it was just the element of surprise, but well done. Is that how you would have gotten the attention of one of your patients at the Royal? I definitely don't remember you doing that to me."

Shamus smiled at the question, knowing that it was offered entirely in jest. "Nope, can't imagine anyone thinking that would have been the best expression of my education. Absolutely would not have tried that on you, Erladoch! It would have only resulted in a bunch of orderlies bursting into the room with needles to calm you down had I done so." The two men shared a knowing smile. "It's just all that I could think of doing in that moment to break the momentum of what was unfolding. But I did feel like I had the power to stop what was happening, even if Anthrac was playing along."

"Well," Erladoch surmised, "sometimes, it really is the simple things which help. Ya sure managed to do it bloody fast." He raised his glass in a toast to his friend.

Shamus happily took him up on it, no longer reacting negatively to the fine flavors of mead as he had once done as a child.

Chapter 30

Dinner was not yet complete when a captain of the Bodeland guard entered the Hall. She went over to Princess Nica straight away.

Andor Seth was not nearly done dragging the end of a large chicken leg across his teeth, but he felt compelled to pay attention to the ensuing exchange.

Alida, who had long since finished supping, had been watching her colossal friend in amused fascination at the bottomlessness of his appetite for both food and drink. She watched him as he listened to the others converse, his powerful jaw still working its way appreciatively through the meat in his mouth.

The conversation between Lady Nica and her captain was short. It had the immediate effect of ruining the Travelers' plan for rest. Without any pause for deliberation, Princess Nica strode over to Erladoch and Shamus, whose attention had already been captured by the earnestness with which the captain had approached her Princess.

"It appears that the malice which nearly consumed our two companions was not confined to this chamber, Erladoch. Reports are coming in that at the same time as our friends were facing off against each other, several pockets of violence among some of my people who were simply going on about their evenings broke out all around Gol. The happening was most prominent the closer the proximity to our tower keep. A number are dead from the sudden infection of minds brought forth by the gaze of the Evil One."

The room fell silent. The announcement was more than troubling; it signified that what the Wigget Bearer had said about this infectious malevolence was bang on. An anxious buzz overtook the room momentarily as those assembled considered their own family members with speculations concerning their individual plight. Nica spoke again to quell the possibility of further ruminations.

"Our company is acting like a beacon to the Evil One. The longer we remain in Gol, the greater the risk to my people's safety."

Hearing Nica's revelation, Erladoch's demeanor became grim. The two of them conducted a brief dialogue in hushed tones. The scrape of Erladoch's heavy chair pushing back across the pristinely maintained wood-hewn floor signaled that a decision had been made. Everyone waited for the Dunbar Prince to speak.

"I know not how much of our secret has been discovered, but we do not have the luxury of time to second guess matters. The cause of what has transpired this night in this hallowed place and the most recent tidings of fighting in the city confirms that the Evil One is hunting us in the mindscape. We must assume that the closer our company is to the people of Bodeland, the more at risk anyone harboring any form of negative thought becomes. His malice now encircles us like a murder of crows waiting to descend and pick the flesh of those about to fall."

No one doubted the correctness of this observation. Shamus himself felt that this only supported further what he had said to O'Mara and Nida. He now waited like everyone else for direction to be given.

"Harn Leafcorn, to you I give this command, which Lady Nica and I agree is necessary. Speak it unto all who bear arms in defense of Bodeland as soon as possible. No person big enough to raise a bow or lift a sword can allow anger into their minds. Even as you pull forth your weapons in battle, feel only the love of your homeland and your families whom you fight for. To do otherwise exposes your minds to His malicious gaze. Even though no one deliberately calls him forth by the utterance of his name, he now reaches into those whose thoughts are black—alas, he has become that powerful!"

Looking back at Lady Nica for confirmation that she agreed with him, he continued, "My friends, we must make for Ara immediately! For everyone's protection, we need to place distance between us and his ever-extending influence. We ride tonight."

Shamus watched the room begin to bustle with heightened activity as the princess's last words landed on his consciousness. "Wait. What? We ride?" he said, even though no one was paying any attention to him in that instant. "Aw, crap!" he whined like a child who'd been told to eat his brussels sprouts.

Nica left Erladoch's shoulder and began instructing various people in the room. A collection of servants began opening the Travelers' packs, which had

281

been resting behind them against the walls of the chamber. They opened them on the nearest open spaces of the massive carved table. Food and flagon alike were being brought into the feasting hall; morsels of meat and dried fruit were wrapped in massive leaves and then further wrapped inside loosely woven cloth before being shoved into their packs.

Here's your hat, what's your hurry? Shamus remarked to himself sarcastically. With perhaps the sadness of having their princess leave so soon after having just arrived in Gol, it was clear that the Bodelanders not only accepted the assessment of the Keepers as to the cause of the mayhem which had just played itself out, they were more than anxious to get such a threat away from the general population as soon as possible.

Shamus registered that when Erladoch said that they should be traveling "immediately" for Ara, this meant that his aching feet, and the weary muscles of all the Travelers, would win no rest tonight. The command that they would be riding rather than walking ought to have come as a relief in the circumstances. For Shamus at least, it did not.

Andor finished the last bites of root vegetables sitting on his plate, carefully drained his tankard, and then rose from the table, wiping his mouth on the sleeve of his woolen overshirt. "Well then, let's get on with it," he said matter-of-factly to his friends.

Nica Bodelander quietly explored plans with the members of the Gol triumvirate. The evacuation plan which she had already ordered in Castra now had to be made patent without delay. She instructed Elhin Overbranch to send runners to all communities in and around Gol to join up with the band of Bodelanders who would be coming down from the North within the next few weeks. She intended that the kingdom's full complement should travel in strength. There had been much discussion about leaving some measure of fighting force behind to attend to the heartbreaking task of defending the flank of those who fled. Worse still was the Order which only she and Erladoch had quietly debated over their journey from Castra to Gol in the three preceding days. That order was to lay waste to anything which could not be carried out by the Bodeland Forresters. This included burning extra food provisions and poisoning the water sources. If a Treborgan horde was, in fact, marching on Bodeland, they could leave nothing behind that could fuel their enemy's advance.

As Nica quietly assigned these orders to her leaders, she could feel the collective 'snapping' of their sense of hope. "If the complete destruction of our beautiful kingdom makes time and space for our people to find safety, you must be unswerving in following this order. Better we live to sing songs of our struggle than to be wiped out of existence, my friends."

Nica placed her forehead against that of each member of the triumvirate in turn. Tears welled up in their eyes, knowing that many who would join the exodus would do so in the belief that the flight from peril was but a temporary thing. "Best not to say anything to the masses about what you've been asked to do once the city is cleared out." Nica assured. "Twill only break the hearts of our kinsmen that much more were they to know."

To those who would not be involved in the rear-guard measures, it would seem the last greatest humiliation. A diversion of massive and catastrophic proportions, all designed to provide the people of Bodeland with the time required to make good their flight.

"T'is nothing less than a deception and a betrayal of my people!" Nica had said in protest to Erladoch during their private moments of debate when they had still been on the road to Gol. Now, but a few days later, she was selling the decision to her subordinates. The news had been horrible to deliver, worse to receive, but ultimately, it would have to be done. She had to trust that no member of the triumvirate would waiver from their orders. These were not idle politicians whom Nica Bodelander commanded. The three of them were skilled Keepers. Every responsibility which had ever been bestowed upon them in their various stations had been based entirely on demonstrated merit. For that reason, Nica felt confident that her missive would be carried out without failure.

***

Hardly a word was exchanged among the Travelers while they were shown a washing area to freshen themselves for the journey. Nothing needed to be said, however. Orders had been given, and action was now required.

The Travelers secured their packs, drew their travel cloaks over themselves, and proceeded to exit from the grand hall. Nica exited last, and for but a nostalgic moment, she looked upon this ancient chamber one last time. She covered her head before crossing over the footbridge. To the hypersensitive hearing of the Galagars, it was plain that the Bodeland princess was weeping softly.

As the party exited the chamber, and a massive bark-covered door was drawn over the opening, fully concealing the entryway to untrained eyes, O'Mara stood aside, waiting for Shamus to approach him. In a few more moments, Shamus did. The Anahimaran made it a point to look under the lip of Shamus's hooded cloak, hoping to meet the eyes of the man who had recently saved him from being consumed by a flood of violent madness. Shamus sensed the ensuing conversation, appreciating that some level of exchange might be inevitable after what had taken place. For reasons that were not yet clear to him, he felt unsettled about having to engage the younger man. Resolving to meet O'Mara Boldar's glance, he could see that a conversation was being organized by the Prince. To his surprise, O'Mara said nothing at first. Instead, they proceeded side by side with their comrades through tree bough and cavern alike until they were being led out into an area which, by its distinctive smell, indicated that they were outdoors again. The night air was cool and damp. It felt refreshing even though Shamus had not thought of the hall as having been stuffy.

As they walked, Shamus divined from the pauses and half-starts at conversation which O'Mara struggled to engage in that the man was troubled. He maintained his pace alongside of O'Mara but decided to wait for him to speak, determining that small talk would not assist the man in coming to his point.

"How'd ya do it?" O'Mara finally began. "I was completely not myself, Wigget Bearer! By what magic did you defeat 'him' and pluck me out of the rage which he was drowning me in?"

Shamus found the question both appropriate and predictable in the circumstances, but everything inside of him was imploring him to use caution. Shamus's life was inextricably tied to all of the Keepers in this company of Travelers, O'Mara included. He, however, occupied a unique role among them as the man who carried Anthrac Aran within his core. Everything that he said and did was now being scrutinized, and Shamus wondered whether it made sense for him to explain to O'Mara that what he had done was both spontaneous, and a product of his training as a psychologist rather than by some trick of 'magic', as O'Mara had implied. He measured the utter futility in trying to explain his professional training of how to contend with a decompensating patient from spiraling further in a counseling setting, knowing that such information would only confuse matters. He chose instead to heed his inner voice. Smiling with an entirely contrived air of confidence, he looked directly at O'Mara.

"A magician never reveals his tricks." Shamus broke off the smile and his gaze before more might be read from his face by the Anahimaran prince. *Jaysus, Shamus!* He chided himself. *That was my best response? Such crap!* He waited for O'Mara to react.

"Uh, fair enough, I guess, Lord Fiorian," O'Mara said, no part of his utterance supporting acceptance of the bizarre answer but also not rejecting it either. "I give you my gratitude. I wonder, however, what it is that powers your ability to have even known that the Evil One's enchantment is what had found us in the room, as opposed to a simple act of pride on my part or that of Nida."

Shamus already did not like this probing but realized that there could easily be a multitude of questions to follow if he didn't give the Anahimaran prince something more to chew on. He assumed that princes were spoiled individuals at heart, after all, and invariably got what they wanted. He also had to accept that O'Mara's pedigree went far beyond that of a simple heir to an ancestral throne; he was, in fact, a highly disciplined and trained Keeper. It thus made sense that his fellow traveler's curiosity had been trained to a level of insight far beyond that of the average person. 'Why' it was important for O'Mara to ferret out whether it was Shamus Bergin who had intervened or Anthrac Aran speaking through him, however, was a question which gnawed at the back of Shamus's mind.

They proceeded in and out of trees, sometimes at dizzying heights somewhere above the ground, only to descend to a dimly lit and cool area. He remarked at his happiness of having a full belly, even though he longed for the rest he was not going to get. His engagement in this conversation with O'Mara made him feel even more tired. He realized that it might not have been the conversation at all that was weighing on him, but rather the princess's earlier comment that they would soon be riding. *Jaysus H, why horses?* He silently protested as he kept up. Whether it was his anxiety over going anywhere on horseback or his being obliged to disclose further to O'Mara, he hoped to retreat from this interrogatory as soon as he could.

"I wish that I could answer your question more plainly, Lord Boldar." Shamus chose to approach him with the respect that he was due and maybe give him something resembling the reality of his experience without committing further. "The truth is that I am never sure where I end and where the White Wigget within me begins. We are one and the same man at times, and, I suppose, his mind is thus mine also. Excuse me a moment, O'Mara. I need to speak to Lady Nica about my choice of horse." With a simple bow of his forehead, Shamus moved forward in the group before O'Mara even had a chance to acknowledge him back. As he sped up his pace, he considered whether, despite the apparent silence of Anthrac within him currently, perhaps his gesture in the Great Hall, like his ability as a psychologist to induce somnolence on his patients in therapy was, in fact, a shared endeavor after all.

Nah, Bull! I'm good at hypnotherapy! He affirmed himself. *Really good at it, in fact!* The skill had come naturally to him right from the get-go as a student. One of his earliest successes in school was his ability to learn 'Neuro-Linguistic Programming'. Showmen who were exceptionally good at this skill were found in places like Las Vegas all the time, making scads of money turning unwitting grown-ups into complete imbeciles for the amusement of crowds. Shamus Bergin came to this skill like a pro. *So,* he mused as Erladoch and Nica came into view beyond Andor's massive frame, '*whether something of Anthrac has rubbed off on me or not, this is a learned and practiced skill all my own.*'

***

Erladoch remained quiet while Shamus and Nica discussed the Wigget Bearer's desired selection of a horse. His opportunity at detaching from O'Mara had been borne on his real desire to make sure that he was favored with a horse of gentle temperament. He had only been horseback riding once when he had been about 10 years of age, and it had not gone well. While he was encouraged on one level that he would not have to travel on this next leg of the journey on foot, he was adamant that he be given a calm beast to carry him.

Twenty years of life can obscure many memories, but Shamus harbored a clear snapshot in his mind of his mother, Katlyn, having to rescue him seconds before a hot-tempered Arabian nearly mashed him against a barn fence. He had only been on the beast maybe three minutes as he and his parents were setting out on a guided ride. Even though he was still young, they felt it important that he acquire horseback riding skills for reasons that were entirely unclear to his child's mind. They had barely left the paddock to start their journey when "Spirit" had apparently decided that he was having none of this nonsense of carrying an inexperienced child for an hour-long country jaunt. Without any obvious signs that the horse had any issue with its mount, Spirit suddenly rose up onto its hind legs, nearly throwing Shamus completely backward onto the ground. By some turn of good luck, 10-year-old and terrified Shamus had looped his arms around the reins just before all hell had broken loose. He found himself with legs out of the stirrups of his western saddle, and his belly bouncing on the glistening black back of a steed that had broken into a full sprint toward the farm's back fence, seemingly terrified of its own shadow. While the entire episode had probably lasted no more than 30 seconds, they had been the longest and most horrifying time of his life to that point. With each doubled-hoof fall, his young body rag-dolled against one side or the other of Spirit's flanks, his arms sustaining leather rope-burns from the reins each time he bounced. Each speeding gallop brought him to the realization that his death was drawing near. Despite this, he also felt the presence of a girl singing a very simple song right beside him as though she were floating in the air beside his ear. The song had been so calming even though he could neither hear it fully nor make sense of even a single solitary word of the melody. For reasons that haunted his mind for years, the song would come to him whenever he found himself feeling lonely or lost. On that first day when the invisible girl and her song first came to his mind, it had buoyed Shamus's courage. For reasons he could not explain to his parents later, he found a level of physical strength and presence of mind that seemed to have been borne upon the wings of the girl's song. The soft melody had come to him in his moment of utter need, making the lactic acid build-up in his arms dissipate. He found himself gaining hold of the horse's flanks with his thighs long enough to prop up and free his arms from the biting leather reins that he had become entangled in even as the horse continued to speed wildly toward his doom. In the last moments before he saw himself careening toward the gnarled and misshapen four-rail-high barn wood beams, he felt a hand snatch the back of his belt from behind, and his mom shouting, "Shamus, let go!" He did so unhesitatingly, not even realizing the magnificence of his mother's actions as she leaned nearly horizontally from her own mount in order to pluck him from Spirit. She had somehow managed to twist herself and him back into a seated position directly in front of her on her horse. "Gotcha, Boy-o!" she'd whispered comfortingly in his ear at the same moment that the girl's song faded away.

Playing the memory back, Shamus now realized that he had never truly considered the complexity of impossible angles and movements his mother, Katlyn, had undertaken to affect such a rescue. They had both been traveling at breakneck speed when she extracted him from certain death. She had pulled this feat off with the practiced skill of an elite trick rider. He mused to himself that he had no memory of either of his parents having been equestrians at all. His focus had, however, not been on that act. Rather, his strongest memory of the incident had always been that this had been the first time of many that this girl's sweet song had come out of nowhere to calm him in a moment of need. Thinking now, however, about the stunt his mom had pulled off, Shamus realized very poignantly the fact that there had been a great many things that had been kept from him his whole life. He bit his lower lip with ironic bitterness for a moment. The only other part of that event that he had ever kept in his memory till now was the sense of safety a boy feels in the arms of his mom—that memory had been more than good enough, he decided. Before he could ruminate further about the childhood incident, he forced himself to smile, and once more capture the loving and relieved looks shared with his parents as they closed the door to their car. As his parents drove away without so much as another word with the farmer, the elder gentleman was sadly left having to end the suffering of his beloved and previously prized and disciplined horse. This award winner had spent the last five years of its existence enjoying a quiet retirement, occasionally carrying children as young as four merrily along well-beaten paths on nature walks. On that fateful day, however, Spirit had become a different horse altogether—one which had no regard for a small child on its back as it ran without consideration from whatever had vexed it. It did not even try to save itself after the boy had been plucked from its back but instead continued on its course without any effort to jump the fence or even turn away. It had run directly into it, impaling itself on the gnarls and twists of natural wood. William and Katlyn Bergin's gray Volvo wagon was already leaving dust behind them on the dirt road from this secluded Renfrew pasture when the distant 'pop, pop' sounded almost inaudibly through the car's window. With their terrified but intact child safely buckled behind them, William and Katlyn had spared Shamus the sight of the final moments of the horse's agonized madness.

***

Lady Nica moved away from Shamus to see what she could do to accommodate his request. He found himself walking on his own near the back of the procession of Bodelandish soldiers, officials and the company of Travelers while others attended to the busy work of preparing to leave Gol.

Earlier, during their ascent to the great ancestral hall from which they had just come, he didn't recall so much walking and wondered where they were going. For more than five minutes, they mostly descended along a network of pathways that were either hewn out of the massive branches of the leafy trees or across rope and wooden bridges. Shamus remarked to himself that the ground below was almost never in sight. Step after step, the procession trod over spectacular undulations of branch networks which, perhaps by force of human manipulation over centuries, intersected into each other to form larger and smaller avenues. They were as broad and smooth as any paved avenue he had ever walked over at home in his timeline, and in places could accommodate as much as ten men walking astride one another. Without clear warning, due to reduced nighttime visibility challenges, he found himself walking right through another set of corridors that spiraled through the inner hollows of the great trees. The Bodelanders knew where they were going, and that was good enough for Shamus as it allowed him to marvel over the architectural and engineering genius that had merged over time with the forest people's own abiding respect for the symmetry of their culture with nature.

"How often has the Wigget whispered to you this night?" came a voice that was catching him up from behind.

Jaysus, Mary and Joseph! Shamus thought privately. *Again with the questions?*

This time, however, it was the familiar voice of Erladoch who had come alongside him. Since leaving the Hall, they had not exchanged words. Erladoch had waited to discuss matters with his friend until all his fellow Keepers had moved quite a number of paces ahead. He was sure that their conversation would be private enough.

"Uh, I don't know, Erladoch," he started, feeling still a bit exasperated about having to explain a phenomenon that he hadn't really worked out for himself yet. "I guess that Anthrac gives me thoughts—thoughts which tell stories all their own. What I do with them is mostly my own choice. At least, I think it's my choice." He considered this a moment and then spoke with more confidence. "Actually, no. I know that I still have the power of my own choice when he emerges. It's been a really rare moment where Anthrac has willed my thoughts or taken control over my physical movements. I definitely think, however, that he has shown me ways to speed up or sometimes even slow things down; just like tonight." More clarity seemed to be coming to Shamus. "I had a moment tonight where, despite the noise of many conversations happening in the room, it was my own intuition which alerted me to the fact that O'Mara and Nida were on a collision course with each other which neither man had control over. It was all that I could focus on, and it was like the pulse of a drumbeat getting louder every second. Once that happened, I knew, and I chose to act. I didn't hear Antrac's voice at all in my ears." Shamus confirmed as much to himself as Erladoch. "My experience was actually my very own." Shamus smiled from his realization.

Erladoch was pleased by this assessment. "If this be the extent of his influence over you, then I am signaled to your growing power. T'is a good thing—a good thing fer sure. I was particularly impressed with how your physical touch seemed to not only weaken O'Mara and Nida's resolve; it clearly stunned them too! When I saw that momentary pulse of energy leave your hands, I was really taken aback. Most impressive, Shamus! Most impressive indeed!"

Shamus hadn't processed this aspect of his intervention. "Shite!" he exclaimed in disappointment; his ego suddenly bruised. "Ok, maybe it's more of a collaboration after all," he conceded. "Let's face it, Erladoch; you know who I am, better than anyone here. I'm a mortal man just like you. There's no special force which flows through me every waking minute. Anthrac only seems to appear when it suits him to do so. I think that my skill from my old life is what equipped me to react to the surging confrontation, but, yah, I had nothing more than that. If they were subdued from my touch, then that was Anthrac. I have no magic in me." He was deflated by the admission, but his professional skill set definitely did not include pulsing energy into people.

Erladoch replayed the moment. "I think yer wrong, my friend. Your destiny involves some relationship to the old magic, not unlike my own. I agree that how it appears to you is still a mystery, but I see gifts emerging inside of you that are akin to my own. Let whatever 'this is' into yourself."

Shamus chewed on the advice, but really didn't know what to say back about the matter. Anything he knew of Louran history had first come from Erladoch, only to be later layered onto by the Keepers in his party. The story of Loura, thus far at least, was entirely a verbal record passed down from one generation to the next. There was nothing written down in any kind of alphabet he would ever be able to access in this timeline which would confirm or deny what he was being told. He would have to accept that anything that anyone told him about this world and his place in it was likely to be both true and factual.

"Though I was not familiar with all the clusters of stars that I could see from my window at the Royal when I lived there, the patterns were clear that you will play a significant role in the coming struggle. It was not clear to me then, but I'm now certain that such events involve more than the rebirth of the Wigget Seed. Mark what I say, Shamus. You wear the cloak of the Grand Wigget for more than the fact that you bear him inside of you. Your presence in this world was predestined; no other could have worn the cloak and lived. There's magic in ya. The uniqueness of your bloodline has made that a reality. Even if it takes a lifetime to work through this, I believe that more will be revealed to you."

Shamus felt unsettled by the assertion and immediately began playing it down. He did not like the 'not-knowing' of what he didn't know. He was here; that should be good enough for now. Erladoch, however, was somewhat exasperated by his friend's unhidden facial reaction.

"Ach! Do not close your mind to the truth so quickly, Shamus! Anthrac said you descend from a prominent line of forgotten warriors. I can feel that your destiny has always been to come to Loura. I know not why this is so any more than you do. I search no longer for such tales, as I have faith that it will be revealed in good time. Heed my words well, friend; in you is hidden an untold story that will come to fruition."

Not knowing whether there was even a point to contradicting his friend, Shamus surrendered to the persistence of Erladoch's argument so he could let the discussion lie. They caught up to the others, who were getting ready for the departure. Servants were assembled in a gathering chamber. They completed a rushed packing job of additional saddle bags for the company and scurried out of the room. Mayor Anisha El entered the hall in the company of several uniformed warriors and bid the party to follow her as the last of the packs had been filled and handed to each of the Travelers. She led them along a number of labyrinthian passages that could have gone in several directions on multiple occasions. It was becoming dizzying to the whole company to even keep track of the countless corridors that appeared and trailed off in multiple directions.

With the exception of the group of warriors who had accompanied the Mayor into the departure hall, every time a seemingly invisible passage was revealed, the numbers of Bodelanders who had accompanied the Travelers diminished. To Shamus's mind, it appeared as though each Bodelander knew, by virtue of their rank, that certain places that they were traversing were simply off-limits to them, and they took their leave and vanished into the shadows behind.

Before entering the next chamber, anyone not familiar with the place they were moving toward in the torchlit shadows could nonetheless detect that they were approaching a horse stable. The air was heavy with the scent of manure. Even upon entering, it was apparent from the continued presence of torchlight that there was no obvious direct access to the outdoors. There the Travelers took control of their horses by grasping the handwoven leather reins given to them by attendants. The workmanship of the reins was unique and intricate. By feel alone, Shamus could discern that a soft fabric cloth had been woven around the stronger strips of ropey leather. It was carefully fitted over the horses' heads and just long enough for a rider to grasp from the ground. There were no saddles and certainly no other appurtenances that Shamus might have expected which might have added to either his or the horse's comfort. In the glimmer of torchlight, he was handed the reins to a ridiculously tall male whose coat was as much white as it was black patch. He felt the animal's warm breath; it was far less unpleasant than he anticipated, and certainly better than the smell of the stables themselves. Rather than let any doubt or anxiety overtake him in the encounter, Shamus immediately placed the palm of his right hand over the horse's long nose, as Nica had counseled him to do. He caressed the massive beast slowly, running his hand up and down its long nose. The physical contact with the quiet horse allowed him to feel considerably more confident than he had expected himself to be in this moment. He cast a brief glance at Lady Nica and whispered a quiet 'thank you' before looking up at the horse again. "Hey," he whispered. "Be good to me, buddy, and I'll be good to you. Okay?" he asked, half expecting a response.

The horse, whom he was told was named 'Uhlwhin', responded with a double mini-twist of his head back and forth and a soft out blow of his nostrils. It would have been impossible not to get horse snot on his hands at that moment, and at first, Shamus was more than a little taken aback, but he decided to stand his ground, keeping his hand steady on Uhlwin's snout. Nica Bodelander had been watching the exchange with amusement from a short distance to Shamus's left. "T'is a sign of respect that is, Lord Shamus," she said, doing her best to conceal an amused giggle.

"Uh, how do I mount him?" Shamus asked, legitimately not knowing how he was possibly going to get up on the back of this tall beast, whose back was easily six feet above the ground.

"Like this." Andor Seth boomed from down the way as he yanked the head of his steed with enough force that Shamus nearly gasped out loud at fear that his friend might break the poor beast's neck. The horse flopped down to half of its height, its forelegs bent at the ready to receive the big man's weight. Andor's horse was bigger than a Belgian workhorse of Shamus's timeline. Its girth was certainly wide and thick enough to accommodate the colossus from the kingdom of Seth. Nonetheless, it steadied itself as he hopped with the weight of himself, his big axe and his pack onto its back. "Well, that was no help," Shamus shared with the room.

"Over here, Wigget Bearer," Alida and Nida said nearly in unison as they leaped without effort to the full height of their respective mounts. Before Shamus could offer another retort that demonstrated that he needed better guidance, Nica Bodelander lead her female until it came alongside Uhlwhin. She pulled gently on her mount's reins, compelling it toward herself. The horse immediately turned to look at her. She placed her left foot onto the left foreleg of her mount. The gentle application of pressure exerted by her, coupled with the turn of her horse's head, created a natural bending motion in the leg, which took on an appearance of a step stool having been created at the joint. With her right hand, she reached onto the hair of the back of her mount's neck and gracefully pulled herself up and over her back. "There, Lord Shamus. Now you try."

"Ok, Uhlwhin," he whispered, looking straight into his eyes as he pulled a little on the reins. "Let's do this."

Uhlwhin immediately bent his left foreleg and created the same natural step for Shamus. In far faster a time than he thought, he found himself and his heavy pack easily settled over his new horse's back, along with the additional provisions bag that he had been given. The procession joined up and walked past one torch after another, all of them projected from 45 degree angles away from the rock and mud walls. Shamus managed to keep a steady heartbeat as he felt every muscle of Uhlwhin's back moving beneath. He was surprised at the sense that he 'fit' reasonably well onto this horse, and he had to concede that the movement didn't bother him nearly as much he expected it might. His focus soon shifted to each torch that was placed ahead, one after what seemed like hundreds of others way off in a great and steady line. The furthest torch still visible to his sight through the blackness was nothing more than a speck of white, and the group made their way slowly toward it.

Although it seemed as though everyone but Shamus knew where they were headed, he caught wind of Andor's exchange with Alida. It was as close to a complaint as he had ever heard from him, and Andor was making his sentiment known that he did not enjoy the confinement of the great tunnel. "It feels like I'm riding directly into the bowels of the world." The others nodded in agreement, as indeed, the tunnel did seem to be gradually descending as they went forward. The ceiling also dropped down from time to time to only inches above their heads, making claustrophobics of everyone other than Lady Nica, who plainly had traversed this tunnel many a time in her life. But for the fact that the wall torches continued to burn unwaveringly, Shamus felt that his lungs were working harder than they should have to as they went along. He hoped for the time when they might find themselves back out in the open air.

Perhaps because the air was indeed thin, very little was exchanged in the way of conversation among any of the Travelers or their Bodelandish guides. Even big Andor, who often had something humorous to report to the collective designed to break the monotony of travel was silent. The 'clop, clop' of hooves reverberated off the walls and echoed out into emptiness, signaling that the tunnel was as yet very long.

The Travelers followed Anisha El in silence. Shamus wondered whether any of them were still working through how two among their sacred ranks had come very close to thrashing the lives out of each other in the Great Meeting Hall. *Perhaps they are just as tired as I am,* he speculated.

Alida finally broke the sound of echoing footsteps. "Mayor El, what is this place we find ourselves in? My people are very familiar with Gol, and yet none has ever spoken of this collection of grand tunnels."

"Fewer and fewer Bodelanders have knowledge of this as well these days," she offered in quick reply. "Yer an honored Galagan indeed. This network of tunnels is thought to have been hewn out of rock and earth by a great magic, perhaps as much as 160 ages ago, maybe by the Strahanas themselves. Howsoever this was made, it lies beneath Gol and extends to the plains just north of the kingdom of Ara. How or by whom it was created involves reasons that are no longer known. Shortly after Gol was constructed in the boughs and ever-stretching branches of the trees above us, the secret of its existence was discovered by the builders of our city. It was decided long ago that it be kept secret from all who do not call themselves Bodelandish. Now, the knowledge of this place and how to navigate through it is not even common to most of our people."

"No offense, Mayor," Andor interrupted as he ducked to avoid hitting his head on a low-hanging portion of the cavern's ceiling, "but it's very tight in here from where I sit, and the air is thin at best. I don't love being so far beneath the ground!"

Anisha accepted Andor's comment in stride without making eye contact. "While t'is true that it's a long journey below the ground, by the time we reach its end, you shall encounter the warmth of Inyi's rise upon your face."

Alida's face lit up from the wonder of such a declaration. "It is that grand then?" She was flummoxed both by the suggested extent of the network as well as her complete lack of foreknowledge of such a place.

"Aye, the tunnel is many yarricks long, and as much as a quarter of a yarrick beneath the surface, hence why the air is a bit thin here. In a moment, we shall round the first corner of the tunnel. Here you may repose a few hours in safety before you move on. That is where I will leave you."

Shamus listened intently to the mayor's exposition even as he focused as best as he could on the walls of the tunnel. He was sure that he had noticed what he understood to be runes etched into the solid rock from time to time. In his mind at least, these scratchings in the rock did not appear to be random juts or edges. It felt like evidence of early written language, or at least some form of deliberate code. If, in fact, they were nothing more than natural striations in the rock walls, the glimmers of torchlight danced so randomly over the smooth and rough surfaces alike that he convinced himself he could have easily been looking at lines of text or even sheet music undulating along his path.

"What is said here?" He added himself to the discussion by pointing to the nearest markings, conveniently located beneath a torch as they rode slowly by. "What do those words say, Mayor El?"

The mayor studied his face quizzically. "I know not what you mean by 'words', Wigget Bearer," she replied blankly.

For reasons that he couldn't explain, Shamus sensed that the mayor was not being forthcoming with him. He pressed. "Those marking there on the wall beneath the torch. Who put them there and why? Do they tell a story?"

Anisha El looked to where he had been pointing. She continued to feign a lack of understanding of his questions for a moment. Then, upon reflection, as though she knew he was testing her, decided to respond as honestly as she could. "We don't know that anyone put them there, Wigget Bearer. They are there because they are there."

"But each time that I have seen such markings, they are unique. Do they not act as a guide for us?"

The wide-eyed shaking of her head indicated that she was ready to come clean with him. "Ah! Yah. I see what yer asking. There are certainly known markings to help guide the knowledgeable traveler; if that is what you mean. For those who don't belong here, they are mere riddles, and likely unsolvable. Those few who are permitted the honor of traveling this hidden highway are taught to memorize the shape of the natural marks from the earliest ages. Even one mistake on the sequence, and you could lose yourself to wandering for many days," she answered softly, the steel of her intense blue eyes glowing almost as bright as the torches themselves. They were very much the color he had been mesmerized by when he first met Nica Bodelander. They had to be close relatives, he surmised.

"I don't see how that is possible, Mayor El. We are going almost entirely straight down one walled path, are we not?"

Anisha El offered a knowing smile. "Not even a little straight, Shamus of Fior. Your mind sees only what it wishes to see because the torches that have been set out along our path have been laid and lit by those knowledgeable of this underground highway to ease your travel. Look past the torches more carefully. You will see passages going off in multiple directions; some which lead back here, and some which go nowhere at all. We like to say that long before Gol Bodeland was built above, there must have been people who lived down here; perhaps even some of the Strahanas."

"If those markings of which you speak are not simply made from nature, then possibly it was they who did this. None of that makes any sense, of course, as the Strahanas had their own land, and it was nowhere near to here, at least not that we know of. We even sometimes speak whimsically of a great spell created by the earliest of walking man, if men they indeed were—men who were here at the arrival of the Strahanas, or perhaps even before. We know not the origin of the markings which appear in certain places along the walls, but we have memorized those that are helpful in guiding us through this place. If a great spell created this place along with the markings which you have noted, then such a spell is surely unfamiliar to anyone who now lives."

"Is it possible that an act of great magic was once employed to create such a thing as this? Sure, t'is possible. But who? Our world has never been this advanced before. Those people who came before our kind are the Scrags. T'is known that they once dwelled in caves before being conscripted into the service of the Master of the Great Pit's puppet. But we've found no evidence that something so foul as a Scrag ever dwelled here. I say truly that Scrags were ne'er a complex or advanced enough people to have constructed such a network of highways below the ground. More likely, these were once underground rivulets that eventually dried up when their connection to the sea was cut off by the passage of time."

"We discovered their existence merely by chance as our city grew and our knowledge of living in harmony with the forest improved, as I began telling Alida here. Who could have known that the tree-dwelling Bodelandish people would look beneath the ground? All that we really know, Lord Shamus, is that this underground highway has allowed Bodelanders to disappear below the ground when all expect to find us in the trees. So, whether t'was a spell cast by the Strahanas, or some other and different people who came before us, or just the force of the earth mother herself, no one knows. The myths nonetheless endure, even though no one has ever found a single item that would prove that this was a dwelling place for anyone ever."

Shamus was anything but content with this explanation from the mayor. Everything about her speculation seemed to distract him from what he knew he was seeing every so often on the walls. Even her instruction to look between the torches toward unseen feeder pathways seemed like a distraction. He was sure that he was seeing the evidence of some form of runic alphabet. His mind went around in circles searching for something he had learned in a history class as a teenager growing up. He was having trouble recalling it until he saw yet another series of lines which seemed to flow, one on top of another, that were no more than five or six inches long, but there was a pattern to them. He was sure of it.

Perhaps another 30 feet down the wall, not far beneath the base of a torch holder, there were once again more of these line scratchings. As he slowly trotted past on Uhlwhin, he screwed up his eyes to focus as best he could on what he was seeing. *Lines; waves really,* He confirmed to himself. This time they seemed to terminate against two vertical lines on one side. Shamus studied this and committed it to memory. As he passed by the markings, he noticed the subtle change in direction that his horse was making under him. *Jaysus! Even the horse knows where to go! This is language! And it's telling us which way to go!* He was miffed at the mayor's half-truth. His instincts told him that he should be bothered by this. At the risk of being considered rude, he chose to follow his instincts. "I know that you're not saying all that there is to be said, Mayor El. Is there a reason?" Shamus offered a half smile, but there was challenge in his tone. "You don't know me, but my companions do. I have earned my place of trust among these people."

Before Anisha El could provide any kind of rebuke, which clearly she was fixing to do in that moment, Nica Bodelander's horse eased in-between them. "Enough of the shite already, cousin Anisha," she interrupted in an informing tone. "Lord Shamus is as much a Keeper as you."

"If that is true, he isn't from any bloody place I've e'er seen!" she answered flatly, more than a little haughtily, too late to remind herself that, elder cousin or not, she was speaking to the princess of all Bodeland.

Nica considered the mistrusting attitude being shown to her and her travel companion. Every bit of news that had made its way to Gol in the past several months had involved tidings of losses of their own kinsmen to Scraggin-borne terror. These former disorganized 'cave-dwellers' were no longer afraid to bring war parties into their sacred lands! Anisha knew the tales regarding the sudden conversions into murderous madness of her Keeper brothers and sisters, possessive of the mind-dancing ábaltacht. She was fully cognizant of the precipitous fall of Anahimara shortly thereafter. Her index of suspicion for anyone asking questions about this secret place was accordingly high. Her outright loss of control in speaking to her princess, however, said something more. A characteristic frown, which she had made no effort to hide, suddenly formed on her face. Nica had seen this look before, but not in response to her, not ever. This was a look that she had reserved for moments just before she would spring into action against an enemy. She was building herself up to something.

Rather than apologize for her tone, Anisha met her cousin's admonishment head-on. "D'ya know who this man really is? Shamus the Fiorian! Hah! Really! His legitimacy is entirely tied to the prince who would be King of all Dunbar one day. How do you know that this is Erladoch of Dunbar at all, and not some deceiver sent to us by the Evil One himself?" As she had been called on the mat, she was prepared to make her anxieties known. "Yer about to embark on yet another journey with these two men, and all I see is blind trust being given by you out of yer need to believe that this be Erladoch." She was shaking her head back and forth, allowing her adrenaline to fuel imminent action. "Oh sure, he looks and sounds like him, and but for the fact that he ought to have been a corpse more than four years ago, maybe it could be him. But I'm less certain, cousin. In fact, I'm not convinced at all!"

Shamus and Alida had not broken stride or departed the conversation. They were without words to add to such an exchange, however.

For his part, Shamus had to accept that the doubts which Anisha El shared were reasonable ones in the circumstances. He had been unconscious for many days after having been brought to Castra by the Bodelanders who had come to his and Erladoch's rescue. He looked around in an attempt to invite Erladoch with his eyes, hoping that he might approach more closely so that he could audit the exchange. As he did so, it suddenly occurred to him that the Bodelanders who were accompanying them were all heavily armed for an escort. *Oh crap! Is this resting place that she has been taking us toward actually a killing ground?* His mind went into overdrive. *Does Erladoch know that Anisha worries that he is an impostor and mistrusts our intentions enough to try to take us out? She thinks that Nica has been enchanted somehow.*

Thoughts of extrication began to race in his mind. *Where the hell would I go to get away if that is what's about to happen here? Oh, I'm so screwed! Erladoch, where the hell are you?* He felt his heart rate climbing as he finally caught his friend's gaze in the shadows. Without attempting to be obvious in his gestures, he slowly relinquished his two-handed hold on Uhlwhin's reins. With exercised calm, he resolved to sneak one hand inside his travel cloak in hopes of being able to draw his katana out, if he had to.

What about the rest of the Travelers? He asked himself. *Surely, she knows at least some of them if she is also a Keeper. Have they sensed that something stinks here too? What's their position going to be in all of this? Oh God! Which side are they going to be on?*

Shamus slowly scanned the entire group of Travelers along with the position of the 'escort'. They were definitely positioned on all sides of the Travelers in such a manner as to be able to mount a stealthy assault on the lot of them with as little as a word from Anisha. *Shite! Has this been her play all along?* Shamus waited for Nica Bodelander to respond to her subordinate. He cautioned himself to take his lead not only from what she would say next but, perhaps more importantly, what Anisha El might do in response.

"State yer grievances once and for all, and let's be done with this, Anisha." Nica's tone was calm but firm. Shamus was pleased to see that she appeared to suspect that something was amiss. She didn't have to wait long for Anisha's reply.

"I look on this man, with his alarmingly strange appearance, as he sits atop one of my prized battle horses, and I have to ask myself, Nica, whether all this trust you have given arises from your need to believe that you have Erladoch back. This man," her finger now stabbed accusingly at Erladoch, who had closed on the conversation even though he continued to trot along in silence, "your great love, this returned-from-the-dead Prince of Dunbar. He just shows up at the edge of your kingdom after four long years! They say that they were pursued to your very door by a Scraggin war party. Your own brother fell to rescue these, these men, and I've heard nary a word of sadness since seeing you 'bout this grievous loss to us all! Have ye even considered that maybe, just maybe, they weren't chased there at all, woman? Perhaps they were escorted to yer door and are actually confederates of the Evil One? Is that not possible? Is it not utterly bizarre and plain to ye that the wave of madness that overtook the grand hall and so many of our people only happened once your group arrived? You must understand that I canna' take the chance of just accepting what you tell me here because you so want it to be him. Someone has brought evil into our very home and your best counsel is that you want us to destroy all that we have built on Erladoch's say-so! Is it not possible that you are playing right into the hands of the Evil One?"

Nica reined up on her horse until it came to a stop. The entire party followed suit. She froze the mayor with a stare which announced: 'Family or not, I will kill you where you sit if you are about to betray us and our mission.'

Anisha El took note of the intention. She was now unsure of herself. Had she previously believed that Nica was under some form of mind control, she was now less sure of it.

"What awaits us around the next turn of this tunnel, cousin? Mind yerself now." Nica took no aggressive action of any kind, but Shamus felt himself let out a breath of partial relief.

At least she is with us! he consoled himself. He carefully shifted his gaze to capture as much of the movements of his fellow Travelers and the escort around them that he could see without allowing his movement to seem abrupt. The Travelers continued to sit calmly, but very much like himself, each and every one of them had allowed a single hand to release their hold from the reins of their respective horses. They were readying themselves for action, but for whom Shamus could not yet tell.

Not so much as a whisper from the Keepers traveling in his company was exchanged, but theirs was a shared readiness brewing inside their cloaks. These were both Nica and Anisha El's sworn brothers and sisters of the Sacred Order! Which side were they about to come down on?

"Answer me now, cousin! You've done something stupid, haven't you?" Nica was not prepared to wait any longer.

Because she was a Keeper, Anisha was immensely bothered by having been excluded from the knowledge which had been shared uniquely among the Travelers. On other matters, she had always accepted that her Order always compartmentalized information about missions. It was not always necessary for every Keeper to know everything all the time. This was an accepted practice designed to keep the members of the Order safe. On this occasion, she had known so little, and yet, so much had been asked of her that she just could not accept her orders without being sure. In the face of Nica's commanding tone, Anisha hesitated, no longer sure of herself or the orders she had secretly given to her warriors to lay in wait at the opening into the next cavern. She recognized Nica's tone. It had been as clear-headed, deliberate and commanding as it had ever been. This was definitely not the voice of a love-drunk or enchanted person who had stopped thinking for herself.

"I…" she stuttered, before letting out the longest possible sigh. Her face reddened—not with heightened adrenaline, but rather with embarrassment. Her lack of faith in the princess had been misguided, and she knew it all at once. "I…I'm sorry, my lady! I'm overcome with doubts! I've been so stupid!"

Nica's face was rapt with disappointment. The hesitation told her everything that she had suspected. A trap had been set, and if Anisha were to give the Order, all but Princess Nica would be slaughtered when they rounded the next turn of the tunnel. She shook her head in dismay and struggled with what she now must do in response to such mutinous behavior.

Erladoch finally spoke, recognizing that he needed to intervene. "You are right, Mayor El!" The sound of his interjection startled them both. "I see it now. You should be vigilant. I would even go so far as to say that you were right to protect Bodeland by preparing a trap for us. Faced with the same lack of information, I might have wanted to assess Princess Nica's clear-headedness too."

Nica scoffed at his suggestion, but in truth, she was relieved that he had stepped in before she had taken punitive action which she would never be able to take back. "Ask what questions you must to satisfy yerself that I am who I say I am and that my friend, bizarre as he currently is in his countenance, is who and what he appears to be."

It was as though a large balloon had just released all its gas. The tension had dissipated significantly, but Shamus wondered whether it was fully gone. There was still the matter of the ambush just ahead of them in the darkness that had not been addressed.

"That's not necessary, Erladoch." Nica admonished. "Anisha's quarrel isn't with you. Not really. Is it, Anisha? You doubted my judgment most of all." Nica was doing her best to control her anger out of love for her cousin, but a part of her wanted to smack her hard enough to unhorse her.

Anisha's head dropped. She appeared genuinely ashamed of herself. Like the princess, she was not one to be prone to acting rashly.

"Did you think that I've done nary but bed Erladoch since he has returned? Have ye not thought about the fact that I too needed to be convinced? Did ya really think me some rutting Brial in heat that's too excited for the return of my mate to think for m'self? Just look at ya now!" Her voice was raised, no longer concerned about the volume. "Ye should be ashamed of yerself! Anisha, even if Erladoch was an utter impostor contrived by some unholy plan of the

Evil One to deceive me, how do you explain Shamus over here? I gave Erladoch the task of placing the bloody Wigget's cloak on the man whom he described to me as one of his truest friends! Whatcha think I might have done had Erladoch either refused or even so much as hesitated to undertake such a task that I bestowed upon him?"

Anisha studied Shamus carefully to confirm for her own mind that he indeed wore the cloak that cannot be worn by a mortal man before responding. Sheepishly, she replied to the princess's challenge, "Ya would've lopped Erladoch's head off knowing that he was an impostor had he hesitated, and you would've let this one here die without so much as a blink by placing the cloak on him yerself to witness what its magic might do to an impostor." She admitted to the ether.

"You see Shamus here with your own eyes, do ya not?" Nica's voice was still raised, but she kept herself under control. "Look at him living and breathing as he is! Would he still be among the living if he did not bear the seed of all our hope within him? Had ye not thought that one through at all in your paranoid imaginings?" She spat on the ground beneath the fore hooves of Anisha El's horse. Both horses stirred restlessly from the act, sensing that it could be a precursor to violence.

Hoping to extricate herself from what she measured would be a fully deserved punishment, Anisha answered, "I am so very sorry to have doubted your judgment, my princess!" Her remorse was real as she withdrew a small, fluted horn. The device was no larger than the palm of her hand. She blew into it once, and only once. In seconds, ten warriors walked out from the shadows ahead, their weapons safely sheathed. A collective look of relief registered on each of their faces as did the entourage that had accompanied the Travelers to this point in the journey.

"What was the plan here?" Nica demanded.

"I would have had your group surrounded, my lady. I would have demanded that you let me interrogate Erladoch and Shamus. I meant to protect you from yourself."

As an elder of Bodeland, Anisha had known that no mortal man could have possibly survived the wearing of such a relic as the White Wigget's cloak—a garment known to instantly kill anyone foolhardy enough to try. It had been kept safely by the Bodelanders for nigh on a thousand years. It should have readily occurred to the mayor that she had nothing to doubt about either man the moment she cast her eyes on the cloak around Shamus's shoulders for the first time. She should have recognized this, but she had been consumed with Lady Nica's order to destroy all that she called 'home'. She couldn't simply accept this without doing something. Anisha's anger and resentment had bubbled over at having been kept out of the loop. That dark thought had worked its way through her mind like an eel in murky waters, swishing away practical thoughts and reason until she felt obliged to take decisive action. She looked upon Shamus as if she was seeing him for the very first time. Her thoughts returned to his actions in the Great Hall, which had skillfully de-escalated imminent violence among her Keeper brethren. His advice to all of them to only think positive thoughts resonated in her ears now as if he had just spoken it. For the first time in hours, her mind was once again clear, rational. She erupted into tears, choking on their liberal flow.

"I am unworthy to lead! I—I have failed all of you!" She apologized through stifling sobs of dismay and grief. "I let the darkness into me. The very darkness which Shamus of Fior here had cautioned us against! Everything about the man tells me that he is not one of us, not a Keeper, and yet, he must be! How else can it be? Most of all, I shouldna' doubted you or Erladoch. My life is forfeit! Ye have every right to punish my actions in accordance with our ways. I don't know how else you could ever forgive me?"

Nica studied her older cousin's face—the deeply felt regret that was washing over her. She knew the power of the Evil One's enchantments. She also knew that Anisha had been right about at least one thing: Evil had attached itself to the Travelers after Shamus had called out the name of the Master's earthly puppet. It was still somehow managing to latch on to them even in the presence of disciplined efforts by the Travelers to exorcise themselves of its insidious hold. Like it or not, Anisha was in the end doing what she was sworn to do—protect Bodeland, and protect her fellow Keepers—even if her method had been sloppy. Kicking her horse's haunches gently to bring it closer alongside her cousin, Nica suddenly threw her arms around her in a gesture of forgiveness and consolation.

"T'is so easy to be consumed by this malice which has been hunting us." Her statement was deliberate and loud enough for all to hear so that she might re-establish the credibility of the mayor of Bodeland by demonstrating that she had fallen under the influence of the same dark enchantment which had fallen over parts of the city. "Had I thought that you acted for the wrong reasons, I would have had to consider you as being so untrustworthy as to not be worthy to continue to call yerself a member of our Order. But I know differently. I know you, cousin." Nica slid her hands from Anisha's shoulders and raised the woman's chin so that they could gaze directly into each other's eyes. "You are and shall always be a trusted member of our Order, and a great protector of our people. What ya did, you did to protect me and all Bodelanders. I see it as plain as the nose on yer face. The matter is done!" She proclaimed so that all would know that there would be no consequences. She then addressed the warriors who had emerged from the shadows, who shifted uncomfortably on their feet as they awaited their princess's pronouncement. "You warriors who came to execute my companions are forgiven. Go back to your families now and begin to make ready to leave along with everyone else, as I have already ordered."

The warriors conscripted for Anisha's dark business didn't need to be told twice to leave. They happily fled away, relieved that they had not been forced to carry out such discordant orders against their princess and her party. As they passed out of earshot, Nica confirmed another correctly identified comment that the mayor had made.

"So that you know, it is complicated." Nica decided to offer some clarification in the hopes of salvaging her cousin's hurt pride. She ventured that while Anisha might simply have been acting under a dark compulsion, she nonetheless had to consider that the source of her rash behavior had been caused at least in part by the discordant information she had had to work with concerning Erladoch and Shamus. She hadn't been entirely wrong to house doubts. "Yer' right, of course, that Shamus is not a Keeper—not at least in the way that we are. He's not from around here either!" She said this a little too enthusiastically. "Mind you, he is in every aspect of his being one of us, and he is vouched for by Prince Erladoch for all the right reasons. Erladoch had been tasked to use the True Knowledge. Even I wasn't told that he was on a mission, and I can tell ya' he's still got some making up to do."

Erladoch's jaw flinched momentarily. He knew that Nica had forgiven him, but he still felt horrible about being forced to keep his mission from her.

"Erladoch traveled a very long way to find Shamus here and bring him back to us. He has been gone because of this and this alone."

Anisha's eyes widened with understanding. While she had not traveled, she was intimately aware of her own family's place of power and had long accepted that if the occasion were ever to come, either she or one of her family members in the Sacred Order would themselves go to their uniquely protected location and travel if it were to ever be deemed necessary by the inner counsel of the Sacred Order. Her tears of self-loathing finally abated.

"Now, you know more than should have been disclosed to ya, but take comfort that Prince Erladoch's return in the company of this man presents us with hope. A decision has already been made as to how many should know the full tale in fear that the Evil One might learn our agenda before we can fulfill it. I'm sorry that you were excluded, cousin, but t'is best this way. We now have hope."

Nica embraced Anisha dearly before making room between their horses.

Anisha felt exhausted from the surge of competing emotions that had run through her. Her princess had not only brought her into the circle of secrecy concerning Shamus's importance to the group; it was clear from the embrace that Nica had already forgiven her. She wondered whether she could have offered up such a kindness so quickly after learning of someone's nefarious plot had it been against her. Nica did understand her, however. It was apparent on her smiling face as she pulled away. She would not ask another thing of Nica; her sovereign had spoken. *Hope,* the princess's last word to her rolled around in her mind like a laughing child spiraling down a grassy hill. Memories of better times filled her. *Hope.* She tried the word on like a familiar garment. It fit her so well that her world felt right once more.

"Now, Shamus, let's clarify a few things." Nica began as she beckoned the party to move along. She was anxious to straighten out her cousin's previous misinformation. "The runes you see here are not a language, as you would consider it. T'is a code, though. It tells those who know of its existence what they must know to traverse these byways. Because this tunnel highway is beneath Bodeland, you might conclude that it was built by our people. T'was not. You could then conclude that it was made by the early members of the Sacred Order of Keepers, and if so, you would be only a little right. The scratchings which you've noted are not natural formations, and their origins aren't wrapped up in legends as this one might've wished ya to believe. That was merely to put you off for obvious reasons." The rebuke to Anisha was intended as humor.

"The Keepers, along with some of the non-Keeper elders of Bodeland, devised a system of etchings to guide anyone who was permitted to travel down here, lest they become horribly lost. The scratchings themselves mean absolutely nothing at all on their own. The order upon which one encounters them, however, is everything. There are etchings that were made by our ancestors on nearly every twist and turn of this labyrinth. That was deliberate, of course. Only if you were afforded an education on the order of which scratching preceded which other scratchings would you ever be able to traverse this place to see the light of day once more. As best we know, there are but two entry points to this network: one in Gol, where we began, and one which pops out at our frontier. Anisha did not wish to share the truth with you for the obvious reason that she was deciding on whether to slay you and Erladoch as agents of the Evil One."

Nica said it so matter-of-factly that Shamus knew that she had already shed her anger over the matter and now wished to trivialize what might have happened into a non-event.

"T'was then that I realized my cousin's plan, of course. When she chose not to share the truth with you, I sensed that she meant to end you." Once more, Nica was not chiding Anisha El. She was simply stating the facts. Anisha rode along, doing her best to avoid eye contact with anyone. Her embarrassment would subside soon enough, but a part of her still smarted at how rash her actions had been. Sensing that Shamus, most of all had to come to terms with her cousin's previous ill-conceived plan, she decided to force the two of them to interact. "Anisha, ye know how this works better than most. Tell the Fiorian how it really works, won't you?"

Recognizing her cousin's intent, Anisha El rejoined the dialogue with a view to nullifying her previous actions. "As ye must know, Lord Shamus, our tales are told in voices trained in the sharing, word for word, over all known Ages of Loura. Applying this ábaltacht to the scratchings you so correctly have identified, our forebears devised a way to navigate a way through this network of tunnels. There are guides whose single job is to commit to memory the pattern of each symbol that has been etched in the rock faces here. All of them are Bodelanders, of course, but not all of them are Keepers, as it was not a Keeper who first discovered this place. There was much deliberation by members of our Order in the early days about this fact, but one of our greatest elders determined long ago that there may come a time when the existence of the tunnels and how to traverse them might need to be shared with a select number of the uninitiated, provided, of course, that they could demonstrate their ability to maintain this knowledge in secret. The practice of exploring and memorizing verbal descriptions of the symbols inside the tunnel system has endured in but a few Bodelandish families ever since."

In his own effort to demonstrate a measure of forgiveness, Shamus replied to Anisha with a further question. "Are such spoken records truly capable of being maintained without alteration?"

Anisha acknowledged Shamus's overture of forgiveness by smiling shyly at him. She knew he could have left the conversation altogether and have nothing more to do with her. He would have been entirely in his rights to never speak to her again, and yet he chose to demonstrate immense maturity by picking back up as though he was capable of moving on. In fact, he was that capable. As a clinical psychologist who had worked with a small subpopulation of schizophrenics who could erupt into violent and deranged behavior patterns, it was an essential part of his skill set to cast away anger and frustration when his patients acted out aggressively toward him. Forgiveness was a prerequisite of his calling.

"Yes, Lord Fiorian." She indulged his question with all seriousness. "The expectation is that Keepers will maintain the historic record in a manner identical to their ancestors. Were this not so, and interpretation or generalizing were to be permitted, we fear that the complete record would be lost. Can you imagine, for example, if the key ingredient in a poultice designed to treat infection were to be forgotten, or its proportion to be lost to time? That would be devastating! Whatever our personal ábaltacht happens to be, we spend our early lives memorizing word for word the Great Tales, which should be told the exact same way until time ends."

Nica smiled in the glimmering darkness at her cousin's effort. She rejoined the educational moment. "Lord Shamus, the knowledge of the 'Toc' is something that is reserved only for the highest and oldest of families of Bodeland. That is what we have come to call these scratchings." As she spoke the three-letter word, it literally sounded in Shamus's ears as if Nica had clucked her tongue at him. "As Anisha said, most Bodelanders would n'er be educated on the meaning of the lines you see before you, but as non-Keepers were involved in the discovery of this underground highway, there have always been non-Keepers in Bodeland who've been allowed to pass this secret."

"But Lady Nica," Shamus inquired. "You have told me that those who are numbered as Keepers are a small group. Do you not have a library where such information could be kept if something were to befall your Order?"

Lady Nica was without understanding. The notion of a 'Library' was something she was unfamiliar with. Clearly, the word did not fit her lexicon. In an effort to answer him, she decided to extol him on the virtues of her Sacred Order. "The House of Dunbar has been our ally for as long as memory can serve, and we its. The same is said for all lands from which the Keepers are drawn. We share an ancient common language, and thus we maintain the record the same way. While I have said that we are but a small group, Lord, we still number in the thousands. I expect that our traditions will carry on unhindered."

Shamus could tell that she was puzzled by his question. Through no fault of her own, her response was going off on a tangent, as she didn't fully comprehend how to provide him with the information he was seeking. Erladoch closed in on the conversation. Unlike his colleagues, his travels had afforded him the ability to offer an answer.

"Allow me to assist, Nica. Shamus, we Keepers 'are' each one of us a library for certain specific things. I've told ya that. before. Unlike your time, we do not 'write' words as you know of them. What must be remembered is told from elder Keeper to younger Keeper. The elder ensures that the record of a thing is maintained perfectly before the young one may even begin to repeat the lore to another. I am a 'library', as you would know of such things." He smiled confidently about his ability. "The members of our Order are each in themselves libraries. Together, our kind comprises a great library of all important knowledge."

Anisha looked at Nica with sudden shared comprehension. A library was somehow a physical repository for the storage of knowledge. Erladoch's explanation had suggested that such a thing was possible, even though they were not sure how that might be so.

Shamus didn't doubt what Erladoch was saying. He had been reasonably certain that, without any help from him, Erladoch had done something that no one from the timeline of Loura had accomplished while he had been in Ottawa; he had taught himself at least the rudiments of written language. He alone knew what a library was in the sense employed by Shamus. His next words confirmed the suspicion.

"What Lord Shamus is referring to involves a very complex system of common symbols that represent the very words we speak. The library then houses those words in one place so that anyone can look at those same symbols and understand the tales that someone else has told."

"So, ya mean groups of pictures to describe what we say to each other?" Nica asked for greater clarity.

"Aye, just that very thing exactly," Erladoch confirmed.

"That must involve a lot of stone?" Anisha ventured.

"They don't use stone like they do down here in the tunnels, Anisha. They cut down trees and make a thing called paper. On that, they apply a colored ink like we might use for dying clothes, but they use that ink to make the symbols on the paper."

Nica considered the magnitude of what she had just been told. "They kill trees. The very thing we draw our food and shelter from? What do they eat then if there are no trees to grow fruit on?"

Shamus could see the conversation was about to go off the rails. "We eat the same things you do, and like yourselves, we use wood to make things like your wagons and beams for housing."

"Is there so much forest in your time that using the trees the way you do doesn't hurt the land, then?" Anisha was very curious about what they were being told.

Shamus didn't have the heart to describe the state of the world he called home to people who venerated the forests. The people of his time had sacrificed much for their modernity. He could not but help to spare them that.

"No. We haven't always protected the forests the way we would like to," he chose to admit, hoping to avoid further elaboration.

"So, the people of your time, Shamus, are doing to your forests what the Galagars did to theirs?" Alida couldn't help but ask, having overheard the discussion.

"Aye," Erladoch offered. "The people of Shamus's time are making the same mistake."

"Bloody inefficient, isn't it? This library making?" Alida offered with knowing regret.

"Yah, what if the place burned down?" Anisha El offered. "T'would all be gone in a flash, wouldn't it?"

"Worse still…" Nica was still working through the implications of words written down rather than meticulously repeated, "what if folks were to get differing impressions of what those symbols meant? Ach, I can foresee nothing but misunderstandings in abundance happening when people canna' agree on what a symbol means!"

Shamus said nothing. These people were truly learned.

Having adjudged that Shamus's world had to be adrift in controversy over libraries containing written words, Anisha El chose to demonstrate the correctness of the Keepers' approach to maintaining the record of things. "Did ya know that Lord Erladoch has always been considered to be one of our greatest scholars? His ábaltacht has equipped him to retell the wonders of Louran history right back to the time of the first Strahanas. When he was believed lost, much more was thought to have perished than just the body of the man. Thankfully, he isn't the only one possessive of that ábaltacht in this generation. We make sure of that."

Shamus nodded his acceptance of what he was being told, but he continued to worry about the ability of the Keepers to hold fast to meticulous records. Hoping to avoid a further bombardment of intelligent questions that he would find difficult to answer, he elected to find a way by which he might close off the discussion. "Thank you for telling me that the Keepers number in the thousands. That gives me hope that all the information which you consider as important will be kept safe. In these difficult times, however, I worry that even Keepers numbering in the thousands might not be enough to do this. Even where I come from, the Keepers continue to thrive, although I do not know their number. I cannot say, however, whether they have maintained this tradition in the same way that you have."

Erladoch understood his friend's point. Being a late arriver to the Order, Shamus had not been exposed to anything approximating the totality of Keeper training. All things being equal, he had been deliberately prevented from membership in the Order for his own protection. Erladoch did what he could to fill in at least some of the gaps. Having met some of the modern Keepers of Shamus's time in his own travels, he felt able to assure his friend that the Order had remained consistent. "If the count of our initiates left to defend the Order were only to number in the handfuls in some future time such as your own, take comfort in knowing that we cultivate only the finest minds of the Age. No initiate can enter the Order of the Keepers unless they are adjudged as being capable of fulfilling the training, and that training involves the ability to remember vast amounts of information. Even if the bloodline of a person were to suggest that they could be initiated due to their connection back to the

Strahanas, we still pick only those from such families as might be able to endure all of the expectations of our Order. As but one example, all warcraft now being taught to the many lands of Loura in anticipation of what is coming are being instructed in exactly the same manner, no matter where such education is taking place."

Before leaping through the void with Erladoch, Shamus had come to understand pretty swiftly that membership in this secret Order required an impressive acumen for warrior craft. It was only after having put more thought to it, even reaching back to the faces of those he had met in his own timeline that numbered themselves among this Order, that he expanded his understanding that the Keepers were far more than elite killing machines; they were highly educated maintainers of a record of all that had once been. He had personally witnessed the swift application of the healing arts by Nida Galagar. The small man had responded to the injury inflicted upon him by the Evil One in the dreamscape as though Shamus's injury had been commonplace. In a matter of seconds, Nida had seamlessly assembled and applied a healing poultice to the wound in his chest as though he were an army medic field dressing a shrapnel wound.

At least in this time, they live every word of their lore, he told himself.

Nica Bodelander's horse closed on Uhlwhin's flank. As it did so, the other horses began to fall into two-by-two pairings without any overt instruction from their riders. Shamus recognized that the way ahead was narrowing into more of a tunnel than the avenue it had just been. As the ceiling and walls tightened more ostensibly, he felt claustrophobic once more. With a beckoning gesture, he resolved to distract himself from the closeness of the air by encouraging his educators to continue to instruct him.

Nica caught the gesture and continued as requested. "One must both embrace and flawlessly recite our code as it is a path of learning undertaken from the time of the Strahanas. One must also commit to memory both a piece of our peoples' story without error, and then determine their unique gift, which must then be worked on throughout the remainder of their lives. In this way, they in turn can become a teacher. Without all these traits, one cannot include themselves among those who are chosen."

"I see?" Shamus offered in initial response to this, expecting that there was about to be more to the point being offered to him. "So what happens when an initiate fails the training?" He found himself incapable of not posing the question to the tight cluster of Keepers closing ranks tightly to one another now as the tunnel narrowed even more oppressively.

"We permit them to meet their deaths with honor by engaging in a battle with confirmed masters of our Order or by accepting the Achroi," he heard Andor say from behind him in the bottlenecked space.

"Their deaths? The Achroi?" Shamus already regretted having asked the previous question, but now he needed to know. "Meaning what? Sorry. Can you elaborate, please?"

"A failed initiate may be permitted to die a swift and honorable death, or they may have their tongue extracted before being released to the wilderness to wander and live as they choose, incapable of revealing our existence. This is the Achroi," Nica offered. Her voice was entirely matter-of-fact.

Shamus was startled by the brutality of the ritual, but nonetheless accepted that it was at least a better choice than death. "Jaysus!" he muttered to himself under his breath. He nodded his appreciation for the information but now regretted having pursued further questioning. "The Achroi." He rolled the word around one final time. "That's some nasty business!" he offered as matter-of-factly as possible.

With no warning, there appeared to be a widening of the torchlit walls ahead. Shamus copied Nica's actions and dug his heels into the sides of Uhlwhin to encourage his horse to hasten forward. He stayed astride of the princess for a few moments, but then pulled up softly on his reins to allow her to get ahead of him. It was, he hoped, the politest way that he could show that he required no further discussion on the practice.

Nica seemed to understand the action. She allowed Shamus to edge away from her. In her own mind, having performed the ritual on more than one failed initiate herself over the years, she repeated Shamus's exclamation quietly to herself. "Nasty business indeed."

As he distanced himself, Shamus wondered whether the practice endured into his timeline. *What is done now with the failed initiates of the Order?* he wondered. The modern Keepers, whom he had been introduced to before making the leap, not only had an ability to use the written word to convey information, but a wide swath of social media options to spread information in milliseconds. Even though every kind of media brimmed with theories about an unknown plethora of secret societies, made movies about them and wrote countless exposés about them, there continued to be absolute radio silence where the Sacred Order of Keepers had been concerned. *Hell!* he confirmed to himself. *My own damned parents and grand-da were initiates, and I never had even the foggiest notion of it!*

As barbaric and stomach-turning a notion as the Achroi had seemed to him only moments ago, he concluded that the modern Keepers were not afforded any way of surviving a failure to measure up. *How could they be allowed to live? There would be no way of assuring that a rejected candidate wouldn't expose the Order.* Chewing on this reality, he accepted that the handling of a failed initiate in the 21st century was likely equally as brutish. At the minimum, a rejected candidate in modern times was without any recourse that equaled 'life'.

It didn't take long at all to connect the dots before he began to develop concern about his own measure. *Would I have made it had I been inducted in the traditional fashion?* The thought blossomed into a fully flowered gasp of anxiety as he considered whether he was, as yet, considered by his travel companions to have been fully inducted into the Order. What did such an induction even look like? He chided himself for such thoughts and made a promise to himself to never bring the topic up again. Despite his disciplined decision to abandon all thoughts about the topic, he couldn't help but be keenly aware for the next fifteen minutes of the weight, heft and dryness of his own tongue as he clopped along in silence.

Chapter 31

"When was this decided?" O'Mara demanded of Erladoch. He had not been made aware of this decision, and neither, he assumed, had his departed father. He was more than a bit irked by the revelation being disclosed to him now. How could it be that the Anahimaran members of the Order had not been afforded the same courtesy? This made no sense! In his mind, he correctly assessed that had his father undertaken the same actions, Anahimara would have stood some measure of a chance to prepare for the Treborgan onslaught that had recently overwhelmed his kingdom.

"This was not my call, O'Mara. I do not sit in the inner council any more than you do." Erladoch tried his best to placate his colleague, even though he knew that this information would be hard to receive. A decision had been made in Lorelai that the existence of the Keepers should be revealed to a very select few outsiders almost half a decade previously. The disclosure had, in fact, only been made to a few of the key politicians who supported the Dunbar monarchy and only in the Kingdom of Dunbar. This disclosure had been undertaken purposively. The inner council of the Order feared that by deploying Erladoch VII, the Brave of Fior Hill, to undertake the mission he had been charged with could create a massive power vacuum in Dunbar were he not to return. Erladoch VI was already of an age. The Keeper leadership had correctly speculated that some civilians simply had to be counted on to support a grieving king as well as carry out the important business of erecting more defensive infrastructure in Baldréimire.

The council knew that the Scrags were more than just flocking to Treborg from all parts of their world in the last half of their age; they were doing so now in numbers that were no longer calculable! The advice they had received from envoys from the future had confirmed their worst fears. As the method of travel chosen by the messengers had been so arduous, they had been severely injured. It had taken them much time to heal, let alone make their message understood in the common tongue of Loura. Once they had recovered and been properly vetted as members of the Order, their message was compelling: the line of Wigget Bearers strong enough to house Anthrac Aran's seed was in peril; not just because of the lack of proximity to the Strahanas' bloodline, but because it had become impossible in the modern age to continue to hide the Angealkind's Bearer. Attempts had already been made on the current Bearer's life more than once. It was clear that there could be no other viable solution: Anthrac's Bearer needed to be found and brought back, and the messengers from the future were unfit to make such perilous travel themselves given their egregious injuries.

Ten years had gone by since the messengers from the future had come to the council with their tidings. As it was, the Keepers had had to wait six years before a porthole was going to be open again just for Erladoch to begin his mission. He would have to find and return the White Wigget or his Bearer to their timeline by the time of the next opening for there even to be a chance of keeping Anthrac alive.

In embarking on this rescue mission, however, it assured that the Master of the Pit would return Enilorac to the human realm in their timeline to wage the final battle for the light. The build-up of Scraggin armies behind the Elecs confirmed that Satan had already made these calculations all on his own, that the Angel would reappear here. Where the Angel went, the stone had to follow.

Dunbar had been given precious time to make preparations to place its kingdom on a war footing, even if that fact had not been communicated quite that way initially by the decision-makers in the Keeper enclave in far-off Lorelai. Anahimara had not been so favored. This revelation would sit with O'Mara Boldar like spoiled milk in his belly.

Rightly or wrongly, it was thought to have been too risky for the Keepers living in the kingdoms directly adjacent to the Elec Mountain range to even be told that the council had quietly begun making disclosures of the Order's existence to select politicians who supported the western royal families. Keepers from the Kingdoms of Seth and Anahimara in particular were not to be told of these decisions until later. Even the Keepers inside those royal families, like that of O'Mara Boldar's, were specifically excluded from the plans which were being made and carried out in Dunbar, and not long afterward, in Ara. It was feared that the sudden emergence of standing armies in these borderlands would be detected by Treborgan spies and possibly escalate timetables unnecessarily. They needed to give Erladoch time to succeed in his mission and, if he were to fail to return, they also needed to take no actions that could be obvious to the Evil One until the western kingdoms had secretly organized for war.

O'Mara had not been the only Keeper to take this advice poorly. Nica Bodelander had been absolutely furious with Erladoch when he had returned to her from apparent death after a four-year absence. Her extended grieving process had nearly robbed her of any ability to be happy ever again. To learn that her kingdom's proximity to the Elec Mountains signified that the governing council of her Order would not share intelligence even with her, her father and her brother rocked her to the core. Like O'Mara, this delay in organizing felt prejudicial as hell to her people's continuity. She struggled for days following Erladoch's return to grapple with his disclosures. *Maybe,* she thought, *it made sense to keep the less noble members of the Keepers out of the loop just so not too many people knew of the operational decision. But did it?* She struggled with this greatly. *Inner council or not, all Keepers were in one way or other descended from the Strahana/Human mix. None of us are supposed to be above any other even if some of us happen to be members of ruling families. That is supposed to be our way!*

She had watched O'Mara shift back and forth on his horse with barely controlled rage as he received the news from Erladoch. It was difficult to be dispassionate about this information, given the consequences that had been visited on the Anahimaran people specifically. Her heart went out to him, even though she had by now resolved the conflict in her mind. At least for Nica, however, the exhilaration of having her great love back in one piece was something that she could find joy in.

"Because of the council's strategic decision, some leaders had gained knowledge of the Order's existence sooner than others." She listened to Erladoch say the words aloud to O'Mara and the others.

Yes, that had happened. She reminded herself as she watched her colleague stew in his resentment over the news. *But every kingdom had become aware of the Order and its continuing mission over the past year. Even Anahimara had begun assembling and training a standing army by the time that Treborg had attacked it.* She justified to herself the same thing which Erladoch had been obliged to justify to her only a few weeks previously. *It just had not been with the same amount of lead time that Dunbar had obtained. He had been riding to the aid of his neighbor with his own newly assembled company of warriors when the invasion of Anahimara happened. He knows this to be true!* She told herself, doing her best to not become directly embroiled in the conversation between the two men. Whether the strategy of gradual disclosures had been well founded or not, it had been the council's decision, and such decisions were final once made. They all must abide such things with the discipline that formed the hallmark of every Keeper's personal makeup. She was accordingly puzzled over how O'Mara could be so angry at Erladoch for simply being honest about the things he had known. *Erladoch had been traveling. It's not like he could have told O'Mara at a time earlier.* She considered Shamus's advice back in Gol when things had nearly gotten out of hand between O'Mara and Nida.

"Enough of this now." She interjected calmly but authoritatively in answer to the reddening face of O'Mara. "Time to think happy thoughts, gentlemen. Heed the Wigget Bearer's advice to us all: only happy thoughts now."

O'Mara released a heavy sigh, almost unaware that he had inhaled so deeply previously. His cheeks became less red as he tipped his forehead in recognition of Nica's point. He wasn't done with the conversation, but his control over his emotions seemed to return to him. "I cannot believe what you are telling me, friend! Though I know your words to be true, we were left exposed with almost no time to build a fighting force capable of repelling even the first level of the Evil One's invasion! That is what is so damned hard to swallow!" He brushed his hand over the long hairy neck of his mount. "My people are all but wiped from existence by this ill-fated decision, ye know?" O'Mara's voice was no longer angry. Instead, it was shattered; it revealed a young man whose outlook was irretrievably damaged. "It's just so hard. So hard," he muttered. "Things might've been different. Different choices coulda' been made". He was sick to his stomach but had nothing more to add.

Erladoch reached from atop his own horse and tapped his fellow traveler on the shoulder consolingly. "For my part, O'Mara, I would have been a dissenting voice among the leadership if I'd been a member of the inner council. As I've said already, friend, I was not part of the decision. It was made just as I was leaving. It took me months to convince my own father and the other members of the council to authorize my journey to the broken shrine of Tine Fhluich, where I made my leap. It felt as though some of them no longer even believed what we were tasked to preserve. So many of our fellow Keepers who had made leaps into different timelines either never came back at all or returned empty-handed in all meaningful sense of the word. The utility of undertaking missions to check in on our future brethren and support them in their struggles to assure that our Order always continues in its purpose seemed to have all but fallen out of favor when the messengers had come to us. It seemed as though the elders of our Order were beginning to think that the White Wigget had vanished from all realms and would not be found despite the mission of the Wigget Bearers to continue his existence. It was disquieting to my heart to think that some of our kind were already losing hope. When the messengers arrived bearing tidings that he still lived, I just knew that I had to be the one to go! I did not think that my absence might act as a trigger for our Order to begin revealing itself to others as it did. For my part in this, I hope that ya can forgive me."

Shamus had not overheard this exchange. Had he been able to, he would have learned something about Erladoch which would have been most unsettling. His friend had been holding on to a piece of truth that had been kept from him; a most important truth which had been a defining element of Shamus's life for better than a decade—possible proof of his parents' survival of their transit.

The minute that Erladoch had uttered the information in his discussion with O'Mara, he recognized the danger of what he had just shared and reflexively looked over both of his shoulders to locate his friend. Shamus was well back from them, examining the stalagmites which loomed precariously overhead in some locations, still feeling the heft of his tongue in his mouth. *In good time, my friend, you will know the rest,* he thought to himself, a pang of guilt over his failure to have not yet fully shared passed over him.

"I recognize yer sentiment to be real," O'Mara confirmed his acceptance of the apology. "I just find this all so hard, Erladoch," he whispered through gritted teeth at a volume that was nearly inaudible. "I carry such a weight upon me! So much has been lost already."

"I know, O'Mara, I know. I journeyed between Taroc and Ataroc's wastes on my way to Bodeland with Shamus. I saw first-hand the devastation which you must've witnessed. When I made my leap in hopes of finding Anthrac in a future timeline described by the messengers, I had studied every small detail of what they had shared with the Order. Or so I had believed."

The expression of doubt caught O'Mara's attention differently. He studied Erladoch's troubled frown. It momentarily distracted him from his own self-pity.

"Even my own Da, knowing that I would be undertaking this mission, didna' share all that the messengers had shared with him and the other members on the council. I have had to guess at some of this over time, and I am fairly certain I am right in my conclusions. But key information was held back from me; information that I am sure would have made my task easier. All I can think is that they feared that if I were to have been captured, they needed for me to not know certain key things which might have made it easier for the enemy to get hold of Anthrac and ultimately his stone. I barely made it back here, and it's all thanks to Shamus. I was pretty sure that I hadn't succeeded in any part of my mission because of those blind spots. T'was only when Anthrac revealed himself as being within Shamus that I could comfort myself that at least some parts of my mission had been fulfilled at all, even though I felt it in my bones that I had made the right decisions. These were some of the truths that I comfort myself with about the way the council operates anyhow."

"Have you figured out those other truths about what was told to ya versus what was not, Erladoch?" O'Mara asked in a dispassionate but curious voice.

Erladoch shook his head in the affirmative. "Aye, I have." Erladoch didn't seem prepared to share further as he briefly paused. Had it not been for the faltering illumination of the surrounding torchlight, O'Mara would have caught the shift in Erladoch's facial expression prior to his continuing.

"What I can say to ye, O'Mara, is that I had hoped to jump, fulfill my mission in a matter of days as the convergence that I was headed for would take me to the exact place and time where I was told, secondhand by the council of course, to seek out the White Wigget. I'd expected him to have already been reborn. Given the passage of time between when the messengers arrived in our time and the beginning of my mission, there was an expectation that the Wigget Bearer might have found a mate and possibly sired Anthrac Aran into flesh already. No one could be sure of that one, but it was a greatly feared prospect. The council believed that there would not be a female member of our Order in the future timeline who could possibly be pure-blooded enough to bring forth the Angealkind; not, at least, without diminishing him in unpredictable ways. I was given no name of whom to look for, only what I should expect him to look like; can ya imagine that nonsense? They actually were satisfied that there'd be enough Keepers on the other side of the portal that I would be bloody escorted to him or some such thing!" Erladoch appeared reflective a moment. Without voicing the words to O'Mara, he realized for the first time that he likely had been handed to Shamus by Keepers after all, albeit not in the way that anyone could have predicted in view of Erladoch's injuries.

"Anyway, I had hoped to either find the man who carried the Angel or the Angel himself and be back at the next convergence that I was told to look for within a matter of weeks. I was even told to take myself and the object of my mission to a place in the southwest of a land they called 'Wales' and make my leap homeward from a place where a stone shrine had been standing for thousands of years in at least the modern timeline. I never anticipated encountering resistance so far west of the Elecs in the form of a war party of Scraggin soldiers. They came on us in strength, O'Mara! Wandering the border lands of Anahimara itself like they already owned the place!"

O'Mara winced noticeably at the comment.

"I certainly never expected to sustain a near mortal wound which robbed me of all health for months; I can tell ya that for sure," Erladoch shared. "T'was nothing short of the efforts made by Lord Shamus and his faith in me that he found us another window home. It might ne'er have been found at all short of his devotion to solving the riddles I had presented him with. He took me on as his personal charge, he did. Clearly, the White Wigget was speaking to him, even though he had not been made manifest in the same way as he has become since we arrived back."

O'Mara was surprised by Erladoch's comment. Noting his surprise, Erladoch offered more. "That's right, the Shamus ya see before ya now looks nothin' like the man I know. That's the presence of the Angealkind we are looking at. I canna' say why he has chosen to alter my friend's countenance so, but there must be a purpose to it."

Erladoch choked back his emotions a moment before speaking again, as he knew that what he was about to say would come as no solace to the Anahimaran prince. "T'is my fault, O'Mara, that your people have been put to the sword. So much time was lost—time that should have been available for us to show the Fiorian to all, and to begin making ready all lands in Loura for the coming evil. Never did I see myself losing four years trying to find a way home, and I'd not be here now at all without his help. Our bond was what drew me to him, and he to me. He trusted in the unspoken knowledge, which had not really been given to him yet by his forebears other than his already mad Grand-da."

"Alas, he was yet too young to receive or even remember what he had been told. In his own timeline, his parents had had to go into hiding for fear that those sworn to the Evil One's purpose had become aware of Anthrac's presence in their time. They chose to keep their own son unaware of his burden, believing he'd be safer that way. He was always under the watchful eye of members of the Order, but he knew none of it! Can you imagine their heartache? They had no way of knowing what might happen to themselves by going through such a tumultuous porthole, and yet they risked everything to find us and make us ready. Knowing their own mission, they refused to put Shamus through the same risk unless the council deemed it correct that he be brought back here at all."

At that confirmation, O'Mara's countenance noticeably changed. "You're saying that the messengers were Shamus's parents?"

Erladoch caught the change in O'Mara's voice even without being able to see his face clearly. "Aye." In a further shushing whisper: "He canna be told this fact, ye understand me? Had the council or even his own parents thought it necessary for him to know, they would'a surely told him, or me, and as you can plainly see, they must have had their own reasons for not doing so. It pains me greatly to keep this to myself!"

O'Mara nodded blankly, acknowledging that a secret made was a secret to be kept.

"The Keepers of Shamus's own time chose to reveal to him only the parts of his own legacy almost too late for it to have even mattered. I had to figure it out for myself, and I know from my chats with him that he suspects all on his own that they lived. In fact, I'm sure that it feeds his hope. I expect that he's worked out that the reason why I came to fetch him is the evidence that he needs to reason out that they survived their own jump; he's not a stupid man. We are here now, friend. The council makes their decisions about what is or is not to remain secret, and it is our job to bide them, just like it is now your task to keep this secret from Shamus if it be a secret at all. Those are the burdens we Keepers live with. It's who we are and how we thrive."

O'Mara could feel the steeliness of Erladoch's gaze upon him now, even though the space between torchlights in the tunnels was spaced at some distance. It dawned on him that the entire exercise was intended for the clear purpose of not only placing the burden of what Erladoch had figured out for himself as a shared secret, but more so to illustrate that the decision made by the inner council of their Order to proceed with making graduated disclosures to each kingdom was not a burden anyone wished to take on but, rather, the best reasoned approach to a difficult responsibility that could only reveal its effects in time.

"Let us not allow the losses of your loved ones to be in vain. The White Wigget will walk among the people of Loura once again. We must protect both Shamus and the secret of his burden at all costs till he can be brought out in time to face the unthinkable evil that now comes."

O'Mara said something so low that it was inaudible to even the razor-sharp hearing of Erladoch or the Galagars, who had otherwise been riding close enough behind the discussion. His eyes, however, met those of Erladoch's through the flickering torch light of the tunnel highway just long enough to show his acceptance of what he had been told. Perhaps because of the stalagmites they were passing under, he ducked his mare's head, and with it his own, in order to not smack right into the largest of them on the wall's outer edge where he was riding.

***

For the better part of another hour, O'Mara chose to ride alongside Andor of Seth. By placing himself in this configuration, he managed to avoid further discussion with Erladoch about the weight of secrets to be borne by any Keeper. He had known all his life what his duties were, and he had never so much as questioned these values until this very day. It was comforting to ride beside Andor, as he ironically never imposed himself—at least not via conversation. As they trotted along, either listening to Andor quietly humming to himself or saying next to nothing at all, he thought much about how various of the members of his Sacred Order had been tasked with responsibilities based, sometimes entirely, upon the geography of their own respective kingdom of origin. Although certainly not exclusively, the Bodelandish and Anahimaran Keepers had been the members of the Order who had been primarily tasked with keeping watch of the western side of the Elec Mountain range. For all intents and purposes, it made the most sense for them to do so given their intimate knowledge of the terrain. Galagars certainly tended to remain tasked, more often than not, with keeping watch over their own lands, and so on and so forth with all of the Keepers.

Unlike O'Mara's homeland, the other Keeper kingdoms were not poised against the frontier between his kingdom and Treborg. Unless tasked with specific missions by the council directly from Lorelai or called back to their secret enclave for other reasons of Keeper interest, it made sense that where the average Keeper would devote much of their time fulfilling their duties would be primarily in their own homelands. For the rest of the Keepers, sorting through the Bodelanders' and Anahimarans' collective paranoia every time a solitary nomadic Scrag was spotted gutting a farmer's sheep within 100 yarricks of the Boldar River Delta made it difficult to assess whether there had, in fact, been any real change in the presence or absence of evil on the other side of the towering Elec Mountains.

After a time, O'Mara sought out Nica Bodelander, not so much to continue to voice his grievances but rather to talk through what he had been feeling about the matter with the one Keeper whom he assessed as having some comprehension of his frustrations. As the underground thoroughfare had once again widened, the Travelers were more astride of one another now versus the two-by-two formation they had been riding in for the past two hours.

Nica listened to what O'Mara wanted to say. She had herself recently bid her brother goodbye as a result of the struggle. Now that O'Mara had found a way to express himself which did not seem to escalate his emotions into a lather, she was sufficiently eager to hear what peace he was able to make with himself over all that had happened in the past few months. It was plain that O'Mara was now doing his best to comment on his own insights on when he should have taken note of the proverbial change in the wind and gone to his Da with concerns that a war might be coming. Nica heard him out for some time before commenting. As a Keeper, listening and compassion were paramount over speechmaking or lecturing.

"It was only when you and I had become old enough to pass the trials Lord Boldar that we could even begin to see the changes for ourselves. This change of which you speak—at least the truly noticeable changes—have not just happened in 'our' age, but in a truly measurable way only very recently. It didn't leave any of us much time to prepare. You can't beat yerself up o'er this forever." This was not the first time Nica had consoled O'Mara. She had been his personal counselor for the many weeks since he and his contingent of refugees had made their way to Bodeland.

"Ach!" O'Mara offered. "The council should'a listened to our paranoia half a generation ago instead of discounting the importance of these sightings. In hindsight, the Treborgans were engaging in planned incursions for some time, testing us, looking for our blind spots. It was our sworn duty to keep watch for this very thing! We are all such fools for not having seen this coming sooner, and I fear that we shall all perish, having been too afraid for our Order to be revealed prematurely in case we were wrong. Our self-interest will prove to be everyone's undoing."

Nica did her best to consider him before responding, but she was not inclined to agree that the Keepers had missed clues. There had been no such clues to be seen. She particularly found his evaluation defeatist, if not downright distasteful. "Looking on it now, O'Mara, I agree that our seeming indecision has left our time short, but no one could have known that the Master of the Pit was planning to send the Evil One back to our timeline to organize for war. Ach, we may not have seen such a thing as that for ten thousand lifetimes! Scrags multiply same as the rest of us. The fact that they were migrating east to answer the Evil One's dark summoning is, in itself, a recent enough thing. There'd been no talk of actual organizing behind the Elecs in far-off Greno until the world was made to shake with the Evil One's screeching return from the Pit. That event could've happened two thousand years from now, or twenty, or never. But I mark yer point that his tearing through the fabric of space and time to arrive back here was message loud enough on its own for all of us to take note, and we have. And now, we are doing all that we can."

"Ya think we have?" O'Mara's retort was about to take shape when Erladoch raised his hand to silence O'Mara Boldar's apparent knee-jerk need to interrupt. "I know the great cost you continue to measure, my friend. I truly do. But so many tidings of single sightings along the edge of the Elecs still measured up to nothing at all. There was nothing that different from what our ancestors in the Order were quietly handling for a thousand years. We are the ones who cultivated the old myths around the nature and behavior of the Scrags, and from what could be seen, the actions of that race of ancient cave-dwellers conformed to the very myths we had constructed about them."

At that, Boldar disobeyed the Dunbar's Prince's command to hear him out and went forth with his interruption. "We blinded ourselves to the danger, even though it was our task to keep the bloody watch!"

"Nah, laddy!" The colossal Sethian now stuck his nose into the heating conversation. "Only in our lifetime has it been clear that the occupants of the Treborgan lands were already under the Master of the Pit's influence. We didn't even know that the defunct kingdom was even occupied any longer! For the first time in memory since their defeat o'er all that time ago, none had seen a grouping of Scrags large enough to be measured as 'organized'. Our predecessor Keepers could not have known that this calamity would arise in our lifetime. Stop measuring the tragedy of Anahimara as a predictable outcome! You will eat yourself alive with such self-blame. Ye know I'm right on this! The Master of the Pit was biding his time, waiting to reinsert the undead Treborgan king when his best chance of recovering the third Itavo became a possibility."

Throughout the conversation that bounced back and forth among the Keepers and O'Mara Boldar, Shamus had ridden along in silence. The longer the Travelers volleyed their thoughts to and fro in an effort to placate O'Mara, the more Shamus worried that his coming to the Louran timeline served as at least part of the explanation for why the Evil One had returned to this moment and place. Time travel was anything but exact. Despite this, it gnawed at him that Enilorac had been sent back to prepare for the White Wigget's return. *Or that's at least how it appears*, he considered.

There had been an anchoring to him all his life that tugged at him in some way. Whether it had been the attempts made to end his life since he was a small child or the comforting echoes of a female voice that soothed him in his dreams so often when he felt himself at his lowest points, the reverberations of those moments danced around in his head now. They were all connected somehow to this time, this place. *Have I drawn this half-human, half-demonic being back here by having called him out in my timeline?* he asked himself. *Jaysus, is this all my fault?*

The possibility of this being his fault was deeply unsettling. *But how does that make any sense?* He attempted to logically organize the events that he was aware of about recent Louran history. The invasion of Anahimara might have coincided with the timing of his having erroneously spoken the Evil One's name back in Ottawa in the late fall. That much was true, but only in the sense of Shamus's accounting of linear time. When he and Erladoch leaped through the portal, he guessed that he had traveled backward perhaps as much as twenty thousand years. His own personal timeline had absolutely nothing to do with anything. *Or did it?*

Could Shamus have actually witnessed the devastation of Saban in the north of Anahimara, followed by the sacking of Taroc and Ataroc on the night that he first came face to face with Enilorac? Was it a remembrance? "Phhheeewww!" He exhaled in a loud, exasperated huff. He simply wasn't sure about anything.

Erladoch looked over at his friend with one raised eyebrow, as did the other Keepers. The look was as much a question of, 'Are you alright, Shamus?' as it was a question of, 'Is there something you would like to contribute to this conversation?'

Shamus did not wish to respond in any way to the questioning looks. He shook his hips awkwardly across Uhlwhin instead, suggesting that the reason for his sudden utterance had been simply a matter of him expressing discomfort over having been on horseback for several hours. Erladoch looked away first, satisfied that no contribution to the group conversation from Shamus was forthcoming.

Without having intended an interruption, the conversation had come to an end following Shamus's surprise utterance. O'Mara looked about at his companions, wondering who would next speak to him about his feelings of woe. No one seemed prepared to continue talking about the matter. Shamus's interruption, intended or not, had acted as an excuse for the pity party to come to an abrupt stop. O'Mara's heart was heavy, but no more was going to be said. No one was prepared to cast blame for what had come to pass. The Anahimaran prince looked at Erladoch and his companions once more to confirm that they had withdrawn from the dialogue as their horses rounded the immense corner spoken of by the Mayor of Gol. More torch lights illuminated the wide-open cavern. The Travelers and their escort came to a halt in front of a storage space. A series of wooden bins containing grain and hay for their horses revealed itself in the heightened illumination. Not far from it was a large pool of icy-cold water, which lay at the base of an underground stream that trickled liberally from somewhere above them. The company dismounted. Given his awkward exclamation only moments ago, Shamus made a show of stretching loudly in hopes that his fellow Travelers would connect his earlier utterance to a display of discomfort rather than an anxious outburst.

He did not have to lead Uhlwhin to a feed box. Once free of his rider, the majestic and massive horse sauntered up to the first available spot and nosed his way methodically through the contents, as did the other horses. They were accustomed to this feed station and needed no invitation to help themselves.

Tracing the well-lit walls of the cavern, Shamus espied yet another space where water flowed down the wall only to gather into a natural cauldron of sorts before rushing away somewhere deeper still into the ground. Containers were filled and passed along to each member of the party so that they could enjoy a proper drink. He pressed the clay receptacle to his lips. The heft of the cup was sufficiently thick that he was taken completely by surprise by the splash of nearly frozen water that poured past his lips. Shamus took a heavy pull on the glass, despite the frigidity of the water as it burst through the dry hollow of his throat. The moment he pulled the now-empty cup away, he felt the familiar brain freeze setting in. It was painful and exhilarating all at once. He waited for his head to clear before filling the cup again. As the assault to his shocked sinuses eased off, he laughed at himself. He had not felt such a powerful sensation since he had been a child. He remembered the hot summer evenings that his parents would take him down Bank Street to the Dairy Queen for an after-dinner treat. He almost always ordered a small Mister Misty and a Peanut Buster Parfait. It was the Mister Misty that always got him—that sudden shock to the system when he took his first draw on his straw of the shaved ice beverage always went straight to his head. *It was horrible!* he told himself as he reminisced. *It was wonderful too! Why didn't I ever learn?* He could hear the voices of his parents chiding him humorously each time that he had done it. Grabbing his nose in feigned horror, crying the words 'brain freeze' sent William and Katlyn into hysterical fits of laughter at their son's utter goofiness. He laughed at himself again. Nobody took notice of Shamus's gesticulations. They were all focused on the piles of hay that lay off in a corner of the cavern. This would serve as their beds for the night. Shamus soon followed his companions to the soft and invitingly spongy surface, himself now anxious to lay his head down to rest. The nearest torches were doused. Soon enough, the Travelers found the long overdue slumber they'd all been craving.

It was, of course, impossible to know whether it was morning when he awoke. Nothing looked any different. Black walls illuminated artificially by well-oiled torches were the only source of light, same as the day before. Shamus had been very pleased to have had an escort through the tunnel highway to this point. Having been underground for so long had given him the heebie-jeebies. They had traveled for so long under the ground that, without people clearly versed in the lore of the Toc, he realized that one could be lost a long time—maybe even forever—beneath the surface. He expected that his sense of claustrophobia was shared by all his fellow Travelers, with perhaps the limited exception of those who actually knew how to navigate their way through these passages.

Given the smoothness of some of the walls, he speculated that some of the areas they had traversed were man-made, or at least enhanced by human hands to make for easier travel. Others were clearly not, however, and Shamus knew that these intersecting honeycombs, which went off in all directions from time to time, were likely evidence of tributaries from a once-great river, or possibly eroded spaces carved out from seawater. *Seawater,* Shamus considered, as he directed Uhlwhin close enough to one of the rock walls to enable himself to run his hand along its surface. *Not rock,* he thought, as his hand felt the ultra-rough and pocked wall. P*etrified coral more like it. Or,* he continued to process the possibilities, *lava rock maybe?* He couldn't be certain. Geology had never really been his thing in school. *Wish now I'd paid attention in Rocks for Jocks.* That had been the expression he and his university classmates used to refer to this field of science. It astounded him how many of his friends who played on sports teams studied Geology, actually. For him, it had been an elective course he had had to take when he was working on his undergrad. Arriving ultimately at the conclusion that the networks of tunnels likely had once been underground rivers leading to some far-off sea, Shamus wondered just how far beneath Bodeland these other dried-out tributaries must extend.

Even with rest, O'Mara Boldar was still speaking about loss to his fellow Keepers, albeit in more reserved tones. His friends continued to listen and give advice where they could, but the magnitude of his loss was not something any of them had yet been forced to face regarding their own people. The carnage they had come upon the previous day in Ardehla before arriving in Gol was still weighing heavily on all of them, however. It was at minimum, a preview of what was to befall their entire world if the Evil One's armies numbered in the magnitude they predicted after the fall of Anahimara.

Shamus followed at a respectful distance from the Travelers directly engaged by O'Mara but did his best to listen to the exchanges. At the very least, it kept his mind off the fact that they were still traveling underground. His professional training instructed him that O'Mara was processing his trauma, and that was a highly positive step. Although he had not been conscious for the first week or more upon arriving in Castra, he wagered that O'Mara was speaking constructively for the first time since his and his remaining soldiers had arrived in the Bodelandish capital several weeks previously following the devastation of his homeland. The slaughter at Ardehla might have been the trigger that caused him to finally open up and begin processing his complex emotions.

Shamus listened carefully to the words being used by the young Prince, doing his best to gain a full measure of the Anahimaran's post-traumatic state of mind. It definitely appeared that O'Mara was indeed sharing in ways he had apparently not yet done till now. Shamus wanted to understand both the 'why' and 'why now' motivators for the discussions being undertaken despite his professional suspicions. He had surmised that Erladoch's disclosure the previous day concerning the staggered approach to organizing for war across the kingdoms could have also been a precipitate of what was now taking place. His psychologist's brain cautioned that other forces might also be at work that should be paid attention to now.

"The Anahimaran race has met its end because of our vanity and blindness to the strategies turning behind the walls of the Black mountains. We failed to see that the Treborgans' had deliberately turned their attentions to kingdoms far beyond our known reach in order to build their armies with such defiled beings. We have dwelled in a cocoon of denial, and now they have me where they want us."

The Travelers nodded supportively, not knowing what else to say to their friend. He was not wrong, of course. Just because they had had no reason to traverse the vast mountainous regions beyond their eastern borders, the Keepers were under no illusions that the world might extend past it. There simply had never been tell of anyone traveling from the far east to visit the Louran kingdoms of the west. It was entirely possible that there were other lands and other kingdoms somewhere beyond the Elecs. It was accordingly also possible that the Evil One was drawing his armies from more than the cave-dwelling people of their known world in the west. What interested Shamus, however, was the turn of phrase employed by O'Mara. "They have me where they want us", he had just said. 'He could have simply made a mistake by saying the word "me" in place of "us" both times,' Shamus acknowledged to himself. 'But this could also have been a parapraxis.' Parapraxes or 'Freudian slips' were a well-known phenomenon in psychology. Sometimes when a patient said one thing when they ought to have said something different, as O'Mara had just done here, it was a signal to the counselor that the subconscious mind was harboring a deeper thought, often connected to trauma yet to be processed. *There's a lot to unpack here*, Shamus told himself. *I'll have to watch this young Prince and do my best to support him where I can.*

O'Mara's less-than-veiled criticism of his fellow Keepers and their sloth at detecting the cancer growing beyond the highest mountain range of their known world was creating a host of different emotions in the Travelers. Each member understood and empathized with O'Mara Boldar's pain, but what they uniquely thought of his criticism was not at all alike. Being highly disciplined, the earlier advice of Shamus to cast negative thoughts aside, lest they open themselves to the Evil One's influence, continued to resonate with them. Alida had heard enough, however. Normally deferential to all, even happy to sit back and let the chips fall where they may in a conversation, she could not help but be a little more like her brother in this moment; albeit, calmer in her approach.

"My dear Lord of the Anahimarans," she interrupted in her incredibly sweet but committed voice, "no one, not even the most cunning of our own Order, could have ever ventured across the Elecs undetected in such foul lands! T'is not reasonable to expect that even a Keeper could have returned alive to speak tales of what lies beyond. The organization of the Scraggin horde may have taken generations for all we know. I cannot agree, however, that we could have seen this coming until they began showing their audacity, and that could only be measured by their having sent large enough bands of warriors through their secret passes for a real threat to have been considered. We all know that the minute that started happening, we stepped up our vigilance. Many lives of many Keepers have now been spent containing the growing threat in secret. Neither in Inyi's cool face nor under Naga's warm kiss, however, could anyone have predicted the true size of the threat. You have to become reconciled with this, Lord Boldar, or ye make yourself of no value at all to those of your people who will need a King to lead them when all of the killing is finally done."

O'Mara was not angry when he next spoke, but he was still a man who was finally coping with his grief. Had the light been more robust in the tunnel, the tears streaming down his face would have been hard to miss. How he choked on his words next betrayed any cloak provided by the weak illumination of the cavernous tunnel.

"Thank you, Alida, but I care not about the Evil One's conquests of wild lands to their eastern borders, if there even be a world that lies beyond. I mourn instead the passing of my proud race, reduced to ash and blood by a wave which could not be stopped. No children, no women were left living in my father's kingdom. What is left of us comprises but a band of deeply saddened soldiers who no longer have a home or family to live for."

Andor grasped solidly at the Anahimaran's arm. He cared for O'Mara and was unable to permit this younger member of their Order to wallow in such a way any longer. Consolingly but firmly, his massive hand enveloped O'Mara's bicep. "Ye speak as a man who is prepared to lay down and surrender his life to the elements of nature. I know the Anahimaran people, O'Mara. Your soldiers will fight simply to avenge their dead and those who have been taken as slaves. Your warriors are proud and strong. They may go to their deaths on the battlefield along with the rest of all the Louran kingdoms before the great struggle is over, but they will go in the knowledge that their final breaths were exhaled in an effort to avenge the souls of those who have fallen to the Scraggin sword, or who were enslaved by the menace that has come out of Greno. This is not O'Mara Boldar who speaks. I have seen yer skill and your courage tested too many times in battle already. Perhaps it is the darkness of this place that blackens your thoughts. We shall all be happier when we finally emerge into the light of day. The endless twists and converging passageways down here are making us all uneasy. Take heart, friend."

O'Mara pulled up on the reins of his horse to bring her to a halt. The Travelers who had been directly engaged in the conversation with him followed suit. Mayor El had left the cluster of Keepers to talk in private with her princess to obtain final commands and instructions. Other than wishing them all a safe journey, she said nothing more to the Travelers. Shamus took this action as a sign that the escort was about to go back the way they had come, whereas the Travelers were about to exit the oppressively long network of tunnels.

When the Bodelander escort had distanced themselves, O'Mara spoke to his companions. "You are right, my good Sethian neighbor. In fact, all of your collective counsel is greatly appreciated. I think that the devastation of the village of Ardehla, and the weight of blackness which nearly overcame me in Gol's Great Hall, has carved a hole in me. I do not wish to feel hopeless; these are alien feelings to me, to be sure. I know that my burden is no greater than anyone else's present. I will think of all your strong words in times of future darkness."

With a quick nicker and tapping of heels on his horse's massive flanks, he hurried ahead. Whether it was a recognition that they were about to crest the end of the tunnel or simply because he had accepted that he had ruminated long enough, O'Mara's actions confirmed that he would not burden himself or his friends any further with negative talk. Only the doctor in Shamus worried that this might not be such a good thing for him to do.

***

Chapter 32

The road to Arana City would be long and perilous but for their having the great benefit of being on horseback. After the Travelers had rested some at the edge of the cloaked opening, they were determined to resume their trek. Nica had called upon her companions to assist with moving the secret door aside. The door, such as it was, consisted of a series of leather hides made from the flanks of woolly mammoths. They draped from the rock ceiling above and extended fully to the ground. As one leather curtain after another was pulled back, the Travelers lead their horses past, only to pull the draping back into place until they encountered the next one. When they finally broached the true door, what they found was a series of overlapping panels of vine-covered wooden panels: living plant walls. There were three heavy panels in all. It took the strength of two Keepers to move each one to permit them to exit one by one through the gap.

With the removal of the first of the three panels, the light burst into the mouth of the cave entrance. The intense power of Inyi's morning illumination stung the party's eyes. It was a revelation, however, to feel the warmth of natural light and inhale air that was not stale. The new day's sun felt like renewal to everyone's souls.

With only a crudely constructed map that he had committed to memory from when he and Erladoch had attempted to define the contours of the Louran kingdoms back at the Browse compound in Calabogie, Shamus calculated correctly that the mouth of the tunnel from whence they had just come now placed them beneath the southernmost border of Bodeland. They were within the contours of the much larger kingdom of Ara.

Nica was leaving her native Bodeland behind with the heaviest of hearts. She registered that it would likely be the last time in her life that she would walk through the peaceful harmony of her forest kingdom ever again. The trees that they had emerged from were sparse here, certainly not thick enough to be considered as part of a forest. As they exited the mouth of the tunnel highway, the Travelers took pains to conceal the entrance from which they had just emerged. Nica cocked her head left, then right, against one of the trees overlaying the mouth of the now closed tunnel. With her ear firmly pressed to the soft bark of a new birch tree whose roots straddled the rocky exterior of the cave mouth, she waited. She repeated the action once more, firmly holding to a stone boulder in hopes of detecting vibrations in the ground which might reveal movement of an enemy in their vicinity. Nothing stirred, no vibrations. With no hint of peril, she mounted her horse and signaled to her friends that it was time to ride. Alida and Nida were surveying their camouflage efforts before they leaped onto the backs of their mounts.

"Niknik M'Lac!" Princess Nica clicked at her jet-black coated horse. The beast, easily standing eight feet above the ground, complied without hesitation and lead the party out of the forest edge at a moderate pace. The Galagans rode on either side of the Bodelander for the balance of the first day. Riding more swiftly when coming upon more flat terrain, they kept astride Nica, singing merry tunes in the rich accent of their own forest homeland. The tone of the Galagans' songs seemed to disregard any part of the reality that their homeland would also be at stake. It was not that they denied themselves consideration of the very real future; it was simply that a Galagan's way of chasing away negative thoughts was to chatter a whole lot. This was their way of suppressing the oppressive forces of doubt and gloom, which would have otherwise weighed down upon them as equally as any other one of the Keepers traveling.

Shamus suspected that the chatter was deliberately made to distract the Bodelandish princess from experiencing undue sadness in leaving her homeland. It also occurred to him that his Galagan companions were doing their best to tell tales of home to each other as a way for making up for the fact that their visit to Gol was cut terribly short, leaving them with no opportunity to seek out members of their own kind to exchange news with.

For her part, Nica Bodelander appreciated the gesture. She did her best to listen to the banter and even participate when she could, knowing that it helped all of them to invest in the well-intentioned efforts of her companions.

While there was an actual very well-traveled road linking Gol to Arana City, Erladoch had been counseled by Andor and the others that they would be well advised to avoid it.

Although the kingdom of Ara was often spoken of as the most civilized and advanced kingdom of Loura, it was an accepted fact that riding out in the open in current times could only attract more attention than they wished to have. There was even a possibility that they might encounter wild people from the Badlands. These were not the Neanderthal communities that had been compelled into the ranks of the Scrags of Treborg. Rather, they were a wild nomadic people who had reputedly come from lands far to the south well beneath the borders of the southern Louran kingdoms. They had traversed a mountain range only a few hundred years ago, moving north into Loura from their home, which had become an arid and inhospitable terrain. Typically, less than a few handfuls of Badlanders were ever seen to be traveling together. They consisted of generally no more than two extended families per band. Fully disinterested in integrating with any of the Louran kingdoms, they avoided contact with other communities whenever possible. The Badlanders wandered the southern half of the Louran kingdoms, spending most of their efforts on hunting deer, buffalo, mammoth and any other wild game which they might come upon. They engaged in no form of trade with any of the kingdoms across Loura and even avoided encounters with the highly traveled Galagan silk traders. The only contact that the people of Loura had ever had with these nomads consisted of lightning raids made upon their trade caravans when the Badlanders' food sources had experienced moments of scarcity. This propensity to prey upon unsuspecting Louran travelers ensured that the Keepers would watch them with the same level of vigilance as marauding Scrags, as people with no allegiances could not be trusted. If they were to encounter Badlanders on their way to Arana City, there was always a chance that they might be set upon given their small number. If there had been any reason for any of the kingdoms to maintain any form of warrior class at all on their own without subtle influence from the Keepers, it would have been as a result of these nomads. As they were so few in numbers, however, and they appeared to mostly shy away from contact with the Lourans as a whole, even this did not trigger a perceived necessity for military organization among the kingdoms of the west. Like everything else related to safety, however, the truth of the Badlanders having remained under control rested squarely upon the concealed efforts of the Keepers to track and quietly police their activities.

With all that had been happening in the current age, the Keepers had resolved to watch more closely for interactions among Badlanders and free-roaming Scrags. Recently enough, there had been surges in such activity. It came as no surprise that Scraggin war parties were successfully traversing parts of the Louran kingdoms undetected. They were getting help from the one nomadic people who knew best how to avoid interaction with Lourans.

Shamus was keenly interested in learning more about the Badlanders, not having been told much of their existence before riding out onto the upper plains of the kingdom of Ara. As usual, Erladoch was happy to oblige his friend's questions. As the Travelers traversed the open landscape, the discussion served as a welcome distraction to the monotony of smacking unevenly into the back of Uhlwhin. It also reminded Shamus to maintain a heightened sense of vigilance.

"During this Age of Loura," Erladoch began, "there are now so many more Scrags and dark bandits about in the western lands. But even before my life, keeping the activities of such dangerous marauders in check formed one of the tasks to which so many of the Keepers had devoted themselves for countless generations. This was one of the ways in which our warrior craft was tested and refined while the kingdoms slept in their ignorance of the dangers that walk in our homelands. We couldn't simply spend our time and efforts hunting brials, you know," he said somewhat sarcastically.

The comment caused an unsolicited shiver down Shamus's spine. He was sure that his grand-da had mentioned them in his storytelling, and Erladoch had confirmed their existence as something more than a mythic beast as they sat around the comfort of a fire in the Browse Cottage at Calabogie, Ontario. He understood a Brial to be a type of large panther. By description, it was somewhat larger than a Bengal Tiger with razor-sharp teeth. With two knife-like fangs protruding several inches below their chins, they were considered the most dangerous predator known to this world. He had not yet seen such a beast. Even though he'd heard the nocturnal calls of wolves since coming to Loura and had even come across the tracks of the occasional bear, he dearly hoped to never have to come face to face with a Brial. As his thoughts lingered a moment on his time of training at John Browse's family cottage, his mouth watered at the thought of eating cheese and drinking a fine red wine. *I hope someday to see John again*, he lamented for another brief moment before Erladoch reclaimed his attention.

"Ya see, Shamus, free-roaming Mountain Scrags were frightened enough of the Keepers' secret war parties that until this age, they really were only known to frequent the lower western slopes of the Elecs; hence the old wives' tales designed to frighten children into not wandering too far afield. Truth is, we needed those wives' tales to be told so that some memory of the dangerousness of these creatures would not be fully forgotten by the world. The Mountain Scrags, like the Badlanders, were basically nomads themselves. They were smaller than the full height of an average man, and they had, for as long as memory could retell for those who kept a record of them, satisfied themselves with sneaking onto farms to steal livestock in the dark of night. They were nothing like the better-fed and trained Scrags of Treborg that we have now witnessed infecting our lands on this side of the Elec Mountains. The Mountain Scrags, for those few of the common folk who knew of them from actual face-to-face encounters that we had not yet dispatched, were considered to be little more than a hateful pest. They were sufficiently dangerous, but all in all, thoroughly unorganized. The same cannot be said of the Scrags of Treborg, as you have seen first-hand enough times now."

While Erladoch had done his best to prepare Shamus to do battle with full-grown Treborgans before they leaped through the void, the memory of his first encounter returned to haunt his thoughts. The scarred and twisted face, the fierce eyes, the frothing blood and foam pouring from him as he slid down Shamus's blade was an image he would never forget. Even with all the violent encounters he had experienced since that first day, this first kill, such as it was, still shook him. As they rode alongside each other over short grasses and heather, a question occurred to him.

"Erladoch, as I have not yet met a mountain Scrag, do they wear the same metal shoes?"

"They do not," he replied. "Or, at least they were not doing so before I left. That is a tradition that has bubbled up from the Pit, I suppose. One that was unique to the Scraggin soldier conscripted into the armies of Treborg. I cannot imagine that such deliberate torment could be inflicted on another in any other place than Hell."

"My nightmares of it are still too fresh in my mind," Shamus shared as he unwittingly brushed over the healed scar on his chest a moment. "I can hear the rumble of those shoes like hammers in my mind, an approaching storm which blots out all other sounds. It's horrifying to me even now, but why do this to your own soldiers? It slows them down and makes them horribly loud when they charge."

Erladoch acknowledged his friend's point. "Well, you'd be right about those things, and I am sure that this is part of it. The infliction of terror as they advance, I mean. But there is more to it than that I have learned from Scrags that I have in the past captured long enough to understand them. It is part of the Evil One's nightmarish routines of torture-training, Shamus. They call it 'shoeing'."

Shamus thought of a horse from his own time. The image of hammering a shoe into the hoof of a horse was said to not hurt the horse. Hammering heated metal into a Neanderthal foot? It would have to be excruciatingly painful.

"The Evil One and his lieutenants shoe all Treborgan Scrags that are able to join in the ranks of their army. T'is done right at the moment a Scrag enters into their adult years. The process of 'shoeing' is all about ultimate submission to the Master of the Pit, I'm told. It involves the hammering of small nails into the bottom of the soldier's foot bones through a plate of metal that would later stay permanently affixed. Remember, Shamus, the Evil One traded away the people of his kingdom to eternal servitude to the King of the Pit in exchange for eternal life and a chance at revenge on the Louran kingdoms. When he ran out of humans to enchant with the powers given to him by Satan, the Scrags were an easy conscript. Treborgans endure a lifetime of torment, burning rituals, random whippings, all designed to toughen the outer shell of a Scrag's skin to make them oblivious to pain in battle. Given to so much suffering over many years, they develop thick and mangled layers of scar tissue over their wounds. After so much abuse, they no longer have nerve endings on the surface of their skin that would register pain by the time they reach adulthood. It creates both madness and a fearlessness in them. The Evil One, however, knows best at how to maintain control over his soldiers. Shoeing is but the final ritual of admitting the Scrag into his dark service. It involves the infliction of a level of agony in the Treborgan that guarantees utter compliance from them. Can ye imagine having someone bang nearly molten nails through plates that will become permanently attached to the soles of your feet?"

Shamus felt his stomach lurch at the question. "Uh, no! I really can't, Erladoch. The thought of it makes me sick actually! Not only for the level of cruelty involved, but at the image of it I can't help but compose in my mind." He felt another quiver in his guts as he tried to shake the thoughts away.

"There is some level of precision to the practice in actual fact," Erladoch went on, seemingly oblivious to Shamus's advice that he'd rather not hear more on the topic. "Different-sized nails are used to attach the metal plates to the soles of the warrior's feet, and they are deftly hammered into the large and small bones of the foot alike in multiple locations. The size of each nail is carefully chosen to avoid destroying the bone it is hammered into. The fiery state of the nails as they are inserted through the pre-made holes in the foot plate is designed to instantly cauterize all bleeding of surrounding tissue as it penetrates deep into the foot bones."

"It's utterly horrible!" Shamus interjected. "I don't understand how anyone could endure such suffering! But seriously, I need you to stop telling me about this before I puke!"

"Come on now, Shamus, ye asked, so now I'm telling ya." Erladoch was determined in his usual way to finish the story. "While it is true that some Scrags die as a result of this horrific ritual from pure shock, the Evil One's lieutenants are ordered to promptly hack a dying Scrag into pieces and pull his flesh apart. The spilled blood of the dead Scrag is drunk by those assembled, and the dismembered flesh is thrown into nearby pens as food for the animals that the Evil One had also bred for his own fiendish pleasure."

Shamus felt a complete and overwhelming sense of revulsion now. His stomach was beginning to fold into knots, listening to Erladoch's overly detailed explanation. He didn't know whether to feel compassion for the Scrags or a more deepening hatred at their collective barbarity.

Having nothing else to do but ride, Erladoch went on with the explanation, paying no attention to the green hue building in Shamus's face. "Most of the Scraggin soldiers survive, obviously," he offered matter-of-factly, "and those that do the least amount of screaming are revered among the Treborgans. They typically are made into the leaders of their squads. They're fed more and better food than any of the less resilient soldiers. It is thus a ritual which they consider as a game of pride. Those Scrags who do not heal well from their life of abuse leading up to adulthood are also used as food, or if they are even less lucky, are forced to act as servants to the soldiers until, ultimately, they too are beaten to death and used as food. I've told ya this more than once; there is nothing of such a creature for you to feel sorrow or compassion for," Erladoch admonished Shamus, having sensed the presence of Shamus's sympathy for them. "For male and female Scraggin soldiers alike, the ritual of submission caused by this process is both all-consuming and assured to achieve unquestioning compliance. Every time a Treborgan Scrag runs, their minds have been so twisted by pain that their brains create an intoxicating substance which fuels them into blind madness and an insatiable lust for murder. There is no humanity in them, Shamus; do not think of them in such terms, as it will be your undoing."

Shamus wondered whether it was his face that gave away his thoughts, or the less-than-subtle act of swallowing back on his own bile. Either way, he accepted the point with a cursory nod, knowing from his skirmishes with these creatures already that they were driven by a lust for murder that would make a sadist in his timeline cower.

Chapter 33

As the Travelers trod along over increasingly more open country, Shamus took note of Lady Nica and the Galagars. Their heads swiveled noticeably and regularly to and fro, scanning the horizon. Several times over the past hour, he caught sight of one or more of them quickly drawing their bows from behind the cloaks on their backs. In seconds, they would fit an arrow to their strings and let loose into the air at some unfortunate solitary bird that had the great misfortune to have been flying overhead. Without any fanfare at all, the one who fired, would then speed off to where the felled bird struck the ground, hang over the side of their mount at a gallop, and, in one smooth action, scoop and stuff it into a cloth bag hanging over their horse's long backs near to their hindquarters. Each time the bag was returned the horses would let out an audible whinny. Given the immense size of these horses as compared to those of Shamus's timeline, he found it hard to believe that adding the weight of even a few extra birds on any one of these formidable equines would annoy them. It occurred to him after this cycle had repeated itself for a third time, that the whinny was not made in protest at all, but rather in celebration of the rider's accomplishment. *These are true war horses!* Shamus told himself as he marveled over the symbiotic relationship between horse and rider. *They count themselves as one with their riders.*

After they'd taken down ten such winged fowl, he began to think that there was more to this exercise than a hunt for their dinner. "Guess we're going to eat well tonight!" Shamus offered to the air, setting the table for someone to comment.

"We won't be dining on these birds at all, Wigget Bearer," Andor Seth offered to his back after a few seconds of empty air. Adjudging himself to have been closest to Shamus when the latter had uttered the statement that was quite obviously a request for information, he took it on himself to respond. "Those are messenger birds, Lord Shamus. They fly with no flock, and it is likely that they are riddled with poison."

"Sorry?" Shamus answered, confused by what he had just been told. "There is no such thing as a venomous bird that I've ever heard of, Andor."

"Yer right. Birds are not venomous on their own, Lord Shamus. But these winged nightmares are in the service of the Evil One. So that their messages are not intercepted, the legs of these carrier ravens are coated in a liquid that, just by touching it with your bare skin, will cause your body to well up with cankers and boils within hours, then lead to a most cruel and violent death not long after."

Shamus was alarmed to hear what Andor had just told him. He replayed the method used by his Keeper colleagues to gather up their kills. As he replayed his companions' actions, it occurred to him that they always grasped the downed birds by their wings or by the shafts of their own arrows when they handled them. "Huh!" he offered to the colossus who continued to gallop beside him. "I see."

Andor remained alongside him, clearly intent on answering any further questions that he expected would now be forthcoming from the Wigget Bearer.

"I'd like to be able to say that this is only the work of Badlanders or free-roaming Scrags that are sending such messages. Truth is though, there are too many of these vile conscripts for this to simply be the work of a couple of enemies. Some of these were crossing in different directions when they were felled. This tells me that there are several pockets or groups of Scrags about this country right now. I believe they are trying to coordinate some kind of plan."

Shamus considered the advice. "You can conclude this simply from the number and directions by which such ravens were flying?" Shamus asked for further confirmation.

"Aye," Andor replied matter-of-factly. "T'is the only sensible conclusion. I reckon that there are multiple Scraggin' war parties lurking all over the plains of Ara right now. They are each sending reports to coordinate what can only be the next phase of their invasion, or at least some form of attack. Either that, or these ravens are controlled by the Evil One himself and were about to rush off and report our presence here. If that be the case, then we've been seen."

"Reports?" Shamus was perplexed. He had been told more than once now that there was no such thing as written language by various of his fellow Travelers. "What kind of reports could they possibly deliver?" he pressed.

Erladoch spat at the ground upon hearing Andor's conclusions. He knew that his friend had been right, possibly on both accounts. "I agree, Andor. There are watchful eyes all about this land in service of Him. If we are to be spotted on the road, such creatures are definitely under the power of enchantment to speed to Greno and make report. I doubt they relate to us, though, as we have only just emerged from the depths beneath Gol."

"What kind of reports then?" Shamus insisted on being heard. He didn't want to allow his anxiety to spiral out of control, but he could feel his breathing increasing in any event.

Erladoch was taken aback by Shamus's frustrated outburst. He looked quizzically at his friend. A moment of realization came to him. "Ah. Images, Shamus. Symbols of images, really. A mountain is squiggled lines, a forest is a tree, a lake a circle, a plain is a horizontal line, a river a vertical line, a tree beside a squiggle signifies a forest beside it, and so on. This is not unlike your mapmaking." He paused momentarily so that Shamus could grasp what he had just been told before resuming his conversation with Andor. "Now that the tree cover is gone, for sure those messages will soon be about us too, no matter what else they might be planning. *'Even if there are not multiple war parties about, you can be sure that the Badlanders and Scrags will be dispatched to interfere with our travel. What is normally an easy four days' ride will have to be compressed into two, if at all possible'.*"

Shamus did not enjoy this news at all. The symbology referred to by Erladoch was rudimentary, but likely effective enough to coordinate war party movements against them. He could already feel a longing to draw his sword out of its scabbard just to have it ready. "If you aren't sure whether these are war party to war party messages versus news of our movements, why bag the birds? Should we not pull the messages off the birds and read them now?" He felt this to be a practical suggestion.

"Whether the messages are about us or not, we still need to make haste to where we are going, Shamus. Now is not the time, under the light of Naga, to find ourselves stationary on the plain," Erladoch offered, kicking his heels into his horse, requesting more haste.

Shamus understood the point but was about to offer protest as he felt that it might yet be important to know if these Badlanders had indeed spotted them and were sending messages to other war parties to lay a trap for them further into their journey. Before he could voice this, Erladoch, sensing that his friend had more to say on the matter, got ahead of him in the exchange. "You probably noticed that neither Lady Nica nor the Galagars touched anything on the downed fowl other than their wings, yes?"

Shamus nodded in agreement. He had worked this out for himself.

"I did, yes." Shamus acknowledged.

"If ye ride up a little closer, m'Lord, you'll notice something else."

"Oh?" Shamus wondered. "And what would that be?" he asked innocently.

"The stench of days-old shite that they use to make the poison," Nida bellowed as he came riding up closer to the group's position, having just returned from a perimeter run.

"There ye go stealing my thunder!" Andor boomed playfully. "Aye. They reek of it! An airing out in the bags is best before we handle them."

"Well, it explains why they fly alone," Shamus offered to the group.

For a moment, everyone glanced at one another without saying a word. Without any warning, the Travelers spontaneously broke into a cacophony of hearty laughter. It took Shamus a moment to recognize that his answer was indeed funny before the infectiousness of his companions' laughter started him going as well. He remarked that this might very well have been the first time he'd seen these otherwise incredibly serious individuals reduced to spontaneous laughter. It felt good. *Actually*, Shamus considered, it *feels better than that. It confirms that these people have the ability to experience joy. Can't say I was sure they were anything other than dour all the time.* As each member then did their best to add to the momentary levity with their own quips, Nica Bodelander brought the tone to an even higher level of amusement by slowing the pace of M'Lac long enough to give everyone a good whiff of what was swinging off either side of the back of her stallion. She then offered to share her quarry by swinging the diseased birds in their direction. *Wow! She's quite stunning!* Shamus thought to himself. All the severity normally lodged in her steel blue eyes now sparkled with a playful brightness, which only made her beaming smile all the wider. Shamus was surprised to see how hearty a laugh Erladoch offered to her antics. Even more heartwarming to him was the measure of the adoring glance that he directed at the Bodelandish princess.

Nida's horse was within but a few feet of the swinging bags. It whinnied in protest, the smell being just that perverse. This made everyone laugh even more as Andor proclaimed, "Even the bloody horses canna' take it!" More laughter and more bag swinging ensued.

What kind of shite could produce such a poison? Shamus puzzled as he watched the reaction of Nida's horse. *Is it actually the odor that is offending the horse's nostrils, or am I missing something?*

"Nida!" Shamus called out. "What kind of animal shite is this that would so offend everyone's noses?"

Nida registered the worry in Shamus's face. "Er, it's likely mouse scat, Lord Fiorian!" he called back.

While working on his PhD, Shamus recalled a course on various naturally occurring toxins that both affected a person's body and mind. His thoughts were suddenly drawn to this learning amidst the continuing laughter of his companions as they all rode closer, then further away from Lady Nica as she waved the sack around at them in playful mockery. He could see the textbook references regarding topics like frog venom used by the ancient Aztecs, who tipped their blowgun darts with the lethal concoction; the passages on snake venom used both as a toxin to stop the heart of a victim when injected via a bite and the paradoxical use of the same toxin, albeit carefully refined down by science, to be used as an anti-toxin. He flipped through pages of text in his memory, recalling the catalogues of poison along with their known antidotes. *Got it!* his mind snapped to attention as if the spin through the catalogue had just come to an abrupt stop at the right page. *Anthrax*, his mind recalled the passage. *An extremely lethal bacterial infection that can be found in feces of various animals. Not just mice, actually,* he recalled, *the list included sheep and cows. Contact with the skin will lead to the formation of extremely painful boils, and upon penetration of the body cavity, will precipitate rapid cascade failure of bodily organs. Anthrax may also become vaporized, and if inhaled, death can ensue at an even more accelerated rate.*

A further thought came rushing in, *Good God! Could it be Anthrax?* Shamus wondered to himself. *They just told me that contact with bare skin, resulting in boils and blisters both inside and out, followed by death, was how this poison worked.* He wondered how such an ancient people could possess the sophistication to create and concentrate such a potent toxin, but then he recognized that the Master of the Pit, who was himself psychically connected in this realm via his once human Treborgan king's body, dwelled in a realm that was not relegated to time or space in the way that humans understood it. He occupied multiple dimensions of time all at once. While the Lord of The Great Pit's pawn had likely possessed none of the tools to fabricate a complex poison, Anthrax, he knew, was a fairly simple and naturally occurring bacterial by-product found in the feces of mice.

"Stop swinging the bloody bags!" He heard himself yelling at Lady Nica, crushing what little fun his companions had likely shared with each other in months, if not years. "Move away from the bags, NOW!" he commanded.

The Travelers were stunned into silence, not knowing what had brought this apparently urgent outburst on. The horses were drawn up to a halt. Erladoch looked none too pleased by the 'kill-joyish' maneuver visited on them by Shamus, but he knew his friend well enough to know that there had to have been a purpose for the dramatic display. The Keepers waited as Shamus continued to keep his right hand raised to them as much to say, "not a word while I work this out."

After a few painfully awkward moments, Shamus lowered his arm. "I'm sorry," he began. "I think that I know what kind of poison this is." He said, gathering himself a little. "If you get too close to this bag and breath in enough of the actual vapors that produce this stench, you will die just as surely as you touch those birds' legs. This is a poison called Anthrax." He offered to dumb, staring eyes. "At least, I'm pretty sure it is. If you get it on your skin, you can possibly be saved, but if you breath it in, you're done for! Waving it around in the air at each other is the worst possible thing you can do right now. It might also act as an aerosolized poison."

The Travelers said nothing, waiting for him to explain. "Did anyone get close enough to have the bag touch their faces?" he asked. None of them seemed to know with certainty. "Alright then," he considered, "let's just burn these infected animals right here and now."

"We can't do that, Shamus. Not yet at least," Nica Bodelander offered. "We have to wait till nightfall so our smoke can't be seen for many yarricks in every direction."

"Alright, we will know soon enough if any of us have been affected. For now, just don't touch the bags again, please," he added, followed by, "Lady Nica, Nida and Alida, you can't afford to let the bags keep bouncing off the sides of your horses any more than you can allow them to touch your skin."

347

In a very real way, the Keepers understood what poison was. Nida was skilled in such things as it paired easily with his herb lore. He was surprised nonetheless by Shamus's advice that one could be made so lethal as to be deadly when inhaled. That was new. For that reason alone, Nida was willing to place his faith in what Shamus was telling them. He was first to loosen the bag and carefully let it drop behind his horse. He considered Shamus's warning with the degree of seriousness that it had been intended. "I've never heard of that word which ye used just now, Wigget Bearer, but I'll take yer word for it that more than just touching the birds can bring about harm. I once saw a man felled into hours-long stupor just by breathing in the fragrance of a red flower that he'd picked in the southern reaches of Seth. He liked the smell so much he threw a whole bunch of 'em into a fire only to make everyone around him behave like lunatics!"

"Poppies," Shamus offered to Nida. "I'd bet anything that you are speaking of poppies. A red flower about so big." He gestured with his hands, "with white tendrils inside the middle."

"Aye." Nida nodded in agreement. He was impressed by Shamus's knowledge. "That'd be them."

"They can be used to help with pain, but they can make a real mess of a person's mind too," Shamus offered.

Nida nodded. This affirmation had just added a further level of respect for the Wigget Bearer in his mental scorecard. "We'll drag the quarry bags by a long rope behind us till nightfall then?"

"Great idea!" Shamus affirmed. "None of us should ride behind the quarry bags either," he added. "Let's hope for the best." He surveyed Nica and the two Galagars for any obvious signs of illness before riding forth. He wanted to place as much distance between himself and the foul odor as he could. Even if there was no risk of an aerosolized poison, he was taking no chances.

Chapter 34

The sound of hooves clomping across the ever-expanding plain was almost as monotonous as the thumping up and down of Shamus's bruised buttocks bouncing against Uhlwhin's broad back. Certain that every muscle in his inner thighs had been stretched to their tearing point, he was at least grateful that Uhlwhin seemed to understand the Wigget Bearer's discomfort. Whenever he felt Shamus crashing upon him out of rhythm, the war horse modified his pace, hoping that his rider would learn to move with him.

Shamus thought that he was singly alone in his discomfort. At first blush, the Travelers all appeared to expertly manage their horses, showing no signs of the teeth gnashing, spine-bouncing repetition that he was enduring—all except Andor. The Sethian complained about his riding experience even more frequently than Shamus.

"Must we ride at this bloody pace?" he heard the colossus protest more than once. "I won't have any teeth by the time we get to Arana City!"

His protests went unheeded. Despite his height and girth, they knew that Andor preferred to be on foot whenever possible.

"Ach! My legs were made for walking and running all on their own! I'm pretty sure I don't need four more of them to help me along!"

Shamus took comfort from Andor's utterances. He imagined that the poor unfortunate horse beneath his massive frame was thinking, "Yah! Get off me already!"

Alida gave Andor the odd "there-there" glance, knowing that this was hard for her dear friend almost as much as it was for the unfortunate beast beneath him, his weighty battle-ax slapping against its forelegs more than any beast of burden would've chosen to voluntarily endure.

Other than contemplating his ongoing discomfort, Shamus had been lost in his own thoughts over the balance of the afternoon. The others had attempted conversation with him, but his short answers conveyed the fact that he was working through something. Given his unique responsibility, he was still very much an oddity to them all, and they politely left him to his thoughts. He struggled with his lack of knowledge for what was coming next. For hours, he'd been trying desperately to communicate with the Wigget Seed. His own inner voice continued to impress upon him that he should better understand the significance of their trip to the capital of Ara. It was of no use. Not being the one to lead the party anymore was disarming for him. Anthrac Aran was nowhere to be found inside his mind currently. He tried to meditate amidst the bumps and robbed breaths of his awkward landings onto Uhlwhin's back. All attempts to place himself into a semi-hypnotic state were useless under these conditions. Any hope of the Wigget Seed within him hearing his pleadings of "Wake up! I need to talk to you!" were futile. The one time that he had felt himself entering a meditative state earlier in the day had nearly resulted in his having been tossed off Uhlwhin's back. Man and horse had briefly found a pace of mutual comfort that had permitted Shamus to relax his breathing. In the very moment he felt the flicker of Anthrac's consciousness working inside of him, Uhlwhin made a surging leap across a ditch, which had been partially obscured by a clump of field flowers and heather. The maneuver had nearly turned him into a projectile.

Shamus wasn't entirely unhappy being left to his own independent musings. On one level, the relative quietude of his mind had been a welcome change. Ironically, however, he also felt lost over why Anthrac had backed away from his conscious thoughts. It was almost as though something else was trying to find prominence in his mind, and Anthrac needed to take a backseat in order for that to happen. Even his highly educated intellect didn't seem to assist him with sorting through the considerations he believed that the White Wigget had seeded into his mind before receding into slumbered silence. His memory resonated with the booming of the White Wiggets' proclamations when he first revealed himself in the tree fortress of Firren in ancient Castra. By Anthrac's proclamation, he'd been bestowed with at least one identifiable task—best as he could make it out anyway. Upon arriving in Arana City, he would need to ascertain the whereabouts of a person who was gifted with an even more expansive grasp on the old teachings of Loura than Erladoch. This 'needle in a haystack' proposition was unsettling, but the reverberations from Anthrac assured him that this individual was required to solve a riddle that would be needed to release the Wigget from his chrysalis. If there was a second imperative, it was one that may have been entirely of his own manufacture: he needed to find a woman—'the woman'. She had presented her ethereal self to him in a dreamscape and as much as told him to find her. The familiarity of her was disarming. *How can I feel so connected to someone whom I've never met before? Oh Christ! What if she's not real? I could be dissociating.* He complained to himself. He had no idea what this all meant. There had been a growing tension within him since coming to Loura, however, and there now continued to be a lingering whisper asking him to sort it out—and soon. It was like an invitation wrapped up in a compulsion to seek out this woman, whomever she might be. Whether that compulsion had been seeded by Anthrac or because he had felt it for himself, Shamus knew that this woman had an intangible hold on his thoughts.

Maybe she always has, he considered. *There was an undeniable familiarity about her the night I saw her in my out-of-body experience, or whatever the hell that was. I'm buggered if I can figure out why she seems to always pop up, though! I'm entirely lost for understanding why this ethereal woman seems to be getting louder in my mind. It's all at once comforting and invasive. Jaysus, Anthrac! Do I have to figure everything out for myself?* he waged in silent protest.

Every time the clouds drifted lazily out of the sun's way, Shamus felt his mood improve. It also seemed to enhance his insight. He speculated that she would be material to his being able to bring the Wizard into life. He had hoped that the 'how to' of this part of the challenge would be obvious enough: he and this woman were going to have to procreate. *Simple enough for this one*, he mused wistfully a moment, *but what if I can't find her? What if she has no idea of her birthright? What if she's a child or a married woman? What if she is hideous?* He shook his head and blew out forcefully trying to slow the flow of questions that he couldn't stop posing to himself. *Jaysus! How is all this going to work? Do we have the time that will be necessary for us to locate her and then for her to carry a child into life? What about raising this Angelic progeny? How will we protect it long enough for*— he hesitated, *for however long enough for it to do whatever it is coming back here to do?*

The exasperation of it made him let out an audible self-rebuke. "Chill the hell out, Shamus!" He looked about. None of the Travelers had taken any obvious note of his outburst. The last in his series of troubled questions was particularly worrisome to him. From everything that he had witnessed since coming to Loura, he'd been forced to conclude that there was an hourglass which was rapidly running out of sand on the kingdoms of Loura. While he had known of these tasks from Anthrac's frightful self-introduction through him in Castra, he struggled with what the Angel had said would happen. He wondered now whether Anthrac had, in fact, spoken of his mission aloud in Castra or whether it was a private instruction given to his thoughts alone while the Wigget bedazzled all those who'd been present to witness him manifest himself? He was no longer sure of this. What he was sure about, however, was that Erladoch and Nica had not discussed these specifics with the rest of the Travelers. *Oh, they know who I am well enough! And they all know that somehow through me the White Wigget will be reborn, but I'm pretty sure that their mission is to support me while I sort out these details for myself.* He mused. *I'm sure they would've told me if they knew more.* He shook his head for clarity. The action startled Uhlwhin beneath him and it let out a protest of its own in the form of a long whinny and a snort. Uhlwhin did not enjoy Shamus's lapses of attention to the task of riding him.

"Ok! Sorry, horsey! I'll pay more attention." He patted Uhlwhin's neck apologetically. The gesture earned him a head tilt followed by a soft "fffffrrrt" from his host, which he interpreted as "I can only carry you if you want to stay on".

Shamus looked around as the Travelers continued to ride unaffected by his exchange. The plains undulated with flowers. He realized that he hadn't paid nearly enough attention to his surroundings. The landscape was lovely—undisturbed. He took this as a good sign that no one had passed by this area for a long time. The tops of long, mustard-colored grains swayed at knee level to the horses. Where the yellow gave way to greenery, the land underfoot felt spongy and mossy. At such times, the Travelers slowed to a near stop to allow their horses to pick their way to small pools of water for brief drinks. Occasionally, copses of trees would present themselves out of the grassy terrain like pop-up mini forests, but they mostly found themselves in open country. Despite the earliness of spring, Shamus noted that many of the trees were already fully flowered. Occasionally, the odd rabbit scurried for its hide-hole while partridges rushed up out of the grass to the safety of the sky at the rumble of their approach. Having been scolded by Uhlwhin to be more present while he sat atop him, he now embraced the pristine beauty of the vistas which he and the Travelers rode across.

Each day that he had been in Loura, Shamus remarked that the air had grown increasingly more comfortable. The sun felt warm on his face when it wasn't obscured by passing cloud or brief mists of rainfall that never lasted long enough to soak him and his fellow Travelers. After having allowed himself and Uhlwhin his full attention for well on two hours, he found himself ruminating once more over the cautionary words which Anthrac had imparted: *Only a woman of pure Angelic bloodline could fit the task. Any other would destroy the Wigget Seed, leaving the potential of Anthrac Aran forever unrealized in a void of silence and emptiness.* That message, at least, had been clear to him. *Jaysus! I better get this right the first time,* he cautioned himself. The future of the civilized world, in fact, of everything, rested on Shamus's finding this one woman. *How will I know her?* he pondered. *How will I be sure?* This unknown variable troubled him increasingly as the journey progressed. It was now front and center in his mind, as if a third party was insisting on his paying proper attention to the point. He wanted confirmation from Anthrac that such a woman actually existed. He wondered if the White Wigget would have the decency to lead him to her so that he would somehow know her instantly. Shamus scoffed at his pampered sense of entitlement. *Might just have to figure this one out for myself,* he concluded half-heartedly.

Anthrac's slumber must have been deep currently. Shamus felt utterly alone inside his head. He calculated whether the previous appearances made by Anthrac may have taken too much of a toll on the Angel seed. He'd literally animated Shamus like a puppet to enhance his chances of surviving mortal combat. He'd filled a bed chamber with Heaven's light when he revealed his presence to the people whom he now counted as friends. It was hard not to fear that these exertions may have drained Anthrac somehow. In a moment of worry, the thought crossed his mind that it may be too late for the seed to be reborn at all. A throb of dread filled him. *Oh Christ! What if my lack of preparation for all of this has used up the Angel's life force? He's had to rescue me a lot! Is it possible that I've needed too much from him in his unrealized state?*

Shamus shook his doubt off like a cold shiver on a hot day. *This second guessing isn't my doing,* he warned himself. *That's the poison of the Evil One trying to take hold of me and ferment doubts that aren't real!* He convinced himself. *Stay where you are, Anthrac, if that's what it takes to be ready,*

Shamus formed the thought with confidence in his mind as a message to the Wigget. *Somehow, I will find a way to get you to where you need to go.*

***

Naga cycled to its repose along the western horizon. The red glitter of its last light flickered brilliantly through the tops of grasses and mossy-covered erratics over the endless rolling plains. Shamus resigned that he could do no more than he had to solve his problem. With only the top of Naga's flaming head still in view, the Travelers found themselves climbing a hill. The scatter of grasses populated by rocks, which wore tiny flowers like fanciful hats, had been exactly like the flat plain around it. With the light failing, it was hard to discern the changing elevation until the Travelers felt their horses incline into it. It seemed to ascend so gradually that the nearly one-hundred-foot rise above the otherwise flat plain that they had been traveling over through the course of the long day seemed more like an optical illusion than a real elevation change. Once they had reached the top, however, an entirely new view revealed itself in all directions for countless miles to the south.

While it was clear in Shamus's mind that travel by horseback had allowed them to cover significantly more ground than if they had been afoot, he was nonetheless weary from just keeping himself on top of Uhlwhin for so many hours. He was accordingly relieved when Erladoch slowed his horse to a stop and announced that this was where they would camp.

In a few very short moments, the entire party had dismounted and located a pool of water for the horses before tying them up to outcroppings of rock. Erladoch placed a droplet of water under his tongue to satisfy himself that it was safe for drinking before allowing the horses to approach. Nica, Alida and Nida gingerly untied the sacks of slain birds, taking them to a location that was, thankfully, deliberately downwind of their position. Holding only the rear tip of their arrows and applying deft slices from their short blades, they carefully liberated the scrolled messages attached to each of the birds' legs, heeding Shamus's earlier advice to also avoid breathing in these fumes when standing so close to them.

Shamus stood at a safe distance from where Nica had carefully unfolded each cloth scroll, using small rocks to hold them open on the moist and somewhat soggy ground. There was just enough natural twilight left to see what the scrolls revealed as they were unfurled. He was most interested to see what might have been contained in such 'messages', given the education Erladoch had provided to him regarding the symbology used for such things.

Once spread out, he wasn't surprised to see that nothing resembling 'words' were actually present. They were crude pictograms that conveyed some level of message. Painted in what appeared to be blood as the medium, Shamus read the messages from over the crouching heads of his fellow Travelers. It was easy enough to recognize geographic images based upon what Erladoch had explained to him. He surmised that they depicted the location of each war party. The point of the exercise, Shamus came to understand, was that these parties were confirming that they were now in position. The terrain signifiers suggested that they might even be converging on one point from various locations across a valley far beneath Bodeland and across the plains of Ara. Based upon where the birds had been coming from, he could tell from both Nica and the others' collective reaction to the information that they were troubled by the number of unchallenged locations that these war parties seemed to occupy across the Aranan plains. War parties didn't comprise more than 20 Scrags typically, and if these were messages from free-roaming Scrags, it was likely that the groupings were even smaller than that. The really troublesome aspect of the combined messages was not just the location of these parties, however. A pictogram of a hill beneath a tree certainly suggested a locale beneath the Bodelandish frontier—that part was easy enough to figure out even for Shamus. The startling aspect of the message was the cloth upon which some of the messages themselves were painted. More specifically, the cloth of each message was carefully torn fragments of clothing garments coming from Anahimara, and, to Andor's utter horror, there were also fragments of fabric recognizable by its double cross-stitched pattern emanating from but one place: Gaduk in Northern Seth. Andor let out an anguished gasp, recognizing that the message could only mean one thing: parts of his homeland kingdom, at least, had recently fallen to invasion.

***

Chapter 35

Nida lay next to Andor throughout the night with eyes wide open as the Travelers took turns getting what sleep they could manage, her right hand sometimes laying softly on his shoulder to comfort him as he quietly wept for his kinsmen. She understood him better than any person living or dead.

The Travelers were safely upon the high ground, and by day, this would have permitted them abundant amounts of time upon which to see an advancing Scraggin war party making a path toward them. The same, of course, could not be said about long sight lines being available to them, even from this vantage point, during the night, however. They would have to rely instead on the finely tuned hearing of the Galagars to sense rustling feet ascending the hill. Given the sudden unevenness of the terrain at the beginning of the rise, both Nida and Alida took comfort knowing that even a soft-footed Badlander or free-roaming Scrag would stumble long before they could reach their campsite. The iron-shod feet of a Treborgan Scrag would give notice of their approach for, at least, a yarrick.

While Scrags were known to patrol under the hungry lash of their commanders during day or night, they were not nocturnal creatures any more than their more evolved occupants of Loura. They suffered from the same frailties of eyesight as anyone. If they chose to travel by night without the assistance of torchlight to gain the element of surprise, even though they were not shod like the Treborgan Scrags, they would nonetheless make sufficient noise from a distance to allow the highly trained Keepers the time they needed to fight or flee into the shadows if the numbers of their opposition were too great.

A fire was made for the express purpose of destroying the poisoned birds 100 yards below the crest of the hilltop and far enough downwind from where they later slept. It was lit just after the last light of day and was quickly extinguished before twilight gave way to total darkness. The Travelers made no fire for their warmth or to even cook a supper. Being located at an elevated height, it made no sense to make a fire that would surely act as a beacon where none should exist in the wilderness. Instead, they remained entirely in darkness, using only each other for warmth. While sleep came to each member of the party in its own turn, the outdoor temperature of a late spring night with no cover from trees to insulate them from wind made for a restless and shivery slumber.

Morning rushed in with a welcoming warmth as Inyi lifted over the horizon. The beams of sunlight were not yet summery warm, but the rays were welcomed by the chittering teeth of the Travelers. Erladoch and Shamus had taken the last watch. They were ready for the day. They roused those of their friends who were still asleep to a meal of fruits and dried meats in a hushed and careful manner, even though there was no obvious movement in any direction.

For the last hour preceding sunrise, Erladoch had been watching the morning sky for something—anything. His ears were cocked to the wind as he performed a stretching and Tai Chi-like routine identical to the one Shamus had seen him do whenever he had arrived at the Royal early enough in the day to observe him as a patient behind the safety of the two-way mirrored wall. Having trained with him for months before making the leap through the Eternal Flame, he joined in with his friend's routine, by now knowing it by heart. It was a dramatic sight for those among the other Keepers who, for several minutes, simply watched in silence as the two men moved entirely in concert atop a hill with beams of sunlight dancing beneath their feet. Had anyone ever doubted the depth of the bond of friendship that had developed between Erladoch the Brave of Fior Hill and Shamus of Fior, it was evident now. This being one of the most recognized training forms of every Keeper for a millennium, each of the Travelers slowly took to their feet as the form was ready to repeat its sequence. They inserted themselves into the dance with ease. Regardless of dramatic body size differentials, the Keepers moved like flowing water on the hilltop, entirely in unison. When the form was completed, Erladoch ceased his melodic singing, which he often added to the dance. He gave his full attention to the surrounding plains below once more, looking for signs of activity, which he fully expected to see. The others had returned to their breakfasts, also eyeing the horizon in every direction. There was now an unspoken but entirely shared uneasiness that permeated the group.

Andor offered a puzzled look to Erladoch and Shamus, who were now sitting back-to-back, each man using the other as a chair while they methodically ran a metal sharpener down the long edges of the blades of their swords.

"What is it with the Lord of Dunbar? What does he see that my eyes fail to detect?"

"Nothing, my Sethian friend," Alida interjected. "That is entirely the problem."

Erladoch diverted his scan of the east and addressed Andor. "There are no birds in the sky and no animals stir anywhere within our gaze. I cannot see the smoke of any cottage hearth anywhere off in the distance either, even though we are simply not that far away from the main highway. Ara is much too inactive! I dislike this!"

"Ah! For sure," Andor acknowledged. "Danger has its own smell."

"I dunna think that our presence has been felt in this land yet, but the wild people that must be here somewhere are themselves silent when one would expect them to be out on a morning hunt. They await something." He moved away from Shamus in order to face him. "Shamus, describe your dreams from last night for me? Did you speak to anyone in them? Did you go anywhere?"

Shamus regarded Erladoch with surprise. "Uh, yes," he paused, "but how could you know that?"

"I didn't know for sure until this moment, but I felt myself being pulled along with you in a dreamscape that I can no longer recall as it seemed to vanish in the moments before I awoke. I felt as though I joined you at one point. Tell me what you recall."

Shamus concentrated, doing his best to recapture his fleeting dream imagery. "I think that the dream was about my thoughts of yesterday, which revolved around the woman that I am supposed to find. You know, the one that was foretold by Anthrac Aran?"

Erladoch and Nica nodded their understanding. It was easy to recall the prophecy that had been revealed back in Firren when Shamus had been enrobed in a blinding aura of white light. The sudden appearance of the essence of the White Wigget flowing around and through Shamus still caused amazement to them when they considered the memory.

"I think that I went looking for her last night," Shamus explained. "To be honest, I think that I've been looking for this person for a very long time. At least, I feel like she's been around in some way, close by, for as long as I can remember. If she is one and the same person as with Anthrac's prophecy, then I think her presence has certainly been more insistent on being found in my dreams of late. When I come to a certain point in my journey, she's always been so far off that I could not see her face, and that's often how it plays itself out. Lately, however, I definitely feel as though I am closing in on her."

The dream was coming back into focus now. "I had this overwhelming sense more than ever last night that I knew this distant image to be the woman that I was being sent to find. I called to her across an empty space. Ugh! I'm not sure if it's a lake or a field or across a cliff, but there is a 'space' between us for sure. Last night, I recall trying my best to explain to her the purpose of our quest as I attempted to cross the expanse. She didn't get closer, though. No matter how fast I ran toward her. As I realized that my efforts seemed fruitless, I called out to her again, telling her that I would find a way to bridge the impossible expanse to find her." Shamus's face filled with the light of recognition now. "I—I now remember being amazed when finally, for the first time ever, I actually heard her voice answering me back across the divide. She said that she would come to me instead and that it was too dangerous for her to reveal her identity except in person. She told me that she could feel that others were growing near. Others were watching her. Yah, that's what she said. In that same instant, I felt as though another person was indeed watching our exchange. Not you, Erladoch, someone malevolent." Shamus then paused once more, suddenly recalling the last part of the dream. "Oh my God, Erladoch!" Revelation was upon him. "You were there! Right at the end of my exchange with her, you were there, pulling me away, trying to warn me to stop my communication. It was like you physically yanked me from the edge of where I was standing."

"That's what I recall of it too. I was pulled into your dream. Your lady summoned my help. Your effort to connect with her in that moment was attracting danger. Oh! I think I may know who she is!" Erladoch reached down to collect his swords and loaded them into the holder affixed to his cloak.

"Ators give us speed!" Nida called out as he leaped to his feet and prepared himself and his horse for departure.

"That's great? But I'm not sure that I understand." Shamus spoke to the air, confused by his travel companions' actions. They were all now rising to their feet, re-fitting their weapons either inside or on top of their respective travel cloaks. In the case of long swords, each of them was fastening their blades to the preferred side of their horses in obvious haste. Shamus rose to his feet despite his confusion, recognizing that the Travelers were making ready for a quick departure.

"Allow me to help you," Princess Nica offered as she assisted Shamus to gather up his personal effects from the ground and secure them to Uhlwhin. "Ya made contact last night with the Aranan woman that you are destined to find. Her blood is of the Strahanas. She, like Lord Dunbar, is clearly a mind dancer. She refused to make her identity known to you for fear that this was the work of the Evil One, conjuring a trap for you both. Shamus," Nica said, taking hold of his arm. "She's been looking for you too! She knows that you are coming, my friend, but she shielded herself from view, sensing the presence of another. I agree with Nida, there is not much time. I believe that she now comes to find you this very day on the road from Arana City, and the absence of movement on the plain warns that a reception of Scrags lie in waiting for her to stop this encounter from happening!"

By the time Nica had finished sharing her dream interpretation, the Travelers had fully broken camp. Within a few short minutes, they were collectively setting their heels into the sides of their horses. Erladoch sang out in an urgent voice to his horse, which seemed to understand exactly what he said, as she nodded her head up and down and began to whine loudly to the other horses. It was clear that whatever song he was singing to his mount was inspiring her and the other horses to ride hard.

While Shamus could only hear the odd word that was being sung into her ear, he heard Erladoch call his horse by name.

"Ka-la!" he cried to her ear. "Nothing in your life is more important than getting us to the Strahana woman! Run like the world will end if you fail!"

It was clear, as Erladoch's mare fell into rhythm with his chant, that she was being hypnotized to find speed and strength at a level she'd never before summoned. The other horses, Uhlwhin included, followed Ka-la as the natural leader. Under Erladoch's mental connection, Ka-la whinnied frantically again. Her legs exploded with energetic strides that accelerated into a furious sprint, almost as though she were ready at any moment to leap into flight, just as her winged ancestors of old had done. She was no regular horse. Ka-la was the descendant of what most believed was an extinct species of flying Manticorn. Her example inspired and empowered the other Travelers' horses to summon all their collective strengths. The speed of the horses was so intense that their riders held on for dear life, despite their otherwise polished equestrian capabilities.

Shamus was instantaneously terrified by the pace Uhlwhin was achieving. This was too reminiscent of his childhood experience with the maddened horse that had been compelled to kill him. Nothing could have been further from the truth, however. Uhlwhin was a proud and highly trained battle horse. She would bear Shamus into fire itself and move in such a way as to keep him on her back, even at the greatest peril to herself if necessary.

Soon enough, Shamus recognized that Uhlwhin's movements were so sleek that she was in no way maddened by enchantment. Rather, she was driven by commitment to serve both rider and Ka-la, their leader. His fear of falling off became overridden by his realization that, if Nica's interpretation was correct, there was precious little time to find the Strahana woman on the road.

The Galagans showed no outward signs of distress from their mode of travel, which, in the circumstances, Shamus considered to be amazing. Given the slightness of their physiques, he'd fully expected that they risked being catapulted from the backs of their horses without even being noticed. Instead, Nida and Alida had shifted themselves to a nearly prone position alongside their horses, so that there was no risk at all of them being launched free. From his sideward glances at them, the Galagars looked like they had become part of their horses. The undulations of their bodies matched the long feverish strides in a way that the shock of collision, which Shamus continued to experience against Uhlwhin's back, was entirely eliminated by their unique riding posture.

Looking to his left, all that Shamus needed to do was catch a glimpse of Andor's eyes. These revealed the story of his personal hell. As a Keeper, he was trained to endure, full stop. That is precisely what he was doing now. He grunted and gnashed his teeth, but he endured.

The rest of the Travelers appeared, at least to Shamus, to be struggling to be comfortable with the breakneck speed being exhibited by their battle horses. While there was no outward expression of distress being registered on their faces, Shamus took comfort that his were not the only knuckles going white from the tightened grasp of hands around reigns.

As yarricks peeled away, his disbelief at their capacity to maintain such a pace increased tenfold. The land passed by the companions at a dizzying rate, so that the best any of them could do was close their eyes or look directly ahead of them. After leaping over a series of undulations, Andor spewed his breakfast liberally into the air. His overwrought belly had told him in protest, "Either stop this madness or you're throwing up!" His belly soon won out, but he continued to endure.

***

The great northern plain of Ara was replaced by a descending roll of hills as the companions traveled further south, far away from the end of the Bodeland mountain chain. After they'd traveled nearly half the day with still no sign of other people or animals, the horses were even now unrelenting as they leaped one after the other onto the well-trodden road of Ara, no longer concerning themselves with the risk of detection.

At this stage of their rapid journey, they had already covered one and a half times the distance traveled the day before. Nica shouted to her friends that they needed to stop for the sake of their animals, but the horses were completely unwilling to heed a call for rest after having been given the challenge communicated by Ka-la in a way that only horses could comprehend. They sped on without breaking stride for another hour.

As the companions flew over the wide and flat road, they could just see the edge of Lake Kitar to the southwest of them. The day was wearing on as the massive landlocked lake came more fully into view. Also, on the horizon north and east of the great lake, the Travelers could now see a slow billow of smoke rising over the land. Erladoch commanded his horse to give him all the speed it had left in an excited and uncharacteristically anxious voice. The ambush had begun. The Travelers risked being late to the party.

Understanding the earnestness of the Travelers, the horses drove forth while beads of sweat poured from every part of them; their legs seemed but moments away from seizing up under the strain of sustained maximum effort. A bloody froth formed around the mouths and nostrils of each horse, and yet Erladoch's singing encouraged them to press on at their continued frenzied pace.

The smoke which they had first seen was now heavy in the air. The Travelers were no more than ten minutes away from closing in on the trap that the Evil One had set for the Aranan woman. She had become the weak link in the chain, the removal of which would dismantle Anthrac's only chance of re-emergence in Loura.

***

In the four years since Erladoch's disappearance, the Evil One had stolen the sanity of as many of the mind-dancers in Loura as he could since making his influence known again. He had hidden within their consciousnesses and manipulated their thoughts, twisting their very wills and turning them into mindless robots. Since the sudden return of the Dunbar prince, the Evil One had put his plans into fast gear. Birds of prey and other impressionable animals had yielded to his dark enchantments that weaved through the ether. They had become his eyes and ears throughout Loura. The Evil One himself was nothing less than an extension of Satan's will on Earth. Whatever the Master of the Pit directed from his fiery domain was to be fulfilled without question. In this moment, it had grown painfully apparent to the Travelers that his entire will was focused on finding the elusive woman. She had managed to remain shielded within the dreamscape when most others had been compromised. While her identity had remained carefully hidden from view by her, her efforts to summon Shamus had revealed where she could be found. He was going to have her killed; she was out of time.

Shamus found himself a whole new level of trauma to process. The emotions of the terrified child on a horse speeding headlong toward his death were replaying themselves like a nightmarish soundtrack caught on a repeating loop. This time, the reasons for his distress were altogether different. Uhlwhin sped along the highway in the direction of some as yet unknown nexus point between where they were now and Arana City. Shamus did all that he could to distract himself from the rush of unrelenting hyperventilation. He could not assess in this moment what was worse: being flung from Uhlwhin's back into the hard ground at a speed which no human could recover from; or fail the faceless woman of his lifelong dreams by not getting to her in time. The memory of her soothing tones replayed in his thoughts until it felt like she was passing a consoling hand slowly up and down his back. She had so many times found her way into his troubled mind at the darkest moments of his life. This was definitely one and the same woman who now beckoned him forth. *Yes!* Shamus assured himself. *I can do this! Failing her would be worse than dying!*

363

He took a firm hold of Uhlwhin's mane so that he could lower his head closer to the horse's ear. "I know what I'm asking of you, beautiful horse, but please, keep going!"

Before Shamus had ever met Erladoch in Ottawa, he found himself finding no comfort with any of the women he had dated. They were simply not 'the one'. Even then, he believed that someone out there was waiting for him. He had told his buddy John Browse this so many times after breakups with girlfriends that it had become a running joke between the two lifelong friends. He was now working out the fact that, since arriving in Loura, the appearances of this ethereal woman had intensified so much that, ironically, it was nearly impossible to accept that this 'presence' would in fact be a real and living person. Putting a face and voice to her had never been part of the equation. This was all about to change. Previously, his approaches to her in the dreamscape had involved nothing more than echoes: oscillations of thought; approaches on a meandering pathway that never got him any closer to reaching her.

The previous night's sleep had been different, though. As Shamus bounced and jostled on Uhlwhin's back, he turned his whole thought to analyzing the most recent dream, sorting through what had made it different than any of its predecessors. *There was a bridge!* He captured the distinction. *There had been a bridge when previously there had only been voids or expanses which had separated us.*

Uhlwhin was running so hard that Shamus had to clench his jaw firmly shut lest his teeth smash up and down into each other. *She had placed a bridge between us and asked me to cross it just as Erladoch snapped me up as some other presence emerged.*

***

They were less than a few minutes' ride away, likely just over the next hill. As they closed on the position, the sounds of a continuing battle raged. The companions had no idea what they would find over this last rise, but the sound of metal crashing on metal was everywhere in the air ahead. From the scale of torn ground that they were speeding across, the Travelers easily concluded that their enemy far outnumbered them. The help that they might add with their small number to repel the massacre unfolding over the next rise was questionable at best. Even as they urged their horses to speed forth, there was a shared expectation that the Travelers would perish in the next few minutes. Such considerations mattered little, however, to the Keepers. Each member of this elite group embraced a common certainty: if this woman of near pure Strahanian blood were to die today, it would not matter in the least whether their lives also ended here. Were she to perish, all hope would disappear for the inhabitants of Loura.

The hope which might flow from the rebirth of Anthrac Aran had to be maintained. Only the last Angel could reveal the location of his Itavo fragment. He alone could lead them to the Great Stone, which had remained hidden for more than a thousand years. He alone could wield such an object with the collective power of the Angealkind. Though no one had a shred of a notion how that wielding might work, the Keepers trusted in their lore. It powered their determination now.

Uhlwhin bellowed to its equine companions what could only be described as the roar of command to 'attack'. The other horses answered with their own labored whinnies, proclaiming their devotion to not falter. As their leaping gallops bounded over 10 yards of torn-up ground at a time, the evidence of Scraggin tracks revealed evidence of both bare-footed and iron-shod enemies somewhere just ahead of them. They'd converged from multiple directions onto this place not long before plunging over the same hill that the members of the Sacred Order of Keepers were about to crest.

With strategy firmly in the forefront of their minds, both O'Mara and Andor drew their great battle horns to their mouths. Paying no attention to the rattling pace of their horses, each man, in their own turn, blew with every ounce of breath in their lungs, one after the other. The echo of their calls could be heard over countless yarricks in such open terrain. Whatever lay over the next ridge might have to face only seven new opponents, but these were seven of the greatest warriors in all of Loura. They wagered that the echoes of their horns might startle the Scrags they expected to come upon momentarily, maybe even unsettle them long enough to create confusion and doubt in the minds of their enemies. Inspiring even a few moments of hesitation might just be enough for the woman they were coming to rescue to have a chance to slip away from the battle.

This, of course, was a flimsy plan, and one, given their very small contingent, that would not maintain the element of surprise for anything more than a few seconds. It was, however, better than no plan at all. Following suit, Erladoch drew a horn which Nica Bodelander had given to him as part of his refreshed equipment back in Castra. It had belonged to his lieutenant from Dunbar, Glorf, who had perished at the hands of Treborgan Scrags not long after announcing what he had believed to have been Erladoch's death at the battle of the ruined Temple of Tine Fhluich.

Erladoch gave three loud blasts all his own on the horn before tossing it behind himself on its thin strap. He threw back his cloak to gain access to his weaponry. Three very distinctive sounds coming from three very distinctive kingdoms of Loura echoed tidings of war coming to meet the battle just beyond.

"Draw your weapons, friends!" Erladoch cried out. "Today we celebrate life!"

With this, he unleashed Fiorling. It flashed brilliantly as it caught the light of descending Naga just as some of the Keepers began to crest the hill's brim.

Shamus pleaded with Uhlwhin to press on, but with each closing stride the great horse deliberately slowed and began changing course even as the remainder of the Travelers were speeding due south ever faster to war.

"Uhlwhin! What the hell are you doing?" Shamus protested loudly. "Follow my friends! To war!"

Uhlwhin refused to listen to its rider. This fearsome war horse had made its own mind up as to what it was going to do.

Shamus caught sight of O'Mara's long Scabber swinging open above his majestic head seconds before he disappeared over the hill ahead of him. The Anahimaran screamed at his foes. He was so filled with rage and a need for revenge that foam was crusting at the edges of his mouth. Shamus heard the young prince's voice echo even as he disappeared from view. "The spirit of Anahimara comes upon youuuu!" His battle cry bellowed over the hilltop. "Take yer-own-foul-lives if you may, for my wrath will not be so kind!"

The Galagars laughed in fitful bursts as they fitted arrows to their bows, rapidly firing them into unknown targets beyond the hill. "For my brothers-in-arms!" Alida called out.

"For my father!" Nida shouted.

Together, the sibling warriors dedicated reasons for why each dart was being fired as arrow after arrow went sailing into the air. "For Ardehla!"..."For all free people!"..."I take my revenge on you, ya black-hearted bastards!"

Nica Bodelander rode proud and defiant upon her mountain of a horse. She had already shouldered her bow after letting loose no less than 10 arrows into the startled Scrags beyond. Bodelander and horse leaped as one over the top of the hill, her sword already flying out from behind her back.

Andor said nothing at first. Instead, he let out a roar like that of a lion. As the battle scene came into view, a smile formed on his face much as it had with the Galagars. He bore the countenance of an athlete who had just heard the starting whistle of a sporting match. He raised his great double-headed axe high above his head, and without a thought to his own survival or hesitation of any kind, went looking for opponents. The only thought which came to him beyond that of rescuing the Aranan woman somewhere ahead was the curiosity as to whether the neck of his first victim would be of a rank high enough to be worthy of such a finely crafted instrument of death.

Shamus was beside himself! He couldn't change the new direction of travel chosen by Uhlwhin for love or money. Tears of distress flowed liberally over his cheeks. More than any other living person, he needed to get to the woman in peril somewhere just over the rise, and yet his defiant horse was now running laterally to the hilltop. In a fit of utter exasperation, Shamus hammered his heels into the furious horse, who continued to run sidelong around the hilltop rather than crest it as all the others had done.

"For the love of all that is holy, Uhlwhin, obey me! What-are-ya-doing?" he shouted at the massive beast between his legs. Blood and froth poured liberally from the war horse's beleaguered nostrils as it let out a cautionary whinny at its rider.

For reasons that would never become clear to Shamus, the whinny sounded all too much like Uhlwhin had spoken a single word in the common language of Loura, and that word was…"Wait!"

End of Book Two